Praise for
STASI CHILD

Winner of the CWA Endeavour Historical Dagger

Longlisted for the Theakstons Old Peculier Crime Novel of the Year

Times Crime **Book of the Month**

Telegraph **Pick of the Week**

'Superb. A thrilling Cold War mystery that **reminded me of Robert Harris at his best**'

> Mason Cross, author of *The Samaritan*

'Deft, assured storytelling, **a compelling new detective** and a fascinating setting – I was up late to finish it!'

> Gilly Macmillan, author of *Burnt Paper Sky*

'One of the best reads I've had in ages. With its masterful intertwining of dual storylines and its stark portrayal of life behind the Berlin Wall, this is **a cracking debut**'

> David Jackson, bestselling author of *Cry Baby*

'Deep and dark, this debut is **utterly gripping**, sucking you in straight from the get go. Fascinating backdrop, well observed characters and a corker of an ending. Superb'

> Nikki Owen, author of *The Spider in the Corner of the Room*

'**Chilling**'

> *Daily Telegraph*

'Extremely **engaging**'

> *Sunday Express*

'Can't get enough cold-war Germany after *Deutschland 83*? This is **your latest reading companion**'

> *Shortlist*

'**A promising debut**, an astutely considered novel of detection and place, redolent of dread, paranoia and suspicion'

> Graeme Blundell, *The Australian, ARTS*

'A self-confessed obsessive, **Young's period detail** – what kind of tyre tracks Stasi official's cars left – **is impressive**'

> Greg Fleming, *New Zealand Herald*

STASI WOLF

David Young was born near Hull and – after dropping out of a Bristol University science degree – studied Humanities at Bristol Polytechnic. Temporary jobs cleaning ferry toilets and driving a butcher's van were followed by a career in journalism with provincial newspapers, a London news agency, and international radio and TV newsrooms. He now writes in his garden shed and in his spare time supports Hull City AFC. You can follow him on Twitter @djy_writer

Also by David Young

Stasi Child

STASI WOLF

DAVID YOUNG

ZAFFRE

First published in Great Britain in 2017 by

ZAFFRE PUBLISHING
80–81 Wimpole St, London W1G 9RE
www.zaffrebooks.co.uk

A CIP catalogue record for this book is available from the British Library.

B Format Paperback ISBN: 978-1-78576-068-6
Trade Paperback ISBN: 978-1-78576-298-7
A Format Paperback ISBN: 978-1-78576-288-8

Also available as an ebook

1 3 5 7 9 10 8 6 4 2

Typeset by IDSUK (Data Connection) Ltd
Printed and bound by Clays Ltd, St Ives Plc

Zaffre Publishing is an imprint of Bonnier Zaffre,
a Bonnier Publishing company
www.bonnierzaffre.co.uk
www.bonnierpublishing.co.uk

For Stephanie, Scarlett and Fergus

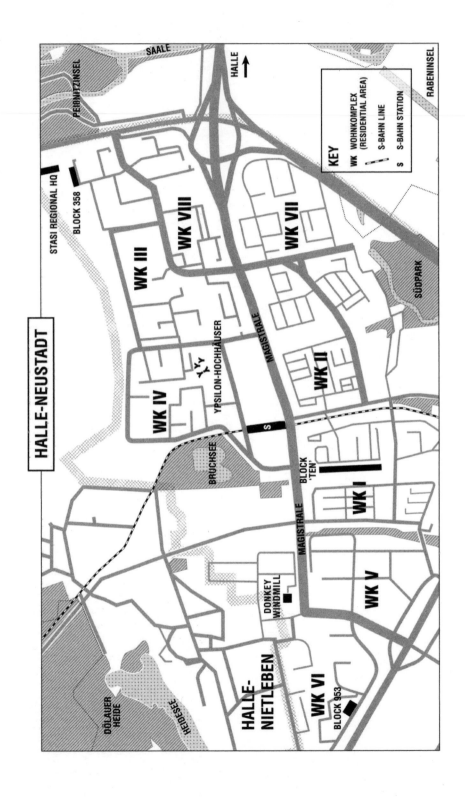

HALLE-NEUSTADT

SAALE

HALLE

PEIßNITZINSEL

RABENINSEL

STASI REGIONAL HQ

BLOCK 358

WK III

WK VIII

WK VII

SÜDPARK

WK IV

YPSILON-HOCHHÄUSER

MAGISTRALE

WK II

S

BRUCHSEE

BLOCK 'TEN'

MAGISTRALE

WK I

DÖLAUER HEIDE

HEIDESEE

DONKEY WINDMILL

WK V

HALLE-NIETLEBEN

WK VI

BLOCK 953

KEY

WK   WOHNKOMPLEX
     (RESIDENTIAL AREA)

     S-BAHN LINE

S   S-BAHN STATION

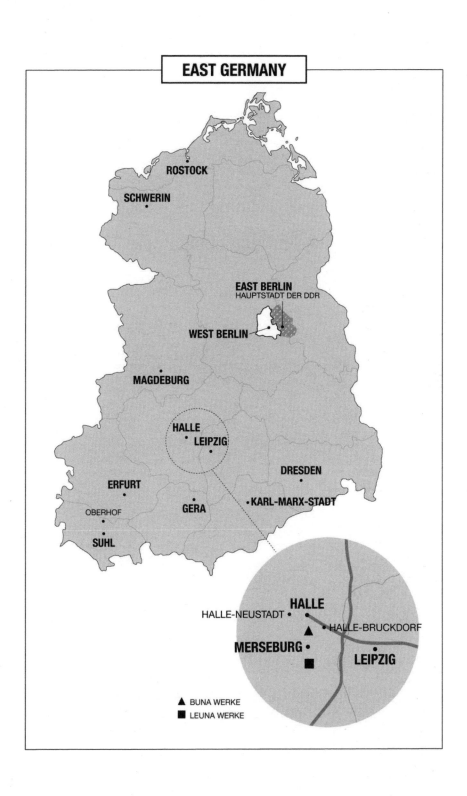

EAST GERMANY

ROSTOCK

SCHWERIN

EAST BERLIN
HAUPTSTADT DER DDR

WEST BERLIN

MAGDEBURG

HALLE
LEIPZIG

DRESDEN

ERFURT

KARL-MARX-STADT

OBERHOF

GERA

SUHL

HALLE

HALLE-NEUSTADT

HALLE-BRUCKDORF

MERSEBURG

LEIPZIG

▲ BUNA WERKE
■ LEUNA WERKE

INTRODUCTION

Welcome to the second instalment of my *Oberleutnant* Karin Müller crime thriller series, set in communist East Germany in the mid-1970s. The story is set a few months after the conclusion of the first novel, *Stasi Child*, but – like the first book – it's a discrete story within the series and I've tried to write it in such a way that anyone starting here will still enjoy it and not feel they've missed out by not reading the first book.

Readers of *Stasi Child* found my introduction there to be useful, so apologies to them as this will repeat some of the same information.

East Germany, or in German the *Deutsche Demokratische Republik* (DDR), was a communist state set up in the years after the Second World War, and very much dominated by the Soviet Union. It had one of the highest standards of living in the eastern bloc and although it was in many ways Moscow's puppet, living there was very different, even if the politics were the same.

My main protagonist, Karin Müller, is an *Oberleutnant* (or first lieutenant) with the state police, the *Volkspolizei* (literally People's Police) – although as a murder squad detective she works for the CID arm, the *Kriminalpolizei*, or *Kripo* (or often just the '*K*', although I've not used that here).

But looming large in the background is the East German secret police, the Ministry for State Security, more commonly known as the Stasi (a contraction of the German name).

Throughout the text I've retained the German ranks for a flavour of authenticity – many are self-explanatory, but for full explanations/translations of these and other East German terms please see the glossary at the back of the novel.

Please note some of the dates of real events used as the basis for this fictional story have been adjusted for the sake of the plot. For more details see the 'Author's Note' at the end of the novel.

Many thanks to everyone who read *Stasi Child*, especially those who reviewed it or blogged about it. It was lovely (and a little overwhelming) that so many of you contacted me to thank me for writing it. There was no need, but it was still great to get your letters and emails.

For contact details and more background, please see my website at www.stasichild.com or follow me on Twitter @djy_writer.

Thanks for reading!

D.Y. (February 2017)

PROLOGUE

July 1945
Halle-Bruckdorf, occupied Germany

Your leg stings as you shuffle along the ledge to try to get comfortable. Frau Sultemeier has fallen against you during the never-ending night. Being squashed together with the others down in the disused mine gives a little warmth, a perhaps mis-placed sense of safety in numbers. So you feel slightly disloyal as you move sideways to get some space – feeling your way in the blackness, where the sun's rays never penetrate, even during the day. You daren't put your foot down because you know your boot will be filled again by the cold, coal-stained water and the pain will be unbearable. You can hear it, sloshing around – the water that seeps in everywhere, into every sore and wound. You can't see it, but you know it's there.

Sultemeier snorts but doesn't wake. You almost wish she did. You want someone to talk to. Someone to calm your fears. Dagna could do that. Your younger sister was never afraid. The drone of the bombers, the explosions of the bombs, the fire in the sky, the dust clouds and rubble. Dagna just used to say: 'We're here.

We're still alive. Be thankful and wait for it to get better.' But Dagna's gone now. With the others. She heard – we all heard – the stories they told in the League of German Girls. About how the Red Army soldiers are worse than wild animals, how they will rape you again and again, tear you limb from limb. The others didn't want to find out if it was true. So they've gone to try to reach the American zone.

Another snort from Sultemeier. She wraps her arm round you, as though you're her lover. Frau Sultemeier, the miserable old shopkeeper who before the war would never let more than two children into her shop at once. Always quick to spot if you tried to pocket a sweet while you thought her eyes were else-where. She, like most of the others here, was too old to run. And you, with your injured foot from the last British bombing raid, you *can't* run. So you had to come down here with them. To the old lignite mine. Most of the brown coal round here they just tear from the ground, huge machines taking big bites directly from the earth, feeding what had seemed like a never-ending war. The war that was once so glorious. Then so dirty, so hate-ful, so exhausting. But you *Kinder des Krieges* knew about the disused underground mine – the cave, you used to call it – when you played down here before the war, you and your sister Dagna astonishing Mutti with how dirty you used to get. 'Black as little negroes,' she used to laugh, playfully patting you on your bums as you ran to the bathtub. Mutti's gone now, of course. Died . . . when was it? A year ago, two? And you've still never seen a black person. Well, apart from in books. You wonder if you'll ever see a real, living one. You wonder if you'll ever get out of here alive.

You see the flash of the torches first, then hear the foreign shouts, the splashing of boots in the waterlogged mine. Frau Sultemeier is awake immediately, gripping your shoulders with her bony hands. To protect you, you think. You hope. You feel the quiver of fear transfer from her body into yours through her fingers.

Then the torch beam dazzling in your eyes, playing along the line of grandmothers, spinsters and widows. Women who've seen too many summers. Too many winters. All except you. Just thirteen winters for you, and this is your fourteenth summer.

'*Frauen! Herkommen!*' The Slavic tongue mangles the pronunciation of the German words, but the message is clear.

Suddenly Sultemeier, the old witch, is pushing you forward. You realise her grip on you was not protectiveness at all. She just wanted to stop you running.

'Here! Here!' she shouts. The torch beam is back, trained on you. 'Take this girl. She's young, pretty – look!' She forces your chin upwards, wrenches your arm away as you try to shield your eyes.

'No,' you say. 'No. I won't go. I don't want to.' But the Soviet soldier is pulling you towards him. In the harsh uplight of the torch, you see his face for the first time. His wild Slavic features. Just as the *Führer* described in his warnings. There is hunger there. Need. A hunger and a need for you.

He shouts at you again, this time in Russian. '*Prikhodite!*'

'I don't understand,' you say. 'I'm only thirteen.'

'*Komm mit mir!*' But he doesn't have to order you, because he just drags you with him, through the waterlogged mine, your undernourished teenage body almost no weight to him at all, each of his strides sending darts of pain through your injured foot. You hear the laughs of his colleagues. 'Pretty girl,' they taunt. 'Pretty girl.'

Outside, even though it's barely after dawn, the light is blinding. Soldiers. Soldiers. Everywhere. Laughing. Whistling. Blowing imaginary kisses. You're trying to walk now, but each stride is more a stumble, and he has your arm locked in his like a vice. You feel the dampness where you've wet yourself.

He's taking you to the hut. The rusting corrugated-metal mine hut where you used to play with Dagna before the war, before all this hell. You were the pretend mother of the house, she your naughty daughter, always playing tricks to try to get you to scold her. He opens the door, throws you inside onto the floor, and then kicks the door closed again behind him.

'Pretty girl,' he says, just staring at you for a moment, echoing the animalistic approval of his fellow soldiers. 'Pretty girl.'

You edge backwards along the floor to the corner of the hut, across the dirt and debris. You see him undoing his belt, lurching towards you as his battledress puddles round his feet. And then he's on you. Ripping your clothes, pinning your arms down as you try to scratch his eyes, thrusting his foul-smelling face towards you for a kiss.

Then you give up. You just flop back and let him do what he wants. Whatever he wants.

Almost as soon as he's finished, he's ready to start again. And then the door opens, and another soldier comes in. With the same hungry look. You realise, through the fog of pain, the shame, and the smell of unwashed man, that what they told you in the League of German Girls was right.

The *Führer* was right.

The Red Army soldiers *are* worse than wild animals.

1

July 1975
East Berlin

Oberleutnant Karin Müller fixed her gaze on the spotty youth sitting opposite her in the Keibelstrasse interview room. He stared back from under a curtain of shoulder-length, greasy black hair with an insolence which she feared wouldn't serve him well in the remand cells of the People's Police.

Müller didn't say anything for a moment, sniffed, and then looked down at her notes.

'You're Stefan Lauterberg, aged nineteen, of Apartment 3019, Block 431, on Fischerinsel in the Hauptstadt. Is that correct?'

'You know it is.'

'And you're the guitarist in a popular music group called . . .' Müller peered down at her notes again, 'Hell Twister. That's correct?' The youth just emitted a careworn sigh. 'Is that correct?' repeated Müller.

'We're a *rock* band,' he said.

'Hmm.' Müller made a point of noting this down, not that she really cared about the youth's pedantry. She had some sympathy for him though. Just as he felt he shouldn't be here, being questioned by a People's Police officer, she believed jobs like this weren't what she'd signed up for. She was a homicide detective. She'd been the first female head of a *Kripo* murder squad in the whole Republic. She'd done well – at least in her opinion – and now they'd moved her from the Mitte Murder Commission and rewarded her with awful little *Vopo* jobs like this. Jobs which should be being done by some uniformed numbskull. Müller sighed, un-clicked her pen, and laid it down on the interview table.

'Look, Stefan. You can make this easy for me, or you can make it difficult. Easy, and you admit the offence, you're given a warning and you're on your way. Back playing with . . .' she peered down at her notes again. She remembered the name of his group perfectly well, but didn't want to give him the satisfaction of knowing it. '. . . with Hell Twister, in no time at all. Or you can make it hard. Play the smart-arse. And then we'll shut you in a cell here for just as long as we want. Any hopes of going to university, of getting a decent job, well, that will all be history.'

Lauterberg snorted. 'A decent job, Comrade *Oberleutnant*?' The use of her rank was laced with sarcasm. 'In this shitty little country?' He shook his head and smiled.

Müller sighed again, ran her hands back through her dirty blond hair, heavy and damp from the oppressive summer heat. 'OK. Have it your way. Stefan Lauterberg, on Sunday, June the fifteenth this year you were reported by Comrade Gerda Hutmacher for making an unreasonable amount of noise in your family's apartment with electrically amplified music. And when she complained to you directly, you made an anti-socialist joke. A joke about Comrade Honecker losing his watch under his bed. Is that correct?'

The youth chuckled. He leaned forward and held Müller's gaze. 'That *is* correct, yes, *Oberleutnant*. He unfortunately loses his watch and thinks it may have been stolen. So he asks the Minister for State Security to investigate.'

Müller placed her elbows on the table and rested her chin on her clasped hands. She hadn't meant for Lauterberg to retell the joke, but clearly he was going to.

'But if I remember correctly,' he continued, 'Comrade Honecker *finds* the watch, and rings the Minister to call off the investigation.' Lauterberg paused for a moment, and stared hard at Müller. 'So, aren't you going to deliver the punch line, *Oberleutnant*?'

Müller gave yet another weary sigh.

'Shall I do it for you? The Minister replies: "Too late, I'm afraid. We've already arrested ten people – and they've all confessed."' Lauterberg rocked back in his chair, laughing.

Müller got to her feet. She'd heard the joke before, didn't think it was particularly funny, and had had quite enough of Stefan Lauterberg for one day. Quite enough of her current job. 'Guards,' she shouted down the corridor. 'Take this one back to his cell.'

Two uniformed police officers entered, one of them cuffing the youth to his arm. Lauterberg looked at Müller in disdain as they passed her in the doorway. Then he turned his head, and spat at her feet.

Müller decided to walk the couple of kilometres back to her Schönhauser Allee apartment, rather than take the U-bahn or tram. The heavy summer heat – so oppressive in the confines of the Keibelstrasse police headquarters – was tempered by an evening breeze. But despite the more pleasant atmosphere, she couldn't shrug off a sense of loneliness, of detachment. At the Mitte Murder Commission, under the arches of Marx-Engels-Platz S-bahn station, she and Werner Tilsner had been a little team. Lovers, one time only, but mainly good friends. But for the moment, Tilsner was out of the picture – laid up in a hospital bed recovering from a near-fatal shooting, with no news on when or whether he would return to police work. Keibelstrasse had many more officers within its walls, but Müller didn't really know any of them well enough to call them a friend – except, perhaps, *Kriminaltechniker* Jonas Schmidt. The forensic officer had worked with her on the case of the murdered girl in the graveyard earlier in the year.

She crossed Prenzlauer Allee at the Ampelmann pedestrian signal, and kept up a rapid walk towards the apartment. With each stride she wondered whether her police career, at one point so promising, had now reached a dead end. And all because she'd refused *Oberstleutnant* Klaus Jäger's offer to join him in the Ministry for State Security, the Stasi. She should have known it was the sort of offer you couldn't turn down.

Arriving at her apartment block's entrance, she gave a wry smile. The surveillance vehicle that had been there for weeks had finally disappeared. It was almost as though she wasn't important enough anymore. And when she climbed the stairs from the lobby to the first-floor landing, the almost ubiquitous click of her neighbour Frau Ostermann's door was also absent. Even Frau Ostermann could no longer be bothered poking her nose into Müller's life.

She turned the key in the lock, and entered the apartment. Once a happy home for her and her husband Gottfried. *Ex*-husband. He'd been allowed – as an enemy of the state for his supposed anti-revolutionary activities – to defect to the West, where he was no doubt carving out a successful teaching career. She wondered how long it would be before the authorities would force her – a single divorcee – to move to a smaller apartment, perhaps even a police hostel. Müller shuddered. She couldn't bear that. It would be like being back at the police college. She didn't want any reminders of her time spent there.

Müller went straight to the bedroom, kicked off her shoes, and lay on the bed staring at cracks in the ornate plaster ceiling. She had to pull herself together. Make a decision. She could either stick with the police, try to get her career back on track, or she could get out. One or the other. She couldn't face many more days trying to get idiots like Lauterberg, with their faux Western hippy attitudes, to confess to petty crimes against the state. It was more exhausting than a murder inquiry.

She took a deep breath. One of those days. It had just been one of those days – the sort you moan about to your husband or wife or family when you finally get back home, letting off steam, allowing the frustration to drift away. But Gottfried was in the past now, and that was partly her own decision. For the first time in as long as she could remember she spared a thought for her family. Not that they were any help – they were hundreds of kilometres south, in Oberhof, and if she hadn't felt like going to visit them at Christmas, she certainly wasn't about to now.

She thought back to events in the Harz mountains, towards the end of her last big case. How she'd tried to be the heroine, leading her and Tilsner into a trap that was within a hair's breadth of seeing her deputy shot dead. Going in without back-up. Now Werner Tilsner lay in a bed in the Charité hospital, unable to speak, unable to walk, barely conscious much of the time.

She got to her feet. A shower and then go and visit Tilsner. That would remind her that there were those worse off than she was. Much worse off.

2

Even before she'd opened the door to his hospital room, Müller could see through the glass pane that Tilsner's condition had improved appreciably. He was sitting up in bed, reading. It wasn't an activity she would normally have associated with her smooth-talking deputy. As she opened the door, her surprise soon evaporated. Tilsner rapidly hid the book under his bedcovers, trying not to get his various feeding and drug tubes tangled in the process. Not before Müller had seen the cover: an erotic novel. Still acting true to form, then, she thought.

'Ka-rin,' he spluttered, still unable to form words properly, four months after the shooting.

Müller sat by the bed and took his hand in hers, careful to avoid the intravenous tube attached to the back of it. 'It's good to see you looking so much better, Werner. And reading, I see.' She jokingly reached to retrieve the hidden book, but Tilsner pressed down hard on the bedclothes, then winced from the resulting pain.

'Much . . . bet-ter, yes.' He nodded. 'Read-ing.' He winked at her, showing little sign of embarrassment.

'I wish I could say the same,' she sighed. 'Work's a nightmare – I'd much rather be in bed reading a book.' She shouldn't really burden Tilsner with her problems. But she missed the day-to-day relationship with her one-time deputy.

'How's . . . things . . . at . . .' The mangled sentence stopped. She could see the effort on his face, his chiselled jaw starting to reassert itself under the bloating from too many days lying in bed. 'At . . . the . . . off-ice?'

Müller's brow creased into a frown for a moment as she tried to make out what he was trying to say. Then it clicked.

She rolled her eyes. 'I'm not at the Marx-Engels-Platz office anymore. I've been moved to Keibelstrasse. Someone else is in charge at the Murder Commission.' She could hear the emotion and hurt in her voice, could see the empathy in Tilsner's eyes. 'They've got me doing the mundane jobs that uniform should be sorting out. I've been sidelined, Werner.' She moved forward to whisper in his ear. 'All because I wouldn't agree to your friend Jäger's job offer. Probably not the most sensible thing I've done in my life.'

Tilsner smiled and squeezed her hand. 'You're . . . bet-ter . . . than . . . that.' Again, it took a moment for Müller to decipher the words that her deputy was struggling so hard to form. Once she'd worked them out, she grinned. 'Don't be too free with the compliments. That's not like you at all.'

The squeal of the double doors to the room opening and closing made them both turn their heads. Tilsner had another visitor. *Oberst* Reiniger. The People's Police colonel who'd originally recommended Müller for promotion, who'd protected her in the previous investigation when she'd thrown the rule book out of the window, but who had now rubber-stamped her move to the Keibelstrasse headquarters. Müller wasn't particularly pleased to see him, but he seemed in a jovial mood.

'Good to see you sitting up, Comrade *Unterleutnant*,' he said to Tilsner, drawing up a chair on the opposite side of the bed to Müller, the buttons on his uniform straining as his belly threatened to burst from his trousers. She watched as he performed his usual ritual of brushing imaginary fluff from his epaulettes, drawing attention to the gold stars of his rank. While Reiniger's eyes were admiring his own shoulders, Tilsner tried to mimic the motion, although the tubes prevented him from doing it particularly effectively. The devilment was still there. He *is* recovering, thought Müller. Reiniger looked up, just as Tilsner dropped his hand back down to his lap. 'At this rate,' said the colonel, 'we'll have you back on your next *Kripo* case in no time at all.'

'Not . . . with-out . . . Ka-rin!' Tilsner's face grimaced – whether from actual pain, or the difficulty of emphasising his point, Müller wasn't sure.

Reiniger frowned, and looked quizzically at Müller. 'What's he saying, Karin? Can you make it out?'

'I think he said "Not without Karin", Comrade *Oberst*.'

She watched Reiniger's face redden. 'Yes, well, that won't be happening for the time being. It's out of my hands, I'm afraid.' Then Reiniger held Müller's gaze. 'Actually, Karin, I'm glad I've caught you here. We need to have a word.'

Tilsner seemed to be about to try to utter another sentence, but before he could get it out, Reiniger rose to his feet and gestured with his eyes to Müller – indicating they should continue the conversation away from her deputy's ears, in the corridor.

He waddled off towards the doors with his peculiar penguin-like, head-down gait, the walk that gave the impression to Müller and whoever else was watching that whatever mission he was on was more important than the last.

As she rose to follow, her eyes met Tilsner's, and they exchanged grins.

Reiniger beckoned Müller over to a row of bench seats along the hospital corridor, sat down, and began to speak in a low voice.

'I might have guessed you'd be here. I came over to Keibel-strasse, but they told me you'd already left for the day.' Müller knew it was an admonishment. But she'd reached the point where she didn't care. 'We've a problem, Karin. I think you might be just the person to help us out. It might be a way of getting you back on a murder inquiry team. I take it you'd like that?'

Müller was immediately suspicious. She'd been left alone in the doghouse of Keibelstrasse for a reason. Why was the colonel now trying to lure her out?

Despite her doubts, she nodded slowly. 'What is it, Comrade *Oberst*?'

'They've got a difficult case down near Leipzig. *Bezirk* Halle. Halle-Neustadt, to be precise. You know it, presumably?'

Müller nodded again. 'Of course, Comrade *Oberst*.' She'd never visited, but she knew it from television programmes and magazines. It was, to some extent, the pride of the Republic.

Eventually almost a hundred thousand citizens would be housed in the brand new town immediately to the west of the city of Halle. A hundred thousand citizens in their own apartments. Row after row of high-rise *Plattenbauten*: concrete slab apartment blocks – with the best community facilities in between. The socialist dream in its living, breathing form. The communist East showing that it could do things better than the corrupt, capitalist West.

'We've had to keep this quite hush-hush,' said Reiniger, his eyes scanning the hospital corridor to make sure no one else was listening in. 'But a couple of babies have gone missing. Twins. The Ministry for State Security is involved, trying to keep a lid on things.' At that, Müller's heart sank. She didn't want to be part of another investigation where she was at the beck and call of the Stasi, however much she craved leaving the drudgery of Keibelstrasse interrogations behind. 'They want a female People's Police detective to help. Your name was mentioned. It will be a chance to get back on the horse, Karin. You're a good detective. I know that, you know that. What happened with Jäger . . . well, that was a little unfortunate. But it's a good sign your name's getting mentioned again.'

Müller sighed. 'The thing is, I've become a Berlin girl, Comrade *Oberst*. It's my home now, my city. I'm not sure I want to work outside the Hauptstadt. Isn't it something best left to the local detectives, rather than bringing in someone from outside?'

Reiniger breathed in slowly, putting even more pressure on his uniform's straining buttons. 'Let's put it this way, Karin. If you ever want to rise above the rank of *Oberleutnant* then you're going to have to say yes occasionally. You're going to have to take on jobs you might not particularly want to do, in places you may not particularly want to go. This is an opportunity. But there can be no errors of judgment like last time. Your performance will be monitored closely – and, as you can imagine, not solely by the People's Police.'

'Can I at least think about it?'

'Briefly, yes. But you can't discuss it with Tilsner.' The police colonel rose from his seated position and waited for Müller to join him by the glazed doors of Tilsner's hospital room. He gestured with his eyes towards her deputy, who seemed to be surreptitiously trying to read his book again. 'I don't want him getting all excited, thinking he's going to be going there with you, and discharging himself. He's getting better, as you've seen – the physical wounds are almost healed. But he's nowhere near ready to return to work. He lost so much blood so rapidly the doctors say it led to a minor stroke. In time, he may still recover completely. And obviously our hope is that it will be in a relatively short period of time. But for now he needs speech therapy, physiotherapy . . . possibly even psychotherapy . . . It will be a matter of months, at the very least, before we can even start to consider a return to work.'

Müller nodded. Then there was a moment's silence, with the two of them standing, shuffling from foot to foot, as though Reiniger was waiting for something.

'So, have you thought about it, Karin?'

She started. 'I meant think about it properly, get back to you with an answer tomorrow?'

Reiniger sighed. 'I don't have time for that. I said I'd get back to the People's Police in Halle by the end of the day.' He glanced at his watch, then met her eyes again. 'In other words, about now.' Müller gave a short laugh, and shook her head in amazement. 'Oh, and one thing I should tell you, Karin, which may help make up your mind. It's not just a missing persons inquiry. One of the babies has been found. Dead. And not from natural causes. This is a murder hunt. If you agree, we'll appoint a new deputy for you – from outside the local area, like yourself. The important thing for you, Karin, is that you will be back in charge of your own Murder Commission.'

Reiniger eyeballed her. He held all the trump cards, and knew she wouldn't be able to resist. It was what she wanted. What they both knew she wanted. To get back to the job she loved.

'Yes, then,' she sighed. 'You always knew I was going to say yes, anyway. But can you tell me more about the case?'

Reiniger gave a weak smile. Müller knew he'd got what he'd come for. 'You know all you need for now. No point in me muddying the waters. They'll give you a full briefing when you get there.'

Müller frowned. An investigation which her boss wasn't prepared to talk about – except in the sketchiest of details – sounded potentially troublesome. And the need to bring in someone from Berlin, highly suspicious. But in her current situation, even the troublesome and suspicious was more attractive then the boredom of doing little more than pen-pushing at headquarters.

After saying their goodbyes to Tilsner, without revealing what the sudden urgency to leave was all about, Müller and the colonel made their way through the hospital corridors towards his car. As they turned a corner, Müller suddenly saw a friendly face. Wollenburg – the doctor she'd met earlier that year, across a particularly harrowing autopsy table. They smiled at each other, but kept walking. Müller couldn't resist a glance back – he was as handsome as she remembered. At that exact moment, Wollenburg did the same, and their eyes locked once more. He broke off from the group of doctors and nurses he was with and ran after Müller and Reiniger.

'Do you have a second, Comrade *Oberleutnant*?' Wollenburg asked.

Müller looked questioningly at her superior officer. 'You can have one minute, *Oberleutnant*,' said Reiniger. 'One minute only. I'll wait for you in the lobby.'

'What was it you wanted?' asked Müller, after Reiniger had walked off. 'I'm in a bit of a hurry.'

'Well ...' The doctor paused, his face reddening. He looks very sweet when he blushes, thought Müller. 'I was just wondering ... Erm, I saw you no longer wear a wedding ring, *Oberleutnant*.'

Müller was surprised at the comment. But it was surprise tinged with a hint of excitement ... and embarrassment. She looked down at her ring finger, then met Wollenburg's eyes with a quizzical expression.

'Well ... this is a little ... um, *awkward*, I must confess,' he continued, stumbling over his words. 'I was just wondering if you might be available for a drink sometime, or to go to the theatre, or ...'

Müller's face softened. He was quite cute. She placed her hand on his arm. 'I'd love to. But I'm afraid I'm being transferred to Halle-Neustadt for a period. I don't know when I'll be back.'

The doctor nodded, and gave a broad smile. 'Halle-Neustadt, you say? Hmm. Well, that might still be a possibility.'

'Why, you're not suddenly being sent there too, are you?'

Wollenburg cocked his head. 'Stranger things have happened.' He turned towards where his colleagues were waiting. 'Anyway I've got to rush, but I'll be in touch. Soon, I hope. I expect I will be able to contact you via the Halle-Neustadt People's Police office. Is that right?'

Müller smiled, then walked off in the direction in which Reiniger had disappeared – without giving Wollenburg a definitive answer.

3

The next day

Reiniger's one concession to Müller was to accede to her request to take her own forensic officer with her from Berlin, and drive down south in an unmarked *Kripo* Wartburg – similar to the one she and Tilsner had used at Marx-Engels-Platz. *Kriminaltechniker* Jonas Schmidt had, in many ways, saved her neck in her previous murder investigation, not to mention saving the life of at least one young girl. She was glad to have him at her side once more.

The autobahn journey from Berlin was one she knew she should have taken more frequently, to go to visit her family in Thuringian forest. Yet she'd avoided it, time and time again, usually using the excuse of her murder squad work. Even at her lowest, after the split from Gottfried, she hadn't confided in her mother, brother or younger sister. In Halle-Neustadt that visit would be harder to put off, she knew. And why did she *want* to put it off? It was something indefinable. The sense that her home was now Berlin and that in the mountain village of Oberhof – indeed within her family itself – she'd somehow never properly belonged. Down the years there had been odd incidents which had left Müller yearning for the sort of mothering she knew that some of her friends had received. The warm, smothering love of a mother, wrapping you in a cosy bath towel, rocking you on her knee as she sang a lullaby. It was something Müller had witnessed her mother do with her sister Sara, but never with her. Was that just jealousy – that Sara, as the baby of the family, got better treatment? Or was it just that she and her mother had never got on, and never would? Many of her memories were of arguments, rather than expressions of love. The look her mother had given her when she questioned her about the disappearance of her childhood friend Johannes and his family. The half-remembered visit from a kindly-looking woman who for some reason wanted to see *her* – Karin – provoking something like rage on the part of her mother. Despite all that, Müller knew that sometime during this investigation, however it played out, she would have to continue this journey further south to the family home.

Glancing across now as they entered the outskirts of Halle city itself, Müller watched Schmidt take his nearest hand from the Wartburg's steering wheel and wipe his brow, something he'd done repeatedly on the two-hour journey from the Hauptstadt. The underarm of his white shirt was stained with sweat, with unsightly tidemark rings at the stain's outer edges. She wondered if Schmidt ever felt the same sense of disconnection from his own family. But although they were friends and work colleagues, she didn't – as his superior in rank – feel it was an appropriate topic of conversation. It would simply undermine her. In any case, Schmidt for the moment seemed more concerned about the summer heat.

'Even with the window open, being cooped up in this tin box isn't pleasant,' he said. 'I'll be glad when we get there.'

Müller gave a half-smile in agreement, turned her thoughts away from her family, and remembered the luxury Mercedes she and Tilsner had travelled in through the border crossing point to West Berlin just a few months earlier. It had been winter then, but she wondered if it was equipped with the latest climate control systems she'd seen previewed on Western motoring programmes. Programmes she'd watched with Gottfried. Programmes that, as an officer of the People's Police, she shouldn't have been watching. Well, Gottfried was in his beloved West now, so he could try out those luxury vehicles first-hand, if he could afford them on his teacher's salary. If *anyone* other than rich businessmen could afford them, thought Müller. Here it was a Trabi, a Wartburg if you were lucky, a Czechoslovak Skoda or Soviet Lada if you were *really* lucky – and then only after a wait of several years. None, as far as she knew, had air conditioning. Certainly none she'd ever driven or been driven in.

They were nearing the centre of Halle now. It seemed an unremarkable city to Müller, though she knew it had history: the composer, Handel, had been born here. Now it was more known for the chemical industry that helped to power the Republic's economy. A pollution haze hanging over the southern skyline above Schmidt's shoulder was testament to that – and an acrid, sharp smell that assaulted the back of her throat like a series of needle stabs.

'There it is,' said Schmidt, pointing straight ahead through the windscreen.

Müller's head turned to follow the direction of the corpulent forensic officer's finger. She raised her hand, almost in salute, shielding her eyes from the low, late evening sun and the pink corona surrounding it. They were driving along a raised dual carriageway – a road that seemed to float in the air. Giant, modernistic street lamps as high as blocks of flats were already casting an orange glow through the dusk over the road. And beyond, over the river Saale, block after block of brand new high-rises. The socialist city of the future. Its right-angled shapes, silhouetted in the rosy hue of dusk, like something from a science fiction film. Another world, in outer space.

'Impressive,' said Müller. 'Have you been here before?'

Schmidt shook his head. 'No, but I've relatives in Dresden. Hoyerswerda's near there. Another new town. This looks very similar. The flats in the new towns are very popular. You get a private bathroom, a private toilet. They even put some Western apartments to shame.'

Schmidt braked sharply to avoid colliding with a truck ahead of them, throwing Müller forward so that she had to brace herself against the dashboard. At the same time, the street map Schmidt had been balancing on his lap to navigate with, fell to the floor.

'Shall I pick it up and map-read?' she asked.

'There's not much point, Comrade *Oberleutnant*. I think I've got my bearings now.'

'I could at least look out for the relevant street name signs?' suggested Müller.

'You'd have a hard job. The road we're on is the Magistrale.' Müller could see they were descending now from the elevated section over the Saale river, or rather, rivers, as there seemed to be more than one waterway, but the dual carriageway continued into the distance, flanked by slab apartment blocks – *Platten-bauten* – on each side. 'And this is really the only street you need to remember.'

'Why?' asked Müller.

'Because none of the others have names, *Oberleutnant*. None of the others have names.'

By the time they'd got to the temporary murder squad office – above the fire station – none of the local police were there. Müller's brow knitted in frustration. The baby girl was still missing. *Shouldn't some of them be putting in a night shift? And shouldn't the local uniform captain be waiting to give her a proper briefing?* If this was the way things were currently being run, then Müller would be having stern words. But at least the reception was manned by a young woman, and an envelope with their accommodation keys and directions had been left for them.

The apartment assigned to Müller and Schmidt was in *Wohnkomplex VI*, on the far western fringe of the new town – divided, Schmidt explained, into eight housing complexes, each made up of several numbered apartment blocks. This was how people found their way round. By memorising 'codes', several digits long, that corresponded to an estate, block and apartment number. But Schmidt wasn't slow in pointing out the illogical nature of the system. As they approached their residential area – designated Complex 6 in Latin numerals – they realised each apartment block – at least those which had their numbers displayed – was in the nine hundreds. The block they were looking for had the number 953.

As Schmidt drove round the nameless road that fringed the *Wohnkomplex*, Müller counted off the numbers, determined not to let this new town and its twilight of nameless streets and near-identical homes defeat her. The apartment blocks here formed a continuous, unbroken curve, one merging into the next. They appeared to be the few in the city not to follow a rigid straight line. The wall of concrete was broken only by occasional open-ings for pedestrian walkways: forbidding areas of blackness in the fast-fading sunlight.

'I can't see 953 anywhere,' complained Schmidt.

Neither could Müller. What she did see, parked at the side of the road, was a red Lada saloon. Something about it seemed odd. The driver was just sitting there, as though he was watch-ing something, or waiting for someone. As they passed, he turned his head and looked straight into her eyes. His flashed in the fading sun just for an instant, and Müller found herself shivering slightly. Perhaps it was just all the perspiration evap-orating, making her body colder. But she felt she'd just been appraised – the same way a fox might stare down a human if suddenly, unexpectedly, it's caught out in the open.

'What do you want to do? Shall we stop and ask someone?'

Müller scanned left and right. The street was deserted. Then she remembered the Lada driver. She turned her head, expecting to see the car in the distance, still parked by the roadside. But it wasn't. The driver had started the car – and now appeared to be following them. If that was the case, and it wasn't just coincidence, she had a good idea who the driver might work for.

4

The next day

The temporary murder squad office above the fire station was a hive of activity by the time the two Berlin officers arrived the next morning, soon after eight o'clock. The local People's Police might not believe in late-night working but they were now under way early enough. The core of the murder squad was being formed by officers from outside the local community: Müller and Schmidt from the Hauptstadt, and another *Unterleutnant* to replace Tilsner as her deputy. Müller didn't as yet know the identity of the missing officer, or indeed his or her gender. But the local uniform team would be staying on to assist.

Müller's initial impression was that the local *Vopo* team also seemed reluctant to relinquish – or even share – control of the case. Various officers were heads down in assorted piles of papers and photographs, and didn't acknowledge Müller's arrival. She knew she would have to assert her authority, take charge, otherwise the policemen here would try to take advantage of her. They wouldn't like a woman being the boss, but that decision had been taken at a higher level. They would just have to live with it.

She banged her briefcase down on the main table and cleared her throat. '*Hauptmann* Eschler? Could I have a private word, please?' This was the *Vopo* captain that Reiniger had said would brief her. She recognised him from the four gold diamonds on each of his silvered epaulettes, and smiled at him.

Without smiling in return, Eschler rose and walked to where Müller was standing by the window, overlooking the town's main street. His eyes had a furtive look, and his facial features were a little sharp, almost mean-looking. But perhaps she was being unkind.

'What can I do for you, Comrade *Oberleutnant*?' asked Eschler. Müller could tell from each of his syllables what an effort it was for him to kowtow to her, given that in rank he was nominally her superior. But here, *Kripo* trumped *Vopo*, and Eschler knew it.

'I need a full briefing about the case, please. I have the barest of details, but I need to know what stage the investigation is at, where you're currently concentrating your efforts, and as much about the family involved as possible.'

Eschler gave a little nod. 'Of course. We've freed up a small office for you, Comrade *Oberleutnant*.' Perhaps Müller was imagining it, but Eschler seemed to emphasise the word 'small', as though wanting to put her in her place. 'I'll show you through,' he continued, 'and I'll bring the files.'

Small was certainly an apt description for her workplace. Once she and Eschler were both inside, it already felt full. There was a desk with a chair behind it in front of the window. On top of the desk, a telephone and typewriter. To one side of the room, a bare wooden stool. It reminded Müller of the interrogation room at Hohenschönhausen in Berlin where she'd had that emotional encounter with Gottfried – the last time they'd seen each other. Müller opted to take the chair – if it was her office, she would decide where to sit. She gestured for Eschler to draw up the stool and sit opposite her.

Eschler placed the files gently on the desk. 'So, Comrade *Oberleutnant*. What would you like to know?'

Müller leant her forearms on the desk and steepled her fingers together. 'Everything, Comrade *Hauptmann*. From the beginning.'

The People's Police captain began to summarise the investigation as Müller sat, arms folded across her beige blouse, prompting him to continue with nods of her head.

The dead baby – Karsten Salzmann – was a male, aged just four weeks. He and his twin sister, Maddelena, had been born prematurely in Halle-Neustadt's main hospital, where because of their sickly condition they'd remained in intensive care until about a week ago, when they'd been moved into a general paediatric ward.

'Their parents were regular visitors,' said Eschler. 'The mother, Klara Salzmann, stayed long hours with the twins, although parents are not permitted to sleep in the hospital overnight. However, just one day after coming out of intensive care, both babies were reported missing.'

Müller frowned. 'They were actually taken from the hospital?'

Eschler nodded. 'I'm afraid so. It doesn't reflect very well on the health service, does it? Even though they were snatched overnight, when there were fewer nurses or doctors on duty. We've questioned them all. No one saw anything untoward – they just claim they don't have enough staff to be on constant watch over every patient, twenty-four hours a day. Someone probably just watched the nurses' movements and waited for an opportune moment to strike. As you can imagine, it's all rather sensitive.'

Sensitive? That didn't begin to describe such an appalling breach of security.

'Go on,' prompted Müller.

'Well, the mother was distraught, as you can imagine, and had to be placed under sedation. And because of the . . . *sensitive* . . . nature of the incident, the Ministry of State Security swung quickly into action, and both parents and all the staff were warned not to talk about the case.'

'So the *MfS* were involved right from the outset?' asked Müller.

'Not only involved,' said Eschler, frowning. 'The Stasi were basically running the investigation from the word go.'

Müller tried hard not to let her facial expression show her disquiet at this news. She hadn't met Eschler's full team of uniform officers yet, and she didn't know which of them would be Stasi IMs – unofficial informers. It was certain someone would be. Perhaps even Eschler himself.

'So at what point did the local *Kriminalpolizei* take over?' asked Müller.

'They didn't. I was just about to get to that.'

'Apologies, Comrade *Hauptmann*. Please continue.'

Eschler gave a half-smile. 'My team – the uniform division in Halle-Neustadt – became involved when Karsten's body was found.' Eschler reached into one of the folders, pulled out two enlarged photographs, and handed them to Müller.

Müller began to examine the uppermost image. It was unremarkable. A battered red suitcase by the side of a railway line, the leather – or more probably faux leather – grazed and torn, either from old age or some kind of impact, or a combination of both.

'That was what his body was found in,' explained Eschler. 'It was discovered by a railway worker three days ago near Angersdorf, at the side of the S-bahn line leading to and from the chemical works at Leuna and Buna, near Merseburg. Fortunately the worker didn't see fit to open it, and simply alerted us, the People's Police. Probably too worried about his own job. And the first of my officers on the scene, feeling the weight and inhaling the odours of rotting flesh, alerted me. So we have concrete evidence to work with. Perhaps even some fingerprints. But the key photograph is the next one.' Eschler gently took hold of both photos, and Müller eased her grip as he moved the upper one aside.

If the first photograph – at least on the surface – looked relatively innocent, the same could not be said for the second. Müller jerked her head back. The image was shocking, even to her – a seasoned murder detective.

The suitcase, as opened at the local police headquarters.

With the body of a baby inside.

The eyes were closed, and the facial expression was almost peaceful. But the ugly purple and red bruises on the baby boy's face told a different story. A young life extinguished, squashed in a case, and dumped from a train. Müller had to breathe deeply for a moment and compose herself.

'Do we know the cause of death?' she asked, finally.

Eschler stretched his arms out and shrugged his shoulders. 'The full official autopsy's not until tomorrow. You'll be able to attend in person. But from his initial look at the body, the pathologist came to the fairly obvious conclusion that the boy was battered to death, as you can see from those horrible bruises. In other words, he was murdered.'

'But you were saying the *Kripo* in Halle have been kept out of the investigation. That seems odd, doesn't it?'

Eschler shrugged again. 'It was at the request of the Ministry for State Security. That's why you were brought in, Comrade *Oberleutnant*. The Stasi wanted the murder squad to be made up of detectives from outside the immediate area. As I understand it, it's part of their attempts to put a lid on any possible panic, before it starts.'

Müller sighed. She wasn't sure it made much sense. She, Schmidt, and the third still-to-be-identified officer were all going to have to contend with building up their local knowledge, working in unfamiliar territory, alongside potentially hostile local officers who wouldn't be impressed that they'd been sidelined by colleagues from the Hauptstadt, and that their own detectives were being kept at arm's length. 'Yet your team is staying on the inquiry, Comrade Eschler. Didn't you ask yourself why?'

If Eschler understood the insinuation behind Müller's words, he was seemingly unmoved. 'Sometimes, Comrade Müller, it's not the wisest thing to question orders.'

'Quite,' said Müller. 'But it must be encouraging for your team that the Stasi obviously trust you.' Müller didn't need to add that there was only one logical reason for the Ministry having such trust in Eschler's men. *They must have someone on the inside. The only question is: who?*

Müller pushed the photographs to one side.

'What about the Salzmanns themselves?' she asked. 'What do we know about them? Presumably we have to consider them as suspects, too?'

Eschler nodded. 'Yes, until and unless we know differently. But we've been going fairly gently with them, for understandable reasons. To be honest, we were going to leave any tougher questioning to you, the *Kripo* team.'

'That's fine,' said Müller. 'We'll be doing that, of course. But come on – tell me what you know about them.'

'They seem model citizens,' said Eschler. 'They were one of the first to be assigned an apartment in Halle-Neustadt, just under eight years ago. Their apartment is virtually directly opposite us.' Eschler flicked his eyes towards the window behind Müller. She turned in her seat to look. 'It's that high-rise – known as an *Ypsilon Hochhaus* because its three wings form a Y-section when viewed from the air. Anyway, they're both Party members. Reinhard Salzmann, the father, is a fork-lift truck driver at the chemical factory, where many of Halle-Neustadt's residents work. The mother, Klara, was still on maternity leave when all this happened – she works at the main *Kaufhalle*, here in the centre.'

'And no police files on them? No record of violence, petty crime?'

'Nothing. As clean as a whistle. As clean as two whistles, in fact. Of course, that's as far as the People's Police are concerned. The Stasi may tell a different story.'

Müller blew out her cheeks. 'So you're saying the Stasi *do* have something on them?'

Eschler shook his head. 'Not at all, Comrade *Oberleutnant*. Not at all. I'm just pointing out that just because neither of them have a record with the People's Police, it doesn't mean they're not known to the authorities in some respect. However, as far as we're concerned, they're clean. No motive for harming their own children that I can see.'

'And no opportunity?' asked Müller.

'No. They both seem to have watertight alibis, from the gentle questioning that we did conduct. On the night in question, they'd been invited round for dinner by some friends. With all the vigils at the hospital, they were both tired – too tired to cook for themselves, and their friends were helping out. It all seems to check out, but you might want to go over it all again.'

Müller nodded slowly, and then picked up the photo of Karsten, and frowned. 'Even if this is a murder, our priority has to lie just as much in trying to find the baby girl, if, as I hope, she's still alive. Are we searching house-to-house?'

Eschler gave her an apologetic look. 'We've been told not to, Comrade *Oberleutnant*. By the Stasi liaison officer, *Hauptmann*

Janowitz, and his boss, *Major* Malkus. They say it will only create panic.'

'We will have to challenge that, then. An apartment-by-apartment search has to be our best way of finding the girl, and stopping the abductor or killer before he, she or they strike again.'

Eschler gave a heavy sigh. 'I've tried to argue the case, believe me. I agree with you. But *Major* Malkus wants our search to use more subtle methods. Have you met Comrade Malkus yet? He was here looking for you last night.'

She thought back to the previous night's encounter with the Lada driver. Had that been the Stasi major or his assistant? She had no idea really. And no evidence the car *had* actually been following her and Schmidt, as opposed to simply driving in the same direction at the same time. She shook her head. 'No. As yet, I haven't had the pleasure.'

Eschler gave her a weak smile. 'I expect he will catch up with you before too long.'

Müller nodded and rose from her seat, drawing herself up to her full height. 'Let's meet the rest of the team, shall we? I'm keen to know exactly what they have been doing instead of a house-to-house search. How about in half-an-hour's time, at nine o'clock? I take it they're all still here, or are they out and about already?'

Eschler looked down at his watch, frowning. 'Some may be going to breakfast around that time. We start early, as you can see.'

Müller breathed in slowly. This whole case felt like trying to push water uphill. 'Please ask them to delay their breakfasts. I'm sure that won't be too much trouble, given that it's a murder inquiry.'

In the event all the officers who'd been detailed to help the investigation arrived promptly, as requested, on the dot of nine. Müller surveyed the room, mentally calculating the numerical strength of the team. There would be herself and the as-yet-unannounced *Kripo Unterleutnant*, Schmidt as the sole forensic officer – but with access to help from the People's Police should he need it – then Eschler as the police captain leading the uniform side. He was assisted by a police sergeant, who Eschler introduced as *Wachtmeister* Fernbach, and three beat constables, as well as various typists and secretaries.

Once everyone had quietened down, Müller cleared her throat and began to speak. 'Thanks very much for agreeing to this meeting, comrades. I'm *Oberleutnant* Karin Müller, from the Hauptstadt *Kripo*, and this . . .' Müller gestured towards Schmidt who was trying to button up in his scientist's white overall, '. . . is *Kriminaltechniker* Jonas Schmidt, again from Berlin, who'll be in charge of forensics. We're also expecting one more *Kripo Unterleutnant* to join us in the next couple of days. Now I dare say you're asking yourselves why a Berlin detective has been brought in – why not someone from Halle-Neustadt or at least from *Bezirk* Halle? I can't give you the definitive answer for that, but I can assure you that the decision has been taken at a high level. So let's deal with it, and make the best of it.'

Müller glanced round the room. She wanted to win the team over, whatever it took. Even if it meant playing to their prejudices against women in leadership roles. She took a breath, smiled, and continued. 'There will be times when Jonas and I will need to rely on your much greater local knowledge. We already had problems finding our apartment last night. The numbering system of the blocks and the lack of street names . . . Well, it was too much for my brain to cope with, anyway.' The admission brought a few gentle laughs. '*Hauptmann* Eschler has just given me a full briefing about the case, and I'm sure you're all completely familiar with it by now. What I want to impress on you is that this is a sensitive inquiry. Halle-Neustadt is a very important city for the Republic. We want people to want to live here, to want to work here. So as well as finding the murderer or murderers as soon as possible, we've got to do it in a subtle way. We don't want to alarm people. I'm sure you understand. That said, I will be asking again about conducting a full apartment-by-apartment search, even though you've been prevented from doing that so far. Anyway, *Wachtmeister* Fernbach, I understand from *Hauptmann* Eschler that you're going to explain to me what the team plans to do today.'

The uniform sergeant – Fernbach – got to his feet and moved in front of a street map on the far wall. Müller and the others gathered round. She could see the plan of the new town had been divided into various colour-coded sections, roughly corresponding to the various *Wohnkomplexe*: eight residential areas – each comprising several apartment blocks.

Fernbach, a ruddy-faced man with bushy eyebrows, cleared his throat. 'If anyone asks us what we're doing, we're telling them it's an operation to secure the city against counter-revolutionary spies. That's what the Stasi's asked us to say, anyway.' The sergeant raised his hirsute brows, clearly indicating his dislike of the subterfuge. 'The story is that the West is so impressed by what we've achieved here in the Neustadt, they want to send spies over to try to copy our architecture and designs. I'm not sure many people believe it, but equally it's fair to say that news of the disappearance of the babies isn't really widely known. Medical staff at the hospital face disciplinary action if they talk about it. The trouble is, there are plenty of hiding places in the new town, if the baby girl is even here. And unfortunately, by and large, many babies look identical to each other. From the face, it's even hard sometimes to tell girls from boys.'

Müller coughed. 'I'm sure the mothers will know.'

'Well, yes. You're right, Comrade *Oberleutnant*. I was forgetting we had a woman present. It's harder for us men.'

Resisting the urge to tear Fernbach off a strip, Müller simply gave a small smile. 'Go on,' she said. 'You were saying there are lots of hiding places. Where, exactly?'

Fernbach started tracing his fingers in straight lines along the map, between the various *Wohnkomplexe*, and then between the strangely numbered apartment blocks in each numbered residential area. 'Underground,' explained Fernbach. 'All the apartment blocks are heated from this plant in the centre of the city. And then the pipes radiate out to take warm air to each block. There are kilometres and kilometres of underground pipe tunnels. But we're also looking at waste ground, scrubland surrounding the new town, and along all the various railway lines, in case it's not just one . . .' Fernbach's voice tailed off, gloomily. Müller knew what he'd been about to say. *In case it wasn't just one murder. In case the second twin, Maddelena, was now also dead.*

'All right, thank you, *Wachtmeister*. For today, I'm going to leave you to continue with all that under *Hauptmann* Eschler's command. Over the next few days, I may want to adjust our priorities. But I want to get fully up to speed today, visiting where Karsten's body was dumped, and – if necessary – meeting with this *Major* Malkus to argue the case for a full search of every home in the city, and the surrounding areas.'

'Good luck with that,' said Fernbach in a loud whisper. Loud enough that Müller could hear – quiet enough that he could claim he'd said something else if he was challenged. Müller let it pass. Until she'd fully appraised herself of the dynamics of the team, she wasn't going to start throwing her weight around.

The short meeting was clearly over, and Müller raised her eyes at Eschler – indicating he should take over from now on. Müller herself moved to the exhibits table, ignoring the battered red suitcase that Karsten Salzmann's tiny body had been discovered in, ignoring the photos of the battered boy himself, and instead stared at the photo of Maddelena Salzmann. His twin sister. The fact that this case involved twins – one missing, one murdered – was too stark a reminder of her own past. Her own aborted twins: the painful memories raked up again, just as they had been in the case of the murdered *Jugendwerkhof* teenager earlier in the year. Maddelena's innocent baby face stared back at her. The girl was smiling, perhaps at her mother. The smile was like a knife into Müller's gut – a sharp, visceral reminder that their ability to solve this case, and solve it quickly, was literally a matter of life . . . and death.

5

Later that day

Müller rocked back on her feet as the express roared by, centimetres from where she'd been peering down at the taped-off square of ballast at the trackside, the shape of the mound of stone chips disturbed where the suitcase had landed – at considerable speed. She'd been concentrating so hard on the crime scene, picturing how it all must have happened, that she hadn't seen the train coming.

'Careful, *Oberleutnant*,' said *Kriminaltechniker* Jonas Schmidt at her side. 'I did warn you they wouldn't be stopping the trains for us.' Müller took a couple of deep breaths, letting her heart rate calm, then smoothed down her windswept hair with her hands. She smiled at the forensic officer. 'Did you bring the photographs, Jonas?'

'Yes, of course, Comrade *Oberleutnant*.'

As Schmidt dug around in his briefcase to retrieve them, Müller looked across at the parallel roadside where the two uniformed *Volkspolizei* officers who'd accompanied them to the scene were leaning against a marked Wartburg patrol car. After their difficulties navigating the nameless streets the previous evening, Müller and Schmidt had been grateful for the chauffeur service. Although she again had a nagging worry that the job of the two *Vopos* might be as much one of surveillance as driving them around. But she'd wanted to come here to see the site for herself. She needed to know that Eschler's conviction that the suitcase had been thrown from the train was well-founded.

'Here you go, *Oberleutnant.*' Schmidt passed over a bundle of plastic-wrapped photographs. Müller had seen them before, of course, in her meeting with Eschler. But this was the way she liked to work. To try to get a visual feel for the scene. She held up the photo of the unopened case across part of her field of vision, lining it up against the view of the railway track, imagining how the body had got there. And then looked again at the tragic picture of little Karsten's battered body.

Then she returned the photos to Schmidt, and he placed them back in his briefcase. What had they told her? Very little. It was just a ritual she liked to perform. After all, this wasn't the location of the actual murder – *if indeed that's what this is.* The autopsy wasn't until the morning. She wasn't prepared to jump to any conclusions.

Müller noticed Schmidt had moved away and was searching the trackside in the direction of Halle-Neustadt town centre. What was he up to? Then she glanced back at the *Vopo* officers at the roadside. Another car, this time unmarked, had drawn up, and both policemen were leaning down talking to the occupants through the open front windows. The new arrivals looked official. Wearing suits. She had a good idea who they might be.

Schmidt ambled back towards her, carrying something in an evidence bag. Two somethings. A disposable lighter and a cigarette butt. The lighter was interesting, thought Müller. Usually only carried by Westerners, or those who had access to *Intershops*.

'I shouldn't think they're connected,' he said. 'But we might as well have a look. The suitcase, although it was heavier, would have travelled further. That's why I was looking back along the track towards Ha-Neu.' Schmidt's use of the nickname for the new town threw Müller for a second. It sounded exactly the same as the German pronunciation of the Vietnamese capital, Hanoi. There were plenty of Vietnamese guest workers in the Republic. No doubt a few of them had invented jokes around it.

'That doesn't make sense, Jonas, does it? Wouldn't the heavier object fall to the ground more quickly?'

'It's hard to explain, *Oberleutnant*, and not really an exact science. In a vacuum, heavy and light objects fall to the ground at the same rate. However the suitcase – and the lighter and butt, if indeed they're from that train, which I expect they aren't – would initially be travelling at the same speed as the train. But the suitcase, being heavier, is less affected by air resistance – so would travel further.'

'Hmm,' murmured Müller, who didn't feel much clearer on the matter than she had before Schmidt's explanation. 'Anyway, I think we're done here. I just wanted to get a feel for where the body was dumped, really. I don't suppose we're going to learn very much that the local *Kripo* don't already know.'

Schmidt nodded, and then the two officers started to pick their way carefully down the embankment to the waiting police car. As they drew closer, the two suited men from the unmarked car alongside got out, and walked towards them.

'Good morning, Comrade *Oberleutnant*,' said the first man, extending his hand towards Müller, and holding her gaze in a vaguely challenging way. 'We were hoping to catch up with you in the People's Police office in Ha-Neu, but they said you'd come out here. I'm *Major* Uwe Malkus, and this is *Hauptmann* Horst Janowitz. We're from the Ministry for State Security office in Halle-Neustadt. We just wanted to let you know we're here, and available to offer you any assistance, should you require it.'

As Müller and Schmidt shook hands with the two men in turn, the high summer sun emerged from behind a rare cloud, illuminating the older man. Müller found she couldn't tear her eyes from his. She was staring, and then she realised why. The sun's glare reflected in his irises – irises that were an unusual yellowy-brown colour. They had a depth to them that almost seemed to have a magnetic pull, sucking her in.

She dropped her gaze, like an animal acknowledging its subservience to a dominant rival before any blows had been struck. Annoyed at herself she raised her eyes again and answered, as firmly as she dared. 'I think we'll be fine with the help of the local People's Police and *Kripo*, Comrade *Major*, but many thanks for your offer.'

Malkus gave a small nod and smile, but Müller was conscious that Janowitz alongside him was unsmiling and still staring fixedly at her, as his boss had been a moment before.

'Nevertheless,' said Malkus, 'there are peculiar sensitivities to this case.' Müller thought about challenging him about what these 'peculiar sensitivities' actually were. Eschler had given an outline, but it still didn't really add up. However, now perhaps wasn't the most opportune time. After a short pause, Malkus continued. 'Ha-Neu is an important project for the Republic, as I'm sure you realise. So I'd be grateful if you'd do me the honour of dropping by the Ministry for State Security office later today so that we can brief you fully.' Malkus handed her his business card. 'Would three o'clock be convenient?'

Müller paused before answering, but knew she had no choice. 'Of course, Comrade *Major*.'

'Good, good,' nodded the Stasi officer. 'We'll see you then.' He glanced slightly disapprovingly at Schmidt, who'd unpacked a sandwich and was chewing on a piece so large his mouth was half open, the contents on show a bit like clothes in one of the latest front-loading washing machines. 'Alone, please, Comrade *Oberleutnant*. I'm sure Comrade Schmidt here will be wanting to get on with his forensic work – once he's finished his early lunch.'

6

Ten years before: 1965
Halle

Hansi is so kind to me. He knows this is a difficult time and that I'm a little frightened about the pregnancy, but he's always reassuring, giving me shoulder massages, making me cups of coffee, visiting the cake counter in the *Kaufhalle* to bring me my favourite apple mousse cake. I shouldn't have so much of it, of course, but Hansi says it's all right. 'After all, you're eating for two now, Franziska,' he'll say, while rubbing my tummy.

A couple of weeks ago, I told him I was worried that I couldn't feel the baby kicking. The other mothers at the antenatal class are always talking about this. 'Ooh, I feel a little kick there,' they'll say. 'I think this one's going to be a footballer when he grows up.' I do worry when I don't feel anything. But Hansi took me for a check-up with his doctor friend and he says the doctor told him there was nothing to worry about. That was such a relief. Although I know I *am* pregnant, I knew as soon as my strawberry weeks stopped. That's such a lovely name for it, isn't it? It's always made me laugh, even though my first strawberry weeks were during . . . No! I'm not going to think about that. Hansi says it's bad for me, remembering those days.

Sometimes now I'll pretend. If Frau Becker says her foot-baller has been kicking again, sometimes I'll say: 'Oh. I felt a little nudge then. Only a very gentle one. I don't think mine's a footballer. She must be a baby girl.' I did that this morning, and Frau Becker laughed. It's so nice to be meeting these new friends. I haven't had many friends these past few years.

Frau Becker of course suffers terribly from morning sickness. I don't feel left out about *that*. Hansi gives me these little pills to prevent it. He's so clever. He works at the chemical factory at Leuna, you know. Has a very good job. Went to university. I was never clever enough for that. And he does some work for the Ministry too – he's quite important. Sometimes he gets me to help with his official Ministry business. You know, if I see any-thing that doesn't look quite right. If anyone's acting oddly, and might need the authorities to help them.

Anyway, that's enough daydreaming. That's my trouble, always daydreaming. Try to stay calm, think of the future, the future with the new baby. We've so much to look forward to, that's what Hansi always says.

There's a new shop they've just opened in Schkeuditz so I'm popping out this afternoon to pay a visit. I won't buy anything, of course. I've promised Hansi I'll try not to buy any more. But it's so exciting. All the tiny, brand new clothes. I love the smell, the feel of them. I've got quite a collection in the chest of drawers in the apartment. Two drawers full. I don't think Hansi knows quite how much stuff I've already got. But it's best to be prepared. What would happen if there was a sudden shortage of baby girls' clothes, just after she was born? And it's only a couple of months away now.

I'm one of the lucky ones who doesn't show that much. I don't like to gossip, but if you had a really obvious bump like Frau Becker's, well, it must be so uncomfortable, mustn't it? I wonder how she gets to sleep at night? I expect she has to sleep on her back. That's another thing that did worry me for a while. But Hansi said the doctor told him that I'm a big girl, and baby bumps don't show so much on big girls. That made me chuckle. I'm not so very big, but I do admit I am rather partial to a slice or two of apple mousse cake. What expectant mother wouldn't be?

There was such a rude woman on the bus to Schkeuditz just now. Who did she think she was? We're all supposed to be equal now, aren't we? But she was tutting and sighing as she sat next to me, claiming I was taking up two seats in the bus, not the one I was entitled to. I said I was expecting, though, and started rubbing my stomach, faking a bit of pain. That soon shut her up. Stupid woman.

The bell that rings as I enter the shop startles me, and just for a moment I wonder where I am. Sudden noises sometimes do that, you know, after . . .

Anyway I soon collect myself, and start to look around. I spot a lovely pink all-in-one, and wander over to take a look. The material is so soft, like brushed wool. I stroke it for a moment.

That's the wonder of our new country. We can produce materials that are even better than the real thing. They'll last longer, I know. Not like the stuff in the throwaway West.

'Can I help you, citizen?' the young shop assistant asks. She's a pretty thing, barely out of school. I expect this is her first real job.

'Ooh, I don't know,' I sigh. 'It's so lovely, but I'm not sure I can afford it.'

'They're the latest style, just in. They're proving very popular,' says the girl. 'Is one of your friends having a baby?'

I feel a bit affronted by this, and point to my stomach. '*I'm* expecting. Surely you can tell? Just two months to go.' The girl reddens. So she should. But then I smile at her. After all, she's not the first to make that mistake. I lower my voice to a whisper. 'I must admit it *is* lovely, but my husband says I shouldn't buy any more baby clothes.'

'He won't know, though, will he?' she whispers back, as though we're two schoolgirls sharing a secret. 'Can't you just hide it away somewhere until the big day?'

Well I suppose I can, I think. I give her a small nod, and we take it to the payment counter.

7

Ten years later: July 1975
Halle-Neustadt, East Germany

Back in the incident room in Ha-Neu, Schmidt busied himself with his railway findings – searching for fingerprints on the cigarette butt and lighter – while Müller got ready for her meeting with Malkus. She looked in the mirror on the back of the door, adjusting her minimal make-up – little more than retouching her black eyeliner – and straightening her short coat. The recent sunny days, first in Berlin, now here in Ha-Neu, had given her skin tone a healthy glow. The trauma of the previous case, her break-up with Gottfried, all had seemed to leave their mark earlier in the year. Now she looked more her usual self. Perhaps too youthful-looking for a murder squad head.

That was the reason for her choice of coat colour. The heat was stifling, but Müller had brought a lightweight red jacket with her from Berlin, and she took it now from the back of the door of the small temporary office Eschler's team had provided her with. She'd deliberately chosen it to make herself stand out, not in meeting the public, but for her dealings with other officers.

The red made her feel more powerful. It was only psychological, perhaps, but she sensed from her earlier meeting with Malkus that winning – or at least competing in – psychological battles might be the key to their relationship.

Malkus might have summoned her to this meeting, leaving her little choice but to attend. But she planned to use it as an opportunity to push for a full and open search for Maddelena. If – as Eschler and his team claimed – the Stasi were resisting this, then she wanted to know exactly why. A desire to avoid panic seemed trivial, set against the welfare of a baby girl for whom time was almost certainly running out.

She grabbed the Wartburg's ignition keys from the table and made her way towards the People's Police car park. As she did so, Eschler rose from his desk to follow, a shopping bag in one hand, a piece of paper in the other.

As they descended the stairs, their footsteps echoing like handclaps on the bare concrete, he handed her the piece of paper. It turned out to be a colour-coded map.

'I thought this might be useful. You're not the only one who gets confused by the numbering system for addresses. I find this helps me. It has all the *Wohnkomplexe* shaded in different colours, similar to the one on the incident room wall. Sometimes it's not easy to see where the boundaries of each residential area are. This should do the trick.'

Müller took the map and nodded her thanks. Hopefully this was a small sign that she was winning the uniform captain over to her side, rather than him treating her as an unwelcome imposter.

Once they were in the car park, Müller got into the Wartburg's driver's seat, and – to her surprise – Eschler climbed into the passenger seat to her right, placing the shopping bag between his legs in the footwell.

'Were you planning on coming with me, Comrade *Hauptmann*?'

Eschler laughed. 'No.' He leaned towards her, took the map from her clasped hand and unfolded it. 'I just thought I'd point out the Stasi regional headquarters for *Bezirk* Halle, which is where Malkus will be meeting you. It's here, easy enough to find, on the eastern edge of the new town. At the edge of *Wohnkomplex VIII* – the one that's shaded blue.'

Müller's eyes followed his finger as he traced the route on the map, then were drawn once more to his bag.

'And while I go to meet Malkus, are you planning a shopping trip?'

Eschler grinned, the smile softening the features that – just a few hours earlier – Müller had found unfriendly, even threatening. 'No, no,' he laughed. 'These are for you.' He opened the bag so Müller could see its contents. 'Some vegetables from my family allotment. I realise you won't have access to anything like that while you're here, and, well, we had a good crop this year.'

'That's really kind of you ...' She paused for a second. '... Bruno. Can I call you Bruno?'

Eschler shifted in the seat and extended his hand to shake Müller's. 'Of course, Comrade *Oberleutnant*. But in front of the team –'

'Don't worry. In front of the team, I shall make sure I use your full title, Bruno. And you . . . you must call me Karin.'

Eschler nodded. 'I'm sorry if I was a little offhand and unwelcoming today at the briefing. I'm sure you appreciate, it's difficult having to relinquish control to a team from outside the local area. But I want us to work together in a friendly, cooperative way, as much as possible.'

'Of course,' said Müller. 'I understand.'

'The vegetables are my little way of saying sorry.'

Müller smiled warmly. 'Much appreciated. Jonas Schmidt and I are off our usual patch. We'll need your team behind us. The gift is very welcome.'

Eschler climbed out of the car, but then ducked his head back in again before closing the door. 'One thing, Karin. Be careful what you agree to with Malkus. I know we're all on the same side, and by and large want the same thing. But they're a funny pair, him and *Hauptmann* Janowitz. The major's OK if you stay on the right side of him. Janowitz, however . . . well, you'll probably find you're dealing with him day to day. And he's a cold fish. It's very hard to stay on the right side of *Hauptmann* Janowitz, take it from me. I would be very careful in your dealings with him.' The police captain gave a gentle bang on the vehicle's roof. 'Anyway, I shouldn't be keeping you. Good luck.' He slammed the door and wandered back towards the incident room.

Müller had left more than enough time to get to her meeting, and now had about twenty minutes to spare. She decided to use it to get her bearings around Ha-Neu in the daylight. The previous evening she and Schmidt had been too busy finding – and settling into – the apartment.

The lack of street names was something that – coming from Berlin – would take a lot of getting used to, but she managed to navigate by referring to Eschler's colour-coded plan and comparing that to the numbering of the apartment blocks. What struck her – from the children cooling off in the fountains, mothers in their short dresses pushing their prams over pedestrian walkways, and Pioneers in their white, blue and red uniforms – was a general air of carefree summer happiness. There was no sign that word of what had happened to the twin babies had affected people's everyday lives. Perhaps the Stasi's policy of a news blackout *was* the right way, thought Müller. But she couldn't shut out the nagging voice in her head that told her that – for the sake of missing baby Maddelena – house-to-house inquiries were necessary. She glanced at another mother with a pram, getting a fleeting look at the baby's face as she drove past. Although she'd nearly pulled him up for it, what Fernbach had said about most babies looking very similar did have an element of truth. If anyone wanted to steal a baby, perhaps the best way of hiding it would be to pretend it was your own. Was that conceivable?

Müller suddenly slammed on the brakes to avoid an elderly woman weaving about on a bicycle, the weighed-down shopping nets attached to each handle causing the old dear to wobble alarmingly. The woman's angry glare reminded Müller of a chore she would rather not face. It was the same sort of thunderous look she'd often been on the receiving end of from her mother. She wouldn't be able to put off the overdue visit to the family home in Thuringia for much longer. It wasn't something she was relishing. Her police career had provided her with an escape from the stifling atmosphere of the family home and those angry looks whenever she did the smallest thing wrong. The angry looks that never seemed to be directed towards her younger sister, Sara, and brother, Roland. *Why?* she wondered. Surely any parent should want to treat their offspring similarly, yet her relationship with her mother had always been fractious at best – occasionally downright hostile. Was that Müller's fault, her mother's fault, or something else?

She'd driven for another few hundred metres almost on autopilot, but now she pulled sharply to a stop and consulted the map. Here, the apartments were newer, uncompleted, with building rubble and dried-up mud between the blocks, and despite trying to follow Eschler's colour codes, she realised she was lost. Not only that, but in this section of the town the people, the citizens of Ha-Neu, all seemed to have disappeared. No proud mothers pushing prams. No Pioneers in their smartly starched uniforms. Müller felt herself give an involuntary shudder. Panic began to constrict her stomach: she'd be late for her meeting with Malkus, and the psychological protection of her red jacket wouldn't be much use. Not the best way to start if she really was having her performance monitored.

Something made her look in the rear-view mirror. Perhaps she was looking for the previous night's red Lada – the one that may or may not have been following her and Schmidt. That

particular car was nowhere to be seen, but some hundred metres
or so behind her, a black Skoda was parked on the same side of
the road, with a figure at the driver's side. Had that been following her this time? If it had, she hadn't noticed. In the sharp
shadow thrown by the nearest apartment block, she couldn't
make out if the occupant was male or female. But she hoped
they would be able to help her – Stasi observer or not.

Müller got out of the Wartburg, and – with Eschler's street
map in her hands – made her way towards the Skoda. As she
entered the same cloak of shadow that was partially obscuring
the car and its occupant, she saw it was a man inside – staring
straight at her. Something about the look was unfriendly, even
though he had no way of knowing she was a police officer. She
was in plain clothes, her car was unmarked. Unless, of course,
he knew exactly who she was, and that was why he was here.
Keeping tabs on her.

For a few seconds, Müller held the man's gaze as she closed
the space between them. But then he broke off the stare, looked
down at the Skoda's dashboard, and Müller heard the roar of the
engine starting up. She raised her arm with the map as he drove
past, but the man ignored her.

She put her hand to her brow, feeling the thump of a headache starting, her body battling the fierce, dry heat and her
mounting anxiety. But as she drew her hand down across her
face, her eyes focussed on the apartment block itself. It was one
of the few in this newly built part of Ha-Neu which had its block
number assigned. Relief flooded through her as she matched
the block number to her map: she had her bearings once more.

The towering concrete apartments – which had seemed to be closing in on her, trapping her in a maze of nameless streets – now once again seemed benign, inanimate.

Müller checked her watch as she studied the map. She'd drifted into the far west of the town, near the apartment assigned to her and Schmidt, although until just now she hadn't realised that. Twenty minutes had been wasted by her unnecessary detour and panic about getting lost. Even if she drove at speed back to the eastern side of town, and the Stasi HQ, next to *Wohnkomplex VIII*, she knew she would be late.

As she turned off the Magistrale, Müller glanced into the Wartburg's rear-view mirror again. Her heart rate quickened when she saw the black Skoda making the same turning towards Stasi HQ. At first, she told herself to stop being so paranoid. That it might just be coincidence that the other vehicle was taking the same route. She decelerated ahead of the barrier at the gated and walled Ministry for State Security compound. As she did so, the Skoda passed her and entered the Stasi zone without stopping.

By the time her pass had been examined and the guard had rung to confirm her appointment, Müller's tardiness verged on being reckless. Not the best way to start what already promised to be a difficult relationship with Malkus and Janowitz. As soon as she was out of the car and had put her red jacket back on, a plain-clothes officer was at her side as her escort, whether she wanted one or not.

'Good afternoon, Comrade *Oberleutnant*. I'm here to take you for your meeting with *Major* Malkus. This way, please.'

As she walked alongside the Stasi operative, Müller looked up at the outside of the building. It was much like the other high-rise blocks of Ha-Neu. Almost brand new, with seven storeys and bands of terracotta-stained render underneath each floor's line of windows – giving the building a horizontally striped appearance. The headquarters was cut into thirds by two towers made up of decorative concrete screen blocks, adorned by a repeating pattern of the Stasi's emblem in the same dull cement grey: the Republic's flag attached to a rifle, held up by a muscular worker's arm.

The entrance towards which the officer was guiding her was under one of the towers. It looked to Müller almost identical to the entrance of the main Stasi HQ in the Hauptstadt at Normannenstrasse. But this would be the first time she'd actually set foot inside a Ministry for State Security premises – other than the jail at Hohenschönhausen where Gottfried had been held earlier in the year. The memory of that, the way they'd tried to use manufactured evidence against her former husband, and her more recent encounter with the agent in the Skoda, made her shiver despite the heat. Malkus had talked of offering her and the team any 'assistance' they needed. In her experience, assistance from an agency like the Ministry for State Security was often a poisoned chalice.

Malkus appeared to greet her warmly, rising from the leather chair behind his desk, shaking her hand, and then inviting her to sit on a low corduroy sofa at the side of the room. He retook the desk seat, his bald head shining as the afternoon sun streamed through the window. His eyeline was a good metre or so above hers. No doubt deliberate, thought Müller, the height differential putting her at an immediate disadvantage.

'Thanks very much for coming, Comrade *Oberleutnant*,' Malkus began, as though she'd had some choice in the matter. 'And don't worry about being late, I realise you and the team must be busy getting to grips with things.' He said this with a thin smile – but it was an admonishment, and Müller knew it.

'Apologies, Comrade *Major*. It's taking me a little while to get used to the fact that there are no street names. It's very different from Berlin.'

'Quite, quite,' said Malkus, sitting back in the chair and twiddling his thumbs slowly. Then he leant forward and pulled up the cuffs of his long-sleeved white shirt a fraction, leaning his arms on the desk. Müller's eyes were drawn to the white bust of the sharp-faced head of the Soviet Cheka, Felix Dzerzhinsky, on the desktop. She knew Stasi members liked to think of themselves as the 'German Cheka'. Alongside the bust was an open vodka bottle with a half-empty glass next to it. Malkus saw her eyeing it, put the top back on the bottle, and then placed it and the glass in one of his desk drawers.

He looked up at her with the same thin smile. 'Now what I wanted to try to agree with you was a framework for this investigation. A framework that suits both the purposes of the People's Police and the Ministry for State Security. I gather you have experience of working with us. *Oberstleutnant* Klaus Jäger, wasn't it, of Department Eight in the Hauptstadt?'

Müller nodded, warily.

'Klaus and I are good friends. We go back all the way to college. He recommended you for this job. Even though you will face some necessary constraints in the inquiry, heading your own murder squad again is preferable to pen-pushing and interviewing no-good little thugs at Keibelstrasse. I'm sure you'll agree with that?'

The knowledge that she'd been chosen by the Stasi, by Jäger in particular, rather than her own People's Police superiors, was like a blow to the stomach for Müller. For the second time in the space of a few months, it looked like she was going to be dancing to the Stasi's tune. Instead of voicing her anguish, Müller gave another slight nod.

'So,' said Malkus, getting a folder from his briefcase and then picking up a ballpoint pen and clicking it. 'Let me take you through some of the issues we face in this inquiry and our suggestions of how to deal with them.' He looked up from his papers and stared directly at Müller. She suddenly realised – as the sun hit his face just as it had by the rail line – what it was about his eyes that looked so odd. They weren't yellowy brown – more a startling, luminescent amber. Müller found them unnerving and had to fight to concentrate on the Stasi officer's words.

'The main concern,' he continued, 'is that we don't want to cause panic. Of course we need to find the killer, the abductor of the babies. We need to find the missing baby . . .' He paused to look down at his notes. '. . . Maddelena. Those should, of course, be priorities. But the avoidance of panic, the avoidance of Ha-Neu getting a bad name, well, that's almost more important, I think you'll agree. So, the main thing I must impress upon you is that there is to be no apartment-by-apartment search.'

She bristled. 'But surely –'

'It's not a matter of negotiation, *Oberleutnant*. It's been agreed at the highest level between the Ministry for State Security and the ministry in charge of the police, the Interior Ministry.'

Müller felt anger course though her body. This wasn't how she imagined the meeting playing out. Her attempts to raise the important issue of a full search were being stonewalled. She made one last attempt to plead her case. 'We are very unlikely to be able to find the girl, to find clues about her whereabouts, without conducting a thorough search of each flat, in each block, in each residential area. I still believe that is what we have to do.'

Malkus started shaking his head even before she'd finished her sentence. 'You will have to use other methods. I'm sure you'll think of something. And if the baby *was* being held somewhere, why would it be in one of the city's residential apartments? Surely that would be too high a risk for the culprit? Anyway, as I say, this aspect of the investigation is non-negotiable. The second-most important thing is that I expect you to share infor-mation with us. When you get a new lead, let us know. If you want to take the investigation in a different direction, talk to us first. That way there will be no misunderstandings.' Malkus put his pen down and rocked back in his chair, with his arms folded over his stomach. 'I gather from Klaus that there were one or two such misunderstandings during your investigation earlier this year.'

Müller said nothing, and just returned the Stasi major's stare.

'Oh, and one other thing before you go. Klaus sends his regards. He was very sorry you turned down the chance to join him in his new job in the Main Intelligence Directorate. He's been promoted to a full colonel now, and assigned to a post in Cuba. But perhaps you felt foreign travel's not really your sort of thing. Not like your ex-husband.'

Müller sighed. It didn't surprise her that the Halle branch of the Stasi knew everything about her. But she wasn't going to give Malkus the satisfaction of knowing that he'd riled her, despite his deliberate attempts to provoke. Müller rearranged her skirt and got to her feet. 'Will that be all for now, Comrade *Major*?'

Malkus waved at her airily from behind his desk. 'Yes, yes, Karin. I don't want to detain you. I know you've got work to be getting on with. Anything important, let me know. For the day-to-day issues, *Hauptmann* Janowitz will be keeping in close contact. Be careful to stay the right side of the captain. He's not always as understanding as I am. You know your way out now, don't you?'

She exited the room without saying goodbye. It had all been a show of power, she was aware of that. Nothing had been said by Malkus that couldn't have been said earlier in the day at the railway embankment. The news that Janowitz would be 'keeping in close contact' was in no way reassuring. The opposite, in fact. The man in the Skoda – perhaps even the driver of the red Lada from the night before – had probably been one of Janowitz's underlings.

As she made her way down the concrete stairs and back out towards the car park, escorted by the same plain-clothes operative, the sense of foreboding she'd felt for much of the *Jugendwerkhof* girl case settled over her again. Perhaps dealing with annoying hippies like Lauterberg at Keibelstrasse hadn't been so bad in comparison after all.

8

Müller decided to make a brief detour to her police apartment on the other side of town before returning to the incident room. She felt she needed to freshen up again after the Malkus meeting. Perhaps wearing the new jacket hadn't been such a good idea after all. Throughout the chat, or lecture, whatever it had been, she'd felt drops of perspiration gathering in her armpits. She glanced up at the rear-view mirror again – so far there was no sign of anyone tailing her. Or if they were, this time it wasn't in plain sight and designed to unnerve her. So on this journey she felt more in control, more confident, despite the discomfort of her clothing.

She turned into *Wohnkomplex VI*, with its idiosyncratic curved wall of apartments, feeling almost a sense of familiarity. To her left, she could see the ring road round the city. Beyond that – she'd been told – lay a park and lake. She made a mental note to visit them in something other than a working capacity, although she would need to make sure Eschler and his team searched them, if they hadn't already. Her head swivelled from side to side, taking in the surroundings. The curved apartment building seemed to extend for ever: uniform windows, uniform doors and uniform grey. But a clean, new grey: not the dirty grey that she was used to and which dominated in Berlin, the Hauptstadt.

The block numbers weren't completely logical and didn't seem to follow a linear pattern. To get her bearings, she watched out for the sudden jump to block 952, which she knew was followed by her block – 953. She parked the car and made her way to the entrance, chewing over in her head what Malkus had said. It was a warning, much as many of Jäger's 'talks' had been in the previous case. In the entrance, she looked around for the lift to get to the fourth floor and then remembered: there wouldn't be one. Only blocks over five storeys high had lifts. She wondered how the young mothers she'd seen earlier in the day, pushing their prams by the fountains, coped with their buggies and the stairs. Perhaps that was the price of being assigned a brand new flat in such a modern city. The sort of start to family life in the Republic that many could only dream of.

Müller climbed the stairs and negotiated what seemed like a never-ending corridor. She glanced over her shoulder before using her key to open the front door of the flat assigned to the *Kripo* team. *What am I worrying about? They've admitted they'll be watching me, and it's not as though I have anything to hide.* Inside, she could hear a male voice humming to himself. It didn't sound like Schmidt, but the timbre was – nonetheless – oddly familiar. As she turned the corner into the kitchen, she came face to face with a curly-haired, wiry young man with spectacles, unpacking tins of food. Simultaneously, both their faces creased into smiles.

'Martin,' she said, pulling him into a hug. 'I wasn't expecting to see you.' It was Vogel, the young *Unterleutnant* who'd helped her and Tilsner in the Harz mountains earlier in the year, during the case of the *Jugendwerkhof* teenagers. 'I didn't expect you to leave the Harz. I thought you were a country detective through and through.'

Vogel pulled back from the embrace, his expression grim. 'It wasn't the same, Comrade *Oberleutnant*. Not without –'

The young officer stopped himself before uttering *Hauptmann* Baumann's name. But Müller could see from his eyes, from the look on his face, what he was thinking about: those last few moments of his People's Police captain's life, deep underground in a mine by the state border, fatally wounded by a gun fired by someone who ought to have been on his side.

Vogel breathed in deeply, and shrugged. 'Anyway, I needed a new challenge. I'd suggested a transfer to Berlin, named you as someone I might like to work for, Comrade *Oberleutnant*.'

'Karin. You must call me Karin, Martin. We know each other well enough by now.'

Vogel grinned. 'Anyway, I didn't get exactly what I wanted. The bright lights of Halle-Neustadt rather than the bright lights of the Hauptstadt. But I am very pleased to be working with you again, Karin. I gather, though, it may be another difficult case.'

Müller nodded, and started preparing the coffee maker. 'Let's have a coffee first, then I'll fill you in on what we know so far. It *is* somewhat sensitive, as with the previous case.'

Vogel pulled back one of the kitchen chairs and sat at the table. 'So I'd heard. I gather the Ministry for State Security is heavily involved again.'

Reaching up to one of the eye-level cupboards to retrieve two coffee mugs, Müller looked quizzically at the young officer who was now her new deputy on the case. 'Who told you that?' she asked.

'I had a phone call. In the Harz. After I'd agreed to come. A Stasi *Hauptmann* – Janowitz? I think that was his name?'

Müller rolled her eyes and nodded slowly. 'Yes. He's the liaison officer. Him and his boss, *Major* Malkus.' So the Stasi had been interfering not just with the investigation, but with her actual team – even before she'd linked up with her new deputy. She hadn't warmed to Malkus, but it sounded as though this Janowitz needed watching equally carefully – if not more so. 'I was hauled in by Malkus an hour or so ago,' she continued. 'I get the impression we'll be seeing rather a lot of them. Our room for manoeuvre in the investigation might be more limited than we'd like.' She put two heaped teaspoonfuls of coffee into the machine, added the water, and then switched it on. 'I'll go through things in a moment. Are you hungry after your journey? I bought a cake yesterday.'

'That sounds lovely, *Oberleutnant*.'

'*Karin*, Martin – please! We're going to be living, as well as working, together until we crack this case. So we can dispense with the formalities, unless we're with other officers.'

'Apologies, *Karin*. Anyway, yes please to the cake.'

Müller opened the fridge door, but couldn't see the cake. 'That's odd. I'm sure it was here yesterday evening.' Then she moved the margarine and milk out of the way and saw the empty plate, with just a few crumbs left. 'Ah, apologies, Martin. Someone seems to have got there first. You'll meet our forensic officer, Jonas Schmidt, later. He's a good officer, and a lovely man. But he does have a rather large appetite.'

Vogel smiled. 'A cup of coffee will be just fine, Karin.'

Müller had needed the break at the apartment after the face-to-face meeting with Malkus. Now – with a new deputy at last in the shape of Vogel – she felt refreshed. The two officers made their way in the Wartburg back to the police incident room in the centre of Ha-Neu. For the time being, at least until they had the results of the next day's autopsy, Müller was content to continue with the series of searches mapped out by the *Vopo* officers. Once she was back in the incident room, Eschler and Fernbach pointed on the office map to the next tunnel they planned to search – along the central heating duct from the Salzmann family's apartment block.

The route took the group of police officers over the majestically curved pedestrian bridge across the Magistrale: the main twin-carriageway road through Halle-Neustadt. The only road in the whole town which actually had a name.

The Salzmanns' apartment was about halfway up one of the tallest buildings, towering fourteen storeys high. With its bright bands of yellow render under each row of windows, it looked to Müller like a giant horizontally striped bath towel. Müller, Vogel and Schmidt kept up a rapid pace behind the handful of uniformed officers, but around them new mothers with prams ambled along, proudly stopping to chat with friends about the latest addition to their model socialist families, paying little heed to the group of policemen. The Salzmanns would have expected to be amongst them, with a double buggy carrying twins. Now their best hope would be that Müller and her team could find Maddelena before it was too late.

The dog-handling team was already in place in the lobby – sent on ahead in vehicles to avoid too obvious a posse marching through the town centre, the dogs already familiarised with Maddelena's scent from her hospital bedding. Müller felt happier having another familiar face in Vogel alongside her. As they descended the stairs of the apartment building, down to the basement, she felt a strong sense of déjà vu from the Harz mountains – going after Vogel down the mineshaft.

The wiry-haired young *Unterleutnant* had obviously guessed what she was thinking. 'It feels strange to be going back underground, Comrade *Oberleutnant*.' Müller could see the moisture shining in his earnest, youthful eyes – another reminder of the traumatic death of *Hauptmann* Baumann.

As Eschler opened a thick steel door, the two dog handlers had to fight to keep their animals from pulling them on ahead. A fug of damp heat wafted over them. With the already scorching temperature above ground, Müller hadn't expected the giant central heating system to be operating. But clearly there was residual heat trapped in the massive tubes that carried hot air to each residential complex.

'I still don't understand why we're not doing a house-to-house search first, *Oberleutnant*,' whispered Vogel, as their torch beams danced along the damp walls of the tunnel, following the dog handlers and uniformed officers. 'Wouldn't that make more sense?'

'I don't disagree, Martin,' Müller replied under her breath. 'But it's out of my hands. This evening we need to brainstorm the case – try to think of a way forward. The trouble is, in a sense it's two cases: an abduction *and* a murder.'

'Unless . . .'

Müller stopped for a moment and eyeballed her junior officer. 'Let's try to stay positive.' Then she set off again, increasing her pace to catch up with Eschler, Fernbach and the others, their silhouettes shuffling along in the torchlight. 'We've got to assume that Maddelena is still alive. That's why we have to act quickly,' continued Müller, as Vogel strode alongside her. 'The first few hours are the most important. They've already gone. So we have to try to make a breakthrough in these early days, before any trail goes cold.'

'Which is why we should be doing a house-to-house search,' insisted Vogel. 'Instead we seem to be aimlessly walking kilometre after kilometre of tunnels under the new town.'

Müller said nothing, although inside her head she was in complete agreement with her new deputy. It just reminded her of the frustrating way Malkus had cut her off when she'd tried to argue the point.

The sudden agitated barking of one of the dogs indicated they both might be wrong. Eschler, Fernbach and the other uniformed officers trained their torches on what the dog had found. It was howling now, ears pricked, straining at its leash as its handler kept it back from the object on a ledge at the tunnel's side.

Müller drew closer, then stopped as the shock hit. It couldn't be, could it? But there, under the *Vopos'* torch beams, in the first tunnel search Müller had been involved in, was a body. A tiny, naked body, splayed out on its back, its lifeless eyes staring at the ceiling.

9

Christmas Eve, 1965
Chemical Workers' City, Halle-West

Oh what a year it's been! It must be my happiest year ever. First there was the news in the autumn that Hansi had succeeded in getting us one of the brand new flats in the new chemical workers' city. I'm sure it helped that I was expecting, and we managed to move in before the big day.

Now we're about to celebrate our first Christmas as a little family. I still need to take it easy, of course, but I can do little bits of cooking, setting out the decorations, that sort of thing.

The flat is looking really lovely. We put up the tree and decorated it early. Hansi put the angel at the top. Although he said we couldn't really call it an angel anymore; apparently it's better to say it's a *Jahresendflügelfigur* – an end of the year winged figurine. He's out at the *Kaufhalle* at the moment, buying the Vienna sausages. We'll have those later with the potato salad I've already made when we settle down to listen to the radio. There's a play on tonight – a traditional story that Hansi likes, called *Auguste, the Christmas Goose*. I'm quite looking forward to it, although

I would perhaps prefer to watch the television. We're lucky to have one. Not many families do, you know, but Hansi's quite important, so we got put on a priority list.

I've also been busy putting up the last of the decorations. The Christmas pyramid on the mantelpiece is already spinning round from the heat of the candle, and I've just lit the *Räuchermännchen* figurines too. That's how I know it's really Christmas – the incense almost makes the living room smell like a gingerbread house. I just love breathing it in! And next to them on the mantelpiece is the Nativity scene. Hansi says I need to hide that away when we have visitors, just in case some of them aren't believers. Hansi isn't, of course – it wouldn't sit well with his Ministry work. But he knows I still like to say a little prayer now and again.

I love the excitement of Christmas. Whatever the *Weihnachtsmann* brings me, it can never compare to the gift I already have. My little Stefanie. My darling, darling Stefanie. She's my real little angel.

She's been crying a lot today, though. I'm not sure why. Ever since Hansi went out to the shops. She does miss her papa! Her tiny face lights up when he's around. She's a little monkey, though. She just won't suck properly on my breasts, so I don't think she's getting the proper nutrition. She seems to like the formula milk better, but I would feel happier if she fed on natural milk. That's the right way, surely? My nipples are really sore now because I was determined to get her to feed earlier. I put a few drops of formula on each one in turn, and it did get her sucking well for a bit, but she soon stopped and started crying again. Perhaps we'll have to take her to the doctor? I'm worried she's starting to lose weight. Hansi says it's best to give her the formula. He makes up the bottles for me before he goes to work each morning. But sometimes I secretly throw them away. I'd rather she had proper milk.

I wonder if it's anything to do with my fall? I hope that isn't what's making her a fussy feeder. That was a big shock, I'll tell you. But it all worked out all right in the end. We'd just moved into the apartment, and of course there's lots and lots of building work going on around us, because eventually they hope nearly a hundred thousand citizens will live in the city. And it's only fair that they build those new homes as soon as possible. We can't start complaining about building work.

Anyway, apparently I had a nasty fall over some pipes. I don't remember anything about it, but Hansi says it knocked me out cold. They were so worried about the baby they had to perform an emergency Caesarean. The scars still hurt a bit. But the good thing is I don't remember a thing about it. One moment there I was, nearly nine months pregnant, the next I'm coming round in bed and Hansi is cradling Stefanie in his arms. What a gift! I'm so lucky. But I was unconscious for a couple of days they say, so no wonder Stefanie had to start on formula for a bottle. Poor little thing.

Ah. A key turning in the lock. Hansi, I think.

'Franzi?' he's calling. Hansi and Franzi, it's our little joke. 'You haven't left Stefanie again have you?' He's slightly breathless, his face flushed, weighed down by the Christmas shopping.

'She just seemed a little out of sorts. I put her in the cot in her bedroom for a sleep.'

'But she's not sleeping, Franzi. She's bawling her head off. We'll get complaints.' I can't believe I haven't realised she's been crying. Oh dear, I don't like it when Hansi gets angry with me. I feel I've let him down. I feel a bit tearful. I hope a turn's not coming on.

'There, there. There, there, little one. Papa's home now.' He's cradling her in his arms, rocking her, shushing her, and already she's quietening a little. Why won't she ever do that for me? 'She's soaked through, Franzi. Didn't you change her? That rash is already quite bad.' I can feel the tears starting to well up, I try to fight them back. Hansi doesn't see because he's taken little Stefanie straight through to the kitchen. I hear him put a bottle in a pan, the click of the electric hob being turned on. Then, after a few minutes, the noise of her sucking greedily. 'There, there, little one. You were just hungry, weren't you?' He comes to the doorway, holding her, frowning. 'You've got to remember to feed her, Franzi. She's half-starved, the poor thing. When was the last time you gave her a bottle?'

I can't really answer because I know my tears will start, and then I won't be able to stop. I don't really want that on Christmas Eve.

'You weren't trying to breastfeed her again, were you, *Liebling*?'

I give a small nod and choke back the tears. I can feel my nipples chafing against my maternity bra. They're horribly sore. I know when I examine them in the mirror they'll be red raw.

Hansi comes over and gives me a half-hug with one arm, careful to avoid my chest, his other still holding Stefanie as she sucks away at the bottle. 'Franzi, Franzi,' he says. 'Whatever are we going to do with you? Whatever are we going to do?'

10

July 1975
Halle-Neustadt

As Eschler reached out to pick up the tiny body from its surrounding blanket, Müller yelled at him to stop, her shout repeating in ever-diminishing echoes along the tunnel.

The People's Police captain turned in surprise. 'It's just a doll, *Oberleutnant*. I doubt it has anything to do with the investigation. Children sometimes manage to break in and play down here. And why would a baby have a life-sized doll, even if she had been here?'

Müller was grateful that the darkness of the underground duct hid her embarrassment. Her face burned. She'd been convinced it was the body of Maddelena, unlikely as it seemed. What was making her so jumpy? 'Nevertheless, Comrade *Hauptmann*. We ought to treat it like any other potential piece of evidence. *Kriminaltechniker* Schmidt, can you do the honours, please?'

Schmidt moved out from behind her, knelt down, and – his hands covered in protective gloves – bagged up the doll. Once he'd done so, Eschler motioned to the dog handlers to continue moving forward, and the search resumed.

The doll was the only thing of note they found, and after a couple of hours' searching, Eschler suggested they resume the next day. It was already mid-evening, so Müller agreed.

The dogs and handlers returned to base, and Fernbach and his men returned to their families at the end of another frustrating day, hampered as the investigation was by the parameters imposed by Malkus and Janowitz. Müller invited Eschler to join her, Vogel and Schmidt for an after-work drink to talk things over. There had to be some way of making progress without incurring the wrath of the Stasi. Eschler suggested a guest house, the Grüne Tanne, in the village of Halle Nietleben, a short drive from the apartment assigned to Müller, Vogel and Schmidt. It had a private back room the local police often used for informal meetings. Eschler rang from the incident room to make sure it was free.

Müller made a point of ordering the drinks for everyone. Although she had warmed more to Eschler, she felt it was important to keep laying down markers that she was in charge. Especially after the embarrassment of the doll incident.

After the waiter had brought their four drinks out, Müller drew her notebook from her case and clicked her ballpoint pen.

'So.' She drew in a long breath. 'I hope you'll agree we need to do something different to move things forward. That's no reflection on the way the case has been run so far, Bruno. I think it was right to concentrate the search on the heating tunnels, waste ground, those sorts of areas. But I want to look at places where mothers congregate. Crèches, kindergartens, play areas.'

Eschler frowned. 'That makes sense, of course. But it's a big assumption that the abductor – who's almost certainly Karsten's killer – would allow Maddelena to be seen anywhere like that. Isn't it more likely they'd have hidden her away?'

'Possibly,' admitted Müller. 'But mothers talk to other mothers about their babies. One of them may have noticed something strange. And I'm convinced we need to treat this primarily as a missing persons inquiry. If we find Maddelena, the chances are we will find Karsten's killer. The trouble is, if we start asking too many people too many questions, the Ministry for State Security will be down on me like a ton of bricks.'

Vogel leaned forward in his chair. 'Why is the search being limited to Halle-Neustadt? What makes us think the person we're hunting comes from this particular city? Why not Halle itself? Leipzig, even?'

Eschler wiped some beer foam from around his mouth with a paper napkin. 'You're right, Comrade *Unterleutnant*. There is no guarantee the person we're hunting comes from Ha-Neu. There's no guarantee that Maddelena is still in the Halle area. And other police districts *have* been informed. Police in the Hauptstadt. That is, after all, why you and Comrades Müller and Schmidt are here. But the suitcase with Karsten's body inside was thrown from a section of the rail line which runs between Ha-Neu and Merseburg and the chemical works at Leuna and Buna. From the angle of impact, and the side of the embankment it was found, we know it was thrown from a train going *from* Ha-Neu. Probably from one of the commuter trains going to the chemical works. They run twenty-four hours a day to service the round-the-clock shifts at both factories.'

Müller nodded slowly and turned towards Schmidt. 'Does that tally with your inspection at the trackside, Jonas?'

'It does, *Oberleutnant*. It does,' said Schmidt, looking up from the food menu.

'Our best guess,' continued Eschler, 'is that the killer threw the case from one of the night trains, just before the train reached Angersdorf. The ground there is quite marshy. Perhaps he was hoping to throw it far enough to clear the embankment and land in the marsh. Maybe he – or she – mistimed the throw slightly. Or the case was heavier than he thought and dropped to the ground more quickly.'

Müller watched Schmidt about to launch into his explanation of how heavy and light objects fall at the same rate in a vacuum. She mouthed a silent 'no' to cut him off, then continued before Eschler realised what was happening.

'And no one on the train saw anything?' she asked.

Eschler shrugged. 'No one that we've managed to find. Or at least, if they did, they're not admitting anything. But we've had to go fairly gently with the questioning, for the same reasons we can't do an apartment-by-apartment search. The Stasi offered to help us out.'

'The Stasi? Who, Malkus?'

Eschler gave a stern-faced nod. 'Last night they had agents on the night trains, showing people photos of the suitcase, without admitting what had been inside it. When people asked too many questions back, the agents – they were posing as police officers – just said they were investigating a robbery.'

Müller took a sip of her wheat beer, savouring the sweet flavour: sweeter than those she was used to in the Hauptstadt. She didn't like the way Malkus and his team seemed to have wormed their way into the very heart of this investigation, an investigation which was still nominally the preserve of the People's Police. 'What about the chemical works themselves? Have you – or the Stasi – questioned people there?'

Eschler sighed. 'We would face the same problems. Many – perhaps most – of those who work at Leuna and Buna live in Halle-Neustadt. As you know, that's why the new town was built. The chemical workers' city – that was always the plan. So if you raise the alarm with too obvious an operation at either of the chemical works, you're in effect doing exactly what the Ministry for State Security has forbidden us to do in Ha-Neu itself. Though I can't answer for the Ministry. They're a law unto themselves, and only tell us what they want us to know.' The People's Police captain paused to take a long draught of beer, as though quenching his thirst might wash away the frustrations of the case. 'I don't want to sound like I'm making excuses, but it's not straightforward.' Müller couldn't help thinking that the Stasi's logic didn't make sense. The levels of secrecy seemed like overkill. *Unless there's some big secret they don't want us to uncover – something else linked to the abductions*, she thought.

Vogel drummed his fingers on the table. 'I'm still not convinced the search should be limited to Ha-Neu. Doesn't the rail line split at Angersdorf? S-bahn trains head towards Halle Süd – it's not just trains going between Ha-Neu and the chemical works and Merseburg.' Müller was impressed that her young deputy was prepared to challenge Eschler's suppositions, but the police captain seemed unmoved.

'It's not just the evidence of where and how the suitcase was dumped,' said Eschler, frowning. 'The baby's body was wrapped in a newspaper. But there was also an advertising flyer in the case for *Kaufhalle* special offers – from the central *Kaufhalle* in Ha-Neu.'

'Where Klara Salzmann works,' said Müller.

Eschler nodded. 'That's right.'

The mention of supermarket special offers seemed to rouse Schmidt, who'd been sitting quietly sipping his beer while still looking longingly at the menu. 'What was the flyer actually for, Comrade *Hauptmann*? Any specific foods?'

Eschler paused, and looked slightly alarmed. '*Scheisse!*' he exclaimed.

'What's wrong, Bruno?' asked Müller.

The police officer held his head in his hands. 'I should have thought. I was concentrating too much on it being something that linked Karsten's killer to Ha-Neu – the fact that it was from the central *Kaufhalle*. But the flyer was for special offers on cooked meats. Hams, salamis, that sort of thing. It's an obvious link to an actual person, isn't it? To a potential suspect.'

'To whom? And what's the link?' asked Schmidt, confusion written on his face.

'The meat counter at the central *Kaufhalle*. That's where Klara Salzmann works.'

Müller furrowed her brow. 'We have to consider the Salzmanns as suspects, of course. But Klara was on maternity leave when the twins were taken. Why would she have one of these leaflets?'

'It may be worth following up, though,' said Vogel. 'Perhaps one of her work colleagues had a grudge against her. Or was jealous of her twins.'

Eschler nodded half-heartedly. 'It's possible. But then to actually abduct them . . . kill one of them? It seems a little far-fetched.'

Müller sighed. 'We need to check it out. Bruno, could your team do that, please?'

'Of course. There's the monthly Party meeting at the office tomorrow – we'll all have to attend that – but we can fit in interviews before and afterwards.'

'Good,' said Müller, breathing in and stretching out the tension from her body. 'Let's hope tomorrow's autopsy gives us something stronger to go on. I shouldn't need to remind you all that in these sorts of cases making an early breakthrough is vital. Karsten's already dead. And poor Maddelena was being kept in hospital for a good reason – because she was a weak and premature baby. Let's just hope she's a fighter. We need to do everything we can to find her, before it's too late.'

11

The next day

Müller spent most of the night tossing and turning, her body sticking to the sweaty sheets, struggling to sleep with the summer night-time temperature not dropping much below twenty degrees. She chewed over the case in her mind, trying to get it into some semblance of order. It nagged her that the questioning on the night trains had been carried out by Stasi agents. She had no way of finding out what – if anything – they'd discovered, beyond what Malkus or Janowitz was prepared to divulge. And there was an unsettling cloud of secrecy hanging over the inquiry, a little like the clouds of pollution belched out by the area's chemical complexes.

By morning, although she didn't feel refreshed, she had at least decided on a way forward, one she would share with the other officers after the autopsy into Karsten Salzmann.

Doctor Albrecht Ebersbach differed from the two forensic pathologists Müller had worked with on her most recent cases in one key respect. The pathologists in the Hauptstadt and the

Harz both, in their own way, kept up a running commentary about what they were doing, what they were finding. Ebersbach didn't. In fact, he said very little at all. It unnerved Müller.

Without the distraction of conversation, of asking questions – Ebersbach's very bearing seemed to discourage them – Müller found herself spending too much time looking at baby Karsten's body. It was so small. So vulnerable. The bruises on his head must have been inflicted by the cruellest of killers. Bruises on the chest too. Who could do that to a baby – a baby of only a few weeks old? Müller tried to look away, look at the mortuary assistant, Vogel standing next to her – anyone, anything. But her eyes kept being drawn back to Karsten, as Ebersbach repeatedly lifted him, turned him, and examined him minutely – without saying a single word. The child's arms and legs flopped around obscenely – unlike the rigidity of the life-sized baby doll they'd found in the heating tunnel.

Müller cleared her throat. She would have to break the silence at some time, and neither Vogel – alongside her – nor the doctor were saying anything. 'Is there anything you can tell us that may help us, Doctor?'

The crown of Ebersbach's ginger head stayed down for a moment, hovering over Karsten's body, almost as though he hadn't heard her question. Then he slowly raised it, but instead of looking directly at Müller or Vogel, he seemed to be staring through his thick horn-rimmed glasses at a point a couple of metres above her. His forehead was creased into a severe frown.

'It's an odd one,' he finally sighed. 'Very odd.' Then he returned his gaze to the baby's body, and started to gently poke it again.

Opening the mouth, lifting the tongue. Opening the eyes and looking under the lids.

Müller wasn't going to let him get away with such an unenlightening response. 'Odd in what way, Doctor Ebersbach?'

Ebersbach lifted his head again and sighed. This time he did meet her eyes, with a quizzical expression. 'Well, on the surface, this seems like a straightforward case of abusive head trauma. You see these bruises on each side of the face?' Ebersbach pointed them out as Müller and Vogel leaned over the tiny body. 'There's also a rib fracture.' The forensic pathologist pressed on the baby's ribcage and Müller watched it give way under the pressure. She felt the bile rise in her throat as nausea gripped her. She tried to concentrate on what the doctor was saying, rather than what he was doing to the body.

'You say *on the surface*. Does that mean you suspect some other cause of death?' asked Müller.

'It depends, really. I won't know for sure until I've actually cut the body up, and while I was happy for you to be here for the initial examination, I'm not going to allow you to stay for that.'

'So what do you expect to find when you do cut the body open?' asked Vogel.

Ebersbach shrugged. 'Expect?' He exhaled dramatically. 'It's not really a question of expectation, Comrade. We deal in facts. Cause and effect.' He paused for a moment, glaring at Vogel, as though he was an imbecile. Then his face softened. 'Sorry, I sometimes get a little too literal. However, if the cause of death was indeed violent, then what you might find – in an infant of this age – are skull fractures, retinal bleeding. Perhaps damage to the liver if we're talking about blows to the body too. Maybe even spinal cord injuries if there was shaking.'

'OK,' said Müller. 'But what makes you have doubts?'

'Well, it's the strange bruising to the boy's lips. See here.' Ebersbach ushered the two detectives close again, cradled Karsten's lifeless head with one arm, and then traced over his lips with the index finger of his other hand, pointing out the bruises. 'It almost looks like someone who's been kissed too fiercely.'

'Kissed?' asked Müller in alarm and horror, hoping her stomach wasn't about to regurgitate her breakfast. 'You mean something sexual?'

'Oh no, no. That's not what I meant at all. Goodness, you Berlin detectives must come across some revolting cases . . .'

'So what *do* you mean?' she asked.

'Well, look at the bruising to the ribcage, where the broken rib is. There are two very defined bruises, almost as though they could have been caused by the tips of someone's fingers.' Ebersbach held the index and middle fingers of his right hand slightly apart, in an inverted 'V' shape, so that the ends of the two digits almost exactly covered the two bruises.

'I don't understand,' Vogel said.

Müller, too, shook her head. 'No. Neither do I, Doctor.'

'Well, I could be mistaken. And as I say, I will need to dissect the body, open the cranium, do all the horrible dirty work which for some reason I trained for all those years ago. But if my suspicions are correct, whoever inflicted these bruises may not have been trying to end this poor child's life.'

'What do you mean?' asked an increasingly frustrated Müller.

'That shape I made with my hands there is the classic position for pushing on an infant's ribs when . . .' Ebersbach paused, as though he couldn't really believe his conclusion himself.

'When what?' prompted Müller.

'When you're trying to perform resuscitation. If I'm right, whoever did this wasn't trying to kill this boy. They were trying to save him.'

12

Müller sent Vogel off to interview witnesses at the hospital's paediatric wing without talking in detail about the implications of the suspicions raised by Doctor Ebersbach in the mortuary room – housed in the same building's basement. Both detectives knew that without the murder investigation aspect of the case, their team was likely to be scaled back. Yet Maddelena was still missing. Müller didn't want any reduction in the number of police officers looking for her and her abductor. Time was paramount. The trail was almost certainly already going cold.

Her next task was one she wasn't really looking forward to: interviewing the twins' parents. She knew they had to treat them as possible suspects. But they were also recently bereaved, and would be frantic and desperate about their still-missing daughter. It would be a fine line to tread. Müller knew that she should have done this sooner, perhaps on the first day. Her personal sympathy for them and their loss had distracted her from doing her job. It was a mistake, and she hoped it didn't come back to haunt her.

The sharp smell of disinfectant made her feel nauseous as she entered the lobby of the Salzmanns' apartment building: it was a reminder of the similar aroma in the autopsy room, although here it barely covered the stench of urine. Having a lift – as Müller already knew – was something of a luxury in Ha-Neu. The 'Y' blocks, with their towering fourteen storeys, easily met the threshold. But clearly those on the upper floors – children, or perhaps the elderly, those who'd had one too many Dunkel beers – couldn't always wait to get to the toilet.

She held her breath for as long as possible as the elevator took her smoothly up to the tenth floor, then walked along the corridor and rang the bell to flat 1024. Karsten and Maddelena's father answered, the tragedy written on his face. Müller showed her *Kripo* ID, and Herr Salzmann ushered her in without saying anything. They both knew what the visit was about.

He guided her to the apartment's tiny kitchen, which Müller knew would be virtually identical to those of the other thirty thousand or so in Ha-Neu. It had all the latest gadgets. A fridge with freezer compartment, electric coffee machine, toast maker. And two high chairs, bought no doubt at great expense – perhaps with loans from Herr Salzmann's comrades at the chemical factory. Everything was in its rightful place. Yet two things were missing. One living, Müller hoped, but one very much dead.

'My wife's taken a pill. She's having a lie-down in the bedroom. Do you want me to get her? I'm not sure what state she'll be in.' As he talked, Reinhard Salzmann juggled a jar of powdered milk between his leathery hands in a frenzied but random fashion. He noticed Müller watching, suddenly realised what he was doing, and shakily placed the jar on the table. 'Sorry,' he said. 'My nerves are shot. Did you want me to fetch my wife?'

'We can leave her a while longer, Comrade Salzmann. I will need to talk to both of you, but why don't we go through into the lounge, and I can interview you first?'

'Can I get you something to drink? A coffee, perhaps? I was just about to make one.' There was a pleading note to his voice, thought Müller. It was as though he needed to be doing something with his hands to take his mind off the horror of what had happened – the trauma that had devastated his family. Müller nodded, and pulled back one of the kitchen chairs to sit down. Salzmann was tanned, with wavy mid-length hair and bushy sideburns worn fashionably long so that they extended beneath his cheeks. He was older than Müller had expected – perhaps late-thirties? Couples in the Republic normally started families at a much younger age. As he spooned out coffee and measured the water, Müller noticed his hands were still shaking. 'I don't know what to do,' he said, with his back to her, almost as though he didn't want to meet her eyes. 'I'm bad enough, but Klara is a complete wreck. She had yearned for children. We'd been trying for so long. We'd married young, made an early mistake, if you understand my meaning, before we were ready to have kids. When we made that decision, little did we know the heartache to follow. Miscarriage after miscarriage. We thought our chance had gone, that we'd thrown it away thanks to our earlier decision.'

'An abortion?' asked Müller.

He gave an almost imperceptible nod. 'And then – after all that time – she became pregnant. Not just that, it was twins. It was like a miracle.' Reinhard Salzmann said all this without turning, almost as though he was addressing the coffee machine as he waited for it to percolate. Then he *did* turn, and held Müller's gaze. 'You are going to be able to find her, aren't you? Klara will never be able to get over the loss of Karsten, but if Maddelena . . .'

Müller was torn. She didn't want to make false promises. The lack of clues to Maddelena's whereabouts, the lack of a trail to her abductor. She took a deep breath. 'You can be sure we will do everything in our power to find her. I will personally make sure of that.'

Salzmann poured the coffee into two mugs, and handed one to Müller. 'Sugar?' he asked, as an afterthought. She shook her head.

They made their way into the neat apartment's lounge and sat down at the dining table. The furniture was similar to that in almost every other new apartment in Ha-Neu, every other new apartment in the Republic. Beige floral wallpaper, sofas and armchairs covered in ribbed forest-green fabric, a television – even a telephone. The latter *was* unusual. Müller, as a People's Police detective, had always had a phone. For ordinary workers like the Salzmanns, they were harder to come by.

'We've only had it the last few days.' Reinhard Salzmann had seen her inspecting it. 'To keep in touch about the investigation. We're very grateful. The trouble is we're always waiting for it to ring. And it doesn't.'

She nodded, and continued to take in the surroundings. Her eyes settled on the mantelpiece, and the saddest sight of all. A split photograph of Reinhard on the left, leaning over one twin's hospital cot and smiling back at the camera, with Klara in an identical pose with the other premature twin on the right. The feeding tubes and apparatus surrounding their tiny bodies reminded Müller of Tilsner, back in his hospital bed in the Hauptstadt. 'Maddelena's on the right – with Klara. That's me . . . with . . .' Reinhard Salzmann couldn't complete the sentence, his words choking in his throat. Instead he just looked up at Müller, his eyes awash with tears. Müller reached out and rested her hand on his muscular forearm, then squeezed, to try to give the man some comfort. If the tears, the grief, were genuine – as Müller felt they were – then it was hard to imagine him being a suspect. If it was an act, it was a very convincing one.

Müller reached down to her briefcase and pulled out her notebook and pen. 'I'm going to have to go over everything again with you, Citizen Salzmann. I know that will be painful.' She gave his arm another gentle squeeze. 'But it could be just one small detail that you've forgotten, or that we've missed, which will help us find Maddelena. So it will be upsetting for you, but try to remember everything. It's the best hope we have.'

Müller questioned the man for about twenty minutes, going exhaustively over every detail the police already knew. The Salzmanns' alibi for when the babies disappeared, their meal with friends; their last visit to the hospital; which nursing staff were normally on duty when they visited; who else from the family had been to see the twins; whether the family was aware of anyone who had a grudge against them who might want to do them harm. Müller made a careful note of all the man's answers and would get the typists in the incident room to prepare a formal statement for him to sign. But she was aware he hadn't really told her anything she didn't already know.

She was just about to draw the interview to a conclusion and ask Herr Salzmann to rouse his wife when the woman appeared, standing wraith-like in the living room doorway, hair tangled and unwashed, dressing gown carelessly wrapped so too much of her bony body was on show. A face so pale she almost looked like she had a terminal illness. Perhaps, thought Müller, in losing both the twins she'd fought so hard for years to give birth to, the hand she'd been dealt was worse even than that.

'This lady's a police detective, *Liebling*.' He turned to Müller. 'Sorry, comrade, I didn't catch your name.'

'*Oberleutnant* Müller, Frau Salzmann. Do you feel well enough to answer some questions?'

The woman didn't answer for a moment, and merely stared – trance-like – at Müller.

'Klara,' said her husband. 'Do you feel well enough to answer the detective's questions?'

Klara Salzmann finally gave a slow nod, and then traipsed towards them to the dining table, dragging each of her slippers behind the other along the floor. She slumped down into the chair opposite Müller and held her head in her hands, her fingers covering her eyes, hiding herself from the horrific reality.

Müller asked much the same questions she had of Klara Salzmann's husband, going over the facts that the police already knew, checking for any anomalies in his wife's account. Klara Salzmann replied in a dull, tranquillised monotone.

Only when Müller mentioned the advertising flyers did her face get more animated. She went off to hunt in the kitchen and came back brandishing one of the promotional pieces of paper.

'Is this what you mean? The *Kaufhalle* has been handing out hundreds of them, and encouraging staff to give them out too. I was given one when I popped in to buy some food – they didn't want me to miss out even though I was on maternity leave. I'm not completely sure why. Half of this stuff is never available anyway, and when it is, the staff themselves buy it first. And prices are controlled, of course. It's more that they are sought-after goods: meats and sausages that we don't always have.'

'So you're saying these leaflets would be widely available across Ha-Neu?'

The woman nodded.

Her husband leant forward, with his arms resting on the melamine table, his face scrunched into a frown. 'What's the relevance of the advertising flyer? How does that help us find Maddelena, or Karsten's killer?'

'Killer?' asked Müller. 'What makes you think Karsten was murdered?' As Müller uttered the M-word, Klara Salzmann took a sharp intake of breath.

'It's what we heard,' said Reinhard Salzmann, sullenly. 'People talk, you know. Wasn't the autopsy this morning? Surely you know the cause of death by now?'

Müller was reluctant to tell the parents more than they needed to know. 'We can't give details of our lines of inquiry. I'm sorry. Not even to you, the parents.'

'Does that mean we're suspects ourselves?' the husband asked. It was met with another gasp by his wife.

'I cannot imagine either of you being involved. The trauma for you both must be terrible.' Müller was aware she hadn't given him a direct answer. She wasn't going to.

'So what exactly *are* your lines of inquiry?' asked Reinhard Salzmann. The tone of his voice had changed – now it was almost menacing. 'There doesn't seem to be much going on at all. Why aren't there police everywhere, knocking on every apartment door? Why aren't there hundreds of officers combing every nook and cranny searching for our baby girl and the killer of our baby boy? There should be posters in every shop window, you should be going round with loudspeakers appealing for information. The newspapers should be full of it. Yet they're not. Why?' During his rant, Herr Salzmann had grabbed both of Müller's forearms, squeezing them ever tighter. Suddenly realising what he'd done, he released them. 'Sorry.'

'You know the answers to your own questions, Citizen Salzmann. The Ministry for State Security have talked to you about it. But I assure you we are doing everything we can.'

Reinhard Salzmann stared at her for a few moments, then lowered his eyes, defeated.

13

When Müller returned to the incident room she was surprised to see the whole team gathered there – including Vogel and Schmidt. The typists, drivers and dog handlers too. Janowitz was at the end of the room. She recognised him from the back of his head as he stared through the window at something in the street below. There was another officer she didn't know, speaking to the room, talking about targets – for clearing up burglaries, thefts from cars, vandalism. None of it relevant to the current investigation. She squeezed in next to Vogel.

He cupped his hand to her ear. 'I made an excuse for you. Didn't you know about it?' Müller frowned, then looked across the room towards Eschler. He raised his brows in amusement, triggering her memory. *Scheisse*. It was the monthly Party meeting. Eschler had mentioned it the previous evening, at their get-together in the Grüne Tanne. With the autopsy, and interviewing the Salzmanns, she'd completely forgotten. It wasn't like this in Berlin, or at least it hadn't been for her and Tilsner at Marx-Engels-Platz. More often than not, they'd have their 'Party meeting' in the nearest bar and then fill in the necessary forms for Reiniger. Tilsner had put himself forward as the local rep and didn't take his duties entirely seriously.

That clearly couldn't be said of the police Party representative here in Halle-Neustadt. The middle-aged man, in a wide-collared beige shirt, had moved on to discussing the month's main stories from *Neues Deutschland* and how they were relevant to police work. He came to the end of a sentence which Müller had paid little attention to, and then turned towards her.

'Ah, Comrade Müller. *Unterleutnant* Vogel explained why you might be late, that you needed to interview the parents of the Salzmann twins. A vital task, I agree. Perhaps you could let us know how the investigation is going, and in particular how you're making sure the Socialist Unity Party's vision is being incorporated into your work.'

Müller looked across at Eschler again, but rather than rushing to intervene and rescue her, he allowed a small smile to play across his face – out of the eyeline of Janowitz and the Party official.

'Well, as you know, Comrade . . .'

'Wiedemann. *Leutnant* Dietmar Wiedemann. I work in the records department. Making sure all the paperwork is filled in and filed properly. I'm sure we'll come across each other during the investigation. If there are any previous cases you need information about, I'm your man. I'm also, for my sins, the local Party representative. Sorry, you were saying?'

'Yes, Comrade Wiedemann. Well, this morning, *Unterleutnant* Vogel and myself attended the autopsy in the mortuary in the basement of the hospital. Unfortunately, we don't yet have a definitive cause of death.'

'But the boy was murdered, surely?' asked Wiedemann.

Müller fixed him with a stare. 'As I said, we don't have a definitive cause of death. Until we do, I wouldn't really like to speculate. What we do know, of course, is that Maddelena is still missing. With a baby of that age, we have to fear for her safety, irrespective of whether anyone actually means her any harm. In Maddelena's case, as you know she was born prematurely. There was a reason she was in hospital receiving care. It must be heart-breaking for the parents.'

Müller paused. A church-like silence had fallen on the room. Wiedemann cleared his throat. 'I understand all that, Comrade *Oberleutnant*. But what are we, the police, doing, and how are we making sure we're meeting Party objectives in the investigation?'

'I've just come back from interviewing the parents. Their alibis seem solid. We still have to regard them as suspects, but personally I believe their grief is genuine. They don't feel we're doing enough. They want a visible police presence out on the streets searching for their daughter. It seems unfair to deny them that, and it's hampering our investigation.'

Stepping forward from the back of the room, Janowitz moved to stand alongside Wiedemann. 'We know your feelings on the matter, *Oberleutnant*. But the Ministry of State Security has not taken this decision lightly. You would be wise not to disregard it.'

Müller tried to make sure she retained a neutral expression. She didn't want either Malkus or his number two to have the excuse to act against her. And Janowitz made her shudder – there was something about the man that unnerved her. She turned to Vogel. He could face the flak for a moment. 'Comrade Vogel has just returned from conducting interviews at the hospital. Any-thing to report from there, *Unterleutnant*?'

If he was annoyed about being forced into the spotlight, Vogel hid it well, and launched into a smooth explanation of his series of interviews with medical staff in the paediatric unit. But just as he was starting the more difficult task of explaining how he'd done this in a way which would meet with Party approval, the phone rang. Eschler reached to answer it. Müller could see the People's Police captain's face crease with worry. He looked up at Müller as the call continued, and beckoned her with his eyes. He held his hand over the mouthpiece and whispered in her ear. 'It's the kindergarten in *Komplex VIII*. Some sort of emergency. The uniforms think it may be of interest to the inquiry, Comrade *Oberleutnant*.'

14

No. No. Not little Stefanie. Oh my God. What will Hansi think of me now?

I mustn't panic. I know I mustn't panic. Come on, Franziska. You were a trained nurse, before you started having your turns. You know what to do.

Tilt her head back. Ear to her mouth. *I can't hear anything. I can't hear anything at all.*

Five rescue breaths. I seal my mouth over hers, hoping I won't be sick. Blow hard, Franzi. Blow hard. One. Breathe. Two. Breathe. Three. Breathe. Four. Breathe. Five. Breathe.

Listen. Watch. *Nothing, nothing.* Oh God. What will everyone think of me? I'd wanted her for so long, for so many years. Don't cry. Keep under control.

What's next? Chest compressions.

Scheisse! I can already see her lips turning purple. Oh Stefi, Stefi, don't go. Mutti's here.

Push, Franzi. Push! Two fingers on the middle of her chest. Push firmly. Release. Do it again. Do it again. Counting. Up to ten. Up to twenty. Still nothing. Still nothing. Please, Stefi. Please. Your Mutti loves you. I didn't mean you any harm.

I'll have to ring Hansi. He'll know what to do. He never likes me calling the doctor directly. He likes to do it. He's calmer. Sometimes I panic, say the wrong things.

Seal her mouth with my lips again, and blow. Blow.

Do it all again, Franzi. Maybe there's still a chance. Two fingers. Middle of Stefi's chest. Push hard. Make sure her chest goes in. Then release. Once more. Twice. Three times.

I'm going to carry on. I'm not going to give up. All I ever wanted was Stefanie. She was my little gift from God. From heaven. I never believed I'd be able to have her. Please, God. Please. That's twenty pushes.

I listen. Still nothing.

Seal her lips again, the taste of the salt from my tears mingling with the taste of stale milk from her lips. Blow, Franzi. Blow. Please breathe, Stefi, my darling. Please breathe.

15

July 1975
Halle-Neustadt

Müller, Vogel and Eschler piled into one of the People's Police's marked squad cars, with Fernbach driving. Ignoring the previous warnings from Malkus and Janowitz not to draw attention to the inquiry, Eschler switched on the flashing light and siren. Müller didn't pull him up for it. The sight of police cars on emergency calls in the Republic was common enough. Lenin's idea that under communism, crime would wither away as the excesses of individuals disappeared . . . well, Müller's own profession wouldn't exist if that was the case.

Fernbach accelerated away, drawing the stares of passers-by. They swung out onto the Magistrale, into the fast lane, as cars and trucks pulled over to let them through. In just a couple of minutes, with a screech of brakes, they were outside the kindergarten, in another of the town's nameless streets.

Saying little, the four police officers rushed inside the building, brandishing their IDs. The staff pointed to a side room, away from the main kindergarten and crèche. As Müller and the others entered, she was unsurprised by who she found. Sitting on a chair, head in her hands, was a clearly distraught Klara Salzmann – surrounded by three uniformed police officers. Maddelena's mother looked up with a half-snarl on her face as she heard Müller's voice.

'It's all right, comrades,' Müller said to the three officers. 'We can deal with it from here.'

The three uniforms started to protest, but Eschler held his hand up to silence them. 'What *Oberleutnant* Müller says is correct. We know this citizen. She's involved in a wider investigation.'

'But she was upsetting the staff and the children,' said one of the three, a young female officer. 'She should be arrested.'

Klara Salzmann snorted. 'Arrested? Me? I'm just trying to do what you should all be doing. Showing everyone this.' Frau Salzmann shrugged off the arm lock she was in and picked up a photograph from the table next to her. Müller could see it was a picture of Maddelena – a close-up of her face. 'All I was doing was asking if anyone had seen this baby. *My* baby. My Maddelena. It's not fair that no one's doing anything. It's not right.'

Eschler motioned with his eyes for the three uniforms to leave the room.

'You're not going to be arrested, Klara,' said Müller. 'But you're not making it easy for us. You must allow us to do our jobs and conduct the investigation *our* way. I can understand why you did what you did, but we can't allow it to go on.' Even as she spoke, Müller could hear her own words ringing false. Malkus's strictures *were* hampering the inquiry. There surely must be more behind the ever-present need for secrecy, something she was determined to uncover. But even Müller couldn't allow Klara Salzmann to go around the town acting like a vigilante.

The fight seemed to go out of the woman. She buried her head in Müller's shoulder and clung to the detective as Müller lightly stroked her back.

As she and Vogel ushered Klara Salzmann into the back of their police vehicle, Müller took a few seconds to scan the surroundings, hoping not too many people had seen the commotion. Like most of the childcare facilities in Ha-Neu, this kindergarten in *Komplex VIII* was in a green square, bounded on three sides by *Plattenbauten*. Mothers didn't have far to go to the crèche or the kindergarten from their apartments. After a few weeks' maternity leave they were expected to be back at their factory or shop jobs, helping the Republic to meet its ever-increasing targets: the majority of them working alongside their menfolk at Leuna and Buna, catching the S-bahn each day from the main station. Thankfully, onlookers and gawpers were absent – it looked as though the Stasi's cloak of secrecy was pretty much intact, at least for now.

Eschler and Fernbach made their own way back to the incident room, while Müller and Vogel took Klara Salzmann to her apartment – Vogel driving, with Müller in the back of the vehicle, still comforting the distraught woman. Vogel took one hand off the wheel and passed his cigarettes and lighter towards Müller. She offered Klara one, and then lit it for her, the woman's fingers shaking as she took a deep drag.

The alcohol fumes hit Müller's nostrils as soon as Klara Salzmann opened the door to her flat. The three of them followed the scent towards the living room. There they found Reinhard Salzmann slumped on the sofa, snoring loudly, a three-quarters-empty bottle of crystal vodka on the coffee table. His trousers were damp at the crotch. Müller at first thought he'd wet himself in his alcoholic stupor, but then noticed the vodka glass on the floor. His last tot of Blue Strangler had ended up spilled on his clothes, rather than adding to what was already a potent mix in his stomach.

'You see why I felt I had to do something,' said his wife. 'He's not capable. He just hits the bottle all the time. That's why he was ranting at you the other day. I'd hidden it from him. He was angry as much about that as about what you're doing to find Maddelena. We're wrecks, *Oberleutnant*, both wrecks. Unless we find her, we're finished. Even if we find her, we've still lost Karsten.' The woman sat down next to her husband and stared hard at Müller. 'I'm sorry for what I did earlier. It won't happen again. But please find her.'

Back at the police headquarters for Ha-Neu, Müller called Vogel and Eschler to a meeting in her office. It was hardly big enough for the three of them. Müller hitched up her skirt and perched on the table, with the two male officers leaning against each side wall.

'Although she didn't go about it the right way, Klara Salzmann had a point,' said Müller. 'We have to do more.'

'I don't see how we can,' said Eschler.

'We can. I've been thinking about it. We need a good reason –
other than an apartment-by-apartment search for a missing
baby – to check on every family with a child of, say, under three
months old.'

'But how would we do that without raising suspicions?' asked
Vogel, pulling a cigarette from his pack of *f6*'s, and then motion-
ing the packet towards Müller and Eschler, who both shook
their heads.

Müller stood and turned to the window, looking out over
the Salzmanns' Y-section high-rise block, and then turned
back towards the other two officers. 'Families with babies will
have health workers checking on them regularly. That's what
we're going to be. Health officials. We'll come up with some
story that local health officials are starting a nutrition drive. To
make sure that all babies are being fed properly. We can use it
as cover. We'll plant a story in the local paper to give it greater
credence.'

'I can't see Malkus and Janowitz allowing that,' said Eschler,
frowning.

Müller fixed him with a stare. 'If you have a better idea, by all
means let me know, Bruno. As for Malkus and Janowitz –'

They were interrupted by a knock on the door.

'Come,' shouted Müller.

It was Wiedemann.

'Ah. Comrade *Oberleutnant*, I'm glad you're back. *Hauptmann* Janowitz wants to talk to you.'

'Can't it wait? You can see we're in the middle of a meeting.'

'No, I don't think it can, Comrade *Oberleutnant*.'

16

Müller followed Wiedemann back to his own office, lined with boxes and boxes of files from previous cases. Janowitz was already sitting there, but so – to Müller's surprise – was Malkus, twirling his pen as he waited. Neither of them rose to greet her. Malkus simply gestured with his eyes to an unoccupied chair across the desk from him and his deputy.

'Thanks for coming so quickly, Comrade *Oberleutnant*, and I'm sorry if I've disrupted your meeting.'

Müller shrugged. 'It's no problem. I wanted to talk to you anyway, Comrade *Major*. But what was it you wanted to see *me* about?'

'It's just that I heard that the Party meeting didn't go quite as smoothly as it usually does,' said Malkus, tapping the end of his pen on his notepad. 'I just wanted to find out why, and whether there's anything we can do to help.'

She looked at the faces of the other two – Wiedemann and Janowitz. They both had identical expressions punctuated by thin, supercilious smiles. 'It seemed to go perfectly well to me, Comrade *Major*,' said Müller. 'But I was conducting an interview and missed the beginning. Was there a problem before I arrived?'

It was Janowitz who spoke first as Malkus sat back in his chair and folded his arms across his chest. 'No. The problem was the fact that you were late. Perhaps we do things differently here.'

Malkus leaned forward now. 'Our monthly Party meetings are compulsory, Comrade *Oberleutnant*, and we expect everyone to take them seriously – especially senior officers such as yourself.'

'I apologise, Comrade *Major*. Next time I will put vital interviews, essential to advancing the case, to one side.'

Malkus's face reddened, but he didn't immediately rebuke Müller. Instead, Janowitz seemed to smell an opportunity to further undermine her.

'The thing is the case *isn't* really advancing, is it?' said the Stasi captain. 'I'm not entirely sure why a team from Berlin is necessary at all. It just seems to complicate things.' He turned to his superior officer. 'My view, Comrade *Major*, is that we should now take this out of the People's Police's hands, and deal with it ourselves.'

Müller found her own face reddening. It was a frustrating case, it was true. But now she was here, she was determined to try to solve it. And she certainly didn't want Janowitz deciding whether or not she, Vogel and Schmidt should be taken off it.

There were a few moments of awkward silence as Malkus sat stroking his chin, calculating his next move. Eventually he turned to Wiedemann and Janowitz. 'Could you two Comrades leave us for a moment, please? I wish to talk to *Oberleutnant* Müller alone.'

When they'd left the office, Malkus locked the door behind them. Then he returned to the desk, but sat on it rather than behind it, so that once again his eyeline was above that of Müller.

'I'd rather you didn't try to show me up in front of more junior colleagues, Karin,' he said, gently. 'The matter was referred to me by *Hauptmann* Janowitz, so I had to deal with it. But while you're here in Halle-Neustadt, you need to play by our rules. We can't just operate on our own terms. It might surprise you to know that I face the same sort of pressures as you. You saw an example of that just now. If I start bending the rules for you and your team, then hardliners such as my deputy will soon be reporting on me, and making my life difficult. So I want you to turn up promptly to the Party meetings in future, and take them seriously, please. Can we agree on that?'

Müller was angry that this slavish adherence to Party doctrine seemed to take precedence over the actual inquiry. But after holding Malkus's gaze for a moment, she nodded.

'Good,' the Stasi major continued. He continued to hold her stare. 'And the incident at the kindergarten involving the mother was unfortunate. That's just the sort of thing we want to avoid. But my agents tell me you dealt with it quickly and well, so I'm grateful.' Müller had to fight back an ironic smile from playing on her face. In damning her with faint praise, Malkus had also demonstrated how the Stasi *did* know everything she and her team did – its tentacles stretching everywhere.

After a pause to let the meaning of his words sink in, it was Malkus's turn to smile ironically. 'Now, what was it you wanted to talk to *me* about?'

Müller got up from her chair, walked towards the window, and then turned back to Malkus. Now she was standing, and he was perched on the desk, she felt she'd removed the psychological advantage he always seemed to be seeking. But she still felt uncomfortable in the glare of his amber eyes.

'We need to move the investigation up a gear, Comrade *Major*. It's getting nowhere very quickly. The incident in the kindergarten was a direct result of the parents' frustrations at the way we're investigating with one hand tied behind our backs. So we need to do something different. I want to search every apartment of every citizen in Ha-Neu with a baby of under three months old. And if possible I'd like to extend that to Halle itself, and surrounding towns such as Merseburg. Perhaps Schkeuditz too. We'll do it in such a way as to avoid raising people's fears. In fact, it may, in its own way, be a force for good.'

Malkus frowned. 'I don't see how you'll be able to do that without specifically countermanding our instructions that there should be no apartment-by-apartment search.'

'It won't be every apartment. It will be very specifically targeted. And we will pose as health workers. It will be a campaign to make sure infants are being fed properly, that they're getting the correct nutrition. That sort of thing. We'll take a trained paediatric nurse with us to weigh each child. All officers involved in the search will be given training to make sure it looks like an authentic campaign. And – with the involvement of the nurse – to some extent it will be.' She held her gaze on the Stasi officer until he looked down at his notepad and sighed.

'Let's for a moment imagine that I'll permit this. Why on earth do you think this missing baby will be hidden in plain sight? Surely it will have been locked away somewhere?'

Müller shrugged. 'Perhaps. But by getting into the homes of parents of new babies, even if we don't find Maddelena herself, we may find some evidence that leads us to her. In any case, for the moment, it's the best we can do.'

Malkus leant back in his chair and clasped his hands together. 'Very well. I'm not going to give you the official green light, but equally I won't stop you. It will be up to you if you want to try to involve the People's Police in Halle itself and the other towns you mentioned. But everyone involved, including any health-care professionals, must be sworn to secrecy over what we're actually doing. If this backfires, on your head be it.' Then his expression relaxed. 'Privately, unofficially, it sounds like a good plan. Well done. Let's hope it produces results, for all our sakes.'

Müller had done a rough calculation of how many babies of the right age there should be: around two hundred and fifty, according to her notes. About one hundred and twenty-five, then, should be girls, assuming an equal division of the sexes. When they'd checked with the hospital and health visitors, the figure was slightly higher. One hundred and forty. She decided the safest policy was to have two teams of two: a detective and a health visitor in each, with herself and Vogel being the obvious choices. Coming from Berlin, they'd be less likely to be recognised, although any of the mothers from *Komplex VIII*'s crèche – where Klara Salzmann had staged her one-woman appeal – could possibly put two and two together. But Müller and Vogel had gone directly to the side room where Frau Salzmann was being held. With a bit of luck, they hadn't been noticed.

Müller calculated that – with a twenty-minute search and interrogation at each address – each team could get through about fifteen visits a day. That meant that, within a week, they should be able to work their way through the whole of Halle-Neustadt. The neighbouring city of Halle itself and surrounding towns and villages were another matter. Halle alone would probably take at least twice as long.

After briefing Vogel and the two health visitors, Müller began her search in her own residential complex – number six. There were around thirty families to visit here: perhaps a couple of days' work.

Müller's sixth home visit was apartment block 956, flat 276, in *Wohnkomplex VI*. Each of the three parts of the address ending in six. Those three sixes – the Devil's number – might have been significant to Müller if she was superstitious or religious. She wasn't. Nevertheless, the visit seemed to have some unspoken significance, even before she and health visitor Kamilla Seidel had rung the apartment's bell. Each of the previous five babies had been towards the upper end of their age range: weighing too much to be Maddelena, and looking nothing like her either.

As they climbed the stairs to the second floor, Kamilla echoed the detective's own thoughts. 'I feel this could be the one, Comrade *Oberleutnant*. I'm not sure why, but . . .' Müller had decided the best policy was to brief the two nurses – in a limited way – about the operation. She hadn't mentioned the death of Karsten, but she had told them about the missing baby – warning them they were not to discuss it with anyone, not even their own families. If they did, their jobs would be at risk.

'Let's wait and see, Kamilla. It would be lovely to find her so soon, but that would feel a bit too easy. Things rarely work out like that.'

The door was opened by a girl who looked like she should still be at school, holding a tiny baby wrapped in a shawl. With her fresh complexion and total lack of make-up, the girl looked far too young to be a mother. Müller already knew from studying the relevant files that the girl's name was Anneliese Haase, and her baby was called Tanja. Müller showed her fake Health Ministry ID card, and explained what they were doing.

'It's nothing to be alarmed about, Anneliese. We simply want to weigh Tanja, do a few simple health checks, and give you some nutritional advice. It's a new government scheme to make sure the Republic's youngest citizens get the best possible start in life.'

The girl looked dubious, but ushered Müller and Kamilla inside. Tanja immediately began bawling, and wouldn't respond to her mother's attempts to calm her with a soft rabbit toy. In the end, an apologetic Anneliese explained she would have to feed her daughter. She sat on the lounge sofa, arranged a towel across her lap while cradling Tanja with her other arm, and then opened her maternity bra for the baby to begin to suckle.

For Müller – although ostensibly this was a perfect example of Tanja getting the required nutrition – it just represented another delay. They were already slipping behind schedule with more than half the day gone, and only five babies 'processed'.

'Is she a good feeder?' asked Kamilla, as she and Müller sat waiting at the dining table.

'Yes. She knows what she likes. She's a very greedy girl, aren't you, *Schatzi*?'

'And how long does she feed for at each session?'

'Usually at least ten minutes – but if she's very hungry it can be as much as an hour. Luckily I produce plenty of milk. I've even started donating some to the milk bank in the centre of Ha-Neu.'

Müller groaned inwardly about the delay, and Kamilla's dull – but necessary – questions. 'We can wait for a few minutes, Frau Haase, but we do need to see other citizens. So let us know as soon as you think we may be able to weigh her without causing too much distress.' She caught Kamilla's gaze and motioned with her eyes to the health visitor's equipment bag. Kamilla took the hint, and started getting the baby scales out. Within a couple of minutes, Anneliese had removed her nipple from Tanya's mouth.

'She should be OK now. She can have more after you've gone if she starts getting upset.'

Kamilla picked Tanya up and began the weighing procedure, noting her weight with and without a nappy. Müller meanwhile got the Foton instant camera from her bag and took two photos of Tanya's face. One, face-on, from above, and the second from the side, in profile. She and Vogel would go through any promising photos later at the incident room.

Reaching into her bag again, Müller pulled out a cellophane-wrapped black-and-white photograph of Maddelena. She passed it to Anneliese.

'This is an example of an undernourished baby we found recently. You haven't seen a baby looking like this, have you? At the crèche, at any mother's groups, when you're out and about with Tanya in her pram. Anything like that?' It was a small deception. One that Malkus wouldn't approve of, but then he didn't need to know the minutiae of what Müller and Vogel were up to.

Anneliese shook her head.

'Well, if you do,' continued Müller, 'please get in touch with Kamilla at the hospital immediately, and she will contact me, then we can take appropriate action.' She passed the young mother a business card with the hospital's logo, but the number was in fact a hotline to the police incident room, staffed by one of the typists and arranged by Müller earlier in the day. 'And thanks for your cooperation, Anneliese. Tanya looks to be a very healthy young lady, and she's clearly a good feeder. Is her weight OK, Kamilla?'

'She's perfect. A little above average for her age, but that's nothing to worry about.'

Anneliese Haase picked up the child, her pride obvious in her beaming face, and then showed the two women to the door.

Müller and Kamilla made the short journey to the northern part of neighbouring *Komplex V* for lunch, at the Donkey Windmill –

the *Eselsmühle*. The cutesy pink-washed mill, with its four blades turning slowly in the summer breeze, made for an anachronistic sight, overshadowed as it was on its eastern flank by towering slab apartment blocks. Modern and ancient made uncomfortable bedfellows, thought Müller, as she parked the Wartburg next to the mill. But she'd chosen it deliberately. It took pride of place on postcards of Ha-Neu, and – thanks to the children's donkey rides offered in the green space alongside – was a popular choice with young families. Young families who might just have even younger babies. One of whom might be the cuckoo in the nest they were looking for: Maddelena Salzmann.

'Do you want to order?' Müller asked Kamilla. 'I'll be with you in a moment. I just need to radio in to the incident room. Could you get me a potato salad and a Vita Cola? And get yourself whatever you'd like.' She handed Kamilla a ten-mark note. After the woman had climbed out of the car and made her way into the restaurant, Müller picked up the radio handset, crouching down to avoid the prying eyes of customers sitting in the afternoon sun outside the mill.

Eschler answered.

What he said immediately sent Müller's heart rate soaring.

The uniform team had made an arrest.

17

Müller radioed Vogel, instructing him to stop what he was doing and make his way back to the incident room. They then drove out of Ha-Neu along the Magistrale, over the two branches of the river Saale, and turned north through the old part of Halle – following the south-to-north line of river tributaries, past the west wing of the imposing Moritzburg castle.

'Where are we heading to?' asked Vogel.

'The *Roter Ochse*,' Müller replied as she swung the Wartburg round another bend.

'I thought that was a Stasi remand centre?'

'It is. But the police don't have any interrogation cells in Ha-Neu, so they use this instead.'

Müller peered to her right. The *Roter Ochse*, or Red Ox, seemed to earn its name: it sat solidly, with its four corner towers looking a bit like the thick-set legs of a bull, its hide formed by millions of red bricks. She felt fear clutch at the bottom of her stomach, but she wasn't sure why.

As they held up their ID cards they were shown to a visitors' parking area, and then found they had a two-man escort by

Stasi officers. At the entrance to the building itself, their escort changed personnel. Then they were climbing the stairs up to the remand centre – in silence, apart from the echoing sounds of their footsteps. It had the same smell of concrete, metal and disinfectant as the prison in the Hauptstadt where Gottfried had been held. The same red and green control lights. The same harsh noises. Every corridor was painted in an identical fashion. An olive-green lower wall, with cream above. After the third corner turn, Müller already knew she was lost and – without the ever-present escort guards – would have struggled to find her way out.

Eventually, they arrived at a cell with an open door. Sitting inside, with a frown on his face, was Eschler. Beside him, Malkus. Müller was immediately on her guard. Malkus gestured to the two other chairs in the room, indicating that Müller and Vogel should sit down.

'Thanks for getting here so quickly, comrades. We might have got a bit of a breakthrough thanks to Comrade Eschler and his team. Eschler, would you like to brief them?'

'Certainly, Comrade *Major*. I think it's a bit early to say it's a breakthrough, though. Anyway, in the next cell we have a prisoner. He's a thirty-five-year-old. We found him in one of the tunnels. Sleeping rough.'

'Homeless?' asked Müller, aware of the note of incredulity in her voice. According to Karl-Eduard von Schnitzler's weekly current affairs programme, *Der schwarze Kanal,* such things only happened in the West. His view seemed to be borne out in the rival Western TV news programmes Gottfried had liked to watch, which for the last few years had been full of miners' strikes, electricity shortages, three-day weeks . . . and homelessness.

Malkus tapped his pen on the desk. 'That's not for broadcast outside this room. I dispute the claim he's homeless. He says he's unemployed too. We all know that doesn't happen in the Republic.'

'Nevertheless,' continued Eschler, 'there was evidence he had indeed been sleeping in this particular heating tunnel for a few weeks. Blankets, discarded vodka bottles, cardboard boxes constructed into a makeshift den to keep himself warm – even though at the moment in the summer heat it's stifling down there.'

'Down where, exactly?' asked Vogel.

'*Wohnkomplex V.* In the heating duct between the Donkey Mill restaurant and Block 815. It's a spur off the main circuit with pretty much waste ground above. It runs under where they do the donkey rides for kids. I think he thought he was safe there. Because it only runs to the Donkey Mill, it probably doesn't get checked by maintenance workers as often as the main ducts between the apartment blocks themselves.'

'OK,' said Müller, realising that was the exact same place she'd just come from. 'But a homeless and unemployed man, though unusual, doesn't necessarily add up to a child abductor. What makes us think he's our man?'

'It was the reaction of the sniffer dog to his bedding,' said Eschler. 'The same dog that found the baby doll wrapped in the blanket. It's been trained to hunt out Maddelena's scent.'

'Maddelena's scent?' queried Müller. 'I thought it had been trained to recognise the smell of the bedding used by Maddelena. That's not necessarily the same thing.'

Before Eschler could answer, Malkus jumped in. 'Let's not get bogged down in details. This is our best lead so far. And if he's guilty, we've solved the case – and got a down-and-out off the streets.'

Müller sighed. 'We won't have *solved* the case, Comrade *Major*, until we find Maddelena. That's our priority now, especially as it looks as though Karsten's death *wasn't* murder.'

Malkus reddened. Müller felt she had perhaps overstepped the mark. But the Stasi major nodded slowly. 'You're correct, of course, Comrade *Oberleutnant*.'

Müller got to her feet and smoothed out her clothing. 'Right. Well, I'd better get in and start questioning him. What's his name?'

Eschler handed her a file. 'Stefan Hildebrand.'

She waved the folder. 'Anything relevant in here?'

'A few petty theft convictions, a spell in jail. Nothing you wouldn't expect.'

'And no form for child abduction or anything remotely connected with it?'

'No,' Eschler said.

Malkus stood up, and made as if to join Müller with the questioning. She held her hand up.

'It's still a police matter at the moment, Comrade *Major*.' She tapped Vogel on the shoulder. 'Martin, why don't you join me in there?' Then she turned to Malkus again. 'Is that OK with you, Comrade *Major*?'

Malkus looked as though he was about to disagree, then sat down in his chair and waved them away. 'Go on, then. But make sure you get something to stick on him. We need results, and quickly.'

18

Stefan Hildebrand looked much as Müller expected. Gaunt face covered with an unkempt salt-and-pepper beard, and sunken eyes with dark shadows under them. Müller found herself holding her breath as she and Vogel sat down opposite the man: he may have managed to find enough food – and certainly enough alcoholic drink – to survive in the heating tunnels, but he clearly hadn't managed to get hold of any personal hygiene products.

He raised his head and looked up at the two detectives. 'Why do they keep asking me about this baby girl?'

'What baby girl?' asked Müller.

'Maddelena? I think that was her name. I don't know anything about any babies.'

Müller gestured with her eyes towards the plastic evidence bag containing the blanket, which Vogel had brought into the room. Her deputy lifted it onto the table and slid it towards Hildebrand.

'We believe this blanket was in her hospital cot,' said Vogel. 'What can you tell us about it?'

Hildebrand reached out towards the package.

'Don't touch it,' warned Müller. 'Just have a look through the plastic. Do you recognise it?'

The sides of Hildebrand's mouth turned downwards, and he frowned. 'I'm not sure.'

'Well, it was found in your possession,' said Vogel. 'And the sniffer dogs smelt Maddelena's scent on it. How do you explain that?'

Hildebrand shrugged. 'I've got a few old blankets. I just collect them as I find them. Don't really need them at the moment, but in the winter –'

'I'm not really interested in your living habits, Citizen Hildebrand,' said Müller. 'What we want to know is where you got this particular blanket.'

The prisoner leant forward on his stool, peering more closely at the package. 'I think I got that quite recently, if it's the one I think it is. From the duct near the hospital, if that helps. It had just been dumped there along with some other bits and bobs. Most of it was rubbish.'

'And why were you near the hospital?' asked Müller.

'It wasn't for any particular reason. During the day I stay in the duct that leads to the Donkey Mill. It feels safer there. No one's ever bothered me, not until today when the *Vopos* came after me. But at night I scout around the other tunnels, occasionally go above ground to see what I can scavenge at the back of the *Kaufhalle*. You'd be amazed how much food gets chucked out.'

'I don't believe you,' said Müller. 'You know as well as I do that there are no jobless, no homeless people in the Republic.

There's a job for everyone, a home for everyone – if you actually want one, Citizen Hildebrand. So I don't believe you. All I want to know is what have you done with Maddelena?'

'And what have you done with her twin brother, Karsten?' added Vogel. 'You realise they were only a few weeks old. They were in hospital for a reason. Without medical attention, they will most probably die. So why don't you tell us where they are?'

Müller saw the fear in Hildebrand's eyes. Vogel's deception about Karsten, not telling the man he was dead, might just trip him up. It might encourage him to reveal vital information. If he was their man.

'Twins? I don't know anything about twin babies. I don't know anything about this Maddelena you keep going on about, or her brother. I accept I've done wrong, that I shouldn't be living down in the tunnels. But I just couldn't stomach the job they gave me after I'd been freed from prison. Sweeping the bloody roads, when I'm a trained scientist. I put in an application to go to the West. I lost my job because of that. And then they started making up stories about me to my wife. She left me.' He sighed, and held his face in his hands. Then he looked up at Müller. 'What would you do if that happened?' Müller thought back to her and Gottfried's troubles: they hadn't been so very different.

'Your personal affairs are no concern of mine, Citizen Hildebrand.' She moved the bag containing the blanket to one side of the table, reached into her briefcase and brought out an envelope. Opening it, she showed it to Hildebrand. A photograph of a battered red suitcase. The case that Karsten's tiny body had been stuffed into.

'Do you recognise this case?'

Hildebrand shook his head.

'Answer, please!' shouted Vogel.

'No, OK? No, I do not recognise that case. Why?'

'Karsten's dead body was dumped in that case,' said Müller.

'Dead? I thought you said he was missing, like his sister?'

Vogel shrugged. 'No. He was killed. Beaten and killed. So I'd have a good long think, Citizen Hildebrand. It will be better for you if you tell us everything. The quicker you do, the more chance the court will be lenient towards you. But murder is a very serious matter.'

Hildebrand's face suddenly looked ashen. 'Murder? I haven't murdered anyone. I haven't taken any babies. What would I want with babies? I have enough trouble feeding myself.'

Müller and Vogel didn't answer the man, but just gathered up the photograph and the evidence bag and left the room.

'Well?' asked Malkus, who was still waiting next door with Eschler.

Müller folded her arms across her chest. 'I can't believe he's our man. Yes, he shouldn't be living down in the tunnels. Yes, he ought to have a proper job and live in a regular apartment, just like everyone else. But we don't really have any evidence against him.'

'The blanket? The dog handlers seemed convinced,' said Eschler.

Müller rolled her eyes. 'As I said earlier, all that means is that it found a similar scent to the one on the blanket that we know was used for Maddelena, Comrade *Hauptmann*. Perhaps the blanket is from the same ward, perhaps it's a particular disinfectant they use in the hospital. It's not really evidence, is it? Yes, we could perhaps build a case against Stefan Hildebrand. But if he's not our man – and I very much doubt that he is – then we'd just be wasting time while the trail to Maddelena gets even colder. Perhaps you could get *Wachtmeister* Fernbach and his men to check with the hospital itself. See if they recognise the blanket. It's got some numbers and letters on. That may mean it belongs to a particular ward.'

Malkus got to his feet, stroking his chin with one hand. 'So what would you recommend we do with Hildebrand?'

'Keep him here for the moment. You can always charge him with vagrancy or theft of food if you want. Meanwhile, *Unterleutnant* Vogel and I will get back to checking on new and recently born babies in Ha-Neu. Maybe we should schedule a catch-up at the incident room this evening?'

Malkus furrowed his brow. 'I'm not sure if *Hauptmann* Janowitz and I can make it, but you go ahead without us.' Then he gave Müller a thin smile. 'After all it is, as you keep telling me, Comrade *Oberleutnant*, your case.' He reached into his bag, pulled out an envelope and handed it to Müller. 'By the way, I need to give you this. It's a list of families who – for security reasons – must not be included your so-called 'nutrition check' campaign. There are only about ten names. Get in touch if it becomes a problem.'

'For security reasons?' Müller felt annoyed that her plan was being compromised before it had really started.

'Exactly. On the orders of the Ministry for State Security. But you can be sure the person we want, and Maddelena, will not be found on this brief list.'

'How can I be sure of that?'

'Because the Ministry for State Security guarantees it, Comrade Müller. That should be good enough for you.'

It wasn't, and Malkus knew it. But there was little Müller could do about it.

The sense that they were going nowhere fast sat heavily on Müller that evening. She and Vogel had completed another three or so visits each to families with young babies following the interrogation of Hildebrand. None of those they had visited so far were on Malkus's list. In fact, she noticed most of the 'forbidden' addresses were located in *Komplex VIII* – the residential area nearest to the Stasi regional headquarters, on the north-east edge of Ha-Neu. It almost certainly wasn't a coincidence. She scanned down it now, comparing the addresses to her street map: families living in Blocks 358, 354, 337, 334. All of them, she knew, were right next to the Ministry for State Security buildings. Only one of those buildings was shown on the map, however. The main headquarters. The rest of the map was blank. A triangle of nothingness, and to the north of that, the main Soviet base. Somewhere else that they really ought to search, but she doubted they'd be able to get permission.

Their evening catch-up had shed no new light on things either. They had no real clues, nothing to crack the case open.

The longer it took, the colder the trail would be. The less likely they were to find Maddelena alive.

Müller surveyed all the photographs on the wall of the incident room again. Then, putting on protective gloves, she shuffled through the various evidence bags. There must be *something* here, she thought. Something that they'd missed. She'd detailed Schmidt to go over everything the local forensic officers had found, but he'd so far failed to come up with anything new.

The summer sun outside was fading now. She reached for the electric light switch, and as she did so the incident room door opened. It was Schmidt.

'Jonas. What are you doing here at this time?'

'I could ask you the same thing, Comrade *Oberleutnant*.' She'd given up on trying to get Schmidt to drop the formalities. Even when there were just the two of them, it was always Comrade this and Comrade that. 'You look tired, if you don't mind me saying,' he added.

Müller moved to the wall mirror and studied her face. The *Kriminaltechniker* was right. The telltale bags under her eyes had returned. Dark circles. Not yet turned thirty, and already bags under the eyes. A bit like the down-and-out, Hildebrand. She smiled at her reflection. 'Some women would take offence at that, Jonas. But you're right.' She moved across to a faux-leather swivel chair and sat heavily into it. 'I don't just look tired. I *am* tired. Tired of this case.'

Instead of replying, Schmidt put on protective gloves and began opening one of the evidence bags.

'What have you got?' she asked.

'Oh, it's probably nothing.'

'Come on, Jonas. We've known each other long enough. Probable nothings with you often turn into probable somethings.'

Schmidt was taking the newspaper which had been found wrapped round Karsten's body from the bag, and what looked like the meat counter advertising flyer from the *Kaufhalle*. The one where Klara Salzmann worked. 'It was the newspaper. Something I saw earlier today, and when I was having dinner just now it came back to me. I had this clear image in my head that wouldn't go away.'

'What was it?'

The forensic officer was smoothing out a double-page spread of the newspaper. 'Look. Here.'

Müller got up, crossed the room, and peered over his shoulder. Schmidt was pointing at the puzzle section in the centre of the paper. What on earth could be the relevance of that? 'And?' prompted Müller.

'The crossword puzzle. It's partially completed.'

Müller looked, as instructed. She could make out a few words, *DEZEMBER* being about the longest. She frowned. 'There doesn't seem to be anything particularly unusual about it.'

'Take a closer look at the capital "E"s.'

Müller bent down. The clues that had been filled in were all in capital letters. All legible. Reasonably neat. 'OK. If it was done in lower-case handwriting, it might be worth getting in a handwriting analyst. But capitals? So many people write them similarly.'

'True, true,' nodded Schmidt. 'But not in this case.'

Müller's heart began to pound. What had Jonas seen that she couldn't? She looked again at the three capital 'E's in *DEZEMBER*. Then it clicked. The 'E's had all been formed like a capital 'L', with the bottom horizontal stroke slanting upwards. The top and middle horizontal strokes also slanted up, but in most of the examples they failed to connect with the vertical downstroke.

Schmidt picked up a pen and a piece of paper and began to write a series of capital 'E's. He offered the pen to Müller. 'You try it. Do it quite quickly, without thinking too much about it.'

She did her own row of about ten letters.

'Now look closely at them, and compare them with the ones in the crossword puzzle.'

Müller did as instructed. 'All the middle strokes of our "E"s either bisect, or at least touch, the downstroke. The top strokes too.'

'Exactly, Comrade *Oberleutnant*. So whoever completed the crossword puzzle has a fairly unusual way of writing the letter "E". That gives us a chance of tracking that person down. And whoever did the puzzle . . .'

'. . . is possibly connected to the abductor of Maddelena?'

'That would be my conclusion, *Oberleutnant*.'

19

Nine years earlier: July 1966
East Berlin

I still think of her all the time. Of course I do. I don't think I'll ever fully get over it. I always worry that it was my fault, even though Hansi tells me it wasn't. It's just one of those things. And she never seemed a very happy child. Almost as though something was missing. She loved her papa, Hansi, but somehow the bond between me and Stefi was never there. Perhaps it was because she had such difficulty feeding. I'm sure I was right, though. It's only natural that a baby should feed from a mother's breasts. I'm not against new ideas, but . . .

The apartment here in Johannisthal is similar to the lovely one we had in Halle-Neustadt, but not quite as new, or as big. In Ha-Neu, Hansi had managed to get us a two-bed, because his doctor friend suspected I might be having twins, I was so large. But in the end, there was just Stefi. And now it's just Hansi and me. If he was annoyed about having to give up his job at the chemical works, he never complained about it to me. Now he seems to be doing more and more work for the Ministry, in

Lichtenberg. He can't really tell me what he gets up to. It's supposed to be secret. But I know it's something important. And as well as the long hours, he has to bring work home. He hides himself away in the bedroom – telling me that because what he's doing is so important, I mustn't interrupt. One evening, there was nothing good on the television, so I went to the bedroom to see what he was up to. There were papers strewn about the floor, although I didn't manage to get a good look at them because he was immediately terribly angry, shouting at me to get out and never come in without knocking in future. I think perhaps he's working too hard, and the stress is getting to him.

It took a long time for the baby weight to come off, even though I've been really trying. It hasn't completely come off even now. But Hansi likes my new shape. After we'd made things up with each other again following the bedroom incident, he bought me a new bikini – my first ever – as a 'thank you' for trying so hard. I've been building up a bit of a tan as a reward to myself. Each day this week I've been going on the S-bahn and tram right up to Weissensee, virtually the whole way across the Hauptstadt. They've got a lovely *Strandbad* there by the shore, with a beach bar and real sand. I was a bit self-conscious at first, revealing myself in the bikini when there were all these younger girls and students with their perfectly toned bodies. But in the end I just went for it, and stretched out on my beach towel. The guy at the beach bar was even eyeing me up, I'm sure of it. Hansi wouldn't have been too happy. Although I don't suppose he could have done much about it. This man was all muscles in his T-shirt, and Hansi . . . well, Hansi isn't. He's more the brainy sort. But he's always been so kind to me, and the other night he was showing interest again. I said no, not yet. It's still a bit soon. After Stefi and everything. He understood. But I can tell he likes the new me. My shapeliness and tan excite him. It's easy to tell with men, isn't it? They can't really hide it. That barman couldn't when he came over just now in his shorts and offered to put up the umbrella for me. I could tell what he actually wanted to do. Anyway, I shouldn't really be thinking like that. It's too soon after Stefi. I'm still upset about it. Of course I am.

But overall, I am feeling much better. My head's clearer. I think those pills I was having to take to prevent any morning sickness made me a bit woozy and unclear sometimes. And my exciting news is that Hansi has sorted me out a new job. Doing what I love best, what I was trained for. Working as a nurse again, and – would you believe it – in a children's hospital, here in the Hauptstadt. With the youngest ones. I love the smell of young babies, their soft skin, their lovely little smiles. It's what I was born to do, I think. I just wish I could have done more for Stefi. But it's not too late. I'm still in my early thirties. Well, just about. Hansi and I can start again. Although I've lost weight, my breasts are still full. Maybe I'll give him a treat and wear his new bikini to bed tonight. He'd like that.

20

July 1975
Halle-Neustadt

Only now, a week after Karsten and Maddelena Salzmann had gone missing, was the investigation truly swinging into gear. Müller's feelings of tiredness had evaporated as soon as Schmidt had pointed out the distinctive capital 'E's in the partially completed crossword. It felt as though the police had simply been treading water so far – now they had at least two fronts to fight on. Müller had got permission for one of the Republic's leading handwriting experts to try to help them match the handwriting. And there was still a chance that the fake nutrition campaign would produce results.

Müller called a meeting with Vogel, Schmidt and Eschler in her office the morning after Schmidt's discovery.

'I thought it would be useful to get our heads together and try to decide on a way forward. You'll have heard by now about what Jonas has found in the crossword. Later today, Professor Karl-Heinz Morgenstern will be arriving from Berlin. He's the Republic's top handwriting expert. He's going to examine the crossword and talk to us about what we need to look out for.'

Eschler scratched his chin. 'We'll need to gather handwriting samples for that to be of much use. Samples from pretty much every adult in Halle-Neustadt, from Halle itself, surrounding towns and villages. It's the same problem we faced with the babies but on a larger scale.'

'I've been thinking about that overnight,' said Müller. 'Although overall in this inquiry I've been keen to keep clear boundaries between us – the People's Police – and the Ministry for State Security, this might be a case where we appeal to them for help.'

'Malkus and Janowitz don't seem that enamoured with us so far,' said Vogel, frowning.

Müller shrugged. 'Maybe. But they have the resources, the personnel, to mount a big operation like that. We don't. And if we ask them to do it, at least they can't accuse *us* of breaking the rules.' While she was saying this out loud, Müller's brain was going over the other aspect of the case which the Stasi – according to Eschler – had already investigated. Checking handwriting samples was all well and good – it was something for which she was content to enlist Stasi helpers. But Eschler's earlier assertion that the Stasi had already questioned people on the night trains to and from Leuna and Buna was something that still nagged at the back of her mind. And there was only one way to dispel that nag. For the moment, though, she kept that to herself.

'But that's only one line of attack,' she continued. 'Our other priority is to visit all the babies of the right age in Ha-Neu.' She smiled at Vogel. 'Martin, I need you to take charge of that on your own now. Jonas and I are going to be busy with Professor

Morgenstern – and hopefully liaising with the Stasi – over the handwriting evidence.'

Vogel nodded.

'Bruno, I want you to continue with the searches of the pipe tunnels and waste ground. How are your men getting on?'

'Well, we found Hildebrand yesterday. But it turns out he has an alibi. At the time the twins went missing, he was being held by a security guard at the *Kaufhalle* on suspicion of shoplifting. He'd managed to give them the slip before we arrived – that's why it didn't show up on his file.'

'But we're sure it was him?' asked Müller.

'Pretty much. Matches the description from the *Kaufhalle* staff. And he independently gave that as his story when we questioned him about his movements on that day.'

'So how much of the pipe complex have you covered?'

'Probably about two thirds of it by now. Once we've finished, we'll move on to the various parks in Ha-Neu, and then we'll start on the Dölauer heathland, but that will be a big job: more than seven hundred hectares.'

'What about the banks of the river Saale, even the Saale itself?' asked Vogel, polishing his glasses with a paper handkerchief.

Blowing out his cheeks, Eschler snorted. 'Pah! We could spend years doing that. How far up- and downstream do we go? We've got the *Vopos* in Halle itself helping. They've combed Peissnitz island in the middle of the river. Ziegelwiese island too.'

'Should we bring in frogmen to search the river itself?' asked Vogel.

Eschler shrugged. 'It's up to *Oberleutnant* Müller here.'

Tidying the papers on her desk, Müller shook her head. 'I want us to assume that Maddelena is still alive, until we have any direct evidence to the contrary. So I want to concentrate on places she might be being held, or hidden. Bringing in divers would be expensive, and the only body they'd be finding at this stage would be a dead one.'

'I fear that's probably the case anyway, *Oberleutnant*.'

Müller said nothing for a moment, slowly breathing in and out. 'You may be right, Bruno. But let's try to stay positive. If nothing else, if the team believes they're searching for a living baby – that they have a chance of saving her, being the hero – I think that will energise them.'

The jangle of her office telephone interrupted her. She reached to answer it. '*Oberleutnant* Müller. Hang on a moment, please.' She cupped her hand over the receiver and then addressed the three other officers. 'OK, so we've all got stuff to be getting on with. Let's have another catch-up this evening.'

Vogel, Schmidt and Eschler took that as their cue to depart, and once they had, Müller removed her hand and spoke into the mouthpiece.

'Sorry about that, I was just finishing a meeting. *Oberleutnant* Müller here.'

'Hello, Karin,' a male voice at the other end of the line said. She didn't recognise the man.

'Who's speaking, please?'

'It's Emil.' Müller racked her brains. She couldn't think of any Emils she knew, not since her school or college days, anyway.

'Sorry. Do I know you?'

'Apologies. You probably don't know my first name. Emil Wollenburg. Doctor Wollenburg. From the Charité hospital in the Hauptstadt. I said I might ring you about meeting up.'

21

That night

Müller's old *Vopo* uniform was something she usually packed for assignments away from the Hauptstadt, and it had been no different for this inquiry in Halle-Neustadt. Now it would come in useful at last.

She checked her make-up in the police apartment mirror, tucking her blond hair under the green People's Police cap. The dark circles under her eyes were less prominent thanks to the action of sun on skin, though still there – as Schmidt had helpfully pointed out. But the face staring back at her – with the prominent cheekbones that had always seemed to her a touch Slavic, rather than Germanic – was, she knew, a lie. Inside, the longer she spent in Ha-Neu without finding Maddelena, the more it felt like her guts were twisting. The streets without names, the forbidding concrete buildings, the ever-watchfulness of Malkus and his team – it all had her longing to be back in Berlin, teamed up with Tilsner again. In charge of her own destiny, if that were ever possible in the Republic. Living in a slightly shabby but historic apartment in Schönhauser Allee. But

then going back to Schönhauser Allee without a successful conclusion to this case would mean going back to the drudgery of
Keibelstrasse.

She breathed in slowly to steel herself and straightened the
collar of her uniform. There was also the complication of Emil
Wollenburg. Yes, she was attracted to him, but his phone call
had come as a shock. It felt too soon after the messy, emotional
split from Gottfried. And now she'd been told the handwriting
professor – Morgenstern – had had to delay his visit. But she still
needed to try to move the inquiry forward. That was why she'd
come up with this new idea.

She continued to stare at her reflection in the mirror. Dressing as a regular beat policewoman would – she knew – arouse
fewer suspicions with what she was about to do. If Tilsner were
here he'd say she was mad: mad to once more set off on a one-
woman mission without back-up. But it was something she
needed to do alone. There was less chance of being watched, less
chance of Stasi interference.

For a few seconds Müller held her breath, straining to hear
the sounds of the television through the thin apartment walls.
The instantly recognisable, hypnotic voice of Karl-Eduard von
Schnitzler presenting *Der schwarze Kanal* told her all she needed
to know. Schmidt – who'd prepared dinner for the three of them
– would be hanging on von Schnitzler's every word, just in case
he was quizzed on it by Weidemann. Vogel was not as slavish a
Party follower – though like all People's Police officers he was
a Party member – and he too was almost certainly glued to the
Republic's Channel One, and its interpretation of stories from

the West. Müller knew she should be too, but tonight she was going to have to miss it.

She exited the bathroom, grabbed her coat from the rack, opened the front door and hurriedly shouted a 'See you later' over her shoulder. Then she slammed it behind her without waiting for a reply.

The S-bahn train heading south towards the chemical works was full, with almost every seat occupied, yet strangely silent, as though there was little joy to be had in going in for another night of work. Amongst the sea of faces, Müller noticed tired eyes aplenty. She wasn't surprised, given the shift work involved to keep the chemical factories operating twenty-four hours a day.

Müller worked methodically, beginning at the front of the train, and working her way backwards. For the first couple of rows there was sullen acceptance of her questions and little interest in the colour photo she passed around of the battered red suitcase in which Karsten's body had been discovered.

But as she worked her way down the aisle, at the fourth row, a middle-aged man in a dark suit challenged her.

'Why are you asking these questions?' he said, holding her gaze, perhaps trying to show that he wasn't afraid of – or had no respect for – the People's Police.

'It's an investigation we're working on,' Müller replied, passing the photo along to the next passenger, a young woman. 'We just want to know if anyone going to work at Leuna or Buna saw someone carrying this case. On Friday evening two weeks ago.'

'It wouldn't have been this shift two weeks ago,' said the man, pushing his dark, greasy hair back from his forehead, and smirking slightly. 'Most of us here would have been on earlies then.'

Müller found herself reddening under his glare. She hadn't thought of that. It was a stupid mistake.

'Not everyone,' interjected the young woman. 'Some of us ask to do more nights to get time off during the day. I have to help my grandparents who are ill. So I do alternate weeks of nights, rather than one week in three. Quite a few here will. There'll even be a few who've asked to do permanent night shifts.'

The greasy-haired man snorted, and then turned his attention back to the puzzle section of his newspaper.

'Thank you,' said Müller to the woman. 'And when you were on this train two weeks ago, did you see anyone carrying that case?'

The woman held the photograph so the weak lighting of the carriage highlighted it better. Then she shook her head. 'No, I'm sorry. Not that I remember.'

Müller had similar conversations with workers through the first half of the train, occasionally having to give a further explanation that the police were investigating a robbery in which the suitcase was thought to have been used. It was a lie, but the cover she needed to ensure she didn't directly alert citizens to the baby abductions. But no one could shed any light on the suitcase; no one had seen it being carried, or being thrown out of the train window.

When she moved through the interconnecting door between carriages two and three, Müller realised the train was approaching the spot near Angersdorf where Karsten's body had been jettisoned. She opened the window of the external door, at the lobby end of the third carriage, to peer out at the scene. The spot where she and Schmidt had been at the trackside – and where she'd first encountered Malkus and Janowitz – was approaching quickly. She held her hands on her head to stop her *Vopo* cap being blown off. The rushing air was warm, pleasant almost, despite the tang of chemical pollution which was evident even here – several kilometres from the chemical works. Darkness had almost fallen, but she could still make out the silhouettes of foliage in the marshy ground of the Saale floodplain. A haunting, wistful beauty in the fading light. It seemed so wrong that the tiny baby's body had just been dumped and abandoned here.

The force that hit her from behind came as an utter shock. Müller tried to turn desperately, fighting to get her arms, neck and head back fully inside the train. But someone stronger was determined she shouldn't. Her cap flew off immediately, then she felt her upper body being lifted as she strained back against whoever was pushing her. She shouted out, but felt the air being squeezed from her lungs as she realised the man – she couldn't turn to see but she assumed it was a man – was lifting her body, trying to push her through the window gap. She felt one of his powerful hands on the back of her head, pushing it downwards. The smell of his warm breath filled her nostrils. Something familiar that made her want to retch, but in her panic she couldn't place it, instead concentrating on gripping the lip of the window to try to stop herself losing her balance and falling to an almost certain death.

Müller tried to wrench her head to the side to see her attacker. She couldn't, but the fractional movement allowed her to see further up the track. Her pulse hammered in her ears as she saw the lights of cars driving along a main road up and over the single-track rail line in the distance. Over a bridge.

As she strained backwards, she suddenly realised the pushing force had stopped, but as she tried to scrabble back inside the train her legs were just kicking against thin air. She couldn't breathe, could feel a panic attack coming on as she realised her body was slowly slipping out of the window. And then she saw the road – now much closer – wasn't crossing a bridge, but a low hill silhouetted in the near darkness, punctured by a black hole. A tunnel. A tunnel fast approaching.

'Help me. Help me,' she tried to shout with what little air she could force from her body. But her screams just died in the onrushing air, as her fingers finally lost their grip.

And then the mouth of the tunnel arrived.

'No, no!' she yelled.

Her eardrums were hit by the pressure rush, she was falling, and all was black.

22

Eight years earlier: July 1967
East Berlin

I wonder if time is running out for me to get what I truly want. Just eighteen months ago, everything seemed so perfect. That Christmas in 1965, back in Halle-Neustadt. Hansi had been a bit annoyed with me on Christmas Eve, but we soon got over it and had a lovely festive period. I even fed little Stefi with the bottles Hansi made up. The thing is, I'd rather have fed her naturally, but as he was home most days, he was keeping watch on me, and he always said that bottle was best. Because he's a scientist, he's hard to disagree with.

For a few days, it was wonderful. But then when Hansi went back to work, it started to go downhill. I try to think of positive things these days, Hansi says it's best, but sometimes I can't help myself going back to that day when Stefi . . .

Sorry. I really shouldn't look back, but it does remind me how things *could* be. If only we could be a little family again. We've been trying, of course. Since last summer, when I got the baby weight off, and once I felt comfortable in my new shape, well . . . it seemed to inspire Hansi. He couldn't keep his hands off me, if truth were told.

'Pass the forceps, Nurse Traugott.'

Gosh. I was daydreaming again. Pull yourself together, Franzi. 'Sorry, Doctor.'

The thing is, this is my last chance, so Hansi says. That's partly why my mind wandered back to that lovely Christmas in Ha-Neu. Things here in the Hauptstadt haven't been going so well, ever since 'the incident'. That's what I call it. Anyway, the incident led to me losing the job in the baby ward at the hospital. It wasn't my fault. At least, I don't think so. But they didn't want to listen. Hansi said I still had to be earning though, he didn't want me moping at home.

So he got me a job here. At Doctor Rothstein's clinic. Only it's not really a clinic. Not in the official sense. And it's not an official job. The doctor pays me cash in hand, without it going through any books. That's how the patients have to pay too. It's all unofficial, of course. That's why Hansi was able to get me in here. The Ministry wanted the place watched. Mostly they turn a blind eye, and there have been moves to try to legalise everything. But it's not legal yet. So it's useful information for the Ministry – for Hansi – to know exactly who comes in here for procedures.

'The curette, please, Nurse Traugott.'

The doctor didn't catch me so unawares that time. I was ready for him, and had the tool in my hand. Horrible thing. Makes me shiver. I remember the definition from my training. *A small hand tool, with a scoop or gouge at the end, for scraping material – usually human tissue.*

I do think it's a bit mean of Hansi to start me working here. He knows what I want. What I've always wanted. What I had for a few, precious months, then lost, or had taken away, or . . . I suppose that was what led to the incident, if I'm honest with myself. Perhaps a baby ward wasn't the best place for me to be working. The temptation was too much. Luckily, Hansi had it all swept under the carpet. In his job, he can do that. Now he's with the Ministry full-time.

We're getting to the end now. I don't like this part. Try not to watch too closely what Doctor Rothstein's doing between the legs. I've got the metal vessels ready for the contents. I know what it will all look like. These late procedures, which have to be by dilation and evacuation if there are complications, they're the worst. It's the eyes you have to try not to look at too closely. The eyes and the face. Especially if they're smiling. Not many people know they can smile so young, but they can, you know. They wouldn't be smiling if they knew what was about to happen. What their mothers are choosing to do to them. They wouldn't be smiling then. Poor little mites.

23

July 1975
From Halle-Neustadt to Oberhof

Falling.

Being sucked into the blackness of the tunnel.

As time had slowed, that was what Müller thought was happening.

But it wasn't.

The guard had yanked her back, out of the window, just as the train plunged into the darkness. She'd fallen back, with him, into the safety of the train.

Disoriented, shaking with shock, but safe.

By the time she reached the hospital, Müller had already resolved to say nothing about the man who had pushed her out of the window – she had no wish to draw the Stasi's attention to her decision to defy them and ask questions on the train. The guard who had so fortunately been passing seemed not to have seen anything, so thinking on her feet she had told him she had simply been looking out of the window and had over-balanced. It was clear he didn't believe her, but luckily Müller wasn't the only one who knew the danger of asking too many questions.

After taking precautionary X-rays, the doctors assured her nothing was broken. Her neck and back ached, and her head pounded, and so she was unsurprised when they advised her to rest. The trouble was, she didn't want to. She couldn't, not until Maddelena – and the person who abducted her and caused the death of her twin brother – was found. Eschler and Vogel agreed, though – she should make sure she took the weekend off. Müller wasn't sure she wanted to do even that, at least not in Halle-Neustadt. She wouldn't be able to relax, knowing the Salzmanns were still frantic with worry, still missing their daughter.

The natural thing at a time like this – in the immediate aftermath of the sort of shock she'd had on the train – would be for someone to seek solace in the bosom of their family. Müller knew, from past experience, there would be precious little solace there for her. She was hesitating: it was a visit she'd told herself she must make, and this was the ideal chance to get it out of the way – although the drive possibly wouldn't be the best prescription for her aching neck and back. What tipped the balance for her was someone she saw – or thought she saw – in the hospital, as she was waiting for her X-ray results.

She'd always had this sense that her brother and sister had been treated more kindly than her in childhood. Perhaps it was her determination to prove herself to her parents that had led her to Berlin and to a career with the police in the Hauptstadt. Sometimes she told herself it was either her imagination, or a mother's natural inclination to favour the only son – Roland – and the baby of the family – Sara. But there were two incidents which stood out in her memory and gave the lie to that notion.

The first happened when she was just five years old, when an elegant, forty-something woman had turned up on the door-step of the family guest house and addressed Müller by her first name, Karin, when she answered the door. Her mother had been so, so angry with her then. Shouting at her, shooing her away. And she'd never understood why. The woman on the doorstep had stayed in Karin's mind ever since – and then who should walk into the hospital waiting room that very afternoon but, so it seemed, the woman herself.

It wasn't her, of course. Müller knew it couldn't be the same person – nearly a quarter of a century had passed, and when she looked more closely she saw at once that the stranger bore only a passing resemblance to the woman she remembered. But see-ing the woman's *Doppelgängerin* was like scratching at an insect bite. It reawakened the memory of the hurt, the look of long-ing she'd fleetingly glimpsed in the woman's eyes. Müller had a family duty to visit her mother, brother and sister. But she also had a duty to herself. She'd suffered in silence long enough – she needed to challenge her mother once and for all.

Müller headed to her home village from the north, skirting Erfurt and Gotha on the autobahn, taking the Wartburg above the national speed limit to allow the natural ventilation through the open driver's window to take the edge off the midday sum-mer heat.

As she drove, she stretched her neck and shoulders from side to side to try to dissipate the ache and hurt that had persisted since the incident on the train. She'd been lucky, she knew that. The guard had yanked her back from the window at the very last second. She'd fallen back against him, into the carriage, as the train catapulted into the blackness of the tunnel. She'd been uncertain what was actually happening, or which way she was falling or being pulled in the fog of panic. It was a few seconds until she'd realised she'd been saved – not sucked out of the train to her death.

More than any physical pain, what was troubling her was the knowledge that someone had tried to at least sabotage the investigation. Even if it wasn't an actual attempt to kill her, it was at best a warning. And she had no idea who had been behind her. There was just some faint recognition on her part. Not visual recognition – she hadn't been able to turn to confront him. It was, instead, the smell of his breath. But try as she might, she couldn't think why it was familiar. When she tried to visualise her attacker, even though she hadn't seen him, the face that danced in front of her eyes, that taunted her, was that of Janowitz. But she had no idea why, it was just a hunch.

Thankfully, the guard had believed her story that she'd simply been checking something through the open window and had got stuck through her own actions. She didn't want to have to explain to Malkus why she'd disregarded his orders, and why she'd been double-checking his own supposed investigation. She was certain now that the Stasi *hadn't* carried out any checks on the trains. Otherwise one of passengers on permanent or semi-permanent night shifts would have recalled it.

The Wartburg finally reached the northern edge of the Thuringian forest at Ohrdruf. As she braked at the town limits, the fumes from the exhaust through the open window stung the back of her throat. Farty Hans – the model's nickname – was living up to its moniker.

Ohrdruf had featured heavily in her school anti-fascist lessons: the concentration camp had been one of the first to be liberated. Thankfully, so her schoolteacher had told the class, the area was one which the Americans had handed over to Soviet forces. The Republic's Soviet friends would ensure no similar atrocities happened in the future.

When Ohrdruf shrank into a speck in the rear-view mirror, the road began to twist and turn, winding through the thick blanket of spruce and pines, broken only occasionally by meadowland. Müller took one hand off the wheel to wipe the sweat from her brow.

This journey south to visit her family had also given her an excuse to stall Emil Wollenburg. The news that the doctor had transferred temporarily to Ha-Neu wasn't really a surprise: he'd implied as much in Berlin. His explanation was that there was a shortage of hospital doctors in Ha-Neu. It seemed suspiciously convenient, and now he wanted to take her out on a date. Müller wasn't sure she was ready for it. Yes, Gottfried – her ex-husband – was in the past, teaching in the Federal Republic as far as she knew. And other than that initial, typewritten letter a few days after he'd arrived she hadn't heard from him. There was no way back for their relationship. But it still seemed far too early to be thinking of beginning a new one.

As the forest finally thinned out, she got her first glimpse of the jagged shards of the Interhotel Panorama, which had now become the most famous landmark of her home village. The glass in its windows sparkled in the summer sun, but its strange ski-jump-shaped roof looked incongruous at this time of the year. Not until the winter snows came in December would it blend in better with the rest of Oberhof. Now it was like two parts of a sunken, disintegrating ocean liner, breaking through the surface of the sea. But the sea here wasn't water, it was the mountain grass and surrounding forest.

Müller pulled over to the side of the road, got out of the car and soaked up the view. She'd seen this vista many times before: in childhood, adolescence, and when returning home from the police training college near the Hauptstadt, although the modernistic Panorama itself had only dominated it since the end of the 1960s. It was a view which always triggered a memory. The second memory that had prompted her to finally make the decision to confront her mother: the day, some twenty-five years ago, when she'd last spoken to her childhood best friend. Müller felt the moisture gather in her eyes. She wiped her hand slowly across her face as the images danced on her brain.

24

November 1951
Oberhof, Thuringia

'You're not doing it right. You need to lie back. Watch me.'

The gangly boy, his height out of proportion to the rest of his appearance, lay flat on his back on the metal tray, using his hands and the heels of his boots to launch himself down the rain-slicked grass slope. The girl – several years younger, an oddly matched playmate – put her hand to her brow below her blond fringe, peering through the mist to where the shape had disappeared.

'Johannes. Where are you? I can't see you. I'm frightened.'

'You'll be fine,' the boy shouted back through the murk. 'It levels out at the bottom here. You won't crash. Just grip hard to the edges of the tray and push yourself off.'

The girl settled her five-year-old frame back against the cold metal tray. She could feel her lips quivering as she wondered if she should do it. If she was brave enough to follow.

'Come on, slowcoach.' The shout echoed up the slope and across the valley, as though scores of Young Pioneers were urging her on. This was it. The World Championships of the Luge. Inside her head – her five-year-old head – she was East Germany's finest female winter athlete, about to take on the world's best.

The girl flexed her legs, and pushed herself off.

Damp late autumn air roared past her ears. Time slowed. She felt every bump of the meadow under her, jolting her back, cracking her head against the tray. On and on it went, as though it would never end. Like a dream. A nightmare.

And then . . . nothing. Quiet, peace. Just the panting of a boy, running towards her.

'Wow! That was amazing. You must have gone fifty metres further than me. I was worried you would go over the next slope.'

The girl got to her feet gingerly, her legs wobbling like jelly. She felt her face redden with pride at the boy's compliments.

He hugged her to him.

The girl decided at that moment that Johannes was the boy for her. That when she was older they would be married. She peered up into his eyes as he towered over her, eyes covered by wire-framed glasses. Even at her tender age, she knew Johannes wasn't a good-looking boy. That he got teased and bullied by his classmates. That he was often left in tears by their meanness. That was how they'd become friends, despite the five-year age difference. When she'd found him crying on the corner by the village sweet shop, and had tried to comfort him.

They both turned towards the village as they heard the sounds. Motors, shouting, screaming. The girl felt the boy tense up. The November mist had cleared. They could see all the way down to the village, to Oberhof, the country's leading winter sports resort.

The girl grabbed the boy's hand, sensing his alarm.

'What is it, Johannes?'

'Soldiers.'

'Soldiers? Fascist soldiers?'

She watched the boy shake his head.

'No. Our soldiers.'

But the alarm didn't leave his voice, and the girl struggled to understand.

'That's all right then, isn't it?'

He shook his head. Then squinted in concentration.

'I've got to get back down there.'

'Why?' she asked.

Johannes's reply was a fast sprint down the sloping meadow. The girl tried to keep up at first, but her shorter legs were no match. When she caught her foot in a cow's hoof print and tumbled to the ground, the tears that came were not caused by the hurt in her leg. They were tears of confusion: of feeling abandoned by her friend. The fear that Farmer Bonz would come and tell her off, and report her to her parents for playing in, and messing up, his field.

The soldiers stood like giants in a line, blocking the way to Mutti, Papa and new baby sister Sara, not that the girl wanted to see her again. The baby was all that Mutti and Papa seemed to talk about these days. That was why the girl spent so much of her time with Johannes in the meadow, pretending they were luge champions. But she was hungry, and frightened. A soldier was shouting at her.

'Halt there, girl.' He looked important, with more stars on his shoulders than the others. He was ticking names off a list. 'What's your name?'

Instead of answering, the child spied a gap through the legs of the line of grey giants. She made a run for it and squeezed through before the soldiers realised what was happening. Home. That's where she had to get to. There was more shouting, but she just ignored it, and ran and ran, splashing through the puddles in the street even though she knew Mutti would be angry that she was now wet, as well as muddy from the meadow.

Her mother was standing, glowering in the doorway of Berg-pension Hanneli, brandishing a wooden spoon.

'Where on earth have you been, young lady? Just look at the state of you. That dress is ruined. And your shoes. Whatever have you been doing?'

The girl tried to run past into the guest house, but her mother grabbed her arm.

'Oh, no, you don't. I'm not having you mess up the house. That boy's been leading you astray again, hasn't he?'

'He's my friend.'

'You should find a friend your own age, young lady. It's not right you playing around with a boy so much older than yourself. Anyway, we won't be having any trouble from him anymore. Now wait here in the porch till I get you cleaned up.'

'Why are the soldiers here? They tried to capture me.'

Her mother's grip tightened. 'That's none of your business.'

The child tried to wriggle free as baby Sara began crying because of all the noise. What did Mutti mean? We won't be having any trouble from him anymore.

'Mannfred!' her mother shouted. 'Come and deal with little Miss Bossyboots here, while I feed the baby. She's covered in mud

and has ruined her clothes.' Then she knelt down and whispered to the girl: 'Your father will give you a good hiding now, madam, just you watch. And you'll have –'

The girl didn't wait for the end of the warning. She yanked her arm from her mother's grip and ran, and ran, as fast as she could. Back towards the shouting. Back towards the line of grey giants. Back towards Johannes's house.

She arrived there just in time to see Johannes's parents being pushed onto the back of an open troop truck. His mother's eyes red-rimmed from tears. And then Johannes himself being led out of Pension Edelweiss – his family's hotel – looking confused, upset. Somewhere he'd lost his characteristic spectacles, and the girl watched his head swivelling from side to side, looking, searching, but unseeing – the world an unfocussed blur.

'Johannes! Johannes!' the girl shouted out. 'What's wrong? Where are they taking you? I want to go with you.'

His head turned in the direction of her call. He seemed to be about to answer back as his eyes desperately tried to focus through a myopic haze, but as he opened his mouth a soldier clasped his hand across it, forced his arm up behind his back, and pushed him into the truck along with his parents.

Then the giant chief soldier, the one with the stars on his shoulder, was back, his huge face peering into the girl's.

'What's your name, girl?' he thundered, his breath warm and foul-smelling, flecks of spittle flying in her face.

The girl didn't pull back. Didn't flinch. And didn't answer, but instead asked a question of her own.

'Where are you taking my friend?'

'They are not your friends, little girl. They are profiteers, rack-eteers. Undermining our socialist republic.' The long words meant nothing to the girl, but she understood the message. Johannes was being taken away. And she wasn't going with him. 'Now, I will ask you just once more.' The girl wiped the spit away from her eyes. 'What is your name?'

The girl spoke clearly, bravely, without fear, staring directly into the mean big chief soldier's eyes, challenging him, matching his stern expression with one of her own. 'My name is Karin Müller. And you are a very nasty man. I will never forgive you for taking away my best friend.'

25

July 1975
Oberhof, Bezirk Suhl

Bergpension Hanneli – the Müller family home – looked much as it always had, almost as though it was constructed with over-sized plastic Pebe bricks, the toy building blocks that Müller had since learned were copied from the Danish originals. The thick log cladding of the ground floor exterior was still coated in blood-red gloss, so shiny that Müller was forced to shield her eyes from the reflected mountain sunlight. The vibrant colour was such a contrast to Ha-Neu's predominant concrete grey. Above it, the guest rooms in the sharply sloping eaves of the nineteenth-century villa were covered in dark grey slate, the pointed central gable above the master suite giving the whole the look of a fairytale witch's cottage.

Müller went to the back door, wiping her shoes on the mat before entering, her eyes drawn to the window boxes full of golden hyacinths. The gold, red and near-black of the roof was striking – an almost perfect representation of the colours of the German flag, both the East's and the West's. She opened the kitchen door softly, and then coughed to attract Sara's attention.

She attempted a smile as her sister looked up from the piles of potatoes she was preparing. There was surprise in Sara's facial expression, but no warmth, and her hands still busied themselves with peeling.

'So you've finally found the way from Berlin, Karin. It's been a long time. Mum misses you.'

Müller stood for a moment on the threshold of the kitchen and looked her younger sister up and down. She wanted to go over and hug Sara, but the look on her face, her tone of voice, and her ever-busy hands seemed designed to ward her off. As sisters, they were so different, and they both knew it. Karin with her looks that the boys always seemed attracted to, and a confidence that had helped her climb the rungs to head her own murder squad in the People's Police. Sara had the ruddy complexion and swarthy figure of a mountain housewife, reddy-brown curls tumbling chaotically from her head, and eyes the colour of pond water. All contrasting with Müller's own Scandinavian or Slavic ice-blue-eyed blondness.

'It's the job, Sara. You know that.'

Her younger sister finally put the potato peeler to one side and moved towards Müller for a lukewarm embrace. 'Is it, though? You didn't even come back at Christmas. It's a lot of work just for Mum and me.'

Müller felt a tug of guilt, but knew it wasn't enough to ever draw her back any more regularly from Berlin to this country village. She grimaced slightly as the pressure of Sara's hands and arms made the pain in her back and neck flare once more. But she held the hug, and squeezed her sister more tightly.

Sara pulled back and stared straight into Müller's eyes, furrowing her brow. 'You look older, Karin. Tired.'

Müller laughed gently. 'I *am* older. I *am* tired.'

'You're sure there's nothing else? Why the unannounced visit? Are you sure there isn't something bothering you? Is it to do with Gottfried?'

Müller felt her stomach tighten at Sara's question. The name of her ex-husband – the man with whom she'd shared a surname even before their marriage, prompting several feeble jokes from him about the two Müllers, or 'millers', joining forces – still had the power to unnerve her, months after their divorce. Even though what was really troubling her was her sense of alienation from her own birth family.

'It's over.'

Sara gasped. 'What's over?'

'The marriage. My marriage. Gottfried was given permission to move to the Federal Republic. The last I heard from him, he was trying to get a teaching job near Heidelberg.'

'Oh Karin. I'm so sorry.' Sara's face had softened, her frown of disapproval replaced by one of concern. 'If there's anything I, Mutti or Roland can do . . . you know we'd always help you.' Müller was touched by the genuineness of Sara's sentiment. She just didn't believe, though, that this sentiment was shared by her mother.

Müller pulled her sister into the hallway of the little hotel and stood beside her, staring into the gilt-framed mirror. 'Look at us. We're so different.'

Sara snorted with laughter. 'Well, I *am* prettier.'

'Of course,' smiled Müller.

Müller's sister stood behind her, looking over her shoulder into the reflective glass. 'All right. I give up. You're the pretty one. You always were.' Then she traced the dark semi-circles under the detective's eyes with her finger. 'But you have aged, Karin.' Müller knew she should be offended. Yet Sara's concern appeared heartfelt. 'I don't think this job's good for you. How can it be? Dealing with dead bodies, horrible murders. I don't know how you do it.'

Müller switched her gaze from the reflection of her sister to the image of her own face. In the last couple of weeks she'd been looking healthier, but now the hallmarks of tiredness and worry were back. The result, no doubt, of the train attack – but she didn't want to worry her sister further by talking about that.

Müller moved away from the mirror. 'Where's Mama? I'd been hoping to surprise her.'

'She's at her flower-arranging class. You should know that.' The gentle admonishment was clear in Sara's tone and words. *You should know that. If you took more interest in the life of your own family.* The last sentence didn't leave Sara's lips, but Müller knew it was implied. 'But she'll be back soon.'

'And Roland?'

'At football. You know that too. Whatever you get up to in Berlin, Karin, life just goes on here. Day after day after day.' They'd moved back into the kitchen, and Sara picked up the potato peeler, rapidly removing the skin from each tuber, then picking up another. Almost as though she were an actual machine on a production line.

Müller moved back out to the hall. Her welcome party was clearly over. She started to climb the stairs to the guest quarters on the first floor, and then a second, narrower step of stairs, right into the eaves. To her bedroom. The one her mother always kept for her, virtually untouched since her teenage years.

The room was tiny, with just a single-width dormer window. Now she was fully grown, two thirds of the floor space was inaccessible without crouching. This had been her haven, and it had been frozen – almost as though in a time capsule – since she'd left Oberhof for her police training in Potsdam some twelve years earlier. It was the room of an early 1960s teenage girl: a poster of a fresh-faced Fab Four still just about stuck to the wall, with one corner curled. The Beatles. One of the few Western pop groups to – at that time – escape the scrutiny of Party bosses. Müller laughed gently to herself. It hadn't lasted long. Only two years later, Walter Ulbricht, the then Party general secretary, had questioned – if it really was a question – why East Germany had to copy every 'yeah, yeah, yeah' that came from the West.

She reached up to the top of the wardrobe, scraping her hand through the dust, searching for her 'secret' key: she'd used the same system years later in the Schönhauser Allee flat. Finally, she located it and brought it down to unlock the desk drawer and pull out her diary. The one she'd kept, almost religiously, since the age of five. Not every day. Not even every month. But each year there were at least a few entries. And that first year had filled nearly a third of the notebook, fuelled by the excitement of learning to write, and later by the realisation that – just like at home in the Bergpension Hanneli – somehow she didn't fit.

Müller leafed through the pages, the smell of the musty paper mingling with the scent of whatever perfume she'd used as a teenager. The aroma was familiar. Brands of cosmetics in the Republic barely changed from year to year. Casino de Luxe, it smelt like: an almost too-flowery scent of roses, with something vaguely unpleasant and sweet behind it.

It didn't take her long to find the entry she wanted from the second of November, 1951. She glanced down it: *Wy did the soljers take Johanas away? Muti wil not tel me. All she torks about is Sara. She is a wich.* Müller wasn't sure whether to laugh at the atrocious spelling and sibling jealousy behind the words, or cry about the truth of the loss of her best friend and feeling of alienation from her family. The slow creak of the stairs instead forced her to hurriedly shut the diary away and lock the drawer.

Face to face, Müller could see in her mother her sister Sara in thirty years' time. Like Sara, Rosamund Müller's smile in greeting for her elder daughter seemed thin and insincere. Müller approached her as though to pull her into a hug, but the middle-aged woman, with the same reddy-brown curly hair as her younger daughter – thanks no doubt to the hairdresser's or her own dye bottle – pulled back, and folded her arms over her fulsome chest.

'It would have been nice to have had some warning, Karin.'

'I'm sorry. I didn't want to let you down again. It's another murder . . . well, missing persons inquiry. I thought it would be worse to announce that I was coming, and then let you down if I had to cancel.'

Rosamund shrugged, then sniffed the air suspiciously. 'What's that smell? It seems familiar.'

'My old perfume. From when I was last living here. I was just testing a bottle I found.' The small lie came easily.

Her mother rolled her eyes. 'Well, I suppose you'll be wanting lunch. You could help Sara with the preparations, you know.'

Müller nodded. 'I'll be down in a moment.'

Rosamund turned as though to retreat down the stairs.

'Mutti. Don't go just yet. Come and sit on the bed. I wanted a chat.'

Her mother eyed her suspiciously, but they sat next to each other, and the bed responded to being disturbed by sending plumes of dust particles into the air that then slowly fell through the shafts of sunlight like miniature snowflakes.

'I was thinking about when I was little, on the journey here.'

'What about it? You were a difficult child. Never made many friends. Always fussy about your food. Always jealous of Sara.'

'You sound as though you hated me.'

'You reap what you sow, Karin. You reap what you sow.' Then her face softened, and she laid her wrinkled, liver-spotted hand on Müller's bare forearm. 'Sorry. That was nasty. It's just I was upset when you didn't thank me for the birthday card or present, or come back for Christmas. You didn't even write.'

Müller in turn laid her own hand on top of her mother's, smoothing out the bulging veins. She'd tried to ignore her birthday as much as possible, but it was still wrong of her not to respond to her mother. 'I'm sorry. I should have. Work was even more of a nightmare. And I was having problems with Gottfried.'

'Oh. I hope it wasn't anything serious?'

Müller didn't say anything. The silence told her mother enough.

'You're still together, I hope?'

The detective shook her head and – to her surprise – found herself fighting back tears. She'd thought she was over it. In her mind, she was. But some deeper tie to her former husband still pulled at her. She wiped at her eyes. Her mother got out a hand-kerchief and handed it to her. That first letter he'd sent from the Federal Republic had been the only letter, and the only piece of actual handwriting was his signature. It troubled her. Maybe others had been intercepted. But, at the end of the day, they *were* now a divorced couple – why should he write?

'Was that what you wanted to talk to me about?'

Müller shook her head again, still not trusting herself to speak.

'What was it then, Katzi?'

Müller clutched her mother's hand more tightly. 'I like it when you call me Katzi. It's what you always used to call me when I was little, before –'

'– before your sister was born?'

Müller nodded, and then breathed in slowly. 'There are a couple of things I was thinking about on the journey down that I wanted to discuss with you.' She saw a shadow of worry cross her mother's face. 'The first was about Johannes.'

'Johannes?' asked her mother in confusion. At the same time, her face relaxed slightly – as though she'd been expecting an altogether more difficult subject to be raised.

'The son of the owners of the Pension Edelweiss. The *former* owners.' Müller couldn't disguise the bitterness in her words.

Rosamund's expression changed as she remembered. 'He was a strange boy. Why he befriended a five-year-old when he was at least six years older than you, I'll never understand.'

'He was a nice boy. We were a good team. But I've never understood why the government took over the Edelweiss – and lots of other hotels here – and handed them to the state tourist authority. And why our little business survived.'

'That was thanks to your father. He'd been through a lot under the Nazis, during the war. It wasn't a pleasant time to be a communist. But he stayed loyal to the Party, to the socialist cause, despite the difficulties it caused.' Rosamund Müller paused, staring vacantly above her daughter's head.

'And?'

Her mother shivered slightly, despite the cloying warmth of the cramped room. 'And he made a lot of friends. Important friends in the Party. He helped them, they helped him. But Johannes's parents . . .'

'Weren't Party members?'

Rosamund shrugged. 'I've no idea. Perhaps not, I never saw them at any meetings. But worse than that, they were racketeers, profiteers, keeping money for themselves that should have been shared with the state. We've never been a rich country, Karin, and we certainly weren't then. The war was not long over. Some people here in the village just carried on like fascist imperialists.' She drew her hand away from her daughter's, and straightened her back. The upright communist convincing herself of her integrity.

'But they didn't have to relocate everyone, surely?'

Her mother gave a weary sigh. 'Sometimes difficult choices must be made for the greater good. You should know that, working for the People's Police.'

They lapsed into silence, sitting uncomfortably now side by side, the brief flash of intimacy and warmth forgotten.

'It wasn't fair, though,' Müller said after a few moments. 'He was my best friend. And he was taken away. You were never sympathetic about it, even though you knew how upset I was. And you say it was odd for me to befriend an awkward boy a few years older than myself. But perhaps there was a reason.' She held her mother's gaze for a moment. 'Perhaps it was because I never really fitted in here.' She gestured round the tiny room. 'Perhaps you didn't do enough to make me feel loved.'

Müller's mother had now removed her hand from her daughter's arm, and stared hard at her in return. 'That's not a very nice thing to say, Karin. And it's not true. We did our best for you. You know that. It wasn't always easy. As I said, you were a difficult child.'

Rosamund Müller's hands were now clasped tightly in her lap. Müller looked into her eyes – there was something almost fearful, cowed about them. Not the image of her mother – a strong-willed, stubborn matriarch – that Müller was used to. Rosamund Müller dropped her gaze. She dropped her voice, almost to a whisper. 'You said there were two things you wanted to talk about. What was the other?'

On the journey, and in the X-ray department of Ha-Neu hospital, Müller's resolve had been clear. She would confront her mother. Confront her about her constant feeling throughout her childhood of being treated differently to her brother and sister. Confront her about that visit by the elegant woman with the fine facial features – whose near double she'd seen in the hospital. The woman who'd stared so hard at her when she – a child of just five years of age – had opened the guest house front door, thinking she was helping her mother by welcoming a paying guest. Only to have her mother shout and scream at her when the woman called out her name, then bundle her inside, before an angry exchange of words with the visitor on the doorstep.

But it had to be done. She let out a long, slow sigh, cleared her throat, and then clasped her mother's hand to hers again.

'The other thing I wanted to talk about was what happened shortly after Johannes was taken away. When that woman visited.'

Rosamund Müller's lips pursed together, her eyes narrowed. 'What woman? I don't know what you mean.' She freed her hand from Müller's and made as if to stand. Müller placed hers on her mother's shoulder.

'Down the years, I've tried to talk about it several times,' said Müller, surprised at the coldness and anger in her own voice. 'The way you reacted, shouting at me, yanking me away from the door. You'd never have treated Sara or Roland like that. I've always felt I was treated differently. I need you to explain why. I need to understand.'

Rosamund threw her daughter's hand off and stood, making towards the bedroom door. 'I said I never want to talk about it, Karin. And I meant it.'

Müller dodged round the older woman, blocking the doorway with her body, her voice rising in frustration. 'I want to know. I need to know.' She gripped her mother's shoulder tightly, watching the other woman wince. So tightly she could feel her pulse. 'I deserve to know.'

Rosamund pulled her head back a fraction, shocked by the venom and desperation in her daughter's words. Then Müller felt the older woman's rigid, upright posture suddenly slump in defeat.

Her mother slowly prised her daughter's fingers away one by one, then took Müller's hand in her own.

'I never wanted it to come to this. Whatever you may think about how badly you feel I treated you, I've always tried to show you love, Karin. I really have.' She exhaled so slowly it sounded as though she was emptying every breath from her wheezing, rattling lungs. 'But perhaps it's time. Time to show you something that I never really wanted to show you. Come with me.'

Müller's parents' bedroom – much as her own – had changed little since her childhood. Her father's side of the bed, even though he no longer slept in it, was still overlooked by a wall emblazoned with an array of medals and certificates for various good communist deeds, and loyal work for the Citizens' Committee.

Since her husband's death some five years earlier, Rosamund Müller clearly hadn't rearranged any of the furniture or sleeping arrangements. She still slept on the far side of the double bed. Müller knew her papa had needed to be nearest the door, especially in his last years when the prostate cancer rampaged and spread through his ailing body. And it was to the far side Rosamund now went, watched closely by Müller. Her mother reached under the bedside table for a hidden key, then opened the top locked drawer and brought out a small, rusty tin box. She thrust it towards Müller, her eyes brimming with tears.

'Here,' she said, her voice shrill and quivering with emotion. 'I never meant to treat you any differently to your brother or sister. I tried not to. But if I did, I'm sorry. This box contains the reason. It's yours. Take it.'

Müller reached out and grasped the object, then loosened her grip with one hand, and examined the rust stains on her fingertips.

'Aren't you going to open it? I thought that was what you wanted? To *know* everything?' There was a bitter edge to her mother's voice. *The sort of nastiness that Sara had never been shown.*

Müller held the box in one hand and began prising the lid off with her other, watching her fingers tremble – partly from the strain of trying to free the fused-on metal, partly from the fear of what she would find.

All of a sudden, the lid came away, sending rust particles into the air. Müller breathed in the tang of metal, felt tingles up her back and neck from the sound – much like her reaction to chalk scraping on a blackboard at school.

'I haven't opened it for years,' admitted her mother. 'I haven't wanted to. I kept it for you. For this day. For this day that I hoped would never come.'

Müller still said nothing, but stared at the tin's contents. There wasn't much. A sepia-tinted, dog-eared black-and-white photo and a piece of folded, yellowing paper. She picked out the photograph first. It showed a young girl – very young, early teens – in a dirty, loose white overall. Cradling a tiny infant, wrapped in a shawl. The girl's eyes were trained on the baby, her expression full of love.

'Who is it?' asked Müller, aware of her own voice crackling with emotion. But in her heart, already knowing the answer.

'That's your natural mother,' sobbed Rosamund. 'It's the only photo I have. With you, just a few hours after you were born.'

26

The revelations in Oberhof hung heavily over Müller for the rest of the weekend. Soon after the discovery made in her mother's tin box, the detective had stormed out of the guest house, unable or unwilling to build bridges with the two women who she'd thought for nearly three decades were her mother and sister.

Throughout the drive back, thoughts raced through her head. Who and where was her real mother? Was it the woman who visited the guest house all those years ago and tried to talk to her? Despite Rosamund Müller giving up some of her secrets, she hadn't been willing – or able – to enlighten Müller on that point. And who and where was her real father? Where had her former best friend Johannes and his family been taken? Were they even still alive?

She felt used. Dirty. Betrayed. And lost. Most of all she felt her whole identity – what she thought of as herself – had been undermined. The emotions made her throat tighten. Tears – perhaps even a breakdown – felt just one misguided comment away.

Yet as she swung the Wartburg left into yet another of Ha-Neu's nameless streets, at the entrance to Residential Area Six, she was also filled with a new sense of determination. She had been parted from her natural mother soon after birth, and hadn't seen her since, not until the photograph shown to her in Oberhof. Now, more than ever, *Oberleutnant* Karin Müller was determined to do her job: to solve the case of baby Maddelena Salzmann and her poor, dead, twin brother Karsten – and return Maddelena to her parents, dead or alive. They had to learn their baby's fate. The not knowing was so unfair, so destructive.

Her resolve did not stop there. She was determined to track down her real mother, whatever the consequences. She was equally certain she would do everything in her power to find her natural father. Perhaps she should have pressed Rosamund Müller further. But the old woman had seemed too upset and angry. Müller had felt the same emotions – leaving what she had thought of as her family home as soon as possible.

As Müller entered the police apartment, she immediately sensed that something had changed. Something was out of place. It felt somehow emptier. She realised as soon as she went past the bathroom. There was only one set of washing, shaving and tooth-brushing equipment there. Someone had left. She checked Schmidt and Vogel's room. Schmidt's bed was messily unmade as usual, snack wrappers discarded on the bedside table. But Vogel's bed was stripped, and his case had disappeared. It must be as she had feared. With the murder element having being ruled out of the inquiry, their People's Police bosses had taken the opportunity to cut back her staffing levels. She wondered if it had been at the insistence of their Stasi 'liaison' officer – Janowitz – whose main role seemed to be to obstruct the inquiry and work towards getting it mothballed. If it was Janowitz, he seemed to have had some success. *Unterleutnant* Martin Vogel – the gentle, student-like detective from the Harz mountains – had been transferred. That only left one fully-fledged *Kripo* officer on the team: herself. It just wouldn't be enough.

Her fears were confirmed as soon as she arrived in the incident room. Eschler handed her a note, from Vogel. She tore it open angrily and began to read.

Dear Karin/Comrade Oberleutnant Müller

Many apologies for dropping you in it like this, without having a chance to talk face to face. I'm very sorry to have had to leave an inquiry before it's complete, and I very much hope that – despite this – you, Schmidt, Eschler and the team will bring things to a successful conclusion and that baby Maddelena will be found safe and well. It's been one of the more harrowing inquiries I've been involved with, but it was a pleasure being able to work with you again.

I have, however, been offered *Hauptmann* Baumann's old job back in Wernigerode. The guy they got in to replace him didn't work out, and for me – as you'll appreciate – it's a big step up. So I couldn't say no. Not that I would have wanted to – or even would have been allowed to!

Anyway, apologies again. Many thanks for having me on your team, and I hope that – one day – our paths will cross again.

Until then, Warmest Greetings

Martin (*Unterleutnant* Vogel)

Müller stuffed the note in her pocket and then looked at Eschler with what she hoped wasn't too defeated an expression.

'So what do we do now?'

'I'm sure we'll cope,' smiled Eschler, seemingly unperturbed. 'And we've set up a new inquiry room specifically for chasing that handwriting lead. It's downstairs in part of the fire station that wasn't being used. The Stasi have given us some manpower to check through everything, and there's someone else down there who wants to see you.'

'Who?' asked Müller. Then she lowered her voice. 'I hope it's not Janowitz again. Or even worse, Wiedemann. I'm not in the best of moods right now. Certainly not in the mood to cope with either of those two.'

'No,' laughed Eschler. 'Don't worry. I think it's someone you'll be pleased to see.'

At first she didn't recognise him. He was sitting with his back to her at a long table, with three other officers – presumably the Stasi operatives that Eschler had mentioned – sitting opposite him and facing her, but with their heads down sorting out what looked to be piles of newspapers.

It was only when one of the other officers looked up questioningly at her that he turned. Perhaps he immediately recognised her heightened emotional state, perhaps the tears were already stinging her eyes. But he was soon on his feet, though a little unsteadily, and when she wrapped her arms round him she could feel him wince.

Then the tears began to flow, and she hid her face in his jacket shoulder.

He ushered her away round a pillar, out of sight of the Stasi team.

'What's wrong?' he asked, wiping a tear away, still unable to enunciate every syllable properly, but with much clearer speech than the last time they'd seen each other. 'Aren't you pleased to see me?'

Müller gripped the hand of his good arm, and stared levelly into his ice-blue eyes. The man she'd thought was dead in a forest in the Harz. The man she'd last seen reading a porno novel and attached to various tubes in a hospital, looking like he wouldn't be back at work for months. But he was. He was here. Her deputy. Her now not-so-smooth-talking deputy. 'Oh, Werner,' she said. 'I'm absolutely delighted to see you. I've just had one of the shittiest weekends of my life. So shitty I'm not really sure who I am anymore. I can't believe you're here. Reiniger said it would be months, perhaps a year, perhaps . . .'

'Perhaps never. That's what he thought. I just nagged him. But I'm not strictly speaking your deputy. I'm not allowed to go haring off with you on lunatic missions without back-up like last time. I've been given strict orders. I've got to stay here. In charge of these Stasi men.' He gestured round the cavernous, bare room. 'No windows. It's going to send me mental. But I was going mental in hospital anyway. Though the nurses helped.' He winked.

Müller rolled her tear-soaked eyes. 'Same old Werner Tilsner. Still, it's good to have you back. You'd better explain what's going on.' As she said it, her eyes were drawn once more to the expensive watch on his wrist – just as they had been so many times during the *Jugendwerkhof* girl murder case – the watch that she was convinced he'd bought, or been awarded, thanks to his freelance work for another of the Republic's agencies. There was a good reason why People's Police *Oberleutnant* Werner Tilsner, even in his enfeebled state, was allowed to take charge of a Stasi team. Because – even though he would never admit it – Tilsner was one of them. Part of the Firm. A carrier of the "sword and shield" protecting the Party. A Stasi operative just like the members of the team he was supervising, despite his official police detective's rank.

If Tilsner knew what she was thinking, it didn't trouble him. Instead, there was a trademark glint in his eye. 'We're moving the handwriting hunt up a gear. I've come up with a little scheme which shouldn't contravene the Stasi's guidelines, but should produce plenty more samples. And you never know, we might find the one we need. The perfect match.'

27

Organising the teams of Pioneers made Müller feel she was more of a schoolteacher – like her former husband Gottfried – than a homicide detective. The buzz of childish giggling and fidgeting lightened her mood. For the children this was a bit of fun: Tilsner's idea of collecting old newspapers and magazines – ostensibly for paper recycling – from outside the various apartment blocks of Ha-Neu's several *Wohnkomplexe*. But both the Young Pioneers, in their blue neckties, and the Thälmann Pioneers, with their corresponding red scarves, had the chance to earn good pocket money from it – paid from the budget of the People's Police. The children weren't aware of this – Müller and Tilsner were in plain clothes. The Pioneers would just assume that the two detectives were authority figures of some description or another.

'Settle down,' she shouted above the din in the Baltic restaurant, where the children had been told to gather for their briefing. For the most part, the Pioneers ignored her.

'Shut up!' roared Tilsner, his face apparently flushed with anger, struggling up from the seat where he'd been resting his fast-healing injuries from March's Harz mountains shoot-out.

That did the trick, and the restaurant quietened. Tilsner winked at his *Oberleutnant*. 'You clearly haven't got my touch,' he whispered in her ear.

The two detectives began to divide the children into eight teams – one for each of the new town's residential areas. They'd already agreed to make sure one team was entirely made up of the possibly more compliant Young Pioneers. Müller wanted to assign this team to *Komplex VIII* – in effect, the Stasi complex; or at least, the area nearest to Stasi regional headquarters in the north-east of Ha-Neu, where most Stasi operatives lived. She hoped Tilsner hadn't yet got his head round the strange urban geography of the new town, and wouldn't grasp what she was trying to do. It was a way to circumvent Malkus's restricted list: the families of Stasi personnel that had been explicitly excluded from the baby health checks. For Müller, it was important that the more politically aware Thälmann Pioneers – older children who would soon go on to join the Free German Youth – were kept away from Complex Eight. They were more likely to be suspicious, more likely to discuss things with their parents. There was also a greater chance that their parents would themselves be connected in some way with the Ministry for State Security.

Once the teams – around twenty children strong – had been formed, Müller and Tilsner appointed a leader from each, and took them to one side for a briefing, sitting around one of the restaurant's oblong melamine tables.

Müller spread out the red-covered street map of Halle and Halle-Neustadt, and placed paper discs with the names of each Pioneer team on the sections of the map corresponding to the various residential areas. Müller's idea of giving each team the name of a flower had been vetoed by Tilsner. He favoured animal names. Unfortunately, the team that were given Complex Eight were the Donkeys. This provoked more name-calling and teasing between the children, with kids from the Tigers, Lions and Rabbits provoking the Young Pioneer team with hee-haw braying sounds.

This time Tilsner looked genuinely annoyed. 'Be quiet, all of you. This is a serious, important project. If you continue to mess around we'll have to inform your parents.'

As a hush finally descended on the group, Müller began to explain to them what they needed to do.

This wasn't strictly detective work – certainly not for someone of her rank – but Müller wanted to get a feel for the newspaper collection operation at first hand. It was a good excuse to visit *Komplex VIII*.

The leader of the little Pioneer team, a blond-haired boy named Andreas, gathered his colleagues around the barrow they would use to ferry the paper in. As the children of Team Donkey stood to attention, Andreas recited the Young Pioneers' slogan: 'For peace and socialism be ready – always ready.' The first part seemed to be ignored by the others, but by the words 'be ready', they all joined in. Müller felt a certain pride in this: community spirit, comradely spirit, was alive and well in the Republic. Even if their real motivation was the promised pocket money.

It was a short walk from the restaurant to Block 321, the nearest of the apartment blocks which belonged to *Komplex VIII*.

This was at the southern edge of the residential area, near to the Magistrale and city limits of Ha-Neu, before the elevated road crossed the Saale, into Halle city itself. The Pioneers formed a walking crocodile of bright white and blue as they marched behind Andreas and his barrow, neckerchiefs fluttering in the summer breeze.

Then they were inside the block and knocking on doors, asking residents if they'd seen the notices about the Pioneers' waste paper collection. Accepting the donations of bundles of papers and magazines with good grace and thanks, Müller looking on with pride as Andreas and his colleagues performed their duties, unaware that they were part of an undercover police operation. An operation to recover one single handwritten capital letter on a crossword puzzle. An 'E' with upwards slanting cross strokes which failed to meet the downstroke. An 'E' that could have been written by the abductor of twin babies from Ha-Neu's hospital. And all the time, Müller kept her eyes peeled: to see if anyone who answered the door was carrying a baby, a particularly small, premature baby.

One that matched the description and photograph of missing Maddelena Salzmann.

28

With the waste newspaper collection safely under way, Müller left Andreas and the other children to their own devices, and returned to the incident room. While the investigation was still making little real progress, at least it hadn't been mothballed. The Stasi might be preventing her and her team from searching for Maddelena door to door, but Müller was trying to ensure she circumvented their restrictions as far as she was able to. The baby health checks, the waste paper collection, the upcoming meetings with the graphologist – Professor Morgenstern. All those initiatives offered the hope of a breakthrough. But every minute, every hour, every day, every week that Maddelena remained undiscovered, her chances of survival diminished. If the baby girl was even still alive.

Professor Morgenstern was – in the end – delayed only by a few days. As she went to greet him, Müller reflected that it was the delay in his visit that had given her the opportunity to visit her family in Oberhof. A visit she now almost regretted making. But it had at least provided her with a window to the truth: the truth about her long-glossed-over real parentage.

Morgenstern wasn't how Müller had pictured him. He was a huge bear of a man, with wild curly hair, a wicked smile and giant hands – one of which proceeded to crush Müller's fingers in a vice-like grip of welcome. Once it was released, she held her arm behind her back and tried to wiggle away the pain.

'I'm delighted you called me down here from Berlin,' Morgenstern growled through an unkempt beard. 'Apologies that I couldn't get here last week as I'd hoped.' He looked round the room at Müller and her team: the core team of herself, Tilsner and Schmidt, the three outsiders drafted in from Berlin, just as Morgenstern himself had been. 'Now, I understand you've got a sample of handwriting which you hope may help you crack a case you're working on.'

'That's right,' nodded Müller. 'Comrade *Kriminaltechniker* Jonas Schmidt will talk you through it.'

Schmidt leant down and pulled various envelopes from his briefcase, from which he then took out a series of photographs. 'It was this that I thought was particularly interesting.' The forensic officer pointed to a monochrome photograph of the crossword puzzle which had been found inside the newspaper used to wrap up Karsten Salzmann's tiny body. 'See here.' Schmidt pointed to the capital 'E's in the completed clue: three of them in the word *DEZEMBER*.

Morgenstern nodded slowly, studying the lettering. He looked a little like an American grizzly sizing up salmon in the rapids, twitching his head back and forth, about to strike. Müller had seen plenty in wildlife programmes on Western TV. Schmidt pointed out the distinctive way the 'E's had been formed, with the sloping pen strokes failing to intersect.

'Hmm . . . yes, yes. I can see that. Interesting, and as you say, unusual.'

'Unusual enough to track someone down from it?' asked Müller.

Morgenstern sat back, resting his elbows on the chair arms and steepling his fingers together. He frowned. 'That depends. Ideally, we'd have a longer sample of writing. A combination of lower- and upper-case letters would help us more. But . . . it's a start. Better than nothing.' He bent his head down again towards the photograph. 'Have you only got this photo, or do you have the original?'

'We do have the original, yes,' said Schmidt.

Morgenstern sighed. 'Could I see it, then? Do you have it with you?'

Schmidt blushed. 'Yes, yes, yes, sorry,' he blustered. 'Of course.' He reached down into the briefcase again, and this time brought out a stained, yellowing newspaper, inside a polythene evidence bag. Morgenstern reached to touch it, but Müller grasped his arm before he could.

'Hang on. Let Comrade Schmidt put on some protective gloves first, then he can open it up for you.'

This time it was the turn of Morgenstern's face to redden. 'Of course, *Oberleutnant*. My sincere apologies.'

Schmidt – his hands now gloved up – unfolded the newspaper to the puzzle page.

Morgenstern peered at it, with his hands carefully tucked under his thighs, presumably to avoid the temptation of touching the evidence. 'Interesting. I just wanted to try to gauge the pressure of the pen strokes – something you can't really do from a photograph. It looks like it's been done quite fiercely, angrily. Although it's often dangerous to ascribe emotions to someone based on their handwriting. Do we know that this was written by your suspect?'

Tilsner snorted. Müller glared at him. If he was getting back to his old self after his hospital stay, fine. But she didn't want the 'ugly cynic Tilsner' rearing his head in front of an important expert from the Hauptstadt.

'We don't, no,' Müller replied. 'Someone else could have filled in the crossword. The abductor could have taken someone else's newspaper to deliberately throw us off the scent. But it's something to be working with. The likelihood is that whoever wrote this . . .' she traced her finger in the air above the letters, mimicking the handwriting, '. . . is somehow connected to the man – or woman – that we're trying to find.'

Morgenstern's ursine head resumed its rapid nod. 'It will be difficult just with these capital letters, but the unusual "E"s are certainly a help. What have you done so far in terms of collecting handwriting samples?'

'We've got teams of volunteers gathering old newspapers,' said Tilsner.

'And have you told them why?'

Müller gave a shake of her blond hair. 'No. We're under instructions to keep our investigation pretty much secret. The Ministry for State Security . . .' Müller tailed off apologetically.

'Ah. I understand. To be honest, it's a good thing that your investigations are secret. If whoever dumped the body realised what was going on, they could seek to compromise the investigation. Fake writing samples, that sort of thing. What I will do is try to examine how these letters are formed. What sort of fine motor skills are being used. Everyone has a unique way of writing. Although this,' Morgenstern glanced down at the crossword again, 'is a fairly old-fashioned style. I would guess it's been written by an older person, perhaps a pensioner.'

Tilsner frowned. 'A pensioner? That wouldn't really fit the usual profile of a baby-snatcher.'

The giant handwriting expert shrugged. 'It's not absolutely certain, of course. Whoever wrote this could have been taught to write by someone elderly. A grandparent, perhaps. Maybe home-schooled for some reason.'

'No one in the Republic is home-schooled,' Müller pointed out.

'Quite so, quite so,' said Morgenstern. 'But our Republic is what – a quarter of a century or so old? Quite young. And you know what came before. When things were going wrong towards the end of the war, people were often home-schooled. And if the parents had been killed . . .'

'Then a grandparent might step in to help?' asked Schmidt.

'Exactly.' Morgenstern sat back in his chair, the wood groaning under his weight. 'But that's all just speculation. This, though,' he jabbed his finger towards the partially completed crossword, 'will be very useful. I will try to pin down the style characteristics. What system of writing the individual learned as a child. And then try to identify the individual characteristics – how the lettering differs from the original learned system. Although it looks like the capital "E"s may be our best way forward, it might be some other letter which provides our solution . . . if we ever get to that stage. You realise, of course, that this will be a Herculean task. Particularly if, as you say, the Ministry for State Security is placing limits on your inquiry.'

Müller gave a long, slow sigh. 'We realise it's not going to be easy.'

'Collecting old newspapers, things like that, that's a good idea. But I think you will need to do more. Government offices and the hospital, that sort of thing. All will have records. You yourselves, the People's Police, will have some handwritten samples – complaints, statements, that sort of thing. Ideally you need something that can secure a handwriting sample from virtually everyone in Halle-Neustadt. And of course there's always the possibility that your abductor is someone from out of town.'

'What do you suggest we do in that case?'

Morgenstern gave a deep laugh that came from somewhere in his ample stomach. 'Well, I know it's not encouraged in the Republic, *Oberleutnant*. But I think your best option then would be to pray. Pray very hard.'

29

Müller's next appointment after the one with Professor Morgenstern was strictly social: an evening rendezvous at last with the doctor from the Charité hospital in Berlin, Emil Wollenburg. This was the third time he'd tried to arrange a date. Müller had cancelled the first two because of the demands of the inquiry – the drink before she went to Oberhof, and the lunch that was supposed to replace it. If she stood him up again, she didn't expect she'd get another chance. That said, it still all felt too early. She wasn't even sure she wanted another chance, the possible start of a new relationship.

Instead of a restaurant meal or a drink in a bar, Emil Wollenburg had suggested a visit to the natural swimming lake – the *Heidesee* – so Müller stopped by the flat in Residential Complex Six to get her swimsuit on the way. It was a short drive from there to the lake on the outskirts of Halle Nietleben.

She had mixed feelings about the date. Emil was visiting the *Kaufhalle* after his hospital stint to buy a picnic, and Müller could certainly do with eating something. She'd skipped lunch, and her only nutritional intake since breakfast had been a couple of biscuits with her mid-morning coffee. The thought of a possible evening swim – if it was still warm enough – certainly held appeal. What she was less sure about were her feelings towards Emil Wollenburg. It almost seemed too convenient, too coincidental that he'd been sent on a temporary attachment to the main hospital in Halle itself, while she'd been despatched to the current case in Halle-Neustadt. Müller was suspicious on two counts: one, that he seemed overeager. The second reason was the same one that always struck her about Tilsner. Was she being watched? By the Stasi? And was Emil Wollenburg – like, she assumed, Werner Tilsner – some form of Stasi employee, official or unofficial?

She saw him before he saw her, leaning against his car in an open-necked shirt, muscles taut against the material. Emil Wollenburg set something off inside her, which was why she knew she had to be even more wary. His smile was warm and welcoming. She wasn't sure if she should move in and kiss him, at least on the cheek. In the end, they both settled on another handshake – thankfully his lacked the bone-crushing grip of the professor from earlier in the day.

'I was wondering if you'd stood me up,' he laughed.

Müller felt herself blushing like a teenager, even though she was only a few minutes late, and felt angry with herself for it. 'Sorry. Busy day. And I thought I might as well get my swimming costume . . . just in case.'

'Ah. My turn to apologise. I'd only planned on having the picnic,' said Emil, his eyes gesturing to the basket he was carrying. 'So I haven't got my trunks. I won't be joining you.'

Müller shrugged and smiled. She wouldn't have objected to him adopting *Freikörperkultur* – and going without. Then she chastised herself for the thought. 'It doesn't matter,' she said, aloud.

'We could take a rowing boat, though? The hire place is still open.'

The last time Müller had been rowed by a man in a boat it had been on the Weisser See, in the northern outskirts of the Hauptstadt. In the depths of winter. By Stasi lieutenant colonel Klaus Jäger. That had been an almost surreal experience, like most of Jäger's meetings. To do it again – this time just for fun and on a sunny summer evening – was much more appealing.

Whether it was because of the wine, or the soporific summer heat, Müller found herself letting Emil Wollenburg do most of the talking. She was concentrating less on his words and more on the way his rather attractive, hard-edged jaw and mouth formed them.

His move to Halle did seem to have been a total, and happy, coincidence. And it had, after all, simply been luck that they had bumped into each other in the corridors of the Charité. At least, that was what the doctor maintained, and Müller realised her guard was down. When Emil leaned in for a kiss, Müller held back for a moment. Did she even need a man in her life? Was it just an added complication when this case, in this strange city of identikit apartments, was already getting her down? But at the same time, she didn't want to reach her thirtieth birthday alone and bitter. Gottfried was in the past now. She wished him well, she hoped he was happy in his new life in the West. But she deserved some happiness too. Emil Wollenburg seemed the sort of man who could provide it.

Emil's flat was right in the centre of Halle old town, overlooking the Handel monument and the market place. The Republic's shining new concrete tower blocks hadn't reached here, and although Müller accepted them as progress, acknowledged the way they could open new lives and opportunities to citizens, there was something so right about these old, historic German buildings.

As she stood at Emil's window admiring them, she felt him come up behind her, the tickle of warm breath on her neck, the smell now more of the wine they'd drunk than the spicy food they'd eaten. They'd shared one bottle of Sekt, then opened another, and she was now warmly tipsy. He wrapped his powerful arms around her, and she let herself fall against him, and felt his desire and need.

It was their first date, but going to bed together felt perfectly natural. Nothing like her sordid romps with Tilsner from a few months earlier, which she had soon regretted. This, she knew, she wouldn't regret. At first, they were just kissing. Kissing and talking. About nonsense most of the time, although he listened attentively when she told him about her visit to Oberhof, the alienation she'd always felt from her family, and her discovering the truth on her most recent trip back home to the Thuringian forest.

'It must be difficult,' he whispered, holding her tightly on top of the bedcovers.

'What must be?' Müller replied, momentarily confused by the alcohol haze.

'Becoming an orphan. That's in effect what's happened. Your father's dead – and now you discover he was never your father after all. And now all your fears that you didn't belong, that there was something different about you, they've been realised.'

Müller was silent for a moment. She thought of the young girl in the photograph and the baby wrapped in a shawl. The girl that was her mother. The baby that was her. Was that girl alive somewhere? And if so, where? And what about her father? She knew with the timing of her conception – right at the end of the war – there was a chance he could be from one of the liberating forces, not German at all.

'You've gone quiet,' said Emil, stroking her cheek. She held his hand a moment, and then kissed it.

When the time came, he paused, and asked if he should wear a condom.

She shook her head. Not trusting herself to speak, to explain why. Just his asking the question grabbed at her heart and brought back the memories of Pawlitzki, the memories of her aborted twins, the memories of Gottfried's unnecessary condom packet hidden on top of the wardrobe. Unnecessary, if indeed they were meant for her, because every gynaecologist she'd ever seen, every second opinion she'd sought, had come back with the same answer. After what had happened at the police college, it was impossible for her to conceive a child. So she'd never discovered what the condoms were about, and now she never would. She didn't really care.

Müller just knew she was ready. Ready for Emil Wollenburg to enter her. Ready to love again.

30

Two months later
September 1975

It felt like old times. She and Tilsner chasing down a new lead – a lead that was taking them back to the place she regarded as home, even more so after the revelations from her adoptive mother in Oberhof. Tilsner driving her in an unmarked People's Police Wartburg along a motorway towards Berlin as rain slanted down. They could hardly see anything through the mist of spray thrown up by a procession of trucks ferrying goods to and from the Hauptstadt.

It felt like old times, but things were very different for Müller. The investigation in Halle-Neustadt had slowed to a crawl, which was why this new information taking them back north had given her fresh hope. The initial impetus of Schmidt's discovery of the crossword clue, the input from the handwriting professor, all had dissipated, and instead an air of gloom and despondency hung over the incident room. Maddelena was still missing, her abductor still at large. The only hope of a breakthrough was in the hands of the Stasi team which Tilsner had been overseeing:

the team cross-checking the handwriting samples gathered by the various Pioneer groups and other volunteers. The handful of people they'd found who wrote their capital 'E's in a similar way to those found in the newspaper that Karsten's body had been wrapped in had all proved to be dead ends: citizens with copper-bottomed alibis, or pensioners with no links to young babies, or any motivation to steal them.

Müller glanced across at Tilsner. He saw her looking, turned and smiled. Then his eyes were back on the road. She'd known – ever since the night they'd shared in the Harz – that there was no future between her and Tilsner. Even if he was prepared to put his marriage at risk, trample all over the feelings of his wife and children, she wasn't going to help him. In any case, Müller was in a new relationship. One that nurtured her, made her feel warm inside. Just picturing Emil now – his square jaw line not unlike Tilsner's, but a decade or so younger – sent a charge of something akin to electricity through her body. That was what had changed. Even though the police inquiry was going nowhere, it had helped to bring her and Emil together through the happy accident of both being sent on job attachments to the Halle area at the same time.

'What are you thinking about?' asked Tilsner.

'Nothing much,' Müller lied. 'Just wondering why they were so happy to let us both go off to Berlin to check out this new lead. When Reiniger sent you down from the Hauptstadt, I thought it was under strict instructions that you could only do a desk job, overseeing the cross-checks of handwriting samples?'

'They didn't really need a detective for that. Anyway, I feel awkward working with the Stasi.' He grinned at her and pulled the sleeve of his jacket up slightly, his other hand still on the wheel. Despite the gloom outside, the expensive watch on his wrist still sparkled.

'You don't have to try to convince me, Werner. I enjoy working with you, wherever your affiliations really lie.' As she said this, she tried to eyeball him, but he just smirked and turned his head back to the road.

Müller had tried to persuade Reiniger and the Halle People's Police to let her take Schmidt with them too. Something seemed to be troubling the forensic officer, and she'd thought a trip back to Berlin might help. But when she'd asked Schmidt about it, he simply brushed it off as a little family trouble: the sort of thing you always get with teenage boys of a certain age. It was another reminder to Müller of the problems families faced day to day. Another reminder that was itself a punch in the gut. Because whatever future she and Emil had together, she knew it wouldn't involve children.

'*Scheisse!*' exclaimed Tilsner over the roar of the Wartburg's motor, wiping his handkerchief across the steamed-up inside of the window. 'I thought September was still supposed to be summer. This reminds me of that day we set off for the Harz.' Müller got a rag out of the car's glove compartment and helped to remove the condensation caused by the unseasonably cold and wet weather.

Their return to the Hauptstadt was thanks to some builders working in the area surrounding the new Palace of the

Republic – the shining new seat of government for the country's leaders, which was due to open in a few months' time. One of the things they'd found was a bus ticket from Halle-Neustadt dating from 1967. By itself, that was nothing remarkable, and nothing to bother the criminal division of the People's Police about. The reason *Kripo* detective *Ober-leutnant* Karin Müller and her deputy *Unterleutnant* Werner Tilsner had been called to the scene was what was found next to the bus ticket, in the cellar of an old war-damaged building which was being demolished as part of the Palace of the Republic project. Side by side, their finger bones arranged to give the impression they were clutching each other, the complete skeletons of two tiny babies.

31

Eight years earlier
September 1967, East Berlin

When I hand the list of names to Hansi I feel slightly disloyal. To my gender. To women who could have been mothers. That thing – that beautiful state – that I have always wanted. That I had once, but which was taken away. In fact not once, but twice. That's what I don't understand. When women like myself yearn so strongly that it hurts, that it takes over our whole lives, how can others throw life away? But still, I feel disloyal.

Hansi smiles at me, looking at my handwritten list almost lovingly. I wish he'd look at *me* that way more often. 'You've done well, Franzi.' He strokes my hair, a bit like you might do to a dog. 'You seem to be happy there. It's all coming together again.'

I smile at him. But inside I want to cry. I hate every day there. It's like a factory. A death factory. The instruments of death are the forceps and curette I hand each day to Doctor Rothstein, which he wields with such precision and devastation.

32

That was how Müller and Tilsner found them. Their finger bones entwined. This hadn't happened by accident, thought Müller. She felt a chill go through her. There was something about this place, something she recognised despite the demolition and rebuilding work. And now two identical baby skeletons, under a taped-off canvas tent, side by side. They'd been left deliberately, to allow Müller to see them *in situ*, because of the Halle-Neustadt bus ticket – the potential link to her case.

But there was something else, here near Marx-Engels-Platz, near the site of her old *Kripo* office, that she found familiar. Almost a sense of déjà vu. And then it came to her in a rush, and she found the nausea and bile welling up, something tight in her stomach. No, deeper. In her womb. The images crowded in on her again. Pawlitzki, his mangled face, his foul breath, his thrusting, and where it had ended up. It had ended up here. In the illegal abortion clinic operated by the quack doctor, Rothstein. It had been her only option, once she'd decided she didn't want a rapist's babies. Abortions hadn't been legalised in the Republic until three years ago, and then only until twelve weeks. In any case, she'd decided much, much later. The only option had been Rothstein's so-called clinic, in reality this cellar, under a bombed-out building which had now been demolished to make way for a shiny new Palace of the Republic.

'Are you OK, Karin?' whispered Tilsner. For once, there was genuine concern in his voice. She realised she'd just been standing there, staring. Willing herself not to vomit. It was the second time this week she'd felt ill: the first time she thought she'd caught a bug. This time . . .

She shook her head, neck and upper back, to try to rid herself of the memories. 'Yes, yes. Sorry, I was miles away. It's such a desperate sight, isn't it?' She turned to the forensic officer who'd been assigned the case. He was young, fresh-faced, looked newly out of college. 'Do we know how old they are? How long they've been there?'

'Well, we didn't want to disturb the remains until you got here, Comrade *Oberleutnant*. But we took some samples away for analysis. My estimate is that they date from approximately the same time as the bus ticket found near them.'

'So, 1967? Eight years ago?'

'Approximately, yes.' The *Kriminaltechniker* nodded his shock of curly brown hair.

It was something of a relief for Müller. For a horrible moment she'd thought they might be *her* babies. *Her* aborted twins. Dumped, or rather, arranged in some bizarre pattern. She knew it wouldn't be the case – it would have been too much of a coincidence – and her own visit here had been at least two years before the bodies of these infants had been dumped. But the thought that Rothstein and his team had carried on working here made her skin crawl.

'You know what this place was, Comrade *Kriminaltechniker*?'

'Well . . . up to a point,' said the young forensic officer. 'It was some sort of part-demolished building, damaged by wartime bombing.'

'Yes, but that's not all,' said Müller. 'It was also an illegal back-street abortion clinic.'

'*Scheisse*,' said Tilsner. 'You're sure about that?'

She watched her deputy look her straight in the eyes, her own watering now, as she fought back tears. Realisation slowly dawned on Tilsner's face. 'Sorry, Karin,' he silently mouthed. Quickly, he asked the forensic officer the question he knew she didn't want to pose.

'So these are aborted babies, then? Therefore it's not going to be anything to do with our Halle-Neustadt inquiry. And more than that, it's not really anything of concern for the *Kriminalpolizei*?'

But even before Tilsner reached the end of his question, Müller could see the young *Kriminaltechniker* shaking his head. 'No, no,' he said. 'We've checked with the pathologist. That's why we brought you up from Ha-Neu.' He crouched down, pointing at the one of the babies' skulls. 'See here, on the top of the head, the fontanelle. It's the soft tissue part that only ossifies later in childhood, although here it's rotted away leaving this cavity. We can tell from the size of the fontanelles. These babies hadn't been aborted. When they died, or were killed, they were three months old.'

Müller had hoped to chew over the case with Tilsner during an evening drink, but after his hospital stay he seemed full of a renewed sense of family values and had returned instead to his family apartment in Prenzlauer Berg. So, after a quick debrief in Müller's Keibelstrasse office, they went their separate ways, Müller returning to the Schönhauser Allee flat.

The forensic officer would check the bus ticket and even the babies' skeletons for the fingerprints of whoever had dumped the children, but Müller was certain the latter would yield nothing. She had higher hopes for the bus ticket: Müller knew from her training that prints could last on paper for several decades *if* they were not exposed to moisture. Unfortunately, a cellar in the throes of demolition would not be the ideal environment for their preservation. But the date, and the skeletons, gave them something to go on. Müller had already phoned Wiedemann – who'd sounded surprisingly helpful given his apparent closeness to Malkus and Janowitz – and instructed him to scour the files in Halle-Neustadt and Halle city to try to find a report of missing babies from the relevant period. They would also have to check out Doctor Rothstein. One possibility was that as well as disposing of unwanted foetuses, Rothstein was involved in something altogether more sinister: the disposal of unwanted babies. It was a train of thought Müller didn't want to follow too far, and she would make sure she delegated any interviewing of him to Tilsner, or another officer. She didn't want any further reminders of her visit to his 'clinic'.

It was the reminders she'd had so far that made her do what she did next. An almost involuntary action. As soon as she was in the apartment, she walked to the bedroom and opened the door. A musty smell of damp assailed her nostrils. Without a human presence for several weeks, the old building's drawbacks had started to reassert themselves. Müller ignored the smell, and instead found herself – in an almost machine-like, robotic way – crossing towards the wardrobe. Pulling up the chair. Feeling on the top for the key, even though – with Gottfried long gone – there was no longer any need to hide it.

She took the key down, then used it to open the locked drawer, and pulled it out. They were still there, those two tiny sets of baby clothes. Ones that would have fitted the two children at the Rothstein clinic, had they been allowed to live. Ones that would have fitted her own twins, had she allowed them to live. This time, Müller just stared at the clothes for a moment, then shut the drawer again. Almost as though this time, she didn't dare to touch them.

Slumping down on the end of the bed, she felt the exhaustion of the last few weeks weighing her down. She felt in her jacket pocket and pulled out the tin box that had been given to her by Rosamund Müller: the box that was the only link she had to her own bloodline. Müller opened the lid and took out the photograph. Had this girl – the nameless girl that she assumed was her birth mother – wanted rid of the baby she cradled in her arms?

It didn't look like it. Not from the love and longing in the girl's eyes as she watched over the child.

The thought that the girl might have fought to keep her, while Müller herself had discarded her own offspring, suddenly led to bile rising in her throat. She put her hand over her mouth, eyes stinging with tears, and ran to the toilet.

Less than half an hour later, as Müller was sitting on the lounge sofa drinking a cup of coffee to try to calm herself down, the shrill jangle of the telephone cut through her thoughts.

She lifted the receiver and immediately recognised Eschler's voice.

'You and Tilsner need to come back to Ha-Neu immediately, Karin. We've found Maddelena.'

Müller's brain immediately conjured up images of the baby girl's face, superimposed on her twin brother's battered, lifeless torso. She wondered how she would be able to break the news to the girl's parents.

'Where did you find the body?' she asked.

'No, no, you misunderstand,' Eschler shouted down the crackly line. 'She's alive . . . and safe . . . and well.'

33

Six months earlier: March 1975
Komplex VIII, Halle-Neustadt

Being back in Halle-Neustadt is a little bittersweet, I must admit. I can't stop thinking of Stefi. I suppose I knew it would be like this, that it would make me sad. I tried to convince Hansi that perhaps it wasn't such a good idea. That it might make me feel a bit funny again. But Hansi says that's what the Ministry want him to do. He'll be going back to his old job at the chemical factory, at Leuna. But as well as that, he's involved in preparations for something important happening here – in Ha-Neu. He won't say what it is.

Of course, we couldn't get exactly the same flat back. Our old one's been reallocated to another young family. Hansi did manage to secure a nice two-bed apartment on the edge of Ha-Neu, near the Ministry for when he needs to go in there. We're on the top floor, facing almost due north, so we don't get as much sun as I'd like. But I still enjoy standing at the window looking out at the view. To the left the Dölauer Heath, and a glimpse of Heidesee. It would have been nice to have taken Stefi there. Still, it wasn't to be. And then in the other direction, the Saale and Peissnitz island. I saw the little train chugging along the river bank the other day. Stefi would have loved that. I used to take her there in the pram some days, you know, when she wouldn't stop crying.

Hansi knows I'm sad. He knows what I really want. But things haven't been very good in that department. I don't know if it's that he's getting older, but he sometimes – what's the phrase again? – oh yes, sometimes he doesn't quite have enough lead in his pencil. I try to be gentle. Try not to put pressure on him. But it's not just men who have needs; women do too, you know.

We've been trying again. For a little one. We have to be careful. The doctor told him last time that there's something wrong with my blood circulation. If I do get pregnant again, then I may have to take some special pills to help with it. Otherwise the pressure of my enlarging womb can apparently squeeze the blood vessels, stop blood getting to my head, and I could faint. I asked Hansi if he thought I was too old now – after all, I'm past forty. If he thought it was all too dangerous. He seems to think everything will be all right, but it may take a long time, and I shouldn't get my hopes up too much. But actually, thinking about it, my strawberry weeks have stopped again. I suppose it's just my age.

Oh my word! You wouldn't believe it. You absolutely wouldn't. You know I said my strawberry weeks had stopped? I thought maybe it was my age, so I wasn't holding out much hope when

Hansi said we should try again for another child. I thought I might have reached the menopause early. Anyway, Hansi said we ought to go to see his doctor friend for a check-up. It's the same one as last time, the one who looked after me with all the upset over Stefi. He's very good, very gentle, and he and Hansi get on like a house on fire – which is nice, because sometimes I think Hansi doesn't have that many friends. Not that I do, either. Anyway, the bombshell news from the doctor is that I'm already pregnant! It's the same as last time. Doesn't show that much because, well, as I told you before, I'm a big girl. I can't quite work out the dates, though, because as I say, Hansi had been having a bit of trouble in that department in our last months in Berlin. He probably had a lot on his mind. But it did affect me. And now I've lost some weight, well, I still attract admirers. In fact, there was a new barman at the Weisser See beach bar this year. Very exotic and very handsome. Quite a charmer, I can tell you. I think he was a foreign student, over from one of the friendly Asian socialist countries, just helping at the bar at week-ends to earn a bit of extra cash. I tried to resist his advances, of course. But he was *very* persistent. And – I'll let you into a little secret here – an *excellent* kisser. There, I've said it. I feel a bit better getting it off my chest. Surely that can't be it, though, can it? You can't get pregnant from a bit of kissing and canoodling. We only did it the once, right at the end of September, and then I felt quite bad about it afterwards. It was terribly disloyal to Hansi. I'll just have to be careful that he never finds out.

34

Six months later: September 1975
Halle-Neustadt

Instead of returning straightaway to the incident room, Müller and Tilsner parked the Wartburg at the back of the Salzmanns' high-rise, the bath-towel-striped *Ypsilon Hochhaus*, and made their way to the lobby. Tilsner summoned the lift. They'd said little to each other on the car journey back from Berlin, and said little now as the lift glided up the ten floors to the Salzmanns' storey. Müller knew that Tilsner would be aware of her unspoken fear: that this strange turn of events in the case was more likely to hinder than help the *Kriminalpolizei* investigation.

As Müller pushed the doorbell for Apartment 1024, the sound of its ring was almost drowned out by the noise of a baby crying. The cries got louder as Reinhard Salzmann opened the latch to let them in, the tension now lifted from his face – which was instead creased in a semi-permanent smile.

'I was wondering when you would get here,' said Maddelena's father. 'It's your colleague, *Hauptmann* Eschler, who we've been dealing with. But I guess I should show you through.'

Müller and Tilsner followed Herr Salzmann towards the source of the baby's cries, to the small apartment's lounge.

Klara Salzmann was sitting on the green corduroy sofa, gazing downwards, beaming with pride. She glanced up at the two detectives, and Müller was immediately struck by the transformation from the desperate woman she had collected from the kindergarten at *Komplex VIII*, a mere two months earlier. That was the joy of motherhood, what it could do for you. Müller wanted to share the woman's elation. She knew she ought to. But instead she felt an emptiness, a desperation, a sharp stab of jealousy that almost physically invaded what was left of her ravaged womb, leaving her almost nauseous. The same sick feeling that had grabbed her in the demolished basement abortion clinic in Berlin. This woman had something that Müller herself wanted, something that now she would always be denied. She tried to empty her head of the thought, but it just wouldn't let go.

Because there, cradled in her mother's arms as she exercised her vocal cords in an almost deafening wail, was the baby they'd been searching for – her sharp, beak-like features unmistakeable, despite *Wachtmeister* Fernbach's contention from a few months earlier that all newborn infants looked the same.

'She's lovely, isn't she?' said Klara.

'Well, she certainly has a fine set of lungs,' replied Tilsner.

Müller herself initially said nothing, trying to get her head round this strange turn of events. She and Tilsner had had the whole journey back from Berlin to contemplate theories. Nothing they'd managed to come up with so far seemed to fit.

Müller forced herself to smile, to try to feel 'sympathetic joy'. It was something Gottfried had talked about after he began going to his church meetings, the meetings that – it was now apparent – had had little to do with actual religion. But that saying, 'sympathetic joy', stuck in her mind. Gottfried had said it had Buddhist origins. The opposite of *Schadenfreude*. Try as she might, Müller just wasn't feeling it. Something was wrong, very wrong, with this happy family scene. But then, something was very wrong with this whole investigation. The sense of some big secret. The Stasi preventing proper searches. Janowitz constantly trying to undermine their investigation. And now this: the miraculous reappearance of the missing baby.

She got her notebook out of her pocket and clicked her retractable pen to the open position. 'Can you tell me again, Frau Salzmann, exactly how and where Maddelena was found?'

'Oh, I've already given a statement,' the woman replied. Maddelena had calmed down now, as Klara bottle-fed her.

'To *Hauptmann* Eschler,' added her husband. 'He was very helpful and understanding.' The pointed implication in Reinhard Salzmann's words was that – in asking the couple to repeat everything – Müller was being anything but helpful.

Müller gave another smile. She tried to make it appear sincere, but it wasn't, and she could tell both the Salzmanns knew it wasn't. 'Nevertheless, I am the lead investigating officer. I'd like to go over everything again, please. After all ...' She glanced up at the mantelpiece, to the photographs of the twins in the hospital: Klara with Maddelena and Reinhard with Karsten. Then she trained her gaze back to Frau Salzmann, and stared hard at the woman. 'After all, someone is still responsible for the death of your son. We're determined to find out who, and to bring them to justice.'

A shadow passed over Klara Salzmann's face. 'That's what we want too,' the woman insisted, her voice cracking. 'Of course it is. But having Maddelena safely back is . . . is something. Something for us to cling on to.'

'It's wonderful you've got her back safe and sound,' said Müller. *Wonderful, but highly suspicious.*

'Nevertheless,' insisted Tilsner, 'you do need to answer our questions. Even if you feel you've been over everything already. So just tell *Oberleutnant* Müller and me everything you told the *Hauptmann*. And if you can remember any extra details, so much the better. It might just be that one tiny detail, the one false move by Maddelena and Karsten's abductor, that helps us to trap him . . . or her . . . Or them, if it was a couple.'

When Tilsner said this, Müller noticed what she took to be a warning glance pass from Reinhard Salzmann to his wife, as their newly found baby continued to make sucking noises at her mother's feeding bottle.

Maddelena had been left on their doorstep late the previous evening, a dummy in her mouth to discourage her from crying.

'Did you see who left her?' asked Müller.

'No. It was only when our neighbours came back from the theatre in Halle that they saw her, and rang our bell,' replied Klara. So they had a witness, thought Müller. But what if the Salzmanns were the actual culprits? What if, for some reason, they had taken Maddelena and Karsten from the hospital back in July, and then something tragic had happened to Karsten? And – to deflect attention – they'd staged Maddelena's disappearance, making it look as though both twins were victims of an abductor? Perhaps the dumping of Karsten's body in the suitcase had been staged by them: again to give the impression of something sinister? As these thoughts raced through her head, Müller attempted to keep a neutral facial expression.

'So she seemed to have been well cared for?' asked Tilsner. 'She wasn't in any distress?'

Reinhard Salzmann gave a throaty laugh. 'Look at her feeding. Does she look to be distressed? I would say she's been very well cared for – don't you agree, *Liebling*?'

His wife nodded rapidly. 'We got in touch with the People's Police straightaway, and the hospital. They sent a health visitor round to check her within a few minutes. Your *Hauptmann* Eschler took her bedding and the Moses basket away with him. I gave him the clothes she was dressed in too, and the pacifier.'

'Did any of the other neighbours see or hear anything unusual?' asked Müller.

Frau Salzmann gave a small shrug, while taking care not to disturb Maddelena. 'We haven't really had a chance to ask. We assumed the police would be doing that.'

Tilsner rubbed the stubble on his chin. 'And when your neighbours rang your bell, you were both in at the time?'

There was a brief pause before Frau Salzmann answered. Müller thought she saw a look pass between the couple. *Is this whole story nothing but a fabrication? Are they in this together?*

'Yes, yes, we were both in. To be honest, we've been in waiting by the phone virtually every evening. Just hoping someone would ring.'

'So,' sighed Müller after a pause. 'Do either of you have any idea who might have been behind all this? Do you have any enemies? Did anyone show any jealousy towards you during your pregnancy, Frau Salzmann, or when they knew you'd had twins?'

The woman stared rather blankly at Müller, shaking her head slowly, almost as though she wasn't fully concentrating on the question. Then Müller realised Frau Salzmann's eyes weren't focussed on her, but on the mantelpiece behind. She followed the woman's eyeline, to the photograph of her husband cradling her now dead son, Karsten, in the hospital ward. They now knew that Karsten had been the weaker of the two twins, the one the hospital staff had been most concerned about. It was almost certainly why he hadn't survived the abduction, while Maddelena had.

Frau Salzmann fixed her eyes on Müller. To the detective it was clear that – for the first time during their visit, perhaps for the first time since Maddelena had been left on the doorstep – the mother was thinking of her dead son, not her living daughter.

The woman stifled a small sob, and when she spoke there was a hard edge to her voice. 'Make sure you find whoever did this, *Oberleutnant*, please. Whoever caused my son to die – even if as the autopsy suggests they made a vain attempt to save him – deserves to be punished. It won't bring our son back, but it might give us some comfort.'

35

Müller couldn't shake off a sense almost of disappointment at Maddelena's reappearance. She knew that was perverse. For the parents, this was little short of a miracle – for an abducted baby, one born several weeks prematurely, to be returned safe and well was almost unprecedented. Especially given what had happened to Karsten. She wanted to share their joy, but Müller suspected the picture of family togetherness was little more than a front. They might have one of their babies back, but something was wrong in the Salzmann marriage. Very wrong.

Müller's other concern was that for her and Tilsner this might mean their People's Police bosses – or the bigwigs from the Ministry for State Security to whom they seemed to kowtow – would simply say there was no case left to investigate. She knew that wasn't true. Someone had still taken both twins, and as a result, one of them had died. For that, they ought to be held to account. But as Müller and Tilsner waited in the incident room for a meeting called by the Halle city People's Police to begin, they both knew the likelihood was that they would be returning to the Hauptstadt, the case unsolved. That Janowitz would finally get his way. For Müller that held an additional problem.

What would now happen to her and Emil? She didn't want to be separated from him, and the fortuitous way they had both ended up in the Halle area at the same time wasn't likely to be repeated in the opposite direction. If she was sent back to the Hauptstadt, she would be on her own. Doing the same shitty jobs in Keibelstrasse that she'd only recently escaped from.

She glanced at Tilsner. He was doodling in his notebook with a vacant expression. He saw her watching and rolled his eyes, then gestured to the open doorway. 'Look out,' he whispered. 'This looks like trouble.'

Dressed in his full People's Police uniform, sharing a joke with *Major* Malkus of the Stasi as they walked down the corridor, was the Halle People's Police colonel. *Oberst* Dieter Frenzel. Müller hadn't met him yet, as until now he seemed to have been happy to leave her to her own devices, perhaps annoyed that his own *Kripo* team hadn't been permitted to investigate the Salzmann twins case. Eschler spoke highly of him, but that was as much as Müller knew.

'Ah, comrades,' he boomed, once he was inside the room, clapping his hands together. 'It's wonderful news about the baby girl, I hope you'll agree.' He surveyed the incident room and everyone inside it: as well as Müller and Tilsner, Eschler and his team were there, Wiedemann from the records department, and – of course – Malkus with his ubiquitous sidekick, Janowitz. 'Although the resolution was perhaps fortuitous, I'd still like to congratulate all of you for your persistence and determination. I know that to some extent your hands were tied, but I hope you understand why.' He gave Müller a hard stare, as Malkus smirked by his side. 'What I've been particularly pleased about is the way we've worked together with the Ministry for State Security – *Major* Malkus and his team – and Comrade Malkus is now going to explain where we go from here.'

'Yes, many thanks, Comrade *Oberst*. What I haven't been able to tell you all so far is the full reason why we needed the police operation in the Salzmann case to be low key.' Müller found herself blushing for no good reason under the Stasi officer's amber-eyed gaze. Perhaps she felt guilty for using every opportunity to stretch the parameters of the investigation. Malkus paused for a moment with his eyes on her. Did he know what she was thinking? 'Yes, the reputation of Halle-Neustadt was important. But that was perhaps something of a smokescreen. The real reason, and the reason why we'll now need to scale down the inquiry even further, is that Ha-Neu is about to play host to an important international visitor. Nothing can undermine this visit – I want to make that absolutely clear.' He glanced down at his watch. 'In a moment, we're going to be joined by a senior officer from the Ministry for State Security, and he will be giving you a full briefing.' A smirk still played on Malkus's face, and Müller noticed that – for much of the time – it appeared to be directed towards her. 'The foreign visitor will be our esteemed socialist comrade, the Prime Minister of Cuba, Fidel Castro.'

Castro's name, and then a knock on the incident room door, told Müller who would be on the other side, even before *Oberst* Frenzel had bellowed the words: 'Come in!'

The tanned features of the Stasi officer who strolled into the room simply confirmed what she already knew. It was Jäger.

Ministry for State Security colonel Klaus Jäger. The man who'd had her pretty much dancing to his own tune throughout their previous big case back in Berlin. She almost didn't recognise him. Instead of looking like a Western television newsreader – his normal mien – now, with a Caribbean suntan and new haircut, he seemed to have moved up into the movie star league.

When she and Tilsner had been back in the Hauptstadt, examining the skeletons of the babies in Rothstein's former illegal abortion clinic, Müller had tried to get back in touch with Jäger to see if he could help in tracking down her birth mother. Her calls had gone unanswered, and she'd assumed he was still on assignment in Cuba, the assignment he'd tried to recruit her for at the end of the previous case. But now he was here, standing in person in front of her. To prepare for the visit of Fidel Castro, and everything that entailed.

Müller found herself grinding her teeth, sitting on her hands, trying to prevent herself doing or saying anything stupid. Tilsner's shoulders had slumped. He looked fed up. She was simply angry. As Jäger and Frenzel's briefing continued, it was clear that only a skeleton team would remain on the Salzmann twins case: Müller and Tilsner themselves, and only a couple of the team of Stasi operatives who until now had been working under Tilsner, ploughing through the piles of handwriting samples from old newspapers and forms. Schmidt would be sent back to the Hauptstadt. Eschler and his men would be working full-time on the Castro visit. Even Müller and Tilsner would have to help out on that as required. Jäger caught her eye, a slight smirk playing on his mouth. Their case was being assigned the lowest possible priority, just as the twin baby skeletons found in Berlin had offered the hope of a possible breakthrough. It was what Janowitz had been pushing for – and Müller had always been suspicious as to why – for some time. Now he'd got what he wanted thanks to Castro's visit. And Maddelena had been 'found' just before that visit commenced. The timing was convenient, to say the least.

As the meeting broke up, Eschler looked over apologetically at Müller. She gave him a wry smile as she, Tilsner and Schmidt retreated to the sanctuary of Müller's small office down the corridor.

'So what do we do now?' asked Tilsner, pulling over a seat and slumping down into it, his arms flopping onto his thighs.

'We keep going,' replied Müller, but she was aware of the lack of enthusiasm in her voice. 'We've only just found an important new lead.'

'What, the baby skeletons by the new Palace of the Republic? It's not much of a lead. The only connection is the bus ticket. It's tenuous, at best. At worst . . .' Tilsner threw his arms open.

'At worst, what?' Müller snapped.

'At worst, ridiculous. Clutching at straws. You know it. I know it.'

Müller pursed her lips. If they were going to get anywhere with a slimmed-down team, everyone needed to be pulling in the same direction. Tilsner's heart didn't seem in it anymore. She felt another wave of nausea rise up from her gut. What was wrong with her? For the last few weeks she'd felt under the weather. Since before the trip to Berlin.

'What about you, Jonas?' asked Tilsner. 'You're keeping very quiet . . . for once. I bet you're thrilled you're going back to Berlin.'

'Hmm. Yes and no,' replied Schmidt. 'It's never ideal leaving a case unsolved. But it will be good to get back to the family, I'll admit. I don't think my wife's been finding it very easy with me away.'

'No serious problems, I hope, Jonas?' asked Müller.

The forensic officer shook his head. 'I hope not. I told you there had been a few issues with Markus. The usual teenage boy stuff . . . I think.'

'You're too soft on him, that's your problem,' said Tilsner.

Schmidt shrugged, and then rose from his seat. 'Anyway. I'd better be getting back to the flat to pack. My train to the Hauptstadt leaves first thing tomorrow morning. Oh, one thing, Comrade *Oberleutnant.*'

'What's that, Jonas?'

'You might want to have a chat to *Leutnant* Wiedemann. As we were going into the meeting just now, he gave me the impression he might have found something of interest.'

'Concerning what?' asked Müller.

'Concerning the baby skeletons in Berlin.'

Leutnant Dieter Wiedemann continued to peer at various documents on his desk for a moment after he barked an 'Enter!' in response to Müller's knock on his office door. When he did look up, his red face broke into a wide smile, like a tomato cut open by a knife.

'Comrade *Oberleutnant*. How fortuitous. I was just about to come and see you.' He rose from his chair and offered her his hand. The officiousness of July's Party meeting seemed forgotten. Müller had, in any case, made sure that she'd turned up on time to all the subsequent Party gatherings, heeding Malkus's warning shot across her bow. 'Did Comrade Schmidt mention anything to you?'

'Yes,' smiled Müller. 'That's why I'm here. What have you got, Dieter?' Müller's use of his first name was deliberate. For those too attached to the use of 'Comrade this, Comrade that' there was no better way of catching them off guard, and getting them to reveal more than they otherwise would have.

'It's very interesting. I've just been going through the file again. It's an incident from 1967, before my time here, I'm afraid. I was an *Unterleutnant* in Leipzig then.'

'An incident?'

'Well, yes.' Wiedemann rotated the file on his desk so that Müller could see it. Then traced his finger over an entry. 'See here. A report of two babies going missing.'

'Twins?' There were so many pairs of twins involved in this strange case. Too many for it to be a coincidence. There had to be a reason.

Wiedemann nodded. 'But,' the lieutenant lowered his voice, 'as with your current investigation, the Ministry for State Security seems to have been involved at an early stage.' Müller was surprised that Wiedemann – as the People's Police Party representative – seemed happy to take her into his confidence over this. 'The babies weren't found – but again, it looks like there was no general alert. From the reports, it appears everything was kept rather hush-hush.'

'As now.'

'Quite. The only conclusion that makes sense is that this was the very dawn, the birth of Halle-Neustadt – before it had actually been given that name. When it was the bright new chemical workers' city. A flat for everyone. The socialist dream. You understand what I'm saying?'

'The authorities didn't want anything detracting from that image.'

'Quite so.'

Müller sat down with the file on her lap, leafing through it.

'You won't find out what happened in there, Comrade *Ober*—'

'Let's dispense with the formalities, Dieter. It makes me nervous. Karin is fine.'

'Well, Karin. The story continues in this file.' Wiedemann riffled through another folder on his desk, and then opened it about halfway through, and again rotated it so Müller could see. 'Look here, the same couple who'd reported the missing babies are charged with child neglect. Both were jailed. The husband for a year, the wife for six months.'

'For neglect of the twins that went missing?' Müller's face screwed up into a puzzled frown.

Again, Wiedemann leaned over the desk to point out the relevant part of the report to Müller. 'Yes. They were accused of allowing their own children to starve to death. Yet according to the People's Police report, the bodies were never found.'

That just didn't make sense to Müller. 'But surely without the bodies there would not be sufficient evidence to convict them?'

Wiedemann sat back down in his chair and shrugged. 'Well . . . the father already had reports in other police files about him. About his supposed counter-revolutionary attitude. But as regards evidence, we don't have all the details in the file, I'm afraid.'

'Why's that?'

'Because the inquiry was taken out of the hands of the Halle *Kripo*, by the –'

'Ministry for State Security.'

'Exactly, Karin. Exactly.'

36

Wiedemann had also managed to find out where the couple concerned – Hannelore and Kaspar Anderegg – lived now, some eight years later. After their jail sentences they'd been permitted to return to Ha-Neu, rehoused in the newly built Block Ten. It seemed a low number to Müller, compared to the numbering system for the other apartment blocks in the new town, so she queried it with Wiedemann before setting off with Tilsner to try to track them down. The block was reputed to be the biggest and longest in the Republic. Part of *Komplex I*, it had been renumbered as Ha-Neu expanded. It was now split into four, each unit separated by a pedestrian passageway to ensure citizens didn't have to walk all the way round to reach the pharmacy and post office at the complex centre. The new block numbers were in the six hundreds, but still the 'Block Ten' tag lived on. The Andereggs lived virtually exactly in the centre, at the southern end of what was now Block 619.

Once they'd climbed the stairs to the third floor, Tilsner hammered on the apartment door. There was no reply. He waited a few seconds, then tried again, rapping even harder. As he was about to shoulder-charge it, Müller placed her hand on his arm and shook her head. Given their inquiry now seemed to be on borrowed time, she didn't want to have to explain away the complication of a broken doorframe, connected to a couple whose case had originally been handled by the Stasi.

They had just turned, and were making their way back down the corridor, when the door opposite the Andereggs' clicked open.

'What's all that racket?' an elderly woman asked. 'I'll report you to the Citizens' Committee. Or the People's Police.'

Müller and Tilsner turned back, and Müller drew out her *Kripo* ID. 'There's no need for that, citizen. We are the police. *Kriminalpolizei*.'

The woman adjusted her housecoat at her neck, and fiddled with her hair, as she peered at the proffered identity card. 'Well, you won't find them here. Not till much later. They both work at the chemical works.'

'Which chemical works?' asked Tilsner.

'That giant one near Merseburg.'

'That's not much help, is it?' Tilsner said sharply. The old woman shrank back. Müller glared at her deputy.

'What the *Unterleutnant* means is, do you know which of the two main factories it is please, citizen? There are two near Merseburg.'

'Leuna, I think. Leuna – not Buna.'

Müller's heart sank. Finding them at the Buna works – to the north of Merseburg – would have been hard enough. But Leuna meant a longer journey – and Leuna was the biggest chemical factory in the whole of the Republic.

'Do you know which part of the complex they work in, citizen?' she asked.

The woman shook her blue-rinsed, thinning hair. 'I'm sorry, no. But they do work together, I can tell you that. Ever since that incident with their children he doesn't let her out of his sight. I think he's frightened.'

'Frightened?' asked Tilsner. 'Of what?'

'Of retaliation, I suppose, comrade. Everyone knows what happened, even though they never talk about it. They keep themselves to themselves.'

'Did you ever see them out with their children, before . . .?' Müller's words trailed off, but the woman knew what she was talking about.

'No.' There was a groaning sound from inside the apartment. 'Sorry, that's my husband. He's bed-ridden. I need to get back to him. But no, by the time they started living here it had all been dealt with. They'd served their sentences. She arrived first. He got longer. Although why that was, I'll never know. Neglect of a child. Two children in this case, poor little mites. That's the mother's fault, don't you think, comrades?' Another groan from inside was this time followed by a feeble shout. 'If that's all, I'd better go.' With that, the woman closed her door before either Müller or Tilsner had time to object.

Given the close links to Halle-Neustadt, Müller realised they should perhaps have visited Leuna before now. But the giant complex had virtually been ruled out of bounds by the Stasi: certainly they hadn't wanted the alarm raised.

The drive in the Wartburg took some thirty minutes – around thirty kilometres – but they were only about halfway there when the acrid chemical smells hit the back of Müller's nose and throat, and triggered a coughing fit. Already from this distance they could see chimneys belching out white smoke into a hazy sky.

'It's worse than one of the Hauptstadt's smogs,' complained Tilsner. Taking one hand off the steering wheel, he reached into his pocket and pulled out a handkerchief. 'Do you want to put this over your nose?'

Müller examined it with distaste without touching. It didn't look clean. She shook her head. 'I'll survive.' But as she said it, she felt another lurch of nausea from deep inside her body, something that had been happening all too often in recent weeks.

As Tilsner stuffed the dirty square of material back into his pocket, he glanced up at the rear-view mirror, and frowned.

'What's wrong?' asked Müller.

Tilsner shrugged. 'Maybe nothing.'

Müller was suddenly thrown forward and to the side as Tilsner took a right-hand turn without warning, and almost without slowing, the Wartburg's tyres sliding and screeching as the rubber burnt its imprint onto the concrete road. Then he slammed on the brakes, throwing her forward.

'What the . . .?'

Tilsner grabbed her head and yanked it round to look back at the junction, just in time to see a black Skoda pass by, its driver staring at them intently.

'It was following us,' explained Tilsner.

Müller glared at him angrily. 'I don't care. Next time warn me when you want to play at being a boy racer. I could have been thrown through the windscreen.'

Tilsner just smiled.

Once they arrived, with the Skoda driver seemingly having got bored of his pursuit – or content with having got his message across – it was pot luck which of the many entrances to the Leuna works might yield success. In the end, they chose Entrance One, with its neoclassical architecture, borrowed no doubt by the Nazis to convey a sense of power and importance. At least, that was the impression Müller got as they were escorted by an official under the entrance façade, with its portico and Doric columns.

In the end, locating the Andereggs was surprisingly easy. Müller and Tilsner were informed that they were eating a meal in the canteen.

If Müller had had to guess who the couple were – without the aid of photographs – she would have succeeded. Because they were eating alone, opposite each other, at one end of a bench table in the giant hangar of a restaurant. An official from VEB Leuna-Werke escorted the two detectives all the way to where the Andereggs were sitting.

Kaspar Anderegg – concentrating hard on his meal of meat and potatoes – didn't deign to look up as Müller, Tilsner and the factory representative approached. But Hannelore did, with a rather cowed expression, thought Müller, as though difficult conversations with officials were something she'd had to get used to over the years.

Once Müller had shown her ID, Kaspar did eventually slam down his knife and fork, and fixed her with a hard stare.

'We don't like talking to the police,' he said. 'We've nothing to say to you.'

The factory official rolled his eyes at the two detectives, and left them alone to conduct what looked as though it was going to be a difficult conversation.

'I can understand that, Herr Anderegg, given what's happened to you both.'

'Understand? You arseholes haven't the first clue. You literally have no idea what it's like to have both your children stolen from you – your only children – and then actually be framed for the crime by the very authorities who are supposed to be helping find them. In other words, you lot.'

Tilsner was about to give the man some choice words back, but Müller gave a slight shake of her head. She wanted to deal with it. And what Kaspar Anderegg didn't know was that – yes – she *did* have some idea what it was like to lose two children. To lose twins. She held her stomach and breathed deeply for a moment, trying to shoo the images away from her brain.

'I appreciate you must feel very bitter about what's gone on, Herr Anderegg.'

'Bitter? Hah! That doesn't cover the half of it.'

Müller tried to give a slight smile, a smile of friendship. But she could see Herr Anderegg was having none of it. Instead, she turned her gaze to his wife.

'Frau Anderegg. We're interested in looking again at your case.'

The woman looked up at Müller. Her eyes were full of sadness, but what Müller said obviously gave her a grain of hope.

'Oh yes. That would be kind of you, wouldn't it Kaspar?'

'Pah!' exclaimed her husband, taking up his fork again and jabbing a piece of potato with it. The meaty smell of the meal suddenly had Müller's salivary glands pumping.

'Have you ever had any indication of your son and daughter's whereabouts, Frau Anderegg?' As soon as the words were out of her mouth – as she saw the smile of joy light up Hannelore Anderegg's face – Müller regretted what she'd said. She couldn't reveal that they'd found two skeletons in Berlin. That would be too cruel when there had been no identification. When there might never be any identification. But she shouldn't have raised the woman's hopes.

'Why? You haven't found them, have you?'

Müller's answering pause – a silence that was pregnant with meaning – was enough to extinguish the woman's renewed hope. How many times had that happened over the last few years, Müller wondered.

Finally, Müller answered. 'It's too early to say. But please don't get your hopes up, Frau Anderegg. What we've found may not be –'

'They're dead, aren't they?' the woman sobbed.

Her husband stabbed his knife into his food, then rose from his seat, and seemed about to launch himself at Tilsner.

'Careful,' warned Müller's deputy as he grabbed the man's arm. 'It's a short trip back to jail.'

'Kaspar!' hissed his wife. 'Don't make a bigger fool of yourself than you have already.'

The man looked sheepish, shrugged his arm from Tilsner's grasp, and then sat back down. 'So what *have* you found?'

Müller looked at Tilsner with a pleading expression. It wasn't supposed to go like this. They were meant to be seeking information, not giving it out. Tilsner shrugged. 'You may as well tell them. They have a right to know.'

Sighing, Müller clasped her fingers together in front of her body, tightening them till the knuckles went white. Why was this so difficult? 'We have found the bodies . . .' she heard Hannelore gasp at this but didn't look up to meet her eyes, instead continuing to concentrate on where her fingers were joined together, '. . . of two babies, skeletons they are now, who could be twins.'

Hannelore Anderegg was sobbing now, her face hidden in her hands. But her husband fixed Müller with a grim stare. 'Where?'

'In the Hauptstadt,' said Tilsner.

'The Hauptstadt?' asked Herr Anderegg. 'Why do you think –'

'There is evidence of a Halle-Neustadt connection,' said Müller.

'What evidence?'

Müller looked at Tilsner. He gave a slight shake of the head. She exhaled. 'We can't say at the moment. It may be nothing. But we wanted to talk to you about the circumstances of your twins' disappearance. We want to try to help you. I know you may not believe that, after what's gone on before. But it's the truth.'

Kaspar Anderegg snorted. But then – after seeing the misery on his wife's face – the fight seemed to go out of him, and he laid his knife and fork to one side and placed his hand on his still-sobbing wife's arm.

'All right,' he said. 'Let's talk.'

37

Once the Andereggs had overcome their initial scepticism – and started to believe that Müller and Tilsner had a genuine interest in discovering the true story of their missing babies – they became much more cooperative. For her part, Müller soon discounted them as potential suspects in the wider investigation. The couple appeared too broken, too damaged by the loss of their children, and the cruel way they'd apparently been treated by the authorities, to inflict that sort of pain on anyone else. It was an assumption – perhaps a dangerous assumption – but Müller was convinced it was true, nonetheless.

The story that emerged was one of genuine misfortune. Frau Anderegg had left her children outside a shop in a double buggy, ostensibly with another mother keeping an eye on them. That woman had become distracted in an animated conversation – against the background of bustle, building noise and overall confusion that had marked the birth of Ha-Neu, as slab apartment blocks rose from what had once been a muddy swamp by the banks of the Saale almost overnight. When she eventually looked round, the double buggy – and the babies inside it – had disappeared. That triggered a nightmare sequence of events for the Andereggs: a frantic, but fruitless, search for their babies – and a flat denial from the other mother that Hannelore had ever asked her to look after them. Or, indeed, that they'd ever been there to start with. Müller could imagine the situation: one in which fear would have been contagious, all-pervasive, and where lies provided a safe harbour for the negligent party.

With no witnesses prepared to back up their story, and with Kaspar already marked down as a troublemaker and potential counter-revolutionary, the fit-up that followed was all too predictable.

Müller's only promise to the Andereggs was that the People's Police would do everything possible to try to identify the skeletons of the twin babies found in the rubble of Doctor Rothstein's illegal abortion clinic. If they were the Andereggs' children, it would extinguish their remaining hopes – but at least it might give them some closure. But Müller knew the likelihood of being able to identify them at all was low.

'Did you buy their story?' asked Tilsner on the drive back to Ha-Neu.

'I think so,' said Müller, relieved to finally get away from the choking atmosphere surrounding Leuna. She rolled down the passenger window of the Wartburg and took a couple of deep breaths of the cleaner air, hoping it would dispel the lingering feeling of nausea. It didn't. 'They seemed angry, but honest. I would be angry if what had happened to them had happened to me.' Her feelings towards the Stasi were conflicted. On the one hand, she was hoping to contact Jäger and persuade him to use his connections to help in her quest to find her natural parents. And of course some form of internal discipline, and security, was necessary in the Republic to guard against its many enemies in the West. Although she couldn't remember the war, she could remember all the endless rebuilding afterwards. She'd seen the scars on countless buildings in Berlin, including the site of the new Palace of the Republic, and what was there before. She didn't want the fascists, the Nazis, to be able to make a comeback. She wanted to help build a fairer future, for *all* the Republic's citizens. But as her eyes honed in once again on Tilsner's Western timepiece, she shuddered at some of the Ministry for State Security's methods. She watched her deputy continually peering into the rear-view mirror to see if the Skoda driver had resumed his surveillance, wondering if this local branch of the Stasi even knew they were keeping tabs on one of their own.

If Müller had had enough of the Stasi, they didn't seem to tire of dealing with her. When she got back to the incident room – which was in the process of being transformed into the control centre for the forthcoming Castro visit – Eschler handed her a note.

He raised one brow as he handed it over, eyes glancing down at the Stasi emblem of the Republic's flag flying from a rifle. Müller shielded it from him as she tore the envelope open. But her face relaxed as she saw it was an 'invitation' to a meeting –

from Jäger – a response to a letter of her own, sent to him at the regional Stasi HQ in Ha-Neu, asking for help in her quest to find information about her real mother. Perhaps he had some news.

The Stasi colonel's choice of meeting place held echoes of their meetings in the Hauptstadt: the Culture Park on Peissnitz island, between the navigable and 'wild' sections of the Saale river.

To get there, Müller had to drive to the north-east of the new town, near Stasi regional headquarters. Perhaps that was why Jäger had chosen the venue: it was convenient for him, nothing more, nothing less. He wanted them to meet near the Swan Bridge, a footbridge connecting the island to Halle West – near the university and, on the other side of Heide Allee, the giant Soviet garrison. Once she'd parked the Wartburg and walked through the woods past the Young Pioneers' clubhouse, she saw him, in plain clothes, sitting in one of the open-top passenger carriages of the miniature narrow-gauge railway.

'You know I like my theme parks,' he laughed as he saw her.

His smile, though, held what appeared to be genuine warmth.

'You look well, Karin. Pleased to be back on a proper case again?' Everyone else had been saying she looked tired. Flattery made a welcome change.

Müller arranged her skirt under herself as she sat next to the Stasi officer on the miniature train. 'Yes, though it's a frustrating one. You presumably know all about it?'

Jäger nodded. 'A little. Though as I think you know, I've been working far away from Berlin.'

'The tan's a bit of a giveaway.' Müller was surprised how easily they lapsed back into friendly conversation given that by the end of the *Jugendwerkhof* case she'd almost grown to hate him. She certainly hated his methods, his ruthlessness. But perhaps, now, some of that could be put to her own advantage.

Müller found herself looking over both shoulders, to each side of the train tracks. What was she expecting to see? The black Skoda parked by the railway line? In any case, what she was about to show Jäger wasn't that controversial. She pulled the rusting metal box from her pocket, opened it, pulled out the photograph and handed it to Jäger. As she did, she caught a faint whiff of Casino de Luxe again. Perhaps her mother – her adoptive mother – had used the same perfume.

'Who's this?' he asked.

'My mother.'

'She barely looks more than a girl. And the baby is –'

'– me . . . as far as I know. And then there's this.'

Müller proffered the yellowing adoption certificate, the legal piece of paper which had allowed her adoptive parents to bring her up as their own child in Oberhof.

'I've written it all down for you. All the details. What my adoptive mother could tell me about my birth mother – which wasn't much.' She handed the piece of paper she'd made her notes on to the Stasi colonel.

He looked at it dubiously. 'What do you expect me to do about it? You know that most of the time I'm stationed abroad now. I've come back only briefly, because of the Castro visit.'

'You're my best chance.' She tried to hold his eyes in her gaze. 'I helped you in the *Jugendwerkhof* case . . .'

'Because you were told to, Karin, by your People's Police superiors. It was your job. And in the Harz, you didn't exactly cover yourself in glory.'

Müller said nothing in reply. She could feel a tightness gripping her throat. The moisture started to well up in her eyes. Jäger noticed, and squeezed her hand.

'Look, I'm sorry. That sounded harsher than I meant it to. But I don't see how I *can* help . . . even if I wanted to.'

Gripping the tin box tightly in her pocket, Müller forced herself not to cry. Tried to sound calm and professional. 'You have plenty of contacts in the Ministry, Klaus – sorry, Comrade *Oberst*.'

'It's OK,' said Jäger. 'This isn't a formal meeting.'

'You knew all about my abortion after the rape at the police college.'

'The *alleged* rape.'

Müller sighed. She wasn't in the mood to get into an argument. 'The point is, you have methods of finding things out that I don't. I'd like your help. To try to identify my birth mother – my birth father too, if his identity is known. I can't force you to do it.' Jäger gave a thin smile at this. 'I'm simply asking you to do what you can.'

The Stasi colonel folded the paper and pushed it into his trouser pocket. 'OK, Karin, I will see what I can do. But if I do a favour for you, you will probably find yourself having to pay me back one day. That's the way things work.'

They watched as another man, in railway engineer's overalls, approached. He gave a slight nod to Jäger, then climbed into the driver's seat.

Jäger looked up at the overcast sky. 'Hopefully the rain will hold off.' He signalled to the driver – the only other person on board – who released the brakes. The miniature train trundled off, with much grinding and clunking of metal.

They were both silent for a few moments as the locomotive pulled them along in a northerly direction. The rhythmic clackety-clack as the train wheels passed over the rail joints had a soporific effect on Müller, so that when Jäger finally spoke again she found herself jolting upright.

'You're probably wondering why I asked for this meeting.'

Müller tried to read the expression in his face. It was his affable Western newsreader look. 'I assumed it was in response to the letter I sent to you. My request for information about my mother.'

Jäger shook his head. 'No, that wasn't it. Though as I've said, I will do what I can – and in return, I expect you to cooperate with me. However, what I really wanted to talk about was the forthcoming state visit.'

'Of Comrade Castro?'

The Stasi colonel gave a single nod. 'We've received information that there may be attempts to disrupt the visit.'

Müller pulled the lapels of her jacket together as the train began to turn the corner at the apex of Peissnitz island. It wasn't particularly cold, but an easterly breeze was enough to raise goosebumps on her forearms. 'And how does that involve my team?'

Jäger rubbed his chin. 'On the actual day, we'll need all hands to the pump. So you and Tilsner will need to be on duty, and put your other investigation to one side. We'll be needing you to watch for anything untoward.'

On the face of it, that seemed to make sense. But why had Jäger felt the need to call her to one of his semi-clandestine meetings?

Sensing her puzzlement, the Stasi officer continued: 'And from now on, I want you to keep your eyes and ears open. Ask questions of the Pioneer teams collecting newspapers for you.' So, as Müller suspected, the Stasi lieutenant colonel *did* know about their investigation – intimately. 'And if there are any more mothers you're visiting as part of this health campaign, try to get them talking. See if you can find anything out. You're from Thuringia, aren't you? Or at least your adoptive family is.'

Müller rolled her eyes. 'You know very well where I'm from. You know everything about me that you want to know, Comrade *Oberst*.'

Jäger smiled. 'You're getting used to our methods, Karin.' Then he turned to her and held her gaze. 'The group who seem to be behind the protests call themselves the Committee for the Dispossessed. Have you ever heard of it?'

The shriek of the train's whistle as it approached Peissnitz Bridge station startled her. She felt her heart rate quicken. Almost as though she felt guilty about something. 'No. I can't say that I have.'

'From the content of their letters we believe the people involved are somehow connected with the drive to eradicate racketeers in tourist areas and our attempts to make sure the Free German Trade Union holiday service had enough properties. In Rügen, where you were earlier this year, and in –'

'– Oberhof, my home village,' interrupted Müller. She turned her head to the station platform as they trundled through. Would-be passengers looked confused that the train wasn't stopping. This, though, was *Oberst* Klaus Jäger's private express.

'So you know about it?'

Müller frowned. 'The Committee for the Dispossessed? No, I've never heard of it, as I said. I *am* aware that some people still bear a grudge about the state taking control of tourist facilities. But tens of thousands of citizens have benefitted from cheap holidays as a result. Workers who otherwise would not have been able to afford it.' She knew this was the answer an authority figure like Jäger would expect to hear. He nodded, as though he could sense she was simply repeating propaganda messages by rote.

'What I'd like you to do – subtly, please, Karin – is ask your family if they've ever heard of this group. If they've heard any grumblings.' Müller knew – even as Jäger was asking the question – that she wouldn't be complying with his request. Relations with what she now knew was her adoptive family were still too raw.

'But the families of the . . .' Müller paused. Johannes, and his family, had been good to her. His mother had always spoiled her as a little girl, when love from her own mother was markedly absent. She didn't want to label them, but she knew what Jäger would expect to hear. 'Families of the racketeers were bussed out. Well, *relocated*. I witnessed it as a little girl.'

What Jäger said next sent a chill through Müller. Had her hunching down in the train seat, wanting to hide.

'I know you did, Karin. Your name is on record. For complaining about it.'

38

Two months earlier: July 1975
Wohnkomplex VIII, Halle-Neustadt

Oh glory of glories. She is *so* pretty. *So* cute.

I still cannot really believe it, even though Hansi had warned me it might be like this. The condition – the pressure of my growing womb – had cut off my blood supply. In effect I'd fainted – so they had to sedate me. I'm told it was touch and go in the hospital. Like last time, when apparently I'd been knocked out after my fall over the building materials, the concrete pipes I think it was, I was completely out of it when I gave birth. By Caesarean, of course.

I rub my tummy as Heike sucks on her bottle. This time I've given in to Hansi. Yes, I'd rather have fed her naturally. But I accept something went wrong last time, with Stefi. Hansi was insistent that this time I should do what he says. And I still feel a little guilty. About Stefi. And about kissing that barman at Weissensee.

The other thing that's slightly odd is that Heike is so small. A tiny little thing. She's pretty. Well, she is to me. But her face is so pinched. She looks a bit like an eagle chick. And so, so tiny. The doctor says it's because she came a few weeks early.

This time I don't go to the normal baby clinic. Hansi arranged for me to go to the one behind the wall, in the special Ministry area – he's important enough for that to happen now. He says Heike will go to the Ministry's kindergarten too, when she's a bit older. Hansi's being so good to me. Bringing me everything I need, doing all the shopping. Because Heike was premature, he says it's not a good idea to take her out shopping with me in Ha-Neu centre. Keep contact with other people to a minimum, that way there'll be less chance of her catching something.

'There, there, precious,' I whisper to Heike, as she starts crying. I think she's got wind from sucking the milk from the bottle too quickly. Greedy little thing. I give her just the lightest of taps on her back. And there, a big burp. 'That's better, darling. Isn't it?'

39

Three months later: October 1975
Halle-Neustadt

Jäger's revelation preyed on Müller for the rest of the day, and made it hard to concentrate. That the army on that day had bothered to note down a five-year-old girl's angry comment was bad enough. The fact that a record of her outburst had been kept, and relayed back to her more than twenty years later, beggared belief.

As she returned to Emil's apartment in Halle market square that evening, she toyed with the idea of discussing it with him. Then she immediately dismissed it. Perhaps she had fallen in love, but that didn't mean she shouldn't be on her guard. The fact was, Emil's move to Halle had been horribly convenient. His seduction of her all too quick and easy. What if he had been sent to watch her, from close quarters? What if Jäger suspected her – with her Oberhof links – of being a member of this so-called Committee for the Dispossessed? She wasn't, of course. In fact, sometimes she wondered if she was too loyal a supporter of the Republic. But in her heart, she still believed in socialism. The greater good for the greater number. She was even prepared to overlook some of the Stasi's methods if that helped the Republic survive and prosper. But that didn't mean she shouldn't be wary.

Müller and Emil had just settled down to begin the evening meal he'd cooked when she heard the siren. She ran to the window to see what was going on. A group of uniforms rushed out of a couple of police Wartburgs, their flashing lights illuminating the Handel monument with eerie pulses of blue. There was a gathering of people outside a restaurant. At the centre, a distraught girl, who looked to be in her late teens. Then the apartment phone rang. Emil held up the handset.

'It's for you. It's *Unterleutnant* Tilsner. He says it's urgent.' Emil threw her a reproachful smile. A look that said to Müller: *This is how it's going to be, isn't it? If we stay together. This is how it's going to be all the time.* 'I'll put your food back in the oven.'

Müller picked up the phone.

'Have you heard?' Tilsner asked over a crackly line.

'I think I've just been watching it.'

'Right by you. In the market place. Another baby's been snatched. I'll drive over straightaway and meet you there.'

Müller had always wondered about the accepted practice in the Republic of leaving infants, in their prams, outside shops or cafés. Yes, usually at least one of the mothers stayed to watch them – as in the Andereggs' case from a decade earlier – but no one was as vigilant as a child's actual mother.

As people milled around, the uniform teams appeared to be trying to get details from a teenage girl who looked to be sobbing into her boyfriend's chest. Only when the girl turned did Müller realise who it was: Anneliese Haase, mother of baby Tanja – the girl from *Wohnkomplex VI* Müller had visited on the first day of the 'nutrition campaign'. Without checking, Müller could remember her block number: 956. The apartment: 276. Perhaps health visitor Kamilla Seidel's superstitions *were* correct after all, but not in a good way.

Anneliese's face, streaked by mascara-stained tears, creased into confusion as she saw Müller, and the deferential way the police officers treated her.

'You . . . you're . . . you're not a health visitor at all, are you?' she said accusingly. 'Where's my baby? What have they done to my baby?'

Tilsner grabbed the girl gently by her shoulders and moved her away from the throng of onlookers. 'Keep your voice down,' he hissed into her ear. 'If you know what's good for you.'

'Let's take her to Emil's flat,' Müller said to her deputy. 'It'll be quieter there. I'll ask Emil to make himself scarce. I just want to get Anneliese away from this lot before she shoots her mouth off any more.'

Anneliese tried to shrug herself out of Tilsner's grip as they moved her off, while the uniforms prevented her boyfriend or any of the others in the crowd from following. 'Where are you taking me? I haven't done anything wrong. Someone's stolen my baby. My Tanja. Why aren't you chasing after –'

The girl's protests stopped as Tilsner yanked her arm up behind her back. 'Be quiet. I won't warn you again. We just want to ask you some questions, get everything clear, away from that mêlée. That's the best way of getting Tanja back safe and sound.'

After having his evening meal interrupted, Emil looked glum at being told by Müller to spend an hour or so at a bar while she and Tilsner used his apartment to interview Anneliese. But – grim-faced – he complied with his police officer girl-friend's request.

Anneliese herself looked frightened – eyes darting every-where, still obviously confused about who Müller actually was, given the detective's deception of three months earlier.

'You'll realise by now that I'm not a health visitor, Anneliese. I'm a detective. But you must under no circumstances tell any-one else that I was involved in that nutrition campaign. Do you understand?'

'Y-y-yes,' the girl stuttered.

Müller got her notebook and clicked her pen. 'Now tell us exactly what happened this evening. Do it slowly, and try to remember everything. I'm sure we will find Tanja safe and well. But we will do it sooner if you are completely honest.'

'W-will I g-g-get into trouble?'

Müller sighed. 'What's important is finding your little girl. Why were you here at a bar in the centre of Halle? It's a long way from your home. *Wohnkomplex VI* is on the far side of Halle-Neustadt.'

'My boyfriend. He works the other side of Halle. This is where we meet – it's about halfway.'

'Why did you bring Tanja with you? Couldn't you have left her with a relative or a friend for the evening? Couldn't you have got a babysitter?'

This question prompted more tears from the girl. 'I did have a babysitter arranged. My aunt. But her son was ill at the last minute. She had to take him to the hospital, and said she couldn't sit for Tanja after all.'

'Couldn't you have found someone else?' asked Tilsner.

The girl shrugged, then hid her face in her hands.

'What's done is done, Anneliese,' said Müller more gently. 'But why couldn't you keep Tanja with you in the bar?'

Anneliese brushed her hair off her face and breathed in slowly, as though trying to keep herself calm. 'I did take her in with me at first. Then she was crying. I tried to breastfeed her, but someone complained. So I took her into the toilet, fed her a bit there until she was sleepy, and then put her to bed in the pram.'

'Outside?' asked Müller.

Anneliese said nothing for a moment, as though she couldn't face what she'd done. 'Yes,' she eventually replied. 'But I made sure she had the rabbit soft toy as a comforter, and went out regularly to check. Every five minutes. I'm not a bad mother, honestly.'

'Is your boyfriend the father?' asked Tilsner.

The girl shook her head.

'Do you have any contact with the father?' continued Tilsner.

Again, a shake of the head. 'He's gone back.'

'Gone back where?' asked Müller.

STASI WOLF | 254

'To Vietnam.'

The revelation silenced Müller and her deputy for a moment. Tilsner threw her a puzzled look.

'Has he ever made any attempts to contact Tanja?' asked Müller. 'Could he have secretly come back to the Republic and attempted to take the baby to Vietnam with him?'

'No. He doesn't even know she exists. He was a student at the university, on the Halle-West Campus. It was just a quick fling and I stupidly got pregnant. He was sharing an apartment in *Wohnkomplex VI*. He'd finished his studies but was staying on for the summer – summer last year.'

'And you never told him he was a father?' asked Tilsner in astonishment.

'I don't even have his address. I just know he lives in Hanoi somewhere – the other Hanoi, the real one, in Vietnam.'

Müller rubbed her chin. The father was obviously a dead end, then. What about the boyfriend?

'What's your boyfriend's name?' she asked.

'I don't want to involve him. We haven't been going out very long. It's hard for a single mother to find a man.'

'Don't be stupid,' snapped Tilsner. 'Officers at the scene will already have his name. He already is involved. We are trying to help you find your baby. A baby you put at risk by leaving her outside while you canoodled inside the bar with your latest love interest. So just answer our questions. All of them.'

The girl stared at Tilsner, open-mouthed. But in Müller's opinion, her deputy was quite right to try to shake her up a bit. 'Come on, Anneliese,' she said. 'Spit it out.'

'It's Georg. Georg Meyer.'

'And how is he with Tanja?' continued Müller.

'What do you mean?'

'Is he accepting of her? Loving towards her? Would he rather you didn't have a baby?'

'He's good with her. But . . .'

'But what?' asked Tilsner.

'Well, any young guy . . . I'm sure they'd rather find a girl *without* a baby. What are you trying to say? That Georg has deliberately arranged for someone to get rid of Tanja? That's ridiculous.'

Müller shook her head vigorously. 'No. We're not trying to say that at all. We're just looking at all possibilities. So Georg was happy enough to be going out with you, even though Tanja sometimes cramped your style, restricted what you could do?'

'Yes. There was no problem.'

'Did he realise that she was half Vietnamese?' asked Tilsner.

'No. It's not obvious. At least not at the moment. She just looks . . . well, she just looks really cute. Adorable.'

Müller thought back to the visit to Anneliese's flat some three months earlier. What the girl was saying was true – Tanja had stood out as a particularly cute baby. An adorable baby. Adorable enough for some woman – some woman desperate for a child of her own – to steal her. But was that what they were dealing with here? A straightforward case of baby-snatching? And did it have any link to the case involving the Salzmann twins, or to the skeletons of the Andereggs' babies in Rothstein's demolished abortion clinic? Surely so many cases of child abduction had to be linked, and couldn't just be coincidence? But if so, why had Maddelena been returned safe and sound?

A cough from Tilsner brought her back to the present. 'Do you have any enemies that you know of, Anneliese?' she asked. 'Anyone who might want to do you or Tanja harm?'

The girl's face creased into a frown. 'Not that I know of. Unless –'

'Unless what?' prompted Tilsner.

'Well . . . there is Georg's ex-girlfriend.'

'What about her?' asked Müller.

'She was really angry that he dumped her to go out with me. We saw her the other day in Halle. She launched herself at me. Georg had to hold her back. Then she started shouting at him. What was it she said? Oh yes: *Watch out, bastard. I'll get you back sooner or later.*'

40

Müller could tell Emil was angry with her, perhaps understand-ably. Once Tilsner and Müller had finished with Anneliese, they contacted the Halle People's Police uniform division and gave them the details of Georg Meyer's ex-girlfriend, asking them to take her in. They'd let her sweat a bit overnight in a police cell before interviewing her the next day. But Emil didn't come back after the hour or so that Müller had suggested he take for a drink. It was nearer midnight before he finally turned up, stink-ing of beer.

While someone like Tilsner seemed to be able to hold his beer, and became jolly and flirtatious when drunk, Emil Wollenburg appeared to be more like Gottfried once he'd had too many. Morose but with a hair-trigger temper. It was a side of him Müller hadn't seen before, and she didn't particularly like it.

Once he'd finished berating Müller for using his flat as an interview room, and for wrecking their supposedly romantic dinner for two, Emil slumped in a chair at the dining table and held his head in his hands.

'I'm not sure this is going to work,' he said, peering up at her.

'It's a two-way thing, Emil. We knew when we started it there would be days like this – for both of us. If you had an emergency at the hospital it would be just the same.'

'I certainly wouldn't be using your flat as a makeshift operating theatre.'

Müller felt her face warming with anger. 'That's unfair. The poor girl's baby had been snatched. I needed to get her into a calm environment, just for thirty minutes, so that we could make sense of everything. You didn't need to stay out until midnight.'

'Hmm.'

'Hmm what?'

'Well, it's just not the same, is it?'

'Same as what?'

'The same as when we started going out together. You seem frazzled all the time. Moody. And what's with all the clutching at your stomach and being sick?'

Müller pulled out the dining chair opposite her boyfriend and slowly sat down on it. 'I don't know what that is. It's worrying me. And having you shouting at me like this won't help.'

Emil laid his hand tenderly on her arm, finally realising how unreasonable he was being. 'Sorry. I was acting like a spoilt brat.'

'So what do we do now?'

He smiled at her. 'Bed? It's the universal panacea, after all.'

Müller laughed, grateful that he'd attempted to defuse the tension. But what *was* wrong with her? She wished she knew. It had been going on for too long. She felt another wave of nausea rise up.

'It's happening again, isn't it?'

She nodded.

'You know, Karin, I think we ought to get you checked out. I'm fairly certain I know what's wrong, even though you swear blind it's not possible.'

She stared into his eyes, her alarm mounting. 'What?'

'You're pregnant.'

If going to bed – and all that it entailed – *was* a universal panacea, then it didn't work for Müller. Emil soon rolled over and was snoring, presumably content in his own mind that physical intimacy had helped to smooth out their row. But Müller couldn't get out of her head his categorical insistence that somehow – flying in the face of everything she'd been told by every other doctor she'd seen – she had fallen pregnant. That her 'illness' was simply morning sickness. Could it be true? If so, how? And was it something she even wanted? The row before bedtime with Emil had surely demonstrated that their relationship wasn't yet ready to be blessed with a child.

The ringing of the phone in the living room cut short her agonising.

'I'll get it,' she said, as Emil groaned and pulled the pillow over his ears.

In the event, it was indeed for her – not him. Tilsner again.

'It's all kicking off, boss, I'm afraid. Anneliese must have blabbed.'

'Where?'

'Outside a dormitory in *Wohnkomplex VIII*. A Vietnamese guest workers' dormitory.'

Müller raced there in the Wartburg, across the bridge over the Saale, blue light on and siren blaring.

She was unsurprised that by the time she got there, the area seemed to have been secured by several leather-jacketed heavies, who were already leading away a mob of male and female demonstrators, tearing their protest banners out of their hands.

'Turn the blue light off please, Karin. We don't want to make this more of a drama than it already is.' It was Jäger, who'd sidled up to her unseen almost as soon as she was out of the car. 'Do you know what this is about?'

Müller could guess, but she wasn't sure she wanted to admit it to Jäger. She was angry, though, that Anneliese didn't seem to have heeded their warnings. The Stasi's fears that the baby abductions might cause unrest seemed to be being borne out. She saw one plain-clothes operative shine a torch on one of the protest banners he'd confiscated. 'GIVE OUR BABY BACK'. She was glad that – in the darkness – Jäger wouldn't be able to see the embarrassment which she was sure was writ large over her face. But he'd seen the words on the banner, just as she had.

'I hope this isn't some fallout from your investigation, Karin. You know we wanted to keep things tightly controlled. We don't want this flaring up again at the weekend when Comrade Castro arrives.'

'Perhaps if we'd done more to start with, Comrade *Oberst*, we wouldn't be facing this mess now.'

They watched as a Stasi operative clapped his hand over the mouth of a woman who'd started shouting again. Müller was shocked to see it was Klara Salzmann. *Why isn't she at home with Maddelena?*

'Do you know her?' asked Jäger, who under the dim street lighting had obviously spotted Müller taking an extra interest.

Müller nodded. 'It's the mother involved in the case of the twin babies who were originally abducted in July. The reason I was brought down here from the Hauptstadt to start with.'

'Do you think she's protesting too much?' asked Jäger.

Müller noticed that Tilsner had joined them at the sidelines, watching the Stasi agents taking the protesters into custody, bundling them into the back of Barkas vans.

'Karin's always been suspicious about them,' said Tilsner.

Müller sighed. 'It's true. But I'm not entirely sure why. It's just something about the looks she and her husband give each other. I don't think they've been entirely truthful with us. As to why she's out with a rabble of protesters in the middle of the night – when she should be at home with her surviving baby – and as to why they've decided to target a Vietnamese dormitory, I'm afraid I've no idea, Comrade *Oberst*.'

The fallout from the dormitory protest the next day was left entirely to the Ministry for State Security. Jäger made it quite clear that Müller and Tilsner's assistance wasn't required. Instead, after a late breakfast, the two Berlin *Kripo* detectives set off for Silberhöhe – to the south of Halle city – to track down Georg Meyer's ex-girlfriend, Kerstin Luitgard, who worked in a clothing factory there. She'd been briefly held by the Halle uniform division, but then allowed back to work after Müller said she and Tilsner would be delayed following their middle of the night call-out.

The factory itself had a run-down appearance. Crumbling red bricks that looked ready to be demolished. Müller knew that that was indeed the plan – this area had been earmarked for another dormitory town of concrete slab apartments, similar to Ha-Neu. In a couple of years the place would be transformed, with apartment after apartment rising from the mud and rubble.

The site forewoman went to fetch Kerstin, after showing Müller and Tilsner into a side room they could use for their interview and complaining that the girl had only just arrived – late for her shift.

When Kerstin was brought back by the woman, she looked exhausted and nervously fiddled with her hair, as Müller performed the introductions.

'This is *Unterleutnant* Tilsner of the *Kriminalpolizei*, and I'm *Oberleutnant* Müller. Do you know why we want to talk to you, Kerstin?'

'Not really,' said the girl in a quiet voice. 'The *Vopos* . . . they wouldn't tell me anything.'

'Do you have a temper, Kerstin?' asked Tilsner.

'Not really. No more than anyone else.'

'Have you ever made any threats against anyone?' asked Müller. She gave the girl a hard stare, until Kerstin dropped her gaze and started wringing her hands.

'No. What's this about? I don't understand. I have to get back to my work.'

'It's about your former boyfriend, Georg Meyer,' continued Müller.

'What about him? I have nothing to do with him anymore. Not after I dumped him.'

'*You* dumped *him*? That's not what we heard,' said Tilsner. 'It's our understanding that *he* left *you*. For another girl. A prettier girl.'

'Anneliese Haase,' said Müller.

The girl said nothing, just continued to wring her hands, eyes downcast.

'Is that correct?' asked Müller.

'Yes, he's with her. What of it? We'd finished. It's nothing to me. But she's not prettier than me – and she's a whore. A whore who fucks Vietnamese guest workers. He's welcome to her.'

'If that's the case, Kerstin,' said Müller, flicking through her notebook, 'why did you get so angry when you saw them together the other day in Halle city centre?'

'Who says I did?'

'We have witnesses,' said Tilsner. 'Witnesses who heard you say to him: "*Watch out, bastard. I'll get you back sooner or later.*" Are you denying you said that?'

Müller could see the tears forming in the girl's eyes. She was obviously jealous, obviously still had feelings for Georg Meyer. But a child-snatcher? Müller didn't think so.

When the girl failed to reply, Tilsner stepped up the pressure. 'You got him back, didn't you? Last night. By stealing his new girlfriend's baby.'

'What!' shouted the girl. 'You're mad. What would I want with a baby? Even if I did want one, I wouldn't want her second-hand mixed-race bastard of a child.'

That flash of anger had revealed part of Kerstin's true character, thought Müller. But she still couldn't see her stealing Tanja from outside the bar.

'Where were you at 7 p.m. last night?' asked Tilsner.

'Here,' spat the girl. 'Ask Frau Garber, the forewoman. She doesn't like me, but she knows I was here.'

41

When the forewoman – as Kerstin had predicted – backed up
the girl's alibi, showing the time sheets and clocking-on information to confirm it, Müller knew the investigation was back to
square one again. Only now they had another baby abduction
to contend with, as well as the first hint of demonstrations and
unrest – something that wouldn't be allowed to interfere with
the weekend's visit of Comrade Castro. Things were no better
at home, with Emil urging her to check out his concerns about
the possible pregnancy – and Müller so far resisting, unable to
believe that what she'd been told by several gynaecologists over
the years was apparently wrong.

The preparations for the visit felt much the same as those for the
May Day or Anniversary of the Republic parades in the Hauptstadt. Müller and Tilsner were drafted in to help Eschler and
his team on what were essentially uniform tasks of organisation
and security. But Müller knew that – beneath the surface – Jäger
and his Stasi operatives would be paying visits to anyone they
suspected of belonging to this shadowy Committee for the
Dispossessed that the Stasi colonel had warned her about. What

Müller had managed to secure, from Jäger himself, was a promise that once the visit was safely out of the way, her investigation
team would be strengthened again – to the level it had been before
Maddelena's safe return. The protest outside the Vietnamese dormitory seemed to have unnerved the Ministry for State Security. If
it helped Müller, so much the better.

Saturday was a bright, late October day. A cloudless sky – and
free, too, of pollution haze. Müller almost wondered if Leuna,
Buna and surrounding plants had been shut down for the day
to ensure no nasty smells upset the Cuban prime minister on
what was said to be the most important day of his visit. Just to
be able to welcome him in Halle-Neustadt, the Republic's model
town for socialist living, filled Müller with pride – although her
pride was tempered by the dark undercurrents in the new town:
the abduction of the Salzmann twins, the death of Karsten, and
now the disappearance of Tanja Haase. All these things had been
cloaked in secrecy to avoid undermining Comrade Castro's visit,
if that was the *real* reason for all the secrecy . . .

Müller and Tilsner watched from the sweeping pedestrian
bridge over the Magistrale as the parade made its way under them:
lines of chemical workers – with their red flags from the various
diverse parts of the giant works – and Pioneers in their crisply
starched white shirts and dazzling blue and red neckerchiefs.

'They'd all be thrilled to be here if it was during work or
school time,' whispered Tilsner. 'Bet they're not as happy doing
all this on a Saturday afternoon.'

Müller screwed her face up at him. It wasn't a day to be cynical. She genuinely hoped everything passed off peacefully. She looked back towards the end of the parade and saw a line of black limousines – looking from the distance a little like beetles, shining in the sunlight as they crossed the bridge over the Saale from Halle city. Surrounding the limousines – Volvos, of course, she could tell from their shapes even at this distance – were columns what looked like ants: the police motorcycle outriders. Müller scanned the skyline. She could see the figures of armed Stasi operatives on the top of the high-rises, no doubt giving radio messages to men on the ground, should they notice anything untoward.

'Do we just stay and watch from here, then?' asked Tilsner. 'If anything does happen, we're not going to be able to do much about it.'

'No, let's make our way to the central hospital. That's where the speeches are going to be. Comrade Castro wants to see how our health service measures up to his.'

'We don't need to rush, then. I've heard his speeches go on for hours.'

Walking across the pedestrian bridge took them directly into *Wohnkomplex IV*, where the hospital was situated, without having to fight their way through the throngs of spectators lining the Magistrale. They then showed their *Kripo* passes to ensure safe passage through the crowd who'd lined up several deep in the hospital's entrance waiting for the speeches.

Müller nodded a greeting to Jäger whom she spotted on the opposite side of the lobby. Emil was there too, in his doctor's coat, but she didn't manage to catch his eye. It was about twenty minutes later when the murmur of voices turned into a roar of acclaim, the flashbulbs of the waiting press fired off in a series of blinding lights, and then he was there, standing at the podium, waving in greeting in his olive-green battle fatigues, with the bespectacled and civilian-suited Erich Honecker at his side. Fidel Castro. The great revolutionary and socialist hero, whose image – along with Che Guevara's – was found on many student T-shirts and posters throughout the Republic. And, bizarrely, in the West too. Müller had seen it on Western news programmes and documentaries.

Tilsner cupped his hand over her ear. 'We've got a sweepstake on this back at People's Police HQ. How long the bloody thing will take. You know he holds the record for the longest speech at the UN? More than four hours.'

Müller rolled her eyes, then tapped his Western watch. 'At least you'll be able to time it accurately with this,' she whispered back. 'Your expensive, *capitalist* timepiece.'

Tilsner sneered in return. Across the concourse, she could see Jäger frowning at her, probably annoyed that the two detectives were joking with each other – rather than keeping their eyes peeled for any members of this shadowy, yet-to-be-seen Committee for the Dispossessed.

In the event, neither Honecker nor Castro started the speeches. That was left to a local Party official.

'Who's he?' Tilsner asked.

Müller shrugged, then a fearsome-looking woman tapped her on the shoulder. 'It's the Ha-Neu district Party secretary, Rolf Strobelt.' Müller nodded her thanks.

Standing in front of a model of the new town, Strobelt began a short speech welcoming Fidel Castro and extolling the virtues of Halle-Neustadt, punctuated by regular breaks for applause. Müller and the rest of the crowd duly clapped. Tilsner – much to Müller's annoyance – raised his eyes to the heavens and kept his hands by his sides, rather than joining the seal-like acclaim. *Doesn't he realise Jäger and his cronies are watching us?*

Then it was Erich Honecker's turn. Müller was surprised his wife Margot wasn't at his side. Müller had been briefed that she was part of the visit. Having been born in Halle, it would have been a chance to catch up with her birthplace – and the labyrinthine all-new concrete city which had now been built alongside it.

Finally – after more pauses for applause – Honecker introduced Castro. As the Cuban leader began to speak, there was a surge in the crowd behind Müller, which separated her from Tilsner. At first she just assumed it was enthusiasm, but then there was more jostling and shouting, and Müller was pushed violently forward, the collision with the person in front like a punch in the gut. She turned to remonstrate and found two leather-jacketed men wrestling with each other, as a shout rang out:

'Give us our homes and businesses back. We want what's rightfully –'

As she clutched her stomach in pain, Müller's eyeline switched to the source of the shouting, from her right-hand side. Another leather-jacketed man – she assumed a Stasi operative – had clasped his hand over the protester's mouth. As confusion in the crowd grew, someone yanked up the volume of the public address system so that Fidel Castro's voice drowned out any further dissent.

More jostling, another push, and Müller found herself stumbling. As she did, from the corner of the eye she spotted a face she was sure she'd seen before. Flashes from her childhood, her youth. *I know him. Who is it?* Before her brain could compute the answer – and with Castro's long-winded words and their German translation echoing between her ears – her head hit the floor with a sickening crash.

42

It was so, so cold. The girl tried to stamp her feet in the unwieldy, specially-adapted ski boots to try to get her blood to circulate. Cloudlets formed in front of her face each time she exhaled. She clapped her hands to generate warmth, her overlong skis wedged in the crook of her arm.

The landing area almost looked like glass, and the early jumpers had struggled to stop before the barriers of tarpaulin-covered straw bales. Hitting them would be like crashing into a brick wall. It would hurt for hours, days afterwards, and it wasn't as though her family were here to comfort her or cheer her on. She'd gone down to feel the straw bales before getting changed: they were frozen solid, the way everything else had been for weeks, months.

It wasn't just here in the heights of the Thuringian forest. Cold held the whole of northern Europe in its grip. She'd seen the pictures in Neues Deutschland: *the frozen waves of the Ostsee, like ripples of icing on a cake. Boats in harbours pushed into impossible angles by wind-blown sheet ice – people walking on the frozen, brackish water to get a closer look. Shop signs and trees in the Hauptstadt decorated with white whiskers that even a midday winter sun wasn't strong enough to melt.*

Now her trainer was in front of her, warming her face with his Wurst-breath, as he talked her through the techniques she already knew by rote. *The explosion at launch with the body and knees, leaning forward towards the ski tips, arms by the sides like fighter jet wings. And then the landing on bent knees, with one leg extended in front of the other* She tried to concentrate on the words, but instead found her eyes following the tributaries of broken blood vessels in his weather- and alcohol-ravaged face.

'Remember,' he shouted, a fleck of undigested sausage flying from his mouth. 'Concentrate. Concentrate. Everyone will be watching. Everyone will be cheering. You can be the champion. You're good enough. Believe it.'

A final clap with his giant gloved hand on her back, and then he pushed her forward to the steps which led to the platform. At the sides of the hill, the rickety wooden grandstands, filled with a sea of faces, steam rising from many as they sipped their coffees or Glühwein mit Schuss. She saw some of her school friends gathered there.

'Come on, Katzi,' they cheered.

Why are you doing this? she asked herself. *What's driving you to prove you're better than the others? That you're the best. Is it your mother's approval you're seeking? Your brother's, your sister's, Pappi's? Why? They're not even here to watch you.*

She was at the top of the steps now. It would be her turn next to shuffle awkwardly over to the bench. *The bench above that fearsome slope of white, with its twin tracks to be followed to the edge . . . of nothing. Nothing but free, mountain air, flying past your ears. The thrill of the adrenalin surge. The magic of soaring through the air – the nearest humans ever got to matching the beauty of birds in flight.*

The girl watched as Lukas Habich prepared to push himself off. Her main rival, the junior champion of Bezirk Suhl. She knew she was better than him – could leap further, get better style points. But when it was all tallied up, hers would be discounted. Because ski-jumping didn't have a category for females, adult women or girls. She was the best, but she wouldn't win any prizes.

As Lukas adjusted his goggles, he got the signal to jump. He pushed himself off, then assumed the traditional crouch down the in-run. The girl watched his take-off, at the same time as moving into the position on the bar that he had vacated moments earlier.

The cheer from the crowd as he landed was huge. It must have been beyond the K-point, with good style marks. Lukas would have set the gold standard, as he always did.

The girl knew that, dotted around the crowd, were not just spectators, but officials from the Republic's Winter Olympic Committee. And they hadn't come to see Lukas. They'd come to see her. To see if what they'd heard about the flying girl from Thuringia was really true. That she could be the spearhead of a new, women-only Olympic ski-jumping competition, and that – by getting in first – the Deutsche Demokratische Republik, *the tiny communist country at the very edge of the Soviet socialist bloc, could rule the world.*

Adjusting her goggles, she tried to blinker herself. To focus solely on a smooth push-off, followed by a controlled, but explosive, take-off. But something was wrong. In the corner of her eye, she noticed one young man staring hard at her from the upper grandstand – a stare that burned with hatred, from behind his wire-rimmed spectacles. She'd seen that face before. So many times. In Farmer Bonz's field as they practised their own version of the luge. And the last time, being pushed onto the back of a People's Army truck, his head looking round in confusion, clouded by myopia. Johannes. It was Johannes.

All of a sudden, the in-run seemed to extend forever. The landing zone looked impossible to hit. The quiver of fear shook her athletic teenage body. Where had that sudden fear come from, when she'd been so fearless before? It was almost as though it had been beamed into her via Johannes's disapproving gaze. The boy she'd been too young and powerless to protect in his own moment of terror. She'd never tried to find out what had become of him – she'd cast him out of her life.

And when they called her name – Karin Müller – she felt that same terror he must have felt when the soldiers took him, his family and his family home away. She sat there, unable to launch herself, perched shivering on the bar.

She knew she couldn't jump, and would never jump again.

43

When she came round, Müller was initially disoriented. Had she – in fact – made that last ski jump? Overcome that sudden fear which had gripped her on seeing what she thought was Johannes's face . . . but then crashed, hitting her head, which hurt like hell. She felt sick just as she had these last few weeks, fearing she was . . .

Pregnant.

As the fog of confusion lifted, she saw not Johannes's face, but Emil's – Emil Wollenburg's – leaning over her bed. Her hospital bed, his eyes and expression full of concern.

'You're back with us then, Karin.'

She started to try to get out of bed, unsure what she was supposed to be doing. Protecting Castro, Honecker. Explaining to Johannes. Why she had been able to stay in Oberhof and he hadn't. Why seeing him on the hill had frozen her with fear, left her unable to jump. And she wanted to ask him questions too. Why was he in Ha-Neu? What was he doing tackling the protester? But had it even been Johannes? She shook her head to try to clear it, then wished she hadn't, the thud of pain like a hammer inside her skull.

'Settle down,' said Emil, pushing her back gently until her head was resting on the pillow once more. 'You're going to have to take it easy for a few days.'

'What happened?'

'You fainted. Hit your head. It must have been the excitement of one of Prime Minister Castro's legendary speeches.'

'No. I saw something. I saw him.'

Emil's face creased in concern. 'Who did you see?'

Johannes, she wanted to say. *You know, the friend I abandoned. The friend I allowed the soldiers to take away.* But no words came out of her mouth. Who was Johannes to Emil? He didn't know him. He wouldn't understand.

When Müller failed to answer, Emil reached over from his seat at the hospital bedside, and held her hand in his.

'While you were unconscious, they performed an ultrasound.'

Müller's eyes opened wide in alarm. 'I don't want to know.' She saw the hurt in Emil's face, his wounded pride. In her befuddled state, she knew she had to repair the damage. 'I don't want to know the sex if . . . if I am pregnant.'

'You are. The scan confirmed it. And all healthy despite your fall. But I didn't want to know if it was a girl or a boy either. I asked them not to tell me anything, other than to confirm whether you were pregnant or not.'

Müller laid her head back on the hospital pillow again, and laughed. 'All those years that I haven't used precautions, because . . .'

'Because you thought it was impossible for you to get pregnant after what happened to you at the police college? Maybe you've just been lucky . . . or unlucky.'

Müller gripped the fingers of Emil's hand. 'What about you, Emil? Are you pleased?'

'Hah!' he laughed. 'Can't you tell from my smile?'

But for Müller, the news was tinged with worry. What would happen now with the investigation into Karsten Salzmann's abduction and death? The snatching of baby Tanja Haase? The Andereggs' stolen and dead twins? If she was being blessed with a child, it seemed horribly unfair to not continue the hunt for the person – or persons – who had wreaked such misery on others.

As if reading her mind, Emil put her fears into words. 'You'll have to take it easy. Especially after that bang on your head, and the fall. You could have miscarried. It won't be safe for you to carry on with your current job.'

'No!' she shouted, digging her nails into the palm of his hand. She watched him wince from the resulting pain, and almost enjoyed it. 'I'm not going to lose my job as head of a murder squad again and become a good little doctor's wife at home. You can forget about that.' Almost as soon as the words were out of her mouth, she regretted them. Emil looked crestfallen. Although she'd been honest, it was presumptuous. There had been no offer of marriage. Perhaps there never would be. 'Sorry,' she said. 'I didn't mean it to come out like that. But I want to work. I enjoy my work. If we're having this baby –'

'If?'

'All right, when. When we have this baby, I'm going to be continuing to work.'

'But surely not as –'

'Yes,' she said, firmly. 'As the head of a murder squad. That's what I do. The People's Police promoted me to that position, and although at one stage they may have regretted it, they're happy enough to trumpet how it shows that equality is very much in place in the *Kripo* – even though there are no women in leadership roles. So you'll need to get used to it, Emil.'

Her doctor boyfriend raised his eyebrows, but said nothing. The semi-argument over her role as a mother had cleared her mind, and she realised he was still wearing his white doctor's coat. He saw her staring at it.

'Yes. I'm still on duty. I just came to see you in my lunch hour.' He glanced down at his watch. 'I need to get back.' He leaned in for a kiss on the cheek, but she rotated her face, held the back of his head, and made sure it was full on the lips.

'Well done, Papa,' she whispered.

He rubbed her belly in turn. 'And well done to you too, Mutti.'

She'd hoped her next visitor would be Tilsner, to bring her up to speed with the case – or cases, if they were unconnected. But instead it was Jäger. On his own. No sign of Malkus or Janowitz, thankfully. Since Jäger's appearance on the scene, the local Stasi officers seemed to have melted into the background. But how long would that continue now that the Castro visit was over?

'You nearly stole the show, Karin,' he laughed. 'Comrade Castro continued manfully over the shouting, but your fall stopped his speech. He had to pause until the medics had safely got you on your way to hospital. What happened?'

Did Jäger need to know she was pregnant? She wasn't going to tell him, at least not until things were so obvious she could no longer hide it. But aside from a slight swelling that she'd previously put down to overeating, nothing was showing yet. 'In all the jostling I lost my balance, Comrade *Oberst*.' She couldn't help herself uttering the formality, despite the unusual – and informal – setting. 'I fell and hit my head. Knocked myself out, apparently, though I remember little of it.'

'How long are they planning to keep you here?'

'I think just a day or two for observation. Tilsner will be able to take charge while I'm away, don't worry. Did you arrest –'

Jäger held his hand up to stop her, while glancing around the hospital ward. He leaned in closer. 'Let's not talk about it here, Karin. But yes, everything was dealt with successfully. I don't think it's part of anything bigger, anything to worry about. I can tell you more once you're out of hospital.'

'What about the other matter?'

Jäger looked puzzled. 'What other matter?'

'The questions I had for you. The information I wanted you to find.'

'Ah. No, I'm sorry. As you can imagine, I've been very busy with the Castro visit. But now that's done and dusted, I may have more time. I haven't forgotten, don't worry.'

With that, he patted the bedclothes over her legs and said his goodbyes.

The lack of progress in finding information about her natural mother – or her father – was a disappointment to Müller. If – and it was a big if – they were still alive, they would soon be grandparents. That made it all the more vital to discover their whereabouts for their sakes, for Müller's sake and – as she rubbed her stomach – for the sake of her unborn child.

44

I knew it couldn't last. Whenever something wonderful happens to me, something horrible follows it – always, always, always. We were so happy. I was feeding Heike properly with the bottles, just as Hansi told me to. I'm sure it wasn't my fault.

But Hansi had always warned me that the doctor had said she was quite a fragile child. What with her being born early after I had my blackout. But to me, she seemed to be doing well.

So it was a horrible shock to learn – after visiting the doctor for a check-up (for myself, not the baby, she stayed with Hansi in the flat) – that Hansi had had to take Heike in to the hospital. And that she'd been admitted. She was very poorly, he said, and had to be put in an isolation ward.

'Can I visit her?' I asked. I'm sure he could see the need in my eyes.

But *his* eyes looked cold, hard. He can get like that sometimes. 'No, Franzi. I'm sorry. She's gone to the Ministry hospital. She'll get the best care there. I hope it will only be for a few weeks.'

'Weeks?! I can't see her for the next few weeks?'

He shook his head. 'Don't make this difficult, Franzi. It's for the best. You know what happened last time.'

There wasn't a lot I could say to that. I know he still blames me for what happened to Stefi. But that was nearly ten years ago, surely he will forgive me at some stage. I did my best. Oh Heike, Heike. I hope you will be all right. I'll pray for you every night.

45

December 1975
Halle-Neustadt

Weeks, then months passed, with little or no progress in the investigation. The handwriting search still seemed their best hope of a breakthrough, but it was a gargantuan task that proceeded with glacial speed. For Müller and Tilsner, working on the inquiry was hampered further by having to pick up some of the more mundane criminal cases in the new town: thefts, assaults and other anti-socialist activity. Janowitz, on behalf of the Stasi, had in a number of meetings openly stated that there was little point in Müller and Tilsner still being seconded from Berlin, and implied that the Stasi could now handle the investigation – or what was left of it – on their own.

Now winter was upon them. If Halle-Neustadt in the summer and autumn was all that was right with the Republic – with the promise of a shining new apartment for all citizens – that couldn't be said to be true in winter. As the calendar turned to December, everyone started to think about Christmas, with decorations already for sale in the *Kaufhalle* and special products on sale at Klara Salzmann's meat counter. But Müller felt anything but festive. The smogs here – with the brown coal and chemical pollution from Leuna and Buna – were as bad as, if not worse than, anything she'd so far encountered in the Hauptstadt. And while her morning sickness had eventually cleared, now her ever-expanding belly was starting to weigh her down. He – or she – was going to be a big one.

The acid smogs had given her a hacking, persistent cough, much to Tilsner's annoyance.

'You need to get that checked out. Or buy some cough mixture, one of the two. I don't want you giving it to me.' Müller threw him a withering look.

They were both heads down, helping the Stasi team wade through the piles and piles of waste newspapers collected by the Pioneers on their barrows. The actual collecting was now at an end, but Müller, Tilsner and the *MfS* operatives were little more than halfway through the giant stacks of newspapers, and the forms obtained by less innocent methods. One of these had been a fake competition at the various *Kaufhalle* around Ha-Neu, where shoppers – if they wanted to win – had to complete a verse in capital letters in their own handwriting: one which contained plenty of capital 'E's.

Tilsner sighed, and slammed the pile of newspapers he'd just been about to check back down on the table. '*Scheisse!* This isn't what I signed up for, Karin. We're getting nowhere.' He got up from the table and went across to make coffees for the team.

Müller moved to his chair and started on his discarded pile – attracted by the photograph on the front of the uppermost paper, a copy of *Neues Deutschland*. It was the report from a couple of months back of Fidel Castro's visit to Ha-Neu. The photograph obviously showed nothing controversial – just the local Party secretary, flanked by Castro and Honecker, in front of a scale model of Ha-Neu. She scanned the report itself. What did she expect to find? Mention of her fall? Mention of the rumoured Committee for the Dispossessed, who Jäger now claimed had disbanded after the arrest of some of their leading members? Unsurprisingly, there was none of that. Just tedious accounts of the various long-winded speeches.

As Tilsner whistled to himself by the coffee machine, Müller idly turned the pages of the paper till she got to the puzzle section. Her eye scanned down to the crossword. Suddenly she felt a pricking sensation on the back of her neck.

'Come and look at this!' she shouted, leaping up at the same time.

The rest of the team huddled round, Tilsner sloshing coffee on the floor from his and Müller's cups as he rushed over. Müller felt the baby in her womb kick out in complaint at being disturbed. She didn't care. He or she would have to get used to it.

Because there they were, as clear as a rare clear day over Ha-Neu. In every completed clue which included an 'E', the hand-writing exactly matched the strange letter 'E's discovered by Schmidt in the newspaper back in the summer. The newspaper which had been used by the killer – or rather the *abductor* – to wrap up Karsten Salzmann's cold, tiny, dead body.

All the piles of waste paper had been labelled by the Pioneer teams with residential complex number, block number, floor number and – where known – the actual apartment number.

That's what Müller and Tilsner had told them they had to do to get their pocket money reward from the People's Police fund. Now their diligence, their accuracy, would be put to the test. Thankfully this pile of papers had the full information: Complex Eight, Block 358, Apartment 329 on the third floor. Without having to check on the street map of Ha-Neu pinned to the wall, Müller knew immediately where Block 358 was. Ha-Neu's strange layout was now almost indelibly printed on her brain. It was in the far north-east of the new town, right on the edge. Bang next to Stasi headquarters.

Tilsner had worked it out too. He cupped his hand to her ear. 'I bet it's on Malkus's forbidden list.'

'I don't care if it is,' whispered Müller, careful not to let their Stasi colleagues hear.

Tilsner was all for haring round there straightaway, blue lights and sirens announcing their coup. But Müller advised caution.

'After six months we're not in any rush. Let's find out as much as possible about who lives there first. Is it a family? A single person? Where do they work? That sort of thing. Once we're armed with the facts, then we can go in and get the bastard.'

'Or bastards.'

Müller nodded, and rubbed her stomach thoughtfully.

Their investigations – with the help of the Stasi – revealed the occupants were an elderly couple, with no connections with the *MfS* despite where they lived. Müller was disappointed at first: they didn't fit the expected profile of baby abductors, although originally the graphology expert Professor Morgenstern had insisted the handwriting may have been a pensioner's. But when they discovered the couple had never had children, and that medical files for the wife – Gertrud Rosenbaum – showed a number of miscarriages, Müller became convinced they were on to something. Her conviction became near certainty when Tilsner revealed that Frau Rosenbaum was a voluntary helper at the paediatric wing of the hospital.

They could have taken a softly-softly approach with the pensioner, but Müller decided to go in hard. She ordered a dawn raid and arrest – with Frau Rosenbaum taken straight to the Red Ox remand centre. Müller knew people in Ha-Neu and Halle itself feared the Red Ox. Frau Rosenbaum was old enough to know its history: originally opened as a penal and reform centre by Prussia in the mid-nineteenth century, under the Nazis it had entered its darkest period – as an execution centre.

Müller and Tilsner sat side by side in the bare interrogation room, behind a desk with a single telephone and single lamp. On the other side of the desk, a lone stool. Guards from Eschler's uniform branch brought the old woman in, and then pushed her down on the stool, cuffing her hands together over her lap. Normally, the two detectives would use a good *Kripo*, bad *Kripo* technique. But Müller couldn't be bothered. She just wanted to frighten the woman, who sat sobbing in front of them.

'What have you done with Tanja?' she barked.

The woman looked startled. 'What do you mean? I've done nothing wrong.'

Tilsner slammed his hand down on the table, vibrating the bell on the plastic phone. 'The baby you stole.'

'I wouldn't do anything like that.' She stared into Müller's eyes. 'You're a woman. You have to believe me. Who is Tanja? Is she a girl from the paediatric ward? I just go there to help out. I don't even get paid. I love little children. I would never harm one, never steal one.'

Müller held the woman's gaze. 'Where were you on the evening of October the twenty-first this year?'

She could see the panic in the woman's eyes as she realised the seriousness of the allegations. Her whole body was shaking with fear. 'I . . . I can't remember. How can you expect me to remember? W-w-what day was it?'

Tilsner started to turn the pages of his notebook to check, but Müller recalled it straightaway. 'It was a Tuesday.'

The woman became even more agitated, holding her hand to her wrinkled brow. 'A Tuesday evening?'

Müller nodded.

'I . . . I would have been at the hospital. I always help out in the ward on Tuesday evenings. I used to be a nurse.'

Drumming his fingers on the table in a fast rhythm, Tilsner took up the attack. 'Do you get a meal break, anything like that? Where would you have been at seven p.m.?'

The woman seemed to relax slightly, knowing she had an alibi for that time. 'In the ward. I would have only started at six p.m. I don't usually take a break until about nine.'

'And can anyone verify that?' asked Müller.

'Yes, of course. We clock in and out.'

Tilsner snorted. 'It's easy enough to get someone to clock in for you, though, isn't it?'

'Why would I want to do that?' asked the woman. Müller noticed the beginning of anger, rather than fear, creeping into her tone. The detective reached into her briefcase and took out a pen and a blank piece of paper.

'Can you write the word "*DEZEMBER*" please, in capitals, in your usual handwriting. And don't try to fake different writing, we will cross-check it against other documents you've filled in.'

The woman's face creased in puzzlement, but she took up the pen and began to write.

'In *capitals*, Citizen Rosenbaum!' shouted Tilsner. 'Didn't you hear what the Comrade *Oberleutnant* said?'

'Sorry, sorry,' said the woman. 'I'll try again.' She crossed out her first effort and Müller watched the pen shake as – this time – she completed the simple task. They'd compare it later with the control sample copied from the newspaper wrapped around Karsten's body. But from memory, Müller knew it was almost identical.

Even if the woman herself had an alibi, had someone from her flat picked up a newspaper containing one of her discarded crosswords? Or had they deliberately taken a thrown-away paper, to try to deflect the blame onto an innocent old woman? Müller softened her voice as she asked her next question.

'Let's assume for a moment that your story checks out, Frau Rosenbaum. What we're interested in is a crossword, completed in a copy of the *Neues Deutschland* newspaper, that is linked to the disappearance of a baby. Possibly a number of babies.'

The woman gasped.

Tilsner banged his hand down on the table again. 'Never repeat that beyond the confines of this room. Not to your husband. Not to anyone.'

'So,' continued Müller, 'do you ever do the newspaper crossword when you're in the hospital?'

Frau Rosenbaum shook her head vigorously. 'No. Never. There's never enough time, really. Apart from a short meal break – when I just go and get a cup of coffee or something – we're busy all the time. Changing nappies, changing bedding, helping the nurses out with whatever they need.'

Tilsner drew in a deep breath. 'OK, Citizen Rosenbaum. What about your husband?'

'What about him?'

Tilsner rolled his eyes. 'Where would *he* have been on the evening of Tuesday, October the twenty-first?'

The woman shrugged. 'Well, I don't know for definite, not without asking him. But Tuesday is skittle night. He plays for a team attached to a bar in Halle Nietleben. The Grüne Tanne.' Müller remembered it as the guest house where she, Vogel and Eschler had held one of their first meetings about the Salzmann twins case. 'So,' said the woman, 'I expect he'd be there. Unless they were playing a team from a different town or village. I can check with him if you like.'

Müller folded her arms across her stomach and sighed. The baby kicked in response. Frau Rosenbaum noticed her grimace.

'Is it a girl, or a boy? . . . That is? . . .' Müller watched her pause as she realised it wasn't her place to be asking the question, her face reddening – obviously wondering if she was mistaken, despite Müller's obviously distended stomach.

'It's OK, Frau Rosenbaum. I *am* pregnant, yes.' She smiled at the woman. If her story checked out – and Müller's instinct was that it would – then, despite the handwriting match, they were no nearer to solving the case. Inside she felt desperate, but it wasn't poor Frau Rosenbaum's fault. 'But I don't want to know what sex the baby is. It'll be a nice surprise.' Müller started gathering her papers together, and placed them back in her briefcase.

'Is that it, then?' asked the woman.

'If your story and your husband's movements check out, then yes,' said Tilsner. 'You both appear to have alibis for the time frame we're looking at. You're free to go.'

Müller gave the woman another smile. 'Thank you for your assistance, Frau Rosenbaum. I'm sorry that some of our initial questioning may have seemed a little tough. As you can appreciate, this is a serious case. And as the Comrade *Unterleutnant* said, do not under any circumstances mention anything about our inquiry to anyone, not even your husband. Otherwise you could get into serious trouble.'

'I understand, *Oberleutnant*. I want to help. I love little children. It's strange that I've been brought in because of a crossword I completed in *Neues Deutschland*. We only buy it on special occasions. I'd wanted a keepsake of Prime Minister Castro's visit.

I certainly didn't mean to put it out with the rubbish. My husband must have done it by mistake.'

Müller nodded. She'd hoped it would provide a breakthrough at last. But she couldn't believe the old woman was a child-snatcher.

Frau Rosenbaum's alibi – once checked – seemed watertight. Müller examined the clocking-in records at the hospital's paediatric unit. They did indeed show that the elderly woman volunteer was on duty the evening Tanja's baby had been snatched from outside the bar in Halle. Yet she hadn't been there when the Salzmann twins were taken. Tilsner had a more difficult job pinning down exactly where the Grüne Tanne's skittle team had been that night. But, eventually, he established that Herr Rosenbaum had been playing that evening – helping the team to a win in an away match in Merseburg. Although old man Rosenbaum wasn't always selected for the team, making way for younger members, teammates remembered that night because he'd been on fire – achieving the highest score of the night, with several clearances.

It left Müller and Tilsner despondent. Not only had another lead turned into a dead end, but they were, if anything, further away than ever from solving the case. If Frau Rosenbaum wasn't the person they were hunting – and it seemed clear she wasn't – then Professor Morgenstern's contention that the handwriting style was highly unusual was wide of the mark.

46

January 1976
Halle

The New Year promised to be a significant one in Müller's home life, as her pregnancy bump grew ever larger. But at work, things were stagnating. They'd exhausted every lead they could think of in searching for Tanja Haase or her abductor. The Salzmann twins investigation now assumed less significance, with Maddelena safe and Karsten's death now confirmed as *not* a result of murder. As for the 'cold' case of the Andereggs' twins, Müller and Tilsner could find nothing to directly link it to the wider investigation. Müller herself felt exhausted most of the time, as her belly expanded at the same time as her appetite. Never mind eating for two, she felt as though she was eating for a whole family.

As she and Emil packed the Christmas decorations away in the flat – his flat – that they now shared, she could tell her boyfriend had something on his mind. He'd been unnaturally quiet, but now – hesitantly – he broke the silence.

'You're struggling with that box, Karin. Just let me do it. You need to rest more. I was thinking the other day that it might be time to –'

'Don't say it, Emil.'

'Well, you're nearly six months gone now. You're exhausted every evening after work. Exhausted and depressed. If the inquiry isn't getting anywhere, perhaps you should consider ... well, slowing down at least.'

Müller pulled a face and sighed. The problem was, she knew he was right. 'We've been called to a meeting tomorrow. I think my decision may be taken for me. But you might not like it. There's a good chance they'll wind things up here, and send me back to the Hauptstadt.'

'Well, we don't want that. At least, I don't want that. I won't be able to free myself from my work here immediately. I can ask for a transfer back to a hospital in Berlin, but it would take time.'

'I don't want it either. Not yet. Although I want to bring up our child in Berlin, not here.'

Emil took the box of decorations out of her hands, placed it on the dining table, and then coaxed Müller down next to him on the sofa. He held both her hands in his, and she found herself staring into his blue eyes. Blue like Tilsner's, blue like her own.

'Why don't you take the initiative? Say you're feeling ill – it's not a lie, I can tell – and ask for some time off.'

'And what about Tilsner?'

'He's still officially recuperating too, isn't he? Perhaps they'd let him keep things going on a semi-mothballed basis. He's probably not fully ready to get back into the thick of things in the Hauptstadt anyway, is he?'

The meeting was scheduled for 9 a.m. the next day at Halle district People's Police HQ, rather than the Ha-Neu police office. Tilsner – who basically had Müller and Schmidt's *Wohnkomplex VI* apartment to himself now Schmidt had gone back to Berlin – picked Müller up from her boyfriend's apartment in the Wartburg. The rush hour traffic was surprisingly heavy, so they had to park quickly and run to the meeting room.

'Hang on!' shouted Müller, leaning against the corridor wall and panting. 'You're forgetting I'm nearly six months gone.'

Tilsner raised his eyebrows. 'I don't think I could forget, Karin. Shall I go on ahead and make your excuses?'

'No, just give me a second to get my breath back.'

When they arrived, the Halle police chief, *Oberst* Frenzel, was sitting behind a long table, flanked by Malkus and Janowitz. Jäger had now returned to Berlin – and possibly back to Cuba, as far as Müller knew – all without providing any of the promised information about her natural mother or father. She'd set that to one side for the moment; her baby had to take precedence.

'Ah, Karin, Werner. Many thanks for joining us,' said Frenzel. His greeting appeared genuinely warm. Malkus wore a thin, unconvincing smile. Janowitz sat there glowering, as usual. How much better it had been for those few weeks when Jäger had been in charge of the Stasi side of things. She didn't think she would ever see eye to eye with Malkus or Janowitz. Maybe they just didn't like women in positions of authority. 'So,' continued Frenzel, 'I wanted us to have a catch-up because I think we need to make some difficult decisions about your investigation. As you know, *Major* Malkus has been very generous in providing manpower, but that's got to come to an end now. And the Ministry for State Security has been given a report by *Hauptmann* Janowitz saying that – in effect – your team doesn't seem to be getting anywhere very quickly.'

'But –' Müller's attempts to interject were cut short by Frenzel raising his hand, palm outwards, and throwing her a fierce stare. But she was angry too – angry that Janowitz was trying to undermine everything.

'As I say, we need to take some difficult decisions. What I've decided is –'

Frenzel was in turn interrupted by someone rapping hard on the office door. He sighed. 'Enter!'

A uniformed officer who looked as though he'd been running all the way from the control room stood panting in the doorway.

'Sorry to interrupt, Comrade *Oberst*, but *Hauptmann* Eschler's on the telephone wanting to speak to *Oberleutnant* Müller.'

Frenzel closed his eyes in annoyance, then drew his hands down over his face. 'You'd better go, Karin. And you, I suppose, Comrade Tilsner. We'll take this up again later today – if we can. And if it's still relevant.'

As they left the room, out of the corner of her eye Karin saw Tilsner wink at Janowitz. It didn't raise a smile.

*

Eschler told Müller to meet him at the boathouse on Rabeninsel – an island in the Saale, south of Peissnitz, and – like its larger cousin – bordered by the wild Saale river to the west, and the navigable watercourse to the east. The only access was from a footbridge in the Böelberg district in Halle city. Members of the rowing club there had reported seeing something suspicious at the back of their clubhouse.

By the time the two Berlin detectives arrived, uniformed officers – led by Eschler and Fernbach – had sealed off the whole of Rabeninsel, and evacuated the café next to the boat- house. They'd cordoned off the back of the building with police tape, and had started to dig, struggling with the semi-frozen ground. Eschler proffered a plastic evidence bag. Müller took it, and almost immediately knew what it was: Tanja Haase's rabbit soft toy – the one she'd seen when they'd first visited Tanja and her mother back in July. The one Anneliese had said was with Tanja in her pram, outside the bar, at the time she disappeared.

'On its own,' said Eschler, 'it wouldn't have been enough to make anyone suspicious or raise the alarm. But it looked like the ground nearby had been freshly dug over. Seeing this, one of the rowers had taken matters into his own hands, got a shovel, and started to dig, even though the ground was partly frozen. His spade hit something solid, he tried to dig through it, and heard a slight crunching sound. As though he'd hit a stone or something. So he reached with his hand into the soil, and pulled this out.'

Eschler held up a second evidence bag. Inside it, severed at the wrist, with soil mixed in with blood, was a human hand. A perfectly formed, dainty, infant child's hand. Despite the dirt, Müller could immediately see the slightly olive, tanned look to the skin. The hand of a mixed-race child. The hand – she was almost certain – of Tanja Haase.

Müller didn't want to take Anneliese to the morgue, but knew it was something she had to do. It wasn't a job she relished at the best of times, getting a parent to identify their dead child. In this case, the pathologist had been able to give an early – and fairly definite – cause of death. Asphyxiation. By manual strangulation. The bruise marks were obvious around the child's neck.

As the baby's body was wheeled out of the cooler on a trolley, Anneliese held on to Muller's right hand tightly, leaning her body against the detective. When the murdered infant's face was uncovered, Anneliese's weight collapsed against Müller. The pregnant detective struggled to hold her up.

'Can you confirm this is Tanja?'

The girl didn't reply.

'Anneliese?' coaxed Müller.

The detective felt as much as saw the slight nod of Anneliese's head. Müller had warned the mortuary assistant ahead of time to make sure the neck was covered – that only the face was showing. She didn't want to add to Anneliese's distress.

'Just to make this absolutely clear, Anneliese. Can you confirm this is the body of your daughter?'

The girl tried to pull forward, to get to her dead baby. Müller struggled to hold her back, and the mortuary assistant intervened.

'I need you to actually answer the question, Anneliese. I'm sorry.'

In between her crying, her attempts to pull away from Müller and the assistant, the girl finally uttered a weak and plaintive 'Yes'.

47

March 1976
Halle-Neustadt

Perhaps as soon as Colonel Frenzel had heard about Eschler's urgent call for Müller he'd known that the decision of the People's Police and the Stasi – to scale back Müller and Tilsner's inquiry – would have to be put on hold. The discovery of Tanja's body on an island in the Saale, one used by walkers, canoeists and rowers, meant that any efforts to maintain a news blackout would prove futile. Once again, Müller was conflicted in the way that only a homicide detective could be: the discovery that baby Tanja had been killed was tragic. The devastation wreaked on Anneliese Haase was cruel beyond words and had Müller stroking her stomach every few minutes, willing her own baby to be safe. But it also offered the hope of new leads. The fact that Rabeninsel was such a popular leisure area – it even had a passenger ferry terminal – gave Müller and Tilsner the hope that someone would have seen the baby either being killed, or being buried.

So while the Stasi team checking for matching handwriting in the Salzmann case redoubled their efforts, Müller, Tilsner and Eschler organised uniformed officers to perform an exhaustive audit of who used Rabeninsel – concentrating particularly on the boathouse.

But as hours became days, and days became weeks, they failed to find anything of significance. This was despite a thorough examination by forensic officers of the area where the body had been found, and of everything that had been buried with Tanja – or accidentally dropped or deliberately planted nearby, such as the toy rabbit. The rabbit became a symbol of the frustrations of the case – or cases – to Müller. An autopsy confirmed that Tanja had been strangled some hours before being buried. But if the killer had managed to cover his or her tracks so well – so that there was no significant forensic evidence, and no witnesses to the dumping and burying of the body – why had the child's soft toy been left in such an obvious place? Did the killer want to be caught? And the only links – so far – to the Salzmann case were tenuous ones of geography and timing. The only link to the Andereggs' twins was . . . what? A Halle-Neustadt bus ticket.

A well-aimed kick from her ever-growing baby inside her womb broke Müller's train of thought.

'Are you OK?' asked Tilsner. 'Maybe –'

'Don't you start, Werner. I've been getting that all the time at the apartment from Emil. Don't worry, I'll know when it's time to stop working.'

They were in the fire station, in the hangar-like room set aside for Tilsner and his Stasi operatives to trawl through the piles of waste newspapers. It was where they came when all other leads had resulted in dead ends, their fallback hope that one of these newspapers would be the golden ticket – containing a crossword completed by someone who wrote their capital 'E's in the same way as whoever had wrapped up Karsten's tiny body. The trouble was, Frau Rosenbaum's handwriting had already looked exactly like that 'golden ticket' – only for her and her husband to have solid alibis.

When Müller returned to Emil's flat at the end of the day, she suddenly felt much worse. The room appeared to be spinning, and she sat down, clutching her stomach, seconds after coming through the front door.

'I'll be OK in a moment,' she said, as Emil rushed to her side.

'No,' he said, getting some apparatus out of his bag, and then pressing his fingers to her face and hands. 'It looks like you've got some swelling. I need to check your blood pressure.'

'Why?' asked Müller, putting her hand to her brow. A sharp headache had suddenly started. 'What's wrong? I'm sure I'll be fine after a sit down.'

Emil wrapped the blood pressure cuff around her arm just above the elbow, and then began to pump the rubber bulb. He listened with his stethoscope as he released the pressure, and Müller saw his face crease in anxiety as he checked the reading.

'It's too high,' he said. 'We need to get you looked at.' Then he felt gently around Müller's wrist, forearm and the sides of her face.

'It's nothing serious, though, is it?' Müller found herself twisting her hair with one hand. Emil carefully pulled her arm down.

'Don't do that. You always do that when you're anxious. I'm sure it's nothing to worry about, but we ought to go to the hospital to check.'

Müller allowed her boyfriend to drive her to the hospital. Her head felt like some great weight was pressing down on the top of it, and Emil's anxious looks were making her worried. She found herself constantly swallowing, fighting a tightness in her throat.

Once in the hospital, Emil's connections meant they were seen almost immediately.

A plump friendly nursing auxiliary fussed over Müller, urging her to lie back on the bed, and getting her files ready for the doctors. As Emil went off to get one of his colleagues, Müller saw the woman staring intently at the file, as though shocked by something.

'There's nothing wrong, is there?' asked Müller.

The woman closed the file quickly, a slightly guilty expression on her face, thought Müller. Or perhaps there *was* something wrong, but it wasn't this junior worker's place to tell Müller.

'No, no, dear. Your man's just gone to get one of the duty paediatricians. I was just checking your notes. Everything's fine. They'll be with you in a moment.'

As Emil returned with a white-coated doctor, the woman rushed from the room.

He frowned at Müller. 'Why was she in such a hurry?'

'I don't know,' Müller replied. 'Just some nurse who was getting me comfortable.'

The doctor started to perform the same tests that Emil had back in the apartment. Taking her blood pressure, pushing down against her skin, then checking her eyes.

He picked up Müller's file and flicked through it, and then placed it down firmly on the bedside table.

'Karin,' he said finally. 'It looks as though we'll want you to stay in hospital for a few days while we run some further tests.'

Müller clutched at her stomach. She'd felt the baby move a few moments ago – surely there was nothing wrong? 'What is it you're worried about?'

Emil took her hand and held it gently, massaging her fingers. 'It's probably nothing, but there appears to be some slight swelling and your blood pressure's on the high side. You've got the symptoms of possible mild pre-eclampsia.'

'What's that?'

'It's a fairly common side-effect of pregnancy,' said the doctor. 'We'll need to take a urine sample to check for protein. What we want to do – given your medical history – is admit you to hospital for a few days just to check everything is OK. It really is very common and nothing to worry about.'

Müller had desperately wanted to stay at work until the very last moment. She felt she owed it to Anneliese Haase, to the

Salzmanns – the Andereggs, even. She and Tilsner had so far failed them. Müller wanted to put that right. But for now her police work would have to wait. She turned onto her side in the bed, and feebly punched the side of the pillow by her head in frustration.

48

Müller's initial alarm at the hospital admission – her fears that once again she might lose her chance of having a child – abated as days passed, and her blood pressure settled. But the medical professionals didn't seem in any hurry to discharge her. With only a month to go until her due date, Emil explained that one option might be a Caesarean section; it wasn't something Müller wanted. He also started to try to tell her more about the ultrasound and what it had found. Müller stopped him mid-sentence.

'I told you, Emil. I don't want to know anything about it. Not whether it's a girl, a boy, any possible disabilities they've picked up on – nothing. I want this child. Whatever will be, will be.'

Amid the boredom of reading trashy novels and magazines borrowed from the hospital bookshelves, Müller was pleased when – on the third day of her stay – Tilsner was allowed to visit. Emil had kept him away before for fear that Müller would once again throw herself into work. She persuaded him that keeping her mind occupied would be good for her.

'You look better than I expected,' said Tilsner, smiling. 'Don't you just want to pump it out now and have done with it?'

'It's still nearly four weeks till I'm due. Anyway, apparently the state I'm in –'

Tilsner held his hands up, palms outward, as Müller gestured towards her groin. 'No. That's enough. I didn't come here to talk about female anatomy, thanks.'

'Don't be such a baby,' laughed Müller. 'Anyway, it looks likely that I'll be having a Caesarean. They think a natural delivery would be too risky.'

'Fantastic,' said Tilsner. 'That's a result, I'd say. Koletta wanted me there and I gave in. Marius was a so-called natural delivery. There was nothing natural about it. All the blood, the pushing and pulling, I thought his head was going to ex—'

This time it was Müller's turn to put her hand up in a 'stop' sign. 'I thought the idea was you were visiting me to take my mind off things. Not to remind me about the horror of childbirth.'

Tilsner grinned. 'Sorry.'

'So, any progress?'

Tilsner cocked his head. Then he reached into his brief-case and pulled out an olive-green cardboard file. It looked to Müller like it had seen better days; the green at the edges had faded from exposure to light over what looked to have been several years.

'What's that?' she asked.

'Something Wiedemann turned up which he said you might be interested in looking at.' Tilsner started leafing through the file until he got to the relevant place. Then he rotated it and passed it to Müller.

She rested it on the blanket covering her baby bump, and began to read.

'It's an accident report. A road accident report. From Halle. *In 1958?* What possible relevance has this got to anything?'

Tilsner snorted. 'To be honest, probably nothing. We've been up so many dead ends in this inquiry already, it's no doubt just another one. But it's not just *any* road accident report. It was a fatal accident.'

'And?'

Tilsner turned the page for Müller.

'Well, it may be nothing. But the victims were twin babies. The parents survived, but the babies died.'

Müller tried to concentrate on the report but her brain felt woolly, her thoughts confused. 'So why is it relevant to our inquiry?'

Tilsner shrugged. 'Fairly early on in the inquiry, we asked Wiedemann to look for any strange reports of baby deaths or baby abductions, particularly involving twins. As you know, in terms of his Party duties, he's nothing if not assiduous. Although actually he's not a bad sort once you get to know him. Wicked sense of humour. And he can drink me under the table. He mentioned this in the bar. He was a bit reticent at first. Wants us to treat it very carefully.'

'Why?'

'Look at the outcome.'

'There is no outcome. It's been taken out of the People's Police hands.'

'Exactly. Like that case on Rügen. The complaint by the *Jugendwerkhof* girl's grandmother. What was the phrase?'

Müller looked down at the file. '"Suggest refer this to the Ministry for State Security" – that's what it says here too.'

'And there's no other conclusion to the case. No prosecution, nothing. No details or name of the other driver. Even the names of the dead babies and their parents have been obscured with correction fluid.'

Müller's brow creased in confusion. 'Even so, this is a road traffic accident. It's not a baby abduction case.'

Tilsner raised his eyebrows. 'Aha. Not so fast. Our friend Comrade Wiedemann did a bit more digging, didn't he? There's another police report from the same evening.' Tilsner turned a few pages of the file, then pointed at the entry for Müller. 'Read that one. Same evening, a couple of hours after the accident.'

Müller read it, as instructed, trying to make sense of the letters which seemed to dance in front of her eyes. A dull pain from inside her skull pressed against her forehead. She breathed in deeply, and wiped her face with her hand.

'Are you OK, Karin?' asked Tilsner. He reached to take the file back. 'I'll go if this is too much for you.'

Tightening her hands on the folder, Müller shook her head. 'It's OK.' She forced herself to concentrate. It was the report of another road incident. A car with a badly damaged front grille and a broken headlight had been stopped while driving in Halle. The occupant had explained he had been in an accident, and was simply taking the vehicle to a safe place. The *Vopos* concerned had allowed the driver on his way without taking further action, even though they'd reported smelling alcohol on his breath and that his eyes seemed unfocussed. A large section of the report had again been covered with correction fluid. Müller held it up towards the window, hoping that with light shining through, a name would become clear. But once again there was nothing. Like the streets that criss-crossed this strange city, these police reports that might help provide a breakthrough in the case had been rendered nameless. But, this time, she had a pretty good idea whose name was missing.

49

Of course, I should have had more faith in my lovely husband, because – oh joy of joys – she's back now in my arms.

Hansi promised it would only be a few weeks, and it was. The Ministry hospital must have worked miracles, because she looks so much better. She's put on a lot of weight and – my, my – isn't she the prettiest thing. I don't know where she gets her looks from. Certainly not from Hansi. And not from her mother either. She is just the absolute definition of cute, and it's wonderful to have her back. I can't stop marvelling at her little button nose, her perfectly symmetrical face – now where did *that* come from? – and the lovely, healthy colour of her skin.

There's just one thing that concerns me slightly. Her eyes. They look different, somehow. I must ask Hansi about them.

Ha! My man is so clever. He could have been a doctor – well, he did train as one to begin with, before becoming a chemist, so perhaps it's not surprising. Anyway, I'd kept my concerns about her eyes to myself. What I was worried about – if truth be told – is that she might have Mongolism. A very mild version, because of the eyes. But Hansi put my mind at rest. He says lots of normal babies are born with what they call epicanthal folds – it's a bit of skin covering the upper eyelid. They should disappear in time. I was silly to worry.

50

Five months later: March 1976
Halle-Neustadt

Müller hadn't expected things to move so quickly, and she'd wanted Emil to be here, but he wasn't. A doctor she hadn't seen before was explaining the procedure. How there would be nothing to worry about. They would give her a pre-med injection to calm her before taking her down to the operating theatre. The nursing auxiliary was preparing it now.

When the woman turned, she smiled encouragingly at her, and Müller was relieved to see a familiar face. It was the same auxiliary who'd been looking at her medical files that first day in hospital. At least she would know Müller's details, why they had to be careful given the detective's previous gynaecological history.

'Couldn't we wait at least until my boyfriend gets here? Have you told him?' Müller asked, as the auxiliary rubbed her upper arm with a cotton wool ball soaked in something cooling.

The doctor looked into her eyes through his black horn-rimmed spectacles. There was something familiar about his eyes, although the rest of his face was hidden by a surgical mask. 'He knows and is on his way, don't worry. But your blood pressure's deteriorated. We can't afford to wait. We need to deliver your baby now.'

The nursing auxiliary strapped a ligature around Müller's arm to locate a suitable vein, and then Müller felt a sharp prick, and almost immediately became drowsy. She'd had a pre-med before when her wisdom teeth had been taken out. She knew it was a bit like feeling slightly tipsy. That nothing mattered. That's how it felt at first. But something was pulling her. Pulling her towards a black hole. She fought against it, fought for consciousness, but she couldn't, and she was sucked deeper and deeper until unconsciousness claimed her.

51

Tilsner had grown utterly fed up, and envied Schmidt's early departure a few months previously. From day one, down here in Halle, they seemed to have been wading through treacle. There was no clear motive for the crime, no obvious suspects, and no real prospect of coming to an end any time soon. Tilsner had also had more than a bellyful of Halle-Neustadt itself. A city with identical apartments for all its citizens might have seemed a good one at the time of Halle-Neustadt's conception – but it wasn't really Tilsner's collar size.

All the time, he was having to report everything back to Jäger's man at Normannenstrasse. He much preferred dealing with Jäger himself, but his former partner in crime – so to speak – had landed himself a cushy new job in the Caribbean. So it was one of his underlings who got the reports. He suspected Karin knew all about it, or that Jäger had told her. She was, after all, always teasing him about his Rolex.

Tilsner had half expected the said underling to warn him off looking further into the strange car accident from 1958 that had got Wiedemann so excited. But, after apparently liaising with Jäger himself, Tilsner got the message back that he had free rein.

Dig as much, and as far, as he wanted to. The message seemed to be that the Ministry for State Security was as fed up with the Halle babies case as Tilsner was: they wanted an end to it, whatever the consequences.

What Tilsner needed was names – names to fill in the deliberate gaps in both reports. The names of the dead babies and their parents, the name of the driver of the other car. The names that had been obscured. He was hoping the forensic science department of Halle city *Kriminalpolizei* would be able to help.

'You do know we were deliberately kept out of this inquiry,' said the *Kripo* captain when Tilsner made his request.

'I know. It seemed odd, us being brought in from the Hauptstadt. To be honest, I wish we never had been. It's a nightmare of a case. But I've a little theory as to why you've been kept out of things.'

The *Hauptmann* stared at him, stony-faced. 'Oh yes? And why's that?'

Tilsner shrugged. 'I can't say for definite ... let's just say I think it may be something to do with these incidents.'

The Halle *Kripo* captain snorted. 'What? A traffic accident from back in the fifties? You're pulling my leg.'

Tilsner smiled. 'No. I could be wrong, of course. But the only way we'll find out is if you allow your forensic scientist to examine the reports. I'm sure there must be some way of scraping this correction fluid off and revealing the names beneath. Tell you what, if I'm wrong, I'll buy you a drink.'

'A bottle.'

'A bottle?'

The *Hauptmann* gave a slow nod and a sly smile. 'Of whisky. Single malt. Or if you can't get that, then a bottle of *Doppelkorn* would do.'

Tilsner sighed. 'OK. Even though that sounds suspiciously like bribery to me.'

Forensic officer Petra Stober immediately had Tilsner wishing he'd come over to the Halle police science labs at an earlier stage in the inquiry. She was tall, blond and gorgeous. About as much of a contrast to the corpulent Jonas Schmidt as it was possible to get. Evidently this *Kriminaltechniker* didn't spend her free time studying and sampling the many different varieties of *Wurst* available in the Republic.

'It's obviously my lucky day,' he smiled. 'Heaven seems to be missing an angel.'

The twenty-something woman rolled her eyes and sighed. 'Who are you? And what do you want? Other than a kick in the balls . . .'

Tilsner explained that *Hauptmann* had given him permission to avail himself of her services. He pulled the fading olive-green file from his briefcase, and then flicked through to the relevant reports.

'See here. All the names have been concealed with correction fluid.' Tilsner unclipped the pages from the file, and then handed them to her.

Kriminaltechniker Stober switched on a desk lamp, held one of the pages up against the light, then reversed the paper.

'Hmm. Not going to be easy. They've put the fluid on both sides of the paper.'

'Both sides?'

'Hmm. The weight of a typeface from the fifties would normally make an indentation in the paper. We'd have been able to read the names backwards from the other side in a mirror. To prevent that, they've covered the reverse with fluid too.'

'So does that mean you can't help? This is really important – I need to know who was originally mentioned in these reports. Their identity may be the key to unlock a case we're working on.'

Stober rolled her eyes. 'Yes, *everyone* tells me what they need is absolutely vital, and they need it yesterday. I *hope* we can help, but it may take a bit of time.'

'How long?'

'By tomorrow morning? Would that do?'

Tilsner had a sudden vision of Petra Stober in the morning. She was wearing minimal make-up now. He imagined her morning face would be much the same – stunningly beautiful.

She knew he was staring. 'Is that OK, *Unterleutnant*?'

'Yes, yes. Of course. Can you ring me with it at the Ha-Neu incident room?'

52

Petra Stober was as good as her word. But there was a problem. She'd managed to uncover the names of the mother and father of the victims of the road traffic accident. But the second report, the one concerning the drunk driver, had been more heavily doctored. Before correction fluid had been applied, the typed name had been scratched out. There was no way Stober could recover any of it. The Stasi had done their job well. What was it – or *who* was it – that they wanted to keep concealed? He was sure it couldn't be coincidence.

Using what information she had managed to find, the next day Tilsner set about trying to track the parents down with Wiedemann's help – if indeed they still lived in the Halle area. After ploughing through various lists of citizens' addresses, Wiedemann found them. 'Here they are, Comrade *Unterleutnant*.'

Tilsner peered over his shoulder at the address. As he did so, a chill ran through him. This looked like a fuck-up, a major fuck-up. His police instinct knew immediately that the apparently innocuous accident report uncovered by Weidemann *was* the key to this whole damn case. He cross-checked the address against Malkus's 'prohibited' list, pulling it out of his pocket – the half a dozen or so names that the Ministry for State Security had banned the People's Police from investigating. They were on that. And that wasn't the only thing that made Tilsner's heart sink. He recognised the address even if he didn't have the same near-photographic memory that Karin possessed. *Komplex VIII*. Block 358. Apartment 328. *The flat that was bang next door to the Rosenbaums*. Somewhere they should have searched straightaway, as soon as the Rosenbaums' alibis had been corroborated. Yes, it *had* been Frau Rosenbaum's newspaper, and her completed crossword puzzle after all. Not the one the Pioneers had collected – that was an issue from when Castro had visited, weeks after Karsten's body had been dumped. But the handwriting in that paper – the one swaddling the baby boy's torso – *was* Rosenbaum's. Of that, Tilsner was now certain. Her next-door neighbour must have picked up one of her discarded newspapers.

They weren't dealing with an armed gang – at least not as far as Tilsner was aware. Nevertheless, after what had happened in the Harz he was taking no chances. He got his Makarov from the drawer, made sure it was loaded and that he had spare ammunition, and then went to get Eschler and Fernbach. He didn't want to give this bastard – or these bastards if there was more than one – any chance of escape.

Tilsner and Eschler left Fernbach guarding the top of the third-floor stairwell – making sure no one could get in or out of the corridor – while they approached the entrance to Apartment 328.

It was one door further on from the Rosenbaums. As Eschler stood to one side, gun drawn, Tilsner slammed his foot against the door, right at the point where the lock married with the frame. Once, twice, three times he kicked the heel of his boot against it until the frame splintered and the door gave way. With his hand holding the Makarov at the ready, he entered, with Eschler following – having already warned nosy neighbours to get back inside their own apartments.

Inside the flat, there was silence. They checked each of the rooms – lounge, both bedrooms, kitchen and bathroom. No one. But in the second bedroom there was something that told Tilsner his suspicions weren't misplaced. A cot. Baby toys. Empty bottles. Nappies and other infant paraphernalia. And in the lounge – on the mantelpiece – something that left Tilsner clenching his jaw, his nostrils flaring. A photograph showing a rather overweight woman who looked too old for motherhood, standing next to a gangly, bespectacled man. Holding a baby that Tilsner immediately recognised – as Tanja Haase. Next to that photograph, another of the same two adults cradling another baby, who again, Tilsner knew at first glance. Maddelena Salzmann. One of the two abducted Salzmann twins. The one who disappeared, then miraculously reappeared, with no one any the wiser. Another photograph alongside that of the same woman, looking a little younger and considerably larger, wearing 1960s fashion, with another baby. And a final one with the woman and man younger still, this time cradling a baby each. Tilsner didn't know for certain – other than in the case of Tanja and Maddelena – who the babies were. But that final photo – he was sure – was of the infants who'd been killed in the collision.

Tilsner turned, and stared Eschler in the face. '*Scheisse*,' he swore. 'We've all fucked up big time here. They've been under our noses all this time. And now they've legged it.'

'Yes, but legged it where?'

Tilsner gave a long sigh and slumped down on the sofa, staring at the photographs of all the babies and the half-crazed adults who'd stolen them. 'I've no idea. No idea at all. But someone's been protecting them, just as someone's trying to protect the drunk who was driving the car.'

53

When Müller regained consciousness, she had an initial rush of joy surge through her. She was alive. And, she knew, she was a mother at last. All the hurt, all the terrible memories of Walter Pawlitzki, all had been wiped away. She knew she wouldn't be having to open her secret drawer anymore in the flat in Schönhauser Allee. No more stroking of those baby clothes. She'd burn them and put the past – finally – to bed.

Müller beamed at the nurse when she arrived for her morning round. She hadn't wanted to know the sex of her child before delivery, but now she needed to know if she had a son or a daughter. She wanted, needed to hold him or her. To cradle her baby in her arms and feed it from her breasts.

'Is it a boy or girl?' she asked, aware she sounded slightly breathless.

'Now then, Frau Müller,' chided the nurse. 'You said you didn't want to know. We're under strict instructions.'

'Yes, but that was before.'

The nurse's sunny face creased in puzzlement. 'Before what?'

Müller found herself getting increasingly frustrated. 'Before my Caesarean. Before my baby –'

The nurse's eyes opened wide. She grabbed the sheet Müller had been holding up towards her chin and yanked it down. The dressings, the contracted state of Müller's stomach told her all she needed to know.

'Oh my God.' The nurse ran over to an alarm button on the side of the wall and pressed it. A siren blared.

As Müller covered her ears, panic coursed through her. 'What's wrong? What's wrong?' she shouted. 'Where's my baby?'

The nurse ignored her. 'Doctor, doctor,' she screamed from the doorway. 'Come here immediately.'

Müller still couldn't understand what was wrong. Why wouldn't they let her hold her child? What was all the panic about? Everything felt like a living nightmare. She wasn't sure what was real and what wasn't.

Only when Emil finally arrived did she start to calm slightly.

'They won't let me hold the baby. They won't even tell me what sex he or she is. Do you know, Emil? Do you know?' She searched her doctor boyfriend's face for an answer, but his appearance was as ashen and pale as everyone else's.

Finally, he took Müller's hands in his own.

'There's no easy way to say this, Karin. You have to stay calm and I'm sure it will all get sorted out. Yes, you have had your Caesarean. You haven't dreamt it. But we don't know who performed it. And we don't know where the babies are.'

'Babies. Oh my God! You mean twins?'

Emil nodded. 'A boy and a girl – the hospital knew all along from the ultrasound, but you insisted you didn't want to know.

But I'm sure we're going to find them. There's just been some horrible mix up.'

'This isn't a mix up. Someone's stolen my twins!' She started to try to get out of bed, her breathing coming in short gasps, but Emil held her down. He gestured with his head to the nurse, who started preparing a sedative injection.

'No!' Müller shouted, fighting against her boyfriend. 'You have to let me up. I have to find them.' But the prick of the needle in her arm defeated her.

54

Two months earlier: January 1976
Komplex VIII, Halle-Neustadt

I don't know what to do. I can't tell Hansi. I can't tell him the truth. He's been so good to me that it can't end like this.

Perhaps I could say she's been stolen. I heard some of the women gossiping about stolen babies. One was taken in Halle a few months ago, they were saying. Right in the city centre, near the Handel monument. Right where everyone could see. Couldn't someone have stopped them?

But then if I said that, the police would come round. They'd find out what really happened. I have nightmares every night about her perfect little face. Perfect in every respect, except for those eyes.

Hansi isn't so perfect himself. I know he isn't. He has his secrets. He must keep them in that metal box that he never lets me look in. The one with the padlock on. Says it's his Ministry work. His Ministry secrets. Well, we all have secrets, Hansi. Perhaps I need to discover a few of yours.

I crash the hammer down on the lock. The neighbours will hear, but I no longer care. Crash. Crash. Crash. Sometimes I can surprise myself with my own strength. I take the hammer up high behind my head and bring it down again, right where the lock, hasp and staple join. Then again.

The noise must have alerted the neighbours. Someone's knocking on the door. Just ignore it, Franzi, they'll go away. It's coming loose. One more big blow. And there we are, the hasp and staple hang free, their attaching bolts severed and bent.

I don't know what I expected to find. Perhaps half of me thought it would just be his Ministry business, secret documents, that sort of thing. What I do find, I don't really understand.

There are newspaper cuttings, taken – it looks like – from the Party newspaper, *Neues Deutschland*. About the opening of new state tourist facilities for winter sports. Well, that's not much of a secret. A photo of a pretty, blond-haired girl. She's aged around five, six . . . seven. It's hard to tell. Is it a secret sister, a secret daughter?

But under that are pamphlets, leaflets. And I suddenly realise this is my bargaining tool. I have my secret and Hansi has his. Because this can't be to do with his Ministry work, not if he was keeping it hidden. I don't understand all the words, but I can tell they are dangerous. Anti-republic. Anti-state. Anti-communist. There are lists of names, addresses, telephone numbers. This is something I can bargain with. All the pamphlets are headed with the name of the same organisation – and it sounds very much like a name the authorities wouldn't approve of. That Hansi's Ministry colleagues wouldn't approve of. *The Committee for the Dispossessed.*

55

Two months later: March 1976
Halle-Neustadt

Tilsner racked his brain over what they could do, where they could look for the couple. *Oberst* Frenzel immediately agreed to an all-bulletins alert across the Republic: their car, a Lada, had its registration circulated. Frenzel even agreed to roadblocks at the entrance and exits to Ha-Neu. The previous policy of keeping everything hush-hush – the one Müller and Tilsner had continually railed against – now seemed to have been abandoned. But then that had been at the behest of the Stasi. Frenzel seemed at last to be willing to put proper policing above the needs of the secret police.

Malkus was less cooperative, initially refusing to get the Ministry for State Security involved in the alert. Tilsner knew he could go over his head, using Jäger's connections in the Hauptstadt, but ideally he needed the head of the local Stasi onside.

'Do you not want us to solve this case and arrest the culprits, Comrade *Major*?'

'Of course I do,' countered Malkus, staring hard at the police detective. 'But the facts remain the same. We don't want the population of this city alarmed. I'll be having words with *Oberst* Frenzel, asking him to remove the roadblocks. We're getting a lot of complaints. People want to know what it's all about.'

'I'm sure they do,' said Tilsner. 'But then you yourself said the reason for keeping our inquiry secret was so as not to spook the Castro visit. Well, that's been and gone a long time, so that excuse won't wash anymore. But before and after that, your good captain Janowitz has seemed suspiciously eager to get the case closed down.' Tilsner knew he was treading a fine line in challenging the Stasi officer. But he also knew that if things got nasty he could exert pressure on Jäger. There were advantages to knowing things about people's pasts, and Tilsner knew plenty about Klaus Jäger. And Jäger – should he choose – could eat Malkus for breakfast.

'What I'd like to know,' continued Tilsner, 'is exactly *why* Janowitz wants to see the back of us.' He didn't know if he should reveal his hand in telling Malkus about the road traffic reports. But if he could drive a wedge between Malkus and his deputy, it might help them. And sometimes, if you wanted to catch an apple, you needed to give the tree a good shake. 'You see, I think we're closer to finding out, thanks to the help of Comrade Wiedemann in the records department.' Tilsner was standing over Malkus's desk, determined to outstare him, having refused the Stasi major's offer of a low seat. He watched now as uncertainty began to enter Malkus's expression.

'What's Wiedemann found?'

'An interesting road traffic accident from the late fifties.'

Malkus crossed his arms over his stomach, drawing his body into itself.

'Why would something like that have any relevance?'

Tilsner watched the man shift uncomfortably. 'It wouldn't look very good if your *Hauptmann* Janowitz was involved in doctoring evidence, would it? Especially as the driver was drunk. And even if it wasn't Janowitz, someone in the Stasi doctored the files. I have the evidence.' Tilsner knew it was a wild shot in the dark. The trouble was, it was all he had.

Malkus's face seemed to have relaxed a little. 'Well, I hope your evidence is strong, Comrade *Oberleutnant*. Otherwise you're playing a dangerous game. Nevertheless, now you've raised the matter, I'm obliged to look into it.'

'Good,' said Tilsner. 'And perhaps you might want to reconsider asking for the roadblocks to be removed. We want to catch these culprits, and I'm sure you do too. Now if *Hauptmann* Janowitz *is* somehow involved, it's very convenient for him to not want a full search, to want the inquiry mothballed, and for *Oberleutnant* Müller and myself to be sent back to Berlin, don't you think?'

Malkus was rising from his chair, and began to usher Tilsner out of his office. 'As I've said, Comrade *Unterleutnant*, I will look into it and consider what you've said. But I can't promise anything. Other than that if you've been making unfounded allegations against one of my officers, there will be hell to pay. You can be sure of that.'

While Frenzel organised Eschler, Fernbach and his men, Tilsner felt he owed it to Karin to bring her up to speed. But when he got to the hospital he realised something was very wrong.

'You can't speak to her,' said her boyfriend, Emil Wollenburg.

'There are things she needs to know,' Tilsner replied.

The doctor boyfriend's shoulders slumped. 'You don't understand. Something awful has happened. We don't know what to do. We're searching everywhere.'

Tilsner grabbed him by the lapels of his jacket. 'What? What's happened? Tell me quickly.'

'Our babies,' sobbed Emil.

'Whose babies?' shouted Tilsner. 'What are you talking about?'

'Karin and my babies.'

'Twins? She's had twins? How can you *lose* them?'

'Someone's stolen them. From her womb.'

Tilsner heard a huge roar, and then realised it came from himself, as he knocked the man aside and rushed into Müller's hospital room. He could see she looked confused, groggy, drugged. Her eyes not properly focussing on him, a nurse by her side.

'Werner. Oh, Werner.'

Tilsner didn't know what to do. He needed her fully functioning. Pushing the nurse to one side, he picked up a glass of water from the bedside table and threw it in Müller's face.

'What! Why the –'

'There's no time to waste, Karin. Pull yourself together and come with me now.'

The nurse started to try to pull him away. 'She's just had a major operation – it's too –'

'Shut it,' said Tilsner. 'She's coming with me.'

Müller had groggily started to get out of bed and was pulling her jacket on over her nightgown. More doctors, and Emil Wollenburg himself, had now surrounded the bedside.

'This is madness, Karin. You don't know where you're going, what –'

At that point, Tilsner's radio crackled into life. He answered it. It was Eschler.

'Come to the incident room immediately. We've got a witness reckons he's spotted the woman – with a baby.'

56

Müller was only barely aware of what was happening. She just had some primal instinct driving her on. The sedatives had numbed her feelings, but she still felt and shared Tilsner's sense of urgency. Emil seemed unable to look her in the eye. The doctors and nurses, too, only made token efforts to try to stop her going with her deputy. One thing, one desperate thing, drove her on: she'd been cheated out of being a mother once, or perhaps – in choosing to abort the children of a rapist – she'd cheated herself. She needed to save her and Emil's children.

Tilsner took her in the Wartburg back to the fire station, even though in the normal course of events it would have been quicker on foot. He drove carefully for once, despite the urgency, and Müller welcomed the fact that she wasn't being thrown around inside the car. She didn't think her bruised and battered body would have coped. But the journey did give her foggy mind the chance to slowly clear.

Once they were in the incident room, Fernbach pointed to the office, while looking in astonishment at the state of Müller, her jacket hanging loose over her hospital gown. Müller almost wished she had her red coat on to at least give her a mental boost, but she'd stopped wearing it in the early stages of pregnancy when it became too tight.

'Eschler's in there with him,' said Fernbach.

'Who?'

'Stefan Hildebrand.'

Müller nodded, but saw Tilsner's frown. 'He's a down-and-out.' Tilsner's forehead creased in further puzzlement. 'Yes, I know, Werner. We don't have homeless people in the Republic. Nevertheless, he is.'

They found Hildebrand – still looking as dishevelled as ever – stumbling breathlessly over his words as he attempted to explain what he'd seen to Eschler. The police captain held up his hand.

'Hang on. You're making no sense. Let's start again. You thought the woman had a doll.'

'Yes. You know, that one that was down in the heating tunnels near the *Ypsilon* block.'

'We took that away as evidence,' said Eschler. 'So where is she – near the "Y" block?'

'No. That's why I took the risk of coming here. I know I wasn't supposed to go back to living in the heating –'

'We don't give a shit about that,' shouted Tilsner. Müller laid a hand on his arm to try to quieten him, even though she was as desperate to know – more desperate to know – than he was. 'Where is she?' said Tilsner, approaching Hildebrand, as though he might hit him.

'In my place.'

'*Your* place. What on earth do you mean?' asked Eschler, getting as frustrated as Tilsner now.

'In my house.'

'Your *house*?'

'He means his den,' said Müller. 'That's it, isn't it, Stefan?' The man nodded in nervous, frightened excitement. 'Your den in the duct by the Donkey Windmill.'

'Yes, yes, *Oberleutnant*. And it isn't a doll she's got. It's a baby. A living baby.'

Tilsner was about to go in, all guns blazing, turning the Wartburg's siren and light on. But Müller stopped him. Whoever this woman with the baby was – and Tilsner still hadn't filled her in on what he knew – she didn't want her scared away. Because Müller had some sixth sense, some signal from her abandoned, damaged womb to her brain, that the baby was hers. Her child. The one she'd always longed for.

The diners and drinkers in the Donkey Windmill looked up in astonishment as the ragtag group of four entered, looking round desperately. Eschler in his People's Police captain's uniform, Tilsner in leather-jacketed detective mode, Hildebrand a hairy, smelly down-and-out, and then Müller. She dreaded to think what she looked like. Probably some escapee from a mental institution. But it didn't matter. Nothing mattered. Except finding her babies alive.

Tilsner shouted to the waitress: 'Where's the entrance to the heating duct?' The girl gestured towards the kitchens.

As they entered, the smell of food, the heat and steam, almost made Müller keel over and faint. She willed herself to stay upright as Tilsner opened the metal door the kitchen staff pointed to. He jabbed Hildebrand forward into the gloom. The fug of damp heat that immediately hit Müller reminded her of that first search, below the *Ypsilon Hochhaus*, the one where she'd thought the doll was a real baby. This time she hoped beyond hope that the baby Hildebrand had seen, being cradled by some madwoman in his den, was alive – and was hers.

Their torch beams bounced along the walls, until up ahead – in the gloom – they saw the collection of cardboard boxes that Hildebrand called his 'house'. Tilsner went forward, lifted up the cardboard flap which served as a makeshift door, and there – illuminated in the beam, with a tiny baby at her breast – was someone Müller recognised from a few days before at the hospital.

Looking scared and confused as the baby – unconcerned – slept on in her arms, was the nursing auxiliary who'd been looking at Müller's files that first day in the hospital. Müller felt overwhelmed as a huge range of emotions surged through her. Delight and happiness that one of her babies was well; rage towards the madwoman who was holding her child; fear about where her other twin was, and its welfare. But she knew she had to control herself. Her legs felt as though they would collapse from under her at any moment, her breathing was rapid, each intake a stab into her lungs. But she had to stay in control. For the sake of her children's welfare, but also for the sake of the investigation in which she'd invested so much.

'Franziska Traugott?' shouted Tilsner.

'Yes,' replied the woman, in a shaky voice.

'Don't move. You're under arrest. Pass the baby to me.'

The woman pulled the bundle back, away from Tilsner's outstretched arms. 'But she's mine now.' Then she stared Müller straight in the face. 'You didn't want her.'

Müller held on to Eschler, feeling once again as though she would collapse. *She.* It was her daughter. The first sight of her daughter. She just wanted her child in her arms. The child that had been stolen from her womb along with her twin brother. 'W-w-what do you mean?' stuttered Müller, struggling to form the words, as her chest heaved like bellows.

The woman continued to cling tightly to the bundle. 'Hansi said you didn't want her. You were on the list.'

Tilsner by now had moved right up to the woman, and had his hands round the wrapped-up baby which still slept on.

'What do you mean, Hansi said I was on the list?'

'Hansi. My husband. He's very important. Works for the Ministry.' As the woman talked, Tilsner had finally managed to prise the baby away. It woke and began screaming, but the woman seemed to not notice now. She was in another world. Her world. 'You know, the Ministry for State Security. I don't think they call him Hansi there, though, they call him –'

Before the woman said the words, they were in Müller's head. Echoing round and around. Traugott. Her surname just uttered by Tilsner. That was the trigger. She found herself slumping against Eschler, no strength in her body. She saw her daughter safe in Tilsner's arms. She felt a huge surge of love for the child, wanted to hold her, but didn't trust herself, and that surname echoed around her brain. With sudden realisation, she knew who had her son. It wasn't Hansi. Not to her. It was Johannes. Johannes Traugott. Gangly Johannes. Bullied, bespectacled Johannes. The childhood best friend she'd allowed to be taken away.

57

Müller found herself biting down hard every few seconds on the inside of her cheek. Willing herself to stay alert, to concentrate, to overcome the pain that still pulsed through her body from the Caesarean wound. As Eschler took Franziska Traugott back to the temporary police HQ to question her, Tilsner took Müller to the hospital.

Emil seemed frozen, unable to decide what to do. Müller handed him their baby daughter, not wanting to let her out of her arms, but knowing she had to – in order to locate and save the baby girl's twin brother.

'Look after her,' she warned. 'Every minute of every hour. Don't let her out of your sight.'

He looked alarmed. He'd obviously assumed her return to the hospital meant that she would be readmitted to receive proper aftercare. To have the surgery on her abdomen and womb checked – they knew now it had been an amateur job, although in the brief questioning of Franziska Traugott that Tilsner had managed so far, the woman had claimed that her husband – Hansi, *Johannes* – had originally trained as a surgeon. Müller doubted it, but hoped it was true.

'Where are you going, Karin? You can't put your health at risk like this.'

'I have to. I have to find my other child. My son.'

Because that was what Traugott had also admitted. After an argument between the pair, Johannes had disappeared with the newly born, stolen baby boy. But she had no idea where, and neither did Tilsner or Müller.

A radio message to the incident room, as Müller sat clutching her dressings – not really knowing what they could do – was the first indication of where Johannes was heading with the baby. A People's Police patrol had spotted his Lada at Straussfurt, heading south towards Erfurt.

Eschler took the message. 'They tried chasing him, but he took off down a side road and gave them the slip. They've heightened the alert in *Bezirke* Erfurt, Gera and Suhl.'

'Did they say where he was heading?' asked Tilsner.

'Other than south? No.'

'I know where he's going,' said Müller.

Tilsner stared at her in astonishment. '*How* do you know? And where?'

She didn't know for certain. It was a hunch. But where did desperate people flee to when they had no options left? 'He's going back to his home village. My home village. To Oberhof.'

'Well, if you're right, he's got a head start of an hour or two. We'll never catch him,' said Tilsner.

'We might,' said Eschler. '*Oberst* Frenzel – as soon as he heard they'd done a flit from their apartment in Residential Complex

Eight – has had a People's Police helicopter on standby. It's in the Südpark – ready to go as soon as needed.'

The Russian KA-26 – in the white and olive-green livery of the People's Police – had its rotor blades already spinning by the time Eschler screeched to a halt at the park's entrance in the Wartburg. Müller held her jacket lapels together to protect her abdomen from the fierce blast of the blades, ducking under them and staggering towards the helicopter. At the door hatch, once Eschler had jumped in, Tilsner lifted Müller and then Eschler hauled her inside as gently as possible. As soon as Tilsner had grabbed the helicopter floor, the pilot took off, angling south, with Tilsner's legs dangling in the air until Eschler finally pulled him fully inside.

'I hope you're right about this, Karin.'

Müller felt the blood pounding where her womb had been cut open. She looked down, could see red seeping through. She had to ignore it, she had to. For the sake of her child. 'I know I'm right. I have to be.'

The helicopter headed south, the pilot angling the rotors – aiming for the last-known sighting of Johannes Traugott's Lada. Meanwhile Eschler, headphones on and microphone in hand, kept in touch with police radio control on the ground.

He turned back towards Müller and Tilsner in the seats behind.

'They've had another sighting,' he shouted above the roar of the helicopter's engines.

'What's that?' Müller shouted back.

Eschler leaned backwards and moved his mouth close to her ear, then repeated what he'd said.

'Where?' shouted Müller.

'Gamstädt,' yelled Eschler. 'Looks like he's deliberately trying to avoid Erfurt. Where do you think it's best for the pilot to head for?'

Müller didn't have to look at a map, she could picture the towns and villages en route.

She lifted the right-hand headphone away from Eschler's ear and brought her mouth close. 'Head for Crawinkel. South-west of Arnstadt. He must be going the back way. We need to cut him off before he reaches the Thuringian forest. If he gets there before us, we'll never find him.'

Eschler relayed the instructions to the pilot, and an anxious conversation ensued.

'He's not sure we'll catch him anyway,' shouted the police captain. 'Even at maximum speed, it's still an hour or so's flying time. He's probably less than an hour's drive away now.'

'Not if he's going the back way.' She pointed down through the glass bubble of the cockpit. 'And look – there's snow lying on the ground even here. By the time we get to the Thuringian forest he might need chains.'

Müller hoped, prayed, that her hunch was right. Because that's all it was. She'd insisted that Eschler radio *Oberst* Frenzel to make sure patrols on the ground didn't start chasing the Lada. She couldn't bear the thought of the son she'd not yet seen being killed in a road accident before she'd had a chance to hold him.

Müller had no real way of knowing where Johannes was going, where he was taking her baby. But the image burned on her mind was the one of Farmer Bonz's field, back in 1952. The day she had been pretending to be the luge champion of the glorious republic of workers and peasants. The day the soldiers had come to take Johannes away. She felt sure he would be going back there to the field above the village. That, or the Pension Edelweiss, his family's old guest house, which had now been converted into a youth hostel for the sons and daughters of loyal Party workers. Back to his home village for some last act of defiance.

During the flight, Tilsner filled her in on the parts of the case that he'd pieced together thanks to the information in the 1950s road traffic reports and the raid on the Traugotts' apartment in Complex Eight. The baby photos on the mantelpiece. Franziska Traugott pictured holding baby Tanja. Baby Maddelena. The unidentified baby from the 1960s who Tilsner suspected was one of the two Anderegg twins. And the final photo – from the late 1950s – of the young Franziska and Johannes Traugott, at the start of their married lives, with their two natural baby children – the ones who would be tragically killed by a drunk driver, but had been denied justice thanks to the account of the accident being doctored by the Republic's authorities.

Another report came through on the ground: the Lada had almost been trapped at a roadblock near Holzhausen, just to the west of Arnstadt, a few kilometres north of the Thuringian forest. But Johannes had evaded capture by heading down a farm track.

Müller held her abdomen as the pilot swooped down, weaving less than a hundred metres above ground level. Pain flared up from her wound. She risked a look and then wished she hadn't. Blood had soaked through the dressings.

Tilsner, sitting next to her in the cramped cockpit behind Eschler and the pilot, squeezed her hand. 'Hold on. We'll get him, don't worry.'

And then they spotted the Lada, a red dot in a sea of white snow, approaching the edge of the forest. Müller could see the pilot forcing a lever to its fullest extent, the helicopter shaking as he pushed the rotors to their maximum velocity, the maximum thrust. They'd nearly caught him. And then they were hovering above the vehicle. The downdraft of the blades was churning the snow into eddies around the car.

All of a sudden, Müller felt as though her womb was being pulled out through the bottom of her body as the pilot banked and climbed. A wall of green spruce trees filled all their vision in front of the cockpit. It looked like they had to crash into the forest. Müller, knuckles white, gripped Tilsner's hand. Then clear sky, and snow-topped trees. They were above the forest canopy, the pilot shouting urgently in Eschler's ear.

The *Hauptmann* turned to Müller to convey the message. 'Sorry, Karin. He got to the forest before us. The pilot had to pull up – couldn't risk colliding with the trees. Where to now? Oberhof?'

As her pulsing heartbeat started to settle, Müller nodded grimly.

Müller had no real idea what madness was churning around in Johannes Traugott's head. But the image she clung to was the image of them as children, playing on the slope in the farmer's field above the Republic's prestige winter sports resort. If it was burned into Müller's brain – as that day when the soldiers came certainly was – then surely it would have had an even greater effect on Johannes. He had been banished, his family had been banished, their business confiscated, their dreams stolen.

As they approached Oberhof, swooping low over the forest canopy, Müller picked out the landmarks. The ski-jump hills and grandstands where ultimately her courage had failed her, to the dismay of the hopeful members of the Republic's Winter Olympics committee. The winding route of the bobsleigh and luge track, the place she and Johannes had imagined winning their medals. And the jagged shards of the ultra-modern, incongruous Interhotel Panorama, where the great and good of the Republic liked to spend their winter holidays.

Eschler turned towards her with a quizzical look. Müller pointed to an area of sloping meadow overlooking the village with a plateau at its summit. As they flew towards it, Müller peered down at the village – concentrating on the former Pension Edelweiss. There was no sign of Johannes's Lada – or her baby son. She looked to the left and saw her adoptive family's guest house, the Hanneli, its blood-red walls a stark contrast to the pristine white of the surrounding snow. And then – as clouds of powdery snow were churned up by the rotor blades – they were slowly descending. Hovering, then gently landing, on the very top of Farmer Bonz's field. The place where – some quarter of a century ago – Johannes Traugott had seen his family's dreams ripped from their hands.

As the whine of the rotors quietened and the spinning blades slowed, Eschler, Tilsner and the pilot all looked at Müller – the dishevelled, damaged People's Police *Oberleutnant*, with her detective's leather jacket failing to fully cover her hospital gown. No one said anything. But Müller knew what they were thinking. The same as she was thinking. *He isn't here, so what the hell do we do next?*

58

Eschler had his headphones unplugged, and with the helicopter's engine just idling, all four of them heard the radio message through the crackle and interference.

'Incident at Interhotel Panorama. Armed man. All units attend. Urgent. Urgent.'

The pain throbbing from the wound in her abdomen suddenly disappeared for Müller as adrenalin kicked in again. Eschler put the headphones back on, and Müller felt a lightness in her chest. She breathed in deeply as the pilot immediately increased the rotor speed – the whine of the engines and the chop-chop-chop noise of the blades speeding into a whir. Time seemed to slow. She didn't understand why they weren't moving. She pulled one of the cans off Eschler's head. 'Why aren't we taking off immediately?' she screamed.

'It takes a good few seconds to get ready,' he shouted back. 'Here we go.'

The craft began to hover, then the pilot tipped the nose forward and they were away, heading for the strange ski-jump-shaped shards that formed the two main buildings of the Interhotel.

*

As they landed on a patch of snow-covered lawn near the entrance, Müller saw the flashing blue lights of the local squad cars. Her heart sank at the sight of armed officers, guns at the ready. She didn't want a shoot-out. Above everything, she needed her baby son unharmed. That was all that really mattered. But after that, her professional pride demanded that Johannes Traugott – her old childhood friend, Johannes – be taken alive to face justice. There were so many questions she needed to ask him.

At first the armed officers were reluctant to let Müller, Tilsner and Eschler through. Once Tilsner explained who Müller was and showed his pass – and Müller had a suspicion that what he'd flashed belonged to the Stasi, not the People's Police – they relented.

They moved as fast as Müller was able through the lobby corridor towards reception, then saw the signs pointing in opposite directions to House One and House Two.

'That way,' shouted a uniformed police officer, pointing to the lifts for House One. 'There's a stand-off on the twelfth floor.'

Eschler took the stairs while Müller and Tilsner waited for one of six lifts. It was there in an instant, and then seemed to whisk them skywards at a rapid rate. But when they got to floor 12, the door wouldn't open.

'*Scheisse*,' screamed Tilsner. 'It must be in lockdown.'

Tilsner jabbed the button for one floor down, the eleventh. After the lift descended the single floor, the door opened and Tilsner helped Müller out. Armed police were in the stairwell leading back to the twelfth storey.

'You can't go up there,' said the captain in charge.

Tilsner again flashed some sort of authority or pass. This time Müller looked over his shoulder and saw the emblem of a muscular arm holding up a rifle, with the flag of the Republic flying from it. Authority from the Stasi, as she'd suspected.

The police officer reluctantly allowed them through.

On floor 12, more police were guarding the entrance to what looked like luxury apartments. Tilsner frowned at Müller.

'They're reserved for the Party bigwigs,' she said. 'Honecker sometimes stays here.'

Tilsner obviously wasn't in the mood for lessons on the Party leadership.

'Where is he?' he asked the policeman who seemed to be in charge.

The officer gestured with his eyes to the stairwell. Tilsner saw there was another flight. 'I thought there were only twelve floors?'

'There are,' said the officer. 'He's on the roof.'

'With the baby?'

The officer nodded.

'The baby's still alive?' asked Müller, her voice high-pitched, panicked.

The officer nodded again. 'The man came up here ranting and raving. Comrade Honecker's here on holiday at the moment. The man was standing at the apartment door, shouting and screaming – something about his family home being stolen from him. Comrade Honecker instituted the emergency procedure.'

Tilsner gestured towards the stairwell. 'We're going up there.'

'You can't,' said the officer. 'I'm under instructions to shoot anyone who tries.'

Tilsner grabbed the man by his lapels. 'Look, fish face. We're going up there. I told you. This is the mother. It's her baby. And this is our authority.' Once again, Tilsner showed the pass – or letter of authority, whatever it was – but this officer seemed unimpressed.

'I have my orders. No one goes up there.'

'Try to stop us and you'll be facing a long stretch in jail, mark my words,' shouted Tilsner, spittle flying from his mouth into the policeman's face.

Clutching her dressed Caesarean wound, Müller moved past them and detached the chain that was the only thing – other than the officer's pointed rifle – stopping anyone from climbing up to the roof. She was sure the policeman wasn't going to shoot. At least she hoped he wasn't.

She heard Tilsner follow as the officer shouted: 'I warned you.' But there was no gunfire to back up his empty threat.

59

As soon as Tilsner opened the emergency door onto the roof of House One, Müller found herself almost being knocked back down the stairs by an icy blast of wind. Late March, but winter still hadn't released its grip.

She crept after Tilsner onto the roof, holding on to the guardrail. She hadn't known what to expect, but this was more terrifying than she imagined. The mock ski-jump structure came to an actual apex. The highest point was a narrow flat section – a ladder's width, no more – with steep slopes falling away on each side.

'Don't move!' The shout was almost lost in the wind. Müller trained her gaze on the figure at the other side of the roof, one arm clutching her baby son, the other with a gun raised, pointing at Tilsner. She tried not to let the height of the building enter her head. Tried not to freeze in fright as she had done as a teenager at the top of the Oberhof ski jump that this strange hotel roof resembled.

'Don't be stupid, Traugott,' screamed Tilsner. 'It's over. It's all over now. Put the gun down and slowly bring the baby to me.'

'No!' Johannes shouted back. 'He's my child. My son. The mother didn't want children.'

Tilsner crouched down, and started to haul himself along the horizontal ladder at the apex of the roof. 'I'm warning you!' screamed Johannes. A shot rang out, ricocheting against the metal tubing of the ladder, a couple of metres in front of Tilsner. The baby started bawling. The sound stopped Müller's heart. She had to save her child. She had to hold her son, if only for one moment.

'I do want my child, Johannes. It's me, Karin.'

The man looked confused, glancing at the baby held tightly in the crook of his arm.

Tilsner took advantage to move another rung on the ladder, but Johannes fired the gun again, this time aiming just a few centimetres from the detective's grip. Müller heard the ricochet slam into the concrete behind her.

'I told you, get back. Now. Otherwise next time it's your head.'

Tilsner released one hand, and held it up. 'OK, OK, I'm going back.'

Müller watched as her deputy tried to negotiate backwards as the wind howled up from the forest, over the top of the bizarrely shaped roof.

'Please let me hold my baby, Johannes,' Müller yelled across the divide. 'Just once. Just for a moment. Please. It's me – Karin. You remember. Little Karin Müller from Bergpension Hanneli. We used to play together in Farmer Bonz's field. Here. Here in Oberhof.'

Johannes peered through the thick lenses of his spectacles, as though he couldn't believe it.

'Karin. Is it really you?' Müller watched his body slump when he recognised something in her dishevelled looks which tallied with his memories of her as a little girl. 'Oh my God,' he cried, clutching her baby ever tighter.

Tilsner had by now negotiated his way slowly back to Müller's side of the roof. 'Keep him talking,' he whispered into Müller's ear. 'I'll go up the other staircase and get behind him.'

Müller pulled him to her. 'Don't do anything to risk the life of my child, Werner. Please.'

'Karin. We have to do something. Your baby won't survive up here with that madman for long. He could throw himself off – with the child – at any moment.'

Müller squeezed Tilsner's arm till she saw him wince. 'Please, Werner. I'm begging you.'

'Just keep him talking. Concentrate on that.'

Johannes had slumped down by the chimney stack which belched out white smoke continually, like the funnel of a ship. He looked as though he was crying, staring down into the baby's eyes.

'It's not true, Johannes, that I didn't want my children. I love them with all my heart.'

'Then why did you kill your twins before?' the man shouted back.

'That's not fair,' sobbed Müller.

'You were on the list, Karin. The Ministry for State Security list of women who chose to have illegal late-term abortions. Franzi found your records in Doctor Rothstein's clinic in Berlin.'

'Yes, but did it say *why* I had to have an abortion?' screamed Müller, her anger now overcoming the pain.

Johannes looked confused again. He said nothing.

'Did it?' yelled Müller. 'Did it say that I'd been raped? That they were the children of a rapist?' The pent-up anger that Müller injected into every word thrown across the apex of the roof suddenly caused something in her body to break. She clutched her womb, the dressing, felt the stitches opening. Blood pulsing out. 'Oh, God!' she screamed, falling to the floor. 'Let me hold my baby one time.'

Johannes saw what was happening, dropped his gun, and ran along the narrow apex, panic concentrating his mind, making his footing sure and exact. In seconds he was there, crouching by her, holding the bawling child for her to kiss and cuddle. 'Karin, Karin. I'm so sorry,' he cried.

As she held her son, Müller could feel her life ebbing away as blood leached out of her onto the now soaked dressings from the split-open C-section.

As she drifted towards unconsciousness, she heard a shout. Tilsner. From the other side of the roof. Then a gunshot.

Johannes had been holding her hand tightly, but now he released his grip. But he hadn't been hit. He was scrabbling to get away. Müller tried to hold on to him, but her strength had gone. 'Don't shoot,' she tried to cry. But as Tilsner raised his gun arm again, as Müller's vision blurred, she saw Johannes slip.

'Karin,' he yelled. 'I'm sorr—'

He didn't reach the end of his screamed apology. As his footing faltered, he fell backwards, down the icy, ski-jump-shaped roof. Over and over his body rolled. At first as if in slow motion, then faster and faster. Müller tried to hold her lower abdomen together as she watched Johannes's spectacles spin off his body. Now, instead of tumbling, he was sliding, frantically scrabbling with his arms to try to cling on. But the iced-up, angled roof was as slick as the in-run had been on the ski jump all those years before. As pain pulsed through her, Müller knew she was power-less to save her one-time friend.

And then he disappeared off the end of the building. No elegant ski-jump take-off, no skis to land on. Nothing.

He'd fallen.

To his death, Müller assumed.

By now Tilsner was at her side. Eschler too. 'You look after her, Bruno. Get her on a stretcher, into the helicopter and to the nearest hospital. We've got to save her. I'll make sure the baby is safe.' Then Tilsner grabbed Müller's as yet unnamed son, turned and ran down the stairs.

In just a few minutes, Müller had been strapped to a stretcher by medics, and was being given an emergency blood trans-fusion even as they were moving through the lobby to the helicopter.

She was barely conscious but her first thought was that she needed to hold her son, in case this was it. In case this was the end. Her second thought – and she knew she shouldn't care, but she did, was: Had Johannes survived?

She struggled to put the question to Eschler.

'Tilsner said he did,' Eschler replied. 'An old snowdrift cush-ioned his fall slightly. But he's in a bad way. Paralysed. They don't think he'll last long.'

'I need to see him,' croaked Müller, her voice fading as she fought to stay conscious.

'But we've got to get you into the helicopter.'

'Take me to him, Bruno, please.'

Eschler indicated to the medics carrying Müller to divert to the side of the building, where Johannes Traugott fell.

He stared up at her stretcher as Müller tried to raise herself.

'Why, Johannes? Why? We were best friends.'

'K-K-Karin,' he spluttered. 'I didn't know –'

His head fell back into the snow. Medics attempted resuscita-tion – and somehow got him breathing again. There was still a chance he would tell Müller his story sometime. But it wouldn't be now.

'That's it, Karin,' shouted Eschler. 'We've got to go. We have to get you to hospital as soon as possible.'

As they raced towards the helicopter, Müller saw a group of armed, leather-jacketed men move towards the area where Johannes was receiving medical treatment. She was surprised to see Malkus and Janowitz amongst them. Lifting her head, she saw them shooing the medics away from Johannes. Then they slipped out of sight as her stretcher was carried round the corner of the hotel. The medical team loaded her onto the KA-26, its rotors already turning manically, its skates just about to lift off. The roar of the engines drowned out virtually everything else, but they were fading as unconsciousness crept up on Müller. Just before she blacked out, she thought she heard a sound above the thwack-thwack-thwack of the rotors. This was different. A double thud.

She couldn't be sure. Her brain wouldn't focus her thoughts, and the noise of the helicopter's engines and rotors overwhelmed virtually every other sound. But something at the back of her mind told her the noise was of pistol shots. Pistol shots muffled by the snow.

60

Tilsner knew he should be interviewing Franziska Traugott, probing her story, finding out to what extent she had been in league with her husband. Could she throw any light on who in the Stasi had doctored the accident reports from the 1950s? But she was safely in custody in the Red Ox. It could wait an hour or so. First he wanted to know how Müller was, wanted to see her in the flesh. To know that she'd survived.

He saw Emil Wollenburg waiting on a chair outside the intensive care unit of Halle hospital, holding his head in his hands. Müller had initially been taken to Suhl – the nearest major medical centre – but transferred up to Halle when staff at Suhl said there was little more they could do for her. The fear was that the massive amount of blood loss could have caused brain damage; although clinging to life, Tilsner's boss was now in a coma.

Tilsner sat down next to Müller's boyfriend and – although he felt uncomfortable doing it – put his arm round the man.

'Any news, Emil?'

The doctor looked up with a defeated expression on his face, shaking his head. 'We're just waiting, hoping.'

'What about the twins?'

Wollenburg gave a wry laugh. 'They're fine. Fit as fiddles – even though they were "born", if you can call it that, a few weeks early. Fine pair of lungs on both of them. They're safe in the paediatric unit. Properly guarded, before you ask.'

'Any names yet?'

'Hah! Do you think my girlfriend would thank me if I tried to name them before she had her say? You know what she's like.' Then his face darkened again. 'Let's just hope she gets a say. They've given her two full blood transfusions already.'

'So can I go in and see her?'

Wollenburg shrugged. 'As far as I know, yes. I've been sitting with her most of the time – reading to her, that sort of thing – but I find it too painful carrying on a one-way conversation after a while. I just wish there was more I could have done. I felt like a spare part staying here with our daughter while Karin went off risking her life.'

Tilsner gave the man's shoulder a squeeze. 'You're a doctor, you save lives every day. Karin did a great job. She saved your son. Whatever happens, you've got a lot to thank –'

Shrugging himself from the detective's grip, Emil Wollenburg stood up. 'Let's not talk about "whatever happens". I need to try to stay positive. Do you want to come in and see her?'

Tilsner was shocked at how pale she looked. Up close, with all the life-support paraphernalia attached to her, he felt her mortality, her vulnerability. Even on the roof of the Interhotel, when it was obvious something had gone horribly wrong and the haemorrhaging had begun, Müller had somehow conveyed the impression that everything would work out in the end. Tilsner rubbed his hands over his wrists, right hand on left wrist, left on right, uncertain what to do – not knowing what could possibly help her.

'It's OK,' said Wollenburg, laying a hand on Tilsner's shoulder – reciprocating the gesture the detective had shown him moments earlier. 'I was shocked the first time I saw her. They say she's stable, but . . .'

Tilsner stared at the various monitors, as they beeped and pulsed in regular patterns, numbers flashing up which he didn't really understand.

'It wasn't the C-section splitting that's caused the blood loss. Some shrapnel from the shooting nicked an artery in her groin.'

Tilsner grimaced at the thought.

'You can sit with her,' said her boyfriend. 'Hold her hand, maybe talk to her, though there's no indication she can hear anything. I find it helps me, even if it's not helping her.'

Tilsner pulled up a chair, and then gently took Müller's hand in his, careful not to dislodge the saline drip tubing where it entered her horribly pale skin.

'Hello, Karin,' he said, squeezing her fingers. 'I miss you at work, you know. I've got to formally interview Franzi Traugott this afternoon, and I'm not really looking forward to it, not without you there. She's an odd one. She's trying to lay it all at Johannes's door. Now she might be right, but I'd be a lot happier if you were there with me. You'd see through her lies, I know.'

He was aware that Emil Wollenburg had moved out of the room again, leaving the two detectives to their tête-à-tête that only one of them was actually participating in. Tilsner looked at Müller's closed eyelids, hoping to see a flicker – some sort of movement – but there was none.

'We've pieced some of it together. It appears he would give her drugs to stop her periods and mimic the effects of pregnancy. And then there'd be some sort of emergency where she'd end up having a fake Caesarean. He'd anaesthetise her, she'd be out cold for a few days, he'd make an incision in her lower abdomen and then sew it up again, and then lo and behold a few days later she'd end up with a baby. Someone else's baby.'

Tilsner squeezed Müller's hand, hoping for some responding pressure from her. But it was limp, only the warmth of the still-circulating blood being pumped round her body – someone else's donated blood – giving any hint of life.

'So the Andereggs' female twin – that was the first time they did it. They called her Stefi. Same as my daughter. But Franzi was a hopeless case. Neglected her, as far as we can gather. We don't know what happened to the boy twin, but he died too, possibly from natural causes or neglect, and then they took them both with them to Berlin when they moved there in the late 1960s. One of them hid the bodies at Rothstein's clinic, probably hoping someone would think they were dumped late-term foetuses. That's what we thought initially, wasn't it? And that's where they chose all their targets – women who'd had abortions, either at that illegal clinic, or another in the Republic that the Stasi had records from.'

Still no response from Müller, but at least the life-support systems kept up their relentless rhythm. Tilsner knew enough about hospitals now to know it was when the waves and pulses and clicks stopped – when the line went flat – that there was trouble. But then, no doubt, there would be some sort of shrieking warning signal.

A nurse came in to check all the readings, but seemed satisfied and left again.

Tilsner resumed his monologue, hoping his update on the case might provoke some response in Müller. 'And then, by last summer, the Traugotts were back in Halle-Neustadt. Hansi – Johannes to you – concocted another fake pregnancy with Franzi, getting help with the charade from a so-called doctor, who was nothing more than a stooge Johannes had some sort of hold over through his Stasi work. Then, lo and behold, their daughter Heike was 'born'. Only she wasn't really Heike, she was Maddelena Salzmann. We can only think that Hansi had planned to give Franzi twins – possibly to replace the ones killed in that car crash in the fifties by that drunken driver. But Karsten was sicklier than his sister. He was the one the medical staff had been concerned about, even while under twenty-four-hour care. Outside hospital, he didn't survive.'

Another hand squeeze from Tilsner.

'But where it starts to get strange is in the case of the half-Vietnamese kid, Tanja Haase.' At the mention of Anneliese's daughter's name – perhaps the most tragic of the abductions and deaths, and the one Tilsner knew was closest to Müller's heart as she'd actually seen the baby girl alive – Tilsner felt something. He thought for a moment that there had been a tiny squeeze back from Müller, but he dismissed it as simply a muscle reaction. 'Pretty little Tanja. Well – according to Franzi – Hansi convinced her that their daughter Heike had to go into hospital for treatment. That was when he returned Maddelena to the Salzmanns by leaving her outside their apartment door. I suspect he'd heard – through his Stasi connections – about the handwriting search. Only when it looked like we'd got the wrong people, in the Rosenbaums, did he feel confident enough to carry out another abduction. So the girl they called "Heike" was suddenly out of hospital – looking healthier, cuter, and presumably with a darker skin. Because this new "Heike" in Franzi's arms was, in fact, Tanja Haase.'

This time there was no doubt. As Tilsner had uttered the name Tanja, Müller had squeezed his hand.

He started squeezing back, in a random pattern, saying – almost shouting – the name Tanja Haase at the same time. He watched Müller's lips, saw she was trying to form a word. Then something came out. He wasn't sure if it was Tanja, or Tilsner or what. But it was something.

'Nurse! Doctor! Emil! Come on, you arseholes. She's trying to speak.'

61

Once he'd alerted everyone, Tilsner didn't think it was his place to hang around and see what transpired. It was fabulous news that Müller had shown signs of communicating. But – from his own experience after the shooting in the Harz the previous year – Tilsner knew it would be a long struggle ahead to full fitness, if that ever happened. In any case, it looked certain things would be changing. Even if – as he and everyone else hoped – Müller was able to play a full and active role as mother to her two newly born twins, she almost certainly wouldn't be able to continue as the head of a murder squad. Of course, that might produce an opening for promotion for himself, but it wasn't something he coveted. He didn't want the responsibility, the form-filling, the necessary kowtowing to superiors.

That was all in the future. For now, he was determined to get some sort of criminal charge to stick against Franziska Traugott, for all her protestations of innocence. The key – he knew – was Tanja Haase. Someone had killed her. He didn't think it had been Johannes. For all Johannes's twisted logic, his mind poisoned by what he saw as the theft of his family home, the killing in a car crash of his only two natural children, nothing Johannes had done pinpointed him as a murderer, although there was still a doubt over the Andereggs' son. And if the killer wasn't Hansi, it had to be Franzi. But it wasn't all about getting her in front of a judge to face justice. Franzi could also prove useful – if, as he suspected, she could tell them more about that drunken driver, more about the doctored accident reports and – most importantly – exactly who had doctored them. Tilsner had a suspect in mind. The man who'd been trying to mothball the *Kripo* inquiry from the start. The odious *Hauptmann* Janowitz. But he needed Franzi to confirm his suspicions.

'So Franziska, do you still maintain that it was your husband who was responsible for Tanja's death?'

The woman gave a high-pitched, utterly inappropriate laugh that set her ample chest wobbling. And Franzi certainly had a lot of wood in front of her shed, thought Tilsner. But it didn't make the package any more attractive. He rolled his eyes at Eschler, sitting by his side in the interview room.

'Yes,' said the woman. 'That must have been what happened. Heike – well, you say she was called Maddelena, but to me she will always be Heike – was taken away. Then she came back. I was always worried she looked a bit different.' She laughed again, but it died in her throat as she caught Tilsner and Eschler's stern expressions. 'So that must have been this Tanja you're going on about. Then Hansi claimed the illness had returned.'

'What illness?' asked Tilsner. More and more he was thinking they weren't going to get anywhere with Franzi. She should be questioned by a psychiatrist, not a detective.

'Ah,' said the woman, looking a little lost. 'I never really asked him.'

Tilsner slammed his fist down on the table. The woman jumped back in her chair. 'This is a load of shit you're telling us, isn't it, Franzi? You're just making it up as you go along.'

'No, honest to God! I'm trying to tell you the truth.'

'Hmm,' said Tilsner. 'You need to try a lot harder.'

His next visit to Müller's hospital bedside, the following day, stunned him. She wasn't in bed anymore, she was sitting in a chair alongside, holding one twin to her right breast, while Emil Wollenburg proffered the other to her left-hand side.

'Should I stay outside for a moment?' he asked.

'No, you're all right, Werner.' Müller smiled at him. All the colour had returned to her cheeks. A picture of motherly radiance.

'Quite a change, isn't it?' laughed Emil.

Tilsner held his hands up. 'A transformation. I don't understand.'

'With a coma triggered by blood loss,' explained Emil, 'if it's only of brief duration, recovery can be quite rapid. Within an hour or so of you leaving yesterday, she was already starting to talk, weren't you, *Liebling*?'

'I don't really remember much of that first hour,' admitted Müller. 'But now, I feel fine. Weak, tired, but fine.'

'Have you decided on names for them yet?'

Tilsner watched a look pass between the couple. 'Not that we've agreed on,' she laughed. 'So, no.' She patted the bedclothes. 'But sit down, Werner. Bring me up to date with the case. Did Johannes surv—'

'No. We've still got his wife in custody, of course. But she's bonkers, not just a bird in her head, but a whole fucking aviary.' He watched Emil raise his eyes at the swear word. 'Sorry,' shrugged Tilsner.

'So he *did* die from his injuries, from the fall?'

Tilsner frowned. 'Why do you ask?'

'As I was losing consciousness, as I was being taken on the stretcher to the helicopter, I could have sworn I heard a sound muffled by the snow and the noise of the helicopter. The sound of gunshots.'

For Müller, recovery was quicker than she could reasonably have expected. The elation of motherhood seemed to banish tiredness. Despite the constant demands of the twins to be fed, the adrenalin racing through her body kept her alert and awake. So much so that she felt annoyed at being denied the chance to join Tilsner in the questioning of Franziska Traugott. She and Emil still hadn't resolved the thorny issue of whether or when she would be going back to work – and in what capacity. It might, in any case, be taken out of her hands. Müller was determined to get back to the Hauptstadt – even if it meant returning to a desk job in Keibelstrasse once she was ready to resume her *Kripo* duties. She pressured Emil to end his temporary posting in Halle as soon as possible so that he could join her and the twins in Berlin.

The twins. Müller smiled to herself. They still hadn't got names; she had rejected all Emil's suggestions – most of them being traditional family names from his side. It meant the visit from Emil's parents passed off awkwardly, with Emil's mother insisting Girl Twin – as Müller thought of her – looked exactly like a Clothilde, her middle name. There was no way Müller was ever going to accept that. Emil and his father's suggestion for Boy Twin – Meinhard – left her equally cold. Müller *did* have ideas for names for both, but thought she had more chance of getting Emil to agree if she left them nameless for a while longer. The nameless twins in the city of nameless streets. Somehow it felt appropriate.

Müller's ecstatic mood – spreading a feeling of warmth and goodwill through her body – changed a couple of days after emerging from the brief coma, when Emil handed her a letter. She saw the emblem of the Ministry for State Security stamped on its front and immediately felt slightly breathless. Her boyfriend looked at her quizzically, but she resisted the temptation to open it straightaway. She knew what she hoped it contained, but it was something private; if it didn't have the information she was searching for inside it, then she didn't want Emil seeing her disappointment.

Finally, when he was out of the room taking the twins to the crèche so Müller could have a rest, she picked up the envelope from the bedside table and ripped it open.

In an instant, she knew Jäger had found what she wanted.

The name of the girl holding the baby in the photo her adoptive mother had given her. The address of her family in Leipzig. And confirmation from Jäger, or his sources within the Stasi, that yes, the baby in the photo was Müller, and yes, the girl was her mother.

62

Müller knew she wasn't yet well enough for a trip to Leipzig. Even if she was physically up to it, she wasn't sure her emotions could cope with more trauma, despite her burning desire to piece her family history together. More than that, the tantalising prospect that she might actually get to meet her real, natural birth mother. Over and over again, she stroked the photo of the girl and baby, scarcely believing it could be true.

As soon as she did feel well enough to travel anywhere, she insisted that Tilsner take her to the Red Ox, where Franziska Traugott was still incarcerated, but only when she was certain that Emil was able to look after the twins. Although she'd missed much of the questioning of the woman, Müller wanted to make up for lost time now. Tilsner had claimed the woman was out of her mind, and that they wouldn't get anywhere with her. Müller was less convinced of her madness. She needed to hear the explanations for the woman's terrible actions – and those of her husband, Müller's childhood friend Johannes – from Franziska's own mouth. If she could begin to understand her, perhaps even to empathise with her, they might yet find the key to this whole perplexing case.

*

'What I don't understand,' said the woman, after repeating the version of events she'd already given Tilsner, 'is where Hansi is. Can't you at least allow him to visit me?'

Müller glared at Tilsner, who shifted uncomfortably in his seat. *Hadn't they told the poor woman what had happened?* Yes she was – at the very least – complicit in child abductions, if not worse. But to hide from her the news about Johannes's fate seemed unnecessarily cruel.

'I'm sorry, Franziska. Hansi won't be visiting you. He's –'

Before she'd completed the sentence, Müller watched Franziska Traugott's face crumple as a terrible wail started from deep within the woman's body.

'No! No!' she screamed, covering her eyes with her hands.

Müller reached out over the interview table and gently stroked her wrist. 'I'm sorry, Franziska. There was a terrible accident.'

When Franziska finally uncovered her eyes, she stared right at Müller. There was an emptiness to them. Müller felt like she was being pulled into a deep pit. 'Why didn't they tell me?' she asked, a flat note in her voice.

Still gripping the woman's wrist, Müller gave a long sigh. 'I'm sorry, Franziska. They should have.' She glared again at Tilsner. He shrugged as though to say it wasn't his fault.

Once the woman had composed herself a little, Müller decided to probe for more information.

'I know it might be painful, Franziska, but I want you to try to cast your mind back nearly twenty years ago. To the late fifties. When you first had children. They were twins, weren't they?'

'I don't like to talk about the past,' she said. 'Hansi says it's not good for me.'

Tilsner slapped the table with his fist. 'That won't wash now, Franziska. He's not here. You need to tell us everything. You have to answer all our questions.'

'All we need to know, Franziska,' said Müller, more gently, 'are a few details.' Müller looked down in her notebook, even though she'd memorised what the children were called immediately. It was just a way of avoiding the woman's stare for a few seconds. 'Monika and Tomas were their names, weren't they?'

The woman didn't say anything, but simply nodded.

'Now, we don't think you've ever got proper justice for what happened to them. It may help your current case if ...' Müller wondered to herself what to say. She didn't want to falsely raise the woman's hopes. '... if we can establish what happened that night.'

Franziska Traugott stared straight ahead, saying nothing – as though she was focussing on a point on the wall behind Müller and Tilsner. Her expression was odd – almost beatific, trance-like. It unnerved Müller.

'Did you hear the *Oberleutnant*?' prompted Tilsner.

Franziska gave an almost imperceptible nod.

'Well – then – what – is – the – answer?' Tilsner enunciated each word, as though he were speaking to a foreigner with limited command of German.

The woman closed her eyes and breathed deeply. Then – still with her eyes tightly shut – she began to speak. 'He was drunk.

Absolutely blind drunk. That's what Hansi said. Never should have been on the road. We were on the crossing, and one second I was pushing the pram, the next –'

Müller stroked the woman's hand again.

'Luckily Hansi was a bit behind us, it missed him. But he saw it all. He was never the same after that. Neither of us were. I was in hospital for weeks. They say I suffered serious brain injuries. When I came round, Hansi broke it to me that . . . that . . . my . . . babies –'

The woman closed her eyes and was almost completely still. Müller could see her repeatedly swallowing, trying to banish the memories.

'It's OK,' said Müller. 'You don't need to tell us every detail, Franziska, not if it's upsetting. Did the driver stop?'

The woman took a long slow breath, then exhaled equally slowly, trying to gather herself. 'Oh yes, Hansi told me he stopped all right, eventually. He got out of the car, staggering up the road towards Hansi, gesticulating angrily. Didn't give two seconds of thought for my babies, or me. He might as well have hit a pile of horse shit for all he cared. And Hansi said his breath stank. Stank to high heaven of drink. Hansi ignored him, rushed over to the remains of the pram, but he could immediately tell there was no hope. No life. But I still had a weak pulse. It was already a miracle that I'd been able to have children, because of what happened –'

The woman stopped speaking suddenly, and began almost hyperventilating. Taking huge, wracking breaths of air into her lungs.

'Sorry. Hansi says I should never think about it, that there's so much to look forward to. That it's bad for me, remembering those days. It can bring on my turns.'

Müller squeezed the woman's fingers. 'Just take your time, Franziska. This is very useful. Just take your time.'

'At the end of the war, when the Red Army came. We were frightened. We hid from them.'

Müller had a mounting sense of dread. What was the woman about to say?

'I was just thirteen. Thirteen! Can you believe it? They raped me again and again and again. I was pregnant – at thirteen!' Müller had a sudden flash of the photograph of her own mother and herself. Was that the fate that had befallen her too? She found her heart breaking for the woman – no wonder Johannes, or Hansi as she knew him, had always urged Franzi not to think about it. More images crowded Müller's brain. Images of her own violation, her own rape. She shuddered. 'I gave birth but there was no one there to help me. My sister had gone to the American zone. My mother had died. It was terrible. There was awful damage to my insides, from the rape and childbirth. They said I'd never be able to have children again. Yet they took my baby daughter away. They took her away. *The bastards.*'

There was such vitriolic force in Franziska Traugott's words that Müller found herself shrinking back. She glanced at Tilsner, could tell he was getting impatient, that in his view the woman had strayed from the point. But Müller could see where the explanation was heading.

'So you can imagine how overjoyed Hansi and I were to discover I was actually pregnant with twins. We couldn't believe
it. It was like a miracle.' Müller thought of her own parallel
situation, the twins she'd aborted all those years ago, conceived
in almost exactly the same set of circumstances, although
her rape had been in the Republic. In one of the Republic's
institutions.

'And then,' Franziska Traugott was spitting out her words
now with absolute fury, 'then that bastard, that drunken bastard killed them. Damn nearly killed me too. How would you
feel? That bastard is responsible for this. For all of this, I tell
you. Everything.'

Müller took a deep breath, glanced at Tilsner and saw him
give a small shake of his head. She knew what he'd be thinking.
That the woman was simply trying to deflect the blame. The
oldest trick in the book. But Müller, for the time being, was
prepared to give her the benefit of the doubt.

'Would you recognise him if you saw him again, Franziska?'

'I don't care if it's nearly twenty years later,' said the woman,
quivering with anger. 'I don't care if I see him on his deathbed.
I would recognise him from his eyes. He'd obviously been too
drunk to turn on the car's headlights. The only thing I saw, and
then just for an instant as he was nearly on us, was the flash of
his eyes in the glare of the streetlights. But people's eyes don't
change.'

'What the hell do you mean by that?' shouted Tilsner.

'He had the eyes of a wolf.'

'What? You're talking nonsense.'

The woman shook her head rapidly from side to side. 'No, no. It's true. A wolf.' Müller could feel her excitement rise. Franziska Traugott might be mad, was most certainly bad, but in this, Müller knew she was right.

Because Müller herself could picture them. Lupine eyes.

The sort of eyes that sucked you in, and watched, and watched, waiting for a weak moment to pounce.

Just like a wolf.

Exactly the same colour.

Amber.

The amber eyes of *Major* Uwe Malkus.

The Stasi Wolf.

63

Tilsner insisted it didn't take them any further forward. In 1958 when the crash had happened in what was then Halle-West, before the new town had been built, Malkus had been protected from prosecution by his bosses at the Ministry for State Security. That's why his name had been scratched from the report, before the correction fluid had been applied. So no one would ever know. Malkus had gone on and risen up the ranks and was now a Stasi major. It wouldn't be any different today, argued Tilsner. In fact, now – in 1976 – he was more senior, and so much time had passed they'd be even less likely to make any case stick against him.

Perhaps Müller was being naïve. Perhaps her deputy was right. But she wasn't so sure. She had seen Malkus, along with Janowitz, in the group of officers who approached Johannes's horribly injured body in Oberhof, after he'd fallen into the snowdrift at the side of the Interhotel Panorama. She was sure she'd heard those muffled gunshots. The shots that finally killed her childhood friend. Müller wasn't prepared to ignore all that – at least not without a fight.

Although Müller was determined to try to do the right thing, the just thing, she knew Tilsner was almost certainly correct in his assessment. But if there was any chance – any sliver of a chance – of bringing Malkus to justice for his drunk drive from almost two decades earlier, well, she knew she had to try to see it through.

Surprisingly, *Oberst* Frenzel listened to what the two Berlin detectives had to say without interruption. At the end, he didn't dismiss their argument, but simply asked them to leave his office for a moment while he made a couple of telephone calls.

A few minutes later, when they were both summoned to enter, they saw the People's Police colonel brandishing a signed, type-written document as he sat at his desk.

'I'd look after this, comrades,' he said. 'You're never likely to see such a document ever again, in your whole careers. It may even be the only time it's ever happened in the history of the Republic. Certainly I've never signed one before. It's authority from me, as the leader of this People's Police district, for you to arrest Uwe Malkus, a Stasi officer.'

'Jesus wept,' said Tilsner. Müller mimed punching the air, like a goal scorer in the *Oberliga*.

'As I say, you'll never see this again. The People's Police never acts against the Ministry for State Security. We always coop-erate. We're on the same side. Luckily there are those in the *Bezirk* Halle branch of the *MfS* who are as eager to see the back of Malkus as I am.'

'As you are?' queried Müller.

Frenzel nodded. 'You know I was unhappy when my own *Kripo* officers were kept off this case. When you two were brought in. Malkus was behind that decision. It'll be nice to pay him back for it. But the key man was Janowitz.'

'Janowitz? He's the one who's been trying to derail this inquiry from the start,' said Tilsner. 'He's just as nasty a piece of work as –'

'Careful, Comrade *Unterleutnant*. You've got what you want, but it doesn't make you fireproof.' Müller shot an angry glare towards Tilsner. They were so close to getting Malkus – she didn't want him messing it up.

'In what way did *Hauptmann* Janowitz help, Comrade *Oberst*?' asked Müller.

'Janowitz might seem dour and humourless, Karin, but he knows which side his bread's buttered on. He was as uncomfortable as anyone with what Malkus did in Oberhof. And he witnessed the shots from Malkus's gun, while covering his own back by advising against it. This gives him a chance to remove Malkus. And probably be promoted in his place.'

Müller watched Tilsner roll his eyes.

'It's the way things work, *Unterleutnant*,' continued Frenzel. 'You know that as well as I do. Anyway, Janowitz will meet you at the regional Stasi HQ entrance. Let's hope Malkus hasn't got wind of this.'

It was Müller's first visit to the Ha-Neu Stasi building since the day after she arrived the previous July, when this whole slow-moving case was just beginning. But this time she wasn't being summoned by Malkus for a warning shot across the bows. This time she and Tilsner held the trump card: the arrest authorisation from *Oberst* Frenzel.

Janowitz gave them a small conspiratorial smile as he welcomed them at the checkpoint at the edge of the Stasi compound. It was the first time Müller had ever seen the Stasi captain's lips curl upwards except when she'd been pulled up for some alleged misdemeanour or another.

'He won't be expecting this,' he said. 'I can't wait to see his face.'

The wide-open office door, the pulled-out drawers at Malkus's desk, papers strewn across the top of it, told Müller all she needed to know.

'*Scheisse*,' yelled Janowitz. 'Someone must have warned him.'

Tilsner raced across to the window. 'There's the bastard. Running towards the car park.'

Janowitz was immediately on the phone, sounding the alert, while Müller and Tilsner ran down the stairs and back towards the Wartburg. Just before they accelerated away, Janowitz jumped inside.

'Any ideas where he'll be heading?' asked Tilsner.

Janowitz shook his head, then shrugged. 'He lives right on the other side of Ha-Neu. *Wohnkomplex VI*. We could try that.'

Tilsner accelerated south, then swung round the corner onto the Magistrale, heading west.

Just then a radio message cut through the crackle.

'*Suspect's Volvo surrounded near the centre of Ha-Neu. He's escaped on foot towards the station.*'

They spotted the abandoned Volvo up ahead by the roadside. Tilsner screeched to a halt directly behind it, then the three clambered out and raced across the square towards the underground S-bahn station. Müller felt her re-stitched C-section wound pulling and her head pounding as she struggled to keep up. They ran down the steps into the station, yelling for passers-by and chemical workers at the end of their shifts to make way.

As they got down to station level, they saw a commotion at the northern end of the platform, as Müller saw the lights of the train coming towards them through the tunnel. Suddenly, the bustling and shouting turned into high-pitched screaming.

Müller could see the horrified look in the driver's eyes, even from this distance.

Time seemed to slow as – at the same time – they saw a body hurl itself in front of the train.

As they reached the end of the platform, Tilsner pulled the surrounding gawpers and rubberneckers out of the way. Müller advanced to the platform edge.

There – lying on his back under the metal train wheels – his torso sliced by the rotating steel, was the upper part of Uwe Malkus's body. A cowardly Stasi officer who had taken the easy way out, rather than face the shame of his downfall.

His eyes staring, lifelessly, at the station roof.

Eyes that even now, in death, were a brilliant amber.

The eyes that, in Franziska Traugott's simple terms, looked like those of a wolf.

64

A few days later

'Are you sure you don't want me to come in with you, Karin?' asked Tilsner, as they sat in the *Kripo* Wartburg outside a turn-of-the-century apartment block in Plagwitz, to the west of Leipzig centre. Tilsner had agreed to drive her the short distance from Halle – she didn't yet feel up to driving herself – but she wanted to do the next bit alone.

'It's all right. It's something I need to do by myself.' She looked up at the building, with its discoloured render, wondering what it had looked like when first built – or what it would look like if the layers of brown-coal-stained crust were cleaned off. It was an imposing building, and the street – Karl-Heine-Strasse – had the feel almost of the Paris boulevards Müller had seen on Western TV. She pulled her jacket tightly around herself and then opened the car door and got out.

'I'll pick you up from here in – what – thirty minutes?'

Müller ducked her head down towards the still-open passenger door to reply. 'OK. But stay for a few moments first, just in case no one's at home.' She hoped that wouldn't be the case.

They had deliberately come in the early evening, when the working day should already be over.

The front door to the apartment block was unlocked. Müller held it open as she rang the bell for apartment 3C, which corresponded to the name – Helga Nonnemacher – that Jäger had provided via his minions. A stern female voice shouted down the staircase from the third floor. 'Who is it?'

Force of habit found Müller responding in her professional, rather than personal, capacity. '*Oberleutnant* Karin Müller. From the *Kriminalpolizei*,' she yelled up into the gloom. As soon as she said it, Müller realised it would put the woman on her guard, rather than encourage her to be open with Müller. 'But I'm here just in a personal capacity. It's nothing to do with police work, there's no need to worry. It's about . . .' *What was it about?* 'It's about family,' shouted Müller, hoping it would be enough to secure an invitation inside.

'You'd better come up, then. Third floor.'

Helga Nonnemacher regarded Müller with a serious expression, but ushered her inside. Her hair was grey, but neatly cut, and Müller imagined that – in her younger years – she had been an attractive woman. She still was, in an elegant but careworn way. Her cheekbones were well defined, so that – even though Müller estimated her to be perhaps in her mid-sixties – her skin was remarkably unlined. Müller saw something in the woman that was familiar. Something that reminded her of herself; of the teenage girl in that black-and-white photo taken soon after the end of the war; and of the mysterious woman who'd come calling on her adoptive family at home in Oberhof all those years ago.

Frau Nonnemacher invited Müller to take a seat in the neat lounge. The furniture was old-fashioned, the decor on the wall fading, but everything was tidy and clean.

The woman took a seat opposite Müller and then leant forward, her hands resting on her knees. 'So if this isn't official police business, what is it about? What did you mean when you said it was to do with family?'

Müller didn't reply immediately. Her mind was racing on an adrenalin high. *Is this her? Is this my real mother? But surely she's too old to be the teenager cradling the baby me?* She pulled the tin box from her jacket pocket. When she brought it into the open, the woman gave it a curious look. Almost a look of recognition, but also of something that spoke of sadness. Of loss. Of longing.

When Müller handed her the monochrome photograph, taken some thirty years earlier, there was no surprise on the woman's face. Instead, Müller saw her dab at the corners of her eyes, left and right in turn, as she held the photo in her other hand.

'You know who it is?' Müller asked.

'Of course,' answered the woman. 'My daughter, Jannika. With . . .' Helga Nonnemacher's words died in her mouth, replaced by a gasp. She covered the lower part of her face with her hand, and stared intently at Müller. 'Oh my God!' She looked down at the photograph again, and then up at Müller once more. 'You're Karin, aren't you?'

Müller nodded, feeling a sudden rush of love for the girl in the photo. She'd assumed – since learning the truth about her adoption the previous year – that her first name had been given to her by her adoptive parents. Evidently, that wasn't the case. No wonder that visitor to the guest house back in the fifties, when she was just a little girl, had known her name.

The woman shook her head in stunned wonder. 'She would have been so proud of you, so, so proud.'

The words were like a stab in the gut for Müller. She found herself clutching her Caesarean wound. 'Would have been?' She had to force herself to say the words. She knew what they meant.

The woman got up from her chair and knelt by Müller, stroking her face. 'I'm sorry, *Liebling*. I'm sorry. It can't be the news you wanted.'

Müller tried to choke back the tears, her hormones already out of balance from the early, forced delivery.

Helga took both of Müller's hands in her own, and squeezed tightly. 'It was a very difficult time after the war. You can see how thin Jannika is here.' She stroked her finger across the image of her daughter. 'She had this faith that your father would come back, but he never did. It broke her heart. And then the Soviet authorities took her baby away – took *you* away. They broke her heart a second time. She never really recovered.'

Müller bit her bottom lip, squeezing the woman's hands in turn, then took a long, deep breath. 'So she's –'

'Passed away? I'm afraid so, dear. Back in forty-nine. Tuberculosis was the official cause, but I never really agreed with that. She just wasted away. When you were taken, it stole her will to live. I managed to track you down a year or so after her death by calling in a lot of favours. I travelled all the way to Oberhof. To try to persuade your adoptive mother to let me play some part in your life. You were the only family I had left.' Then, curiously, the woman laughed and shook her head. 'And now – twenty-five years later – you've found me. It's a miracle. And Jannika would have been so proud of you. To see you now, a beautiful young woman.'

The woman was smiling, lighting up her features, so that Müller got a glimpse of how Helga Nonnemacher would have looked in her own youth. Müller could see herself – like looking through a time-warped mirror. And now – like a camera shot slowly brought into focus – she realised with certainty that Helga Nonnemacher was a part of her. She'd found her own flesh and blood at last. She'd found her home. Her true home.

'I'm very pleased to meet you, Karin. At last. After all these years.'

Müller took a long swallow. 'And you're my grandmother.' Despite the devastating news about the fate of Jannika – her natural mother – Müller raised a weak smile. 'Oma,' she laughed. 'I will have to call you Oma.'

'Don't, don't,' said Helga, reaching out and embracing Müller, pulling her granddaughter into a tight hug. 'I don't feel old enough to be a grandmother. Not yet.'

Müller raised her eyebrows, then reached into her pocket for her purse, and drew out a small photograph – of her, Emil and the twins. 'Then this might be even worse news,' she grinned. 'This is your great-granddaughter, and your great-grandson.'

'Oh Karin, Karin,' cried the woman. 'I can see so much of Jannika in them. So, so much. She would have loved them. Loved them to bits, just as she did you, my darling.' She stroked the photo, as though by doing it she could make some contact with her lost daughter, Müller's mother, the mother that the detective would now never meet. 'What are the names of the little beauties?'

Müller grinned. 'You won't believe it. They're already nearly a week old, and they still don't have names. My boyfriend and I can't agree.'

'Boyfriend, not husband?'

'Not yet. So you've that to look forward to – if he ever asks me.'

'Don't stand on ceremony. Ask him. That was what I did with my Helmut.'

'My grandfather?'

'Of course. But he's gone now, dear. In the war, like so many. The Eastern Front. I don't like to think of it, what they must have gone through. And after that, and you being taken away, and Jannika . . . well, I just didn't have the heart anymore. To start again.' She fingered the photo of the twins lovingly. 'But I never, ever believed I would be so blessed. To find you again, is . . . well, it's a miracle. And I can't wait to meet these two. *Their* Oma might be dead, poor things, but *your* Oma is here, and would be very honoured to do her best to fill my daughter's place in your little family.'

The two women – grandmother and granddaughter – traded smiles and tears in almost equal measure as they began to fill in the gaps in their lives, until Müller realised the thirty minutes Tilsner had allowed her was on the point of expiring.

'Is there anything you can tell me about my father, Helga?'

The woman stared at Müller for a moment, delaying her answer. 'Well, Karin. I don't like to speak ill of him. I never knew him. At the time you must have been conceived, Jannika and I had been split up in the confusion that followed the war. But Jannika was always waiting for him to come back, and he didn't.'

The woman continued to hold the detective's eyes in her gaze, as though wondering whether to trust her.

Müller knew something of the post-war horrors. They were never spoken about publicly, never admitted. It was just known that some Germans – especially women – had been left horribly damaged. She hoped that wasn't the real tragedy behind her mother's abruptly shortened life.

She could tell Helga had noticed the look of fear that must have crossed her face. The woman held out her hand. 'Come here. I've got something to give you.'

As Helga opened the top drawer in her bedroom dressing table, Müller was surprised to see her pull out an identical tin box to the one her adoptive mother had given her in Oberhof the previous summer. She handed it to Müller.

'You ought to have this,' she said. 'You have more claim over it than I do. Though if you could do me a copy, I would appreciate it.'

Müller picked up the photograph and examined it. It was almost exactly the same shot as the one Rosamund Müller had given her. Only the changed expression on Jannika's face – a broader smile – indicated that had been taken at a fractionally different time. Perhaps seconds later, or earlier, than the one already in Müller's possession.

A flash of metal in the bottom of the rusting tin caught Müller's eye.

'What's this?'

'I don't know for certain. It's just something Jannika got from their first . . . meeting. The first meeting with your father. She kept it hidden. Look at the writing.'

Müller swivelled the octagonal metal disc in her fingers so that the inscription or stamp was facing her. Then realisation dawned. From her Russian lessons at school. It was Cyrillic. Müller slowly drew her finger across the indentations in the metal as she translated, her excitement growing in tandem with her fear. *Litshnyi Znak* – the two longest words. That loosely translated as identification tag. Then numbers and more letters. Second Company, 404 Battalion, soldier number 105.

She stared at her grandmother open-mouthed.

'You said "meeting". Is that *really* what you meant?'

Helga Nonnemacher lowered her eyes.

'No!' shouted Müller. 'Don't tell me she was ra—'

The woman clasped her hand to Müller's mouth, and held her tightly. 'Don't say it, Karin. Don't think about it. As I say, it wasn't until a few months after the war that Jannika and I were reunited. By then, something had happened, he'd had to move away. But Jannika never gave me the impression that there was any element of coercion. I told you, she was heartbroken he didn't come back for her.'

'Did he know about me?' asked Müller, balling her hands into fists, trying to fight back the tears.

'I don't think so, Karin. I don't think so.'

65

After packing Emil's car and safely strapping the twins inside, Müller requested that they drive over the Saale and along the Magistrale – to take one last look at the strange concrete city that had been her working home for the best part of a year. With spring now arrived, the atmosphere felt similar to Müller to when the case had started. Ha-Neu's numerous fountains were now working again, their cleansing plumes almost literally washing away the smogs of winter. Mothers were out with their prams showing off their new offspring – just as they had been in July the previous year – and the tiled murals decorating the sides of the slab apartment blocks were illuminated by the sunlight. Mosaics of colour breaking up the otherwise monotonous drabness of cement and concrete grey.

'I thought you were pleased to be getting back to Berlin,' said Emil, 'but you look almost wistful.'

Müller reached over and squeezed his thigh. 'I *am* pleased. The Hauptstadt is my home.' Then she glanced at the twins, sleeping peacefully on the back seat. Her time in this city had changed her life. She wasn't sure if it represented the future, with its streets without names, its peculiar numbering system for addresses, and block after block of identical apartments. But with the arrival of spring, Ha-Neu – which had closed in on her during the dark winter nights – now had a much more benign feel. It was where her children had been born. The children she'd been told she'd never be able to have. And perhaps it would always hold a place in her heart.

EPILOGUE

Four months later: July 1976
Halle-Neustadt

The pretty policewoman's words in court – the little speech the authorities tried to stop her giving – must have done some good, Dagna. I know you'd have done the same, spoken up for me like her. And what the doctor said, after her. That the accident had left me brain-damaged. I don't agree with that. I feel fine. But if it saved my life, well . . .

Whenever I have these conversations with myself in my head, it's you I'm thinking of, Dagna. It was always funny that you were two years younger than me, but so, so much more sensible. That's what Mutti used to say. I still remember fondly us playing in the corrugated-metal mine hut. We had such fun. Even though that place, I suppose, should be a place of terror for me, it's not. Because I remember our games there before the war, as young children. Not what happened that day the Red Army came.

I still have to attend the hospital regularly for tests, I still have to report to the police station. All those sorts of things I can put up with. But what I find hard to deal with is the fact that I'll never see you again. So I'm sitting here, with the only photo I have of you on the desk, talking into this machine. It's one Hansi used to have for his Ministry work. For some reason they didn't take it away.

So I thought I'd record this last conversation with you, even though I don't think you'll ever hear it. All my attempts to find out about you, and where you are in the Federal Republic, come back with the answer 'Whereabouts Unknown'. So maybe I won't try to talk to you in my head anymore, just this last time into the machine.

You see I wanted to tell you something, something that only you would understand.

It was those eyes that did it. Those eyes and the epicanthal folds. It became obvious a few weeks after she came back from the hospital that she wasn't Hansi's. She was that Berlin barman's. You see we didn't *just* kiss and cuddle. I wasn't really being completely honest then. I think I was lying to myself.

Oh, poor, poor Heike. They keep saying she was called Tanja, but she wasn't. She was my Heike. And I couldn't let Hansi find out. That's why I had to do it. The poor little mite would have been disowned by him. I would have been too, and I don't think I could have survived without Hansi. I'm not sure I can now.

You see, life is very fragile. I learned that soon after the war, when they took my baby away, before I'd even had a chance to give her a name. I couldn't let that happen again. So I had to protect her in the only way I could, by helping her go to sleep.

I hope you'll find it in your heart to forgive me, Dagna. Hansi would have known. I'm sure he would.

It was her eyes.

GLOSSARY

Ampelmann	East German pedestrian traffic light symbol
Barkas	East German van model
Bezirk	District
Der schwarze Kanal	*The Black Channel* – East German weekly current affairs programme
Doppelkorn	Distilled alcoholic drink, usually from rye
f6	East German cigarette brand
Freikörperkultur	Naturism
Ha-Neu	Short form for Halle-Neustadt
Hauptmann	Captain
Hauptstadt	Capital city (in this book, East Berlin)

Interhotel	East German chain of luxury hotels
Intershop	Chain of government-run stores selling luxury goods where only foreign hard currency was accepted
Jugendwerkhof	Reform school or youth workhouse
Kaufhalle	East German term for supermarket
Keibelstrasse	The People's Police headquarters near Alexanderplatz – the East German equivalent of Scotland Yard
Kinder des Krieges	War children
Kriminalpolizei	Criminal Police or CID
Kriminaltechniker	Forensic officer
Kripo	CID (short form) – also known as the 'K'
Liebling	Darling
Main Intelligence Directorate	The Stasi's foreign arm – the East German equivalent of MI6

Ministry for State Security (*MfS*)	The East German secret police, abbreviated to *MfS* from the German initials, and colloquially known as the Stasi – a contraction of the German name
Mutti	Mum, or Mummy
Neues Deutschland	The official East German Communist Party newspaper
Oberleutnant	First Lieutenant
Oberliga	Top division of the East German football league
Oberst	Colonel
Oma	Grandma, granny
People's Police	The regular East German state police (*Volkspolizei* in German)
Pioneers	Organisation for children operated by the Communist Party in the Soviet Union and East Germany
Plattenbauten	Concrete slab apartment blocks
Räuchermännchen	Incense-burning figurine

Roter Ochse	Red Ox
S-bahn	Rapid transit railway
Scheisse	Shit
Sekt	German sparkling wine
Stasi	Colloquial term for the Ministry for State Security (see above)
Strandbad	Lido or bathing beach
U-bahn	Underground railway
Unterleutnant	Sub-lieutenant
Volkspolizei	See People's Police above
Vopo	Short form of *Volkspolizei*, usually referring to uniformed police officers, as opposed to detectives
Wachtmeister	Police sergeant
Weihnachtsmann	Father Christmas
Wohnkomplex	Housing estate
Ypsilon Hochhaus	Y-section high-rise apartment block

AUTHOR'S NOTE

This is a work of fiction, and although the socialist city of Halle-Neustadt existed – and still exists in the capitalist united Germany as part of neighbouring Halle – all the events that happened in this book are products of my imagination.

I have very loosely used a few true stories from real life East Germany as springboards for the plot. Halle-Neustadt was the scene of a horrific murder in the early 1980s, one of the most notorious in the former DDR. The so-called Crossword Puzzle Murder (the *Kreuzworträtselmord*) saw a young boy's torso found in a suitcase dumped by a railway line. The case was eventually solved by the local Halle *Kripo* team under the leadership of *Hauptmann* Siegfried Schwarz (see the Acknowledgements which follow) – not by detectives brought in from Berlin. They cracked it thanks to handwriting in a crossword in the newspaper used to wrap the body – but only after an exhaustive check of hundreds of thousands of writing samples (it's cited as the largest sampling of handwriting in history). The murder of seven-year-old Lars Bense is still raw in the Halle area – indeed in 2013 a case was reopened against the girlfriend of the youth convicted of the killing, although it was set aside a year later due to lack of evidence. In using some of the background to the Crossword Puzzle Murder in my fictional story, my intention is not to reopen old wounds or to use tragic events as the basis for entertainment, and I hope I haven't crossed that line.

The plot line of babies going missing from a hospital was based on a story told to me by DDR crime expert Dr Remo Kroll about how the Stasi took over the investigation into infant murders in a Leipzig hospital – because they didn't want the public to become alarmed. The Palace of the Republic in Berlin was completed in 1976, but as far as I know it wasn't built near or on top of a former illegal abortion clinic – the latter is fictional.

Cases of foetal abduction anywhere in the world are incredibly rare, and on almost every occasion the mother-to-be does not survive being mutilated. As far as I'm aware, there has never been a foetal abduction within a hospital, and the one involving Karin is obviously fictitious.

Karin Müller's 'home village', Oberhof, *was* the subject of a private guest house confiscation programme but in 1950, not 1951, as in the book, although the Müller and Traugott guest houses are fictional. A handful of the owners managed to get their property back a few years later, but most did not – at least in DDR times – and the episode remains controversial to this day. A similar but better-known nationalisation operation (*Aktion Rose*) was carried out on the island of Rügen in February 1953.

The geography I've used of Halle-Neustadt is reasonably accurate, although I've cheated a little for the sake of the plot. For example, as far as I know *Wohnkomplex VI* had not been completed by 1975 – although it appears on a 1977 street map.

Similarly, the high-rise 'Y' blocks are not opposite the fire station. Fidel Castro did visit – but a few years earlier than in my fictional account, in 1972. I've 'cheated' in a few other places to help the plot, for example, *Der schwarze Kanal*, was – I think – broadcast on Mondays rather than Fridays, so please don't write complaining about that one!

Although my prologue is fictional, a similar atrocity involving Red Army soldiers did happen in a mine in Halle-Bruckdorf at that time (I suspect a disused *opencast* mine – although a few underground brown coal mines do exist, they are the exception, and there are none I know of in the Halle area). The story was finally told in 2009 by the then eighty-three-year-old Ruth Schumacher. Ruth – then aged eighteen – was gang-raped by five Russian soldiers in the waterlogged Halle-Bruckdorf mine. But in communist East Germany, Ruth says she was forced to sign a statement denying the rapes ever happened, because the Soviets were regarded as 'liberators' and 'friends'. The rapes left Ruth unable to have children – and in 2009 she was living alone as a widow in a cramped flat in Leipzig, having survived her former U-boat captain husband. They were married for forty-nine years, but she told American National Public Radio they didn't marry out of love. Instead, recalls Ruth: 'When I told him "I'm not pure and innocent anymore", he didn't walk away from me.'

ACKNOWLEDGEMENTS

A lot of people have helped with this book, and I'm very grateful to all of them. In Germany, I had a wonderful time chatting to former Halle murder squad head, Siegfried Schwarz – whose team solved the Crossword Puzzle Murder. 'Sigi', as he's known, is something of a minor celebrity and an incredible character who took me on a guided tour of his old patch in Ha-Neu, and then invited me for tea in his hunting lodge home. Also many thanks to his friend, Jana Reissmann – who was born and brought up in Halle-Neustadt (and still lives on the edge of the town and remembers her childhood fondly) – for kindly taking a day off work to help with the interpreting.

In Berlin, the former head of the DDR's serious crimes squad, Berndt Marmulla, gave me plenty of useful advice (interpreted by Thomas Abrams).

BBC World Service journalist and former East German citizen Oliver Berlau kindly read the first draft to check for inaccuracies (although all remaining errors are mine), as did Stephanie Smith and former City University writing colleagues Rod Reynolds (whose own excellent detective stories, including *The Dark Inside*, are published by Faber) and Steph Broadribb (aka blogger Crime Thriller Girl, whose *Deep Down Dead* is being published by Orenda Books). Many thanks also to the remaining members of the City University 12–14 Crime Thriller MA writing group: Rob, Laura, Seun, James and Jody.

Special thanks of course to my agent Adam Gauntlett and the other agents at Peters, Fraser and Dunlop, and to the team at Bonnier Zaffre, particularly my editor, Joel Richardson.

STASI CHILD

East Berlin, 1975

When Oberleutnant Karin Müller is called to investigate a teenage girl's body at the foot of the Wall, she imagines she's seen it all before. But when she arrives she realises this is a death like no other. It seems the girl was trying to escape – but from the West.

Müller is a member of the People's Police, but in East Germany her power only stretches so far. The Stasi want her to discover the identity of the girl, but assure her the case is otherwise closed – and strongly discourage her from asking questions.

The evidence doesn't add up, and it soon becomes clear the crime scene has been staged. But this is not a regime that tolerates a curious mind, and Müller doesn't realise that the trail she's following will lead her dangerously close to home . . .

Available in paperback and ebook now